The Resonance

Michelle Medhat

Mindblowing Books Ltd © 2019

MINDBLOWING
BOOKS LTD

THANK YOU FROM MICHELLE MEDHAT

I would like to thank you for reading this book.

If you've picked this up, and you haven't read the earlier books, please check out The Trusted (book one) and The Dominant (book two). Direct links to The Trusted and The Dominant can be found at the end of this book.

Also, at the end of this book you can find details on how to get the free eBook **Operation Snowdrop**. This book is only through sign up to my newsletter *'Fearless Spies, Amazing Realms and Ice-Cold Villains'*. It's not available anywhere else. Operation Snowdrop is the mission that is cited throughout *The Trusted Thriller Series*. Together with this free eBook you'll get early bird discounts, the latest news on this series and access to incredible free thrillers bundles to keep you entertained.

But for now....

Dive in, hold on tight and enjoy!

Chapter 1

March 26, 2017

Ellie clutched to life like a stray, starving cat clutches to a chicken bone. Her time to go wasn't yet. She wasn't letting go of the life she held so precious. After her torture, reality swam in and out. One minute she was in the broadcast room. The next, she lay in a shiny, sterile medical lab.

People encircled. Her clothes were removed. Injections were given. Valium to calm her frenzy and morphine to douse her pain. Someone gave her water. Someone else wrapped her naked, shaking, and hysterical frame in a medical gown.

Ellie moved her head and watched helplessly as a young man injected her. She was too weak to struggle, too immersed in pain she'd never believed she would ever feel. She didn't care what any of them did.

"I'm a doctor. It's an anesthetic," said the man, who smiled in half-hearted way.

The others left him to deal with Ellie on his own.

Suddenly, Ellie was aware of his behavior. Despite her pain, she couldn't help being struck by the situation. It was surreal and ironic. Here was a doctor who administered a local anesthetic to treat wounds that his paymasters had so enjoyed inflicting. It was a masquerade of a real hospital, and she was being tended to by a caring and compassionate doctor.

Ellie felt awkward. The young doctor was gentle. He was totally out of place in the hellhole around her. Ellie knew he could sense her awkwardness and chose to remain silent. She stared at him, incredulous at how a professional could provide their life-saving skills to an organization hell-bent on making people suffer.

The doctor avoided the woman's stare. He knew what she was thinking. She knew that he didn't belong and that what he did was wrong, like when his brother forced him to superglue back on the wings of butterflies only for them to be ripped off again. Only now, he patched up injuries, not to save himself from being beaten but to feed his heroin craving.

He'd been a good doctor. Had it not been for the one case of malpractice, he'd still have been on the right path. But the girl had died. His colleagues had given evidence claiming they had seen him 'chase' just before prepping for theatre. It wasn't true. But it was all they needed. Dealers came out of the woodwork. His respectable façade, like an onionskin, peeled away, revealing his shadowy other life. And he was struck off.

Unable to practice, but with an addiction leading him further into debt, he'd been desperate. When Al Nadir approached him, they were like a godsend.

Now he knew they were the devil incarnate.

He'd seen what atrocities they were capable of. Thinking back, he shuddered. No human should have to endure or witness such barbarism. He was fully aware that his role was to provide just enough medical care to keep his patients alive so Al Nadir could continue their torture and prolong their suffering.

He looked at the woman and knew her story was no different. After he'd finished sewing her leg, he turned to look at her. The woman's hypnotic stare held him. It hooked him like his soul had been adrift and it reeled him in.

"Let me go," she whispered. The woman gazed into his pale eyes as he leant over. Her eyes burned into him. "Please. Let me go."

The doctor caught her frantic stare. His emotions rose as he realized the captured creature before him had no hope of surviving.

"Please," she implored, her face desperate and terrified. He knew he was her last hope.

The doctor held onto her clamps, staring into her eyes. Her pain was tangible. He paused. He could let her go. Although he doubted, with her injuries, that she'd get far. That wasn't his concern.

His hand rested on her wrists. He was indecisive and deeply confused.

The doctor heard her. He could sense her reaching into him, trying to connect with his good side. The part that had made him become a doctor. She pleaded persistently for release. Her persistence penetrated. Trance-like, he started to unclamp the woman from the trolley, first her left leg and then her right. Then he proceeded to unlock her wrists. The woman's whispered, breathless "thank you" had barely left her lips when the doctor recognized what he was doing. He clocked the back of a guard in the doorway and started to sweat. Looking down at the empty clamp in his hands, he realized the enormous risk he was taking.

He knew Al Nadir were inhuman sadists. If they discovered he'd helped one of their captives escape, he could expect the same treatment the woman had received. He locked the clamp back around the woman's ankle.

As the lock sprung back into place, the woman gasped. The doctor wasn't facing the woman but her sense of sheer horror was palpable. Her engulfing desolation seeped into him as he returned the clamp wrists.

"For Christ's sake. No. Don't do this. You know you could let me go."

But the doctor knew he couldn't. After years of narcotics abuse, he was malleable, vulnerable, and weak. He'd killed his conscience to survive. He'd buried it the moment he mainlined his first wage from Al Nadir.

"Please, help me. You know they're going to kill me. You can't want to see that happen. You're a good person. I feel it. You're not like them. You're not evil. You know you want to help me. Please, for God's sake, help me. Please, let me go. I won't say anything. Just let me go."

The doctor listened to the woman's hysterical pleas.

"They're planning a floorshow with me in it. I don't know what it means, but I know it's not good."

The doctor shuddered instinctively on hearing the word floorshow.

"Oh dear God, no," he muttered, and the woman's eyes widened at his exclamation.

"They're going to kill me, aren't they?" whispered the woman.

The doctor stopped clamping and stared back at the woman waiting on his answer. Kill her. If only that's all they were going to do. Before he could stop them, scenes of the last floorshow that he had been a guest at stumbled into his mind and, as bile rose in his throat, he wanted to physically vomit.

The woman eyed his reaction with terror.

"Oh God! You *do* know what it is, don't you?"

The doctor shook his head, too frightened to face the woman for fear his emotions would leak and he would tell her the whole story of what she would be enduring.

Silently, he continued to secure the clamps, fastening them to the sides of the trolley in turn.

The woman continued her incessant pleading, focusing on the floorshow to force him to change his mind. He couldn't, lest he become the central attraction of a future show.

Her eyes followed him as he secured the last clamp. He felt her silent anger. She accused him, blamed him for the eventual fate he knew she'd soon meet. She said he wasn't evil. That was true. But he was lost…very, very lost.

Ashamed, the doctor couldn't meet her eyes. But he did not have to; he could feel their intensity burning into his heart. Her attempts fruitless, the woman turned to him, her face full of contempt and disgust.

"How do you live with yourself?"

Finally, the doctor revolved to face her, his eyes wretched, his face sallow and lined with the years of misery he had seen.

Slowly, he replied, "I don't."

The silhouette of the doctor's retreating back defined for Ellie a total lack of hope. Falling back into the softness of the pillow, a lump like a pomegranate welled up in her throat. Harsh fabrics would have been less painful. But the soft cotton brought back home. Along with the feeling, memories flooded. Waking up with Sam, playing mischievously, leisurely making love on a Saturday morning, walking along the Thames, watching the ducks, going on seaside drives and country treks, sipping wine, eating curries, watching TV, having rows about who had the remote control.

All these normal, natural, simple things were now lost. Her days with Sam were over.

Lying there, waiting for the return of Sabena and her constant, cruel intentions, Ellie knew she had taken so much for granted. Alone, out of the mean, remorseless eyes of her captors, Ellie cried.

The tears came in powerful throes. Sobbing deeply, she set free the pain in her heart. Closing her eyes, Sam was there, smiling, holding her, caressing her hair, kissing her.

Ellie's tears flowed.

"I love you," she whispered. "See you on the other side, my darling."

Chapter 2

The Peace Summit had been hurriedly moved to Malta, a country completely free from the yolk of terrorism. Upon Sam's grave and foreboding instructions to UK Prime Minister Richard Ashton, the Parliament House state building in Valletta now housed the UN members. Within minutes of receiving the formal ok from the US President Jonathan Treeborne, officials around the world sprang into action. With the summit less than twenty-four hours away, speed and spontaneity were active defenses against Al Nadir.

Knowing their transmissions were constantly being intercepted, intelligence agencies washed their airways with a barrage of misinformation. Complex cryptics and multidimensional coded structures hiding secret, but totally false location information created a labyrinth where false was true and true was false, and Al Nadir remained confounded.

Back in the early days of Al Nadir's reign, such confusion would not have existed. In two years, everything had changed. The UN ratified Resolution 458, which delivered a global ban on the coverage of any event that impacted international security, and now media blanketing was commonplace despite the power of the internet. The technologies the security agencies now possessed could efficiently root out any news events that could impact international security. Use of quantum computing enabled a different level of processing, and artificial intelligence gave the security agencies a granular search capability where no one could hide anymore. Policing of the internet had become a reality. Freedom was no longer an option.

Of course, at the time of the ban, protests came from all directions: the press, the socialists, the academics, the geeks. Everyone claimed freedom of information was a human right. But their demonstrations shrank in pull power and potency as the vicious, heartless attacks by Al Nadir operatives entrenched in the international press community increased.

Day after day, reporters would be broadcasting and suddenly a member of the press team would detonate a bomb or open fire, killing everyone in shot. Neighborhood kids receiving medals or US troops fighting in a war zone, it was all the same to Al Nadir. They knew their own act of evil destruction would be the definitive headline.

After a string of these attacks, urgent and unprecedented action was taken to curb the world's press. Screening of new media recruits was handled by the military. Existing members were systematically scrutinized and forced, under law, to go through lie detection procedures to confirm that they were not Al Nadir operatives.

The problem was made more acute by the fact that Al Nadir recruited its operatives from existing members. They did not infiltrate their own operatives. Instead, they turned reporters, cameramen, researchers, and technicians into Al Nadir operatives. How they achieved this was never completely discovered. Intel agencies found evidence to confirm a combination of influencing drugs and money.

Very soon, the focus changed from how they did it to how they could be stopped. Using the UN ban, no media company was allowed to cover any event that threatened national or international security. Any company or individual seen broadcasting or talking about a prohibited event would, under Resolution 458, face the full force of the international security agencies. In the case of a media company, they would be pulled off the air immediately and both criminal and civil proceedings would be filed against the company to shut them down and place their executives into custody. It didn't matter if the company was using television, radio, new media, or the internet, their actions would constitute a breach of UN legislation and they would be prosecuted to the full extent of international law.

In the case of an individual trying their luck on promoting an event over social media, that person would be labelled a terrorist, their bank accounts frozen, their ability to travel removed (they would be placed on global security blacklists), and their employers informed of their insurgent behavior. Their life would, basically, be ruined.

In the beginning, media companies had been blasé, considering that they were above the law and untouchable. That was until the giant CNN irresponsibly broadcast the location of a meeting of the US president, the British PM, and the president of France. Before the reporter had finished his delivery, CNN had been pulled off the air by the National Security Agency.

It took a barrage of lawyers to get the station back on the air. Weeks went by before CNN was permitted to broadcast again. They were the example and it worked. No one became blasé again.

There were hundreds of episodes of smart-aleck students and hot-shot bloggers putting out sensitive information to test the security agencies and the UN. One by one, they were identified, taken, interrogated, given a black list status, and relegated to being unable to work, travel, or live a normal life. All were security tagged and all were publicly ridiculed. When it was made clear by the security agencies that their actions had resulted in the death of innocents, many were lucky to escape the lynch mobs that quickly formed in the towns and cities. And all because of some irresponsible Tweet or Facebook post.

Al Nadir was such a force, the only way the world could cope was by application of such stringent measures. Although it wasn't tasteful, individuals around the world, on hearing the stories put out by the establishment of those who had transgressed, eventually acquiesced. No longer was the internet a platform of fun and freedom. It became a place of dark fear.

The Peace Summit directly addressed the global threat of Al Nadir, and thus, under the ban, no media could attend, know, or tell the location of the summit. And those attending were bound to absolute secrecy with the threat of treason (and therefore, death) if one attempted to reveal the location. To the world outside, including Al Nadir, the Peace Summit was totally concealed.

Chapter 3

The haggard face of Al Nadir's resident physician slipped past Sabena's large office window as she tapped the air furiously. With her SmartLens in place, her HoloTab app suite was in full Augmented Reality function, and thus, what she was working on was for her eyes only. The beauty of SmartLens was that she could keep a watch on everything around her whilst working on her calculations. As the doctor walked briskly into her eye line, she yelled out, making him jump visibly. Sabena grinned, enjoying the nervousness she generated in others.

"Doc, is my girl done yet?"

The doctor stopped mid-stride and turned around. "Erm…yes," he stuttered. "She's all done. The stitches need some time to heal. Give it a day or two."

Sabena shook her head, her long brunette locks swishing back and forth. "Not possible, doc."

The doctor stood at the threshold to Sabena's office. She beckoned him in and he entered. Every step, she noted with amusement, was loaded with measured caution.

"Erm, well…at least keep any…physical exertion to a minimum." The doctor averted his eyes and stared at the floor.

"Physical exertion to a minimum, eh?" Sabena smirked, licking her lips. "I'm not sure that's going to be possible."

The doctor kept his eyes down and his face flushed pink.

Sabena loved his show of gentle sensitivity to the subject. She approached him, purring, "After all, doc, you know what's planned."

He nodded, his eyes still staring at the floor.

"So make sure she can take some serious exertion. Superglue her or something."

"Dr. Sanantoni, she's not an ornament," said the doctor, piping up and showing a glimmer of courage.

Sabena raised an eyebrow at his response. "No, but she is an *objet d'art*!" replied Sabena, breathing faster as she remembered Ellie's gorgeous body.

The doctor flushed a deeper pink and Sabena detected a shiver on his lips.

"You like her, don't you?"

The doctor turned his face away, and Sabena read his shyness. She found it rather cndcaring.

She reached out and pulled his chin up, forcing him to look at her. In his terrified eyes, sadness flickered. Sabena moved forward, so close she could feel the doctor's breath on her lips. She swept a glance up and down his body, and her hand danced down his torso towards his stomach and beyond. Her eyes sparkled with evil intent.

"You could join in too. If you like?"

The doctor swallowed deeply and stood as still as stone. Sabena's hand rested on his crotch. She could feel little tremors ripple through him. His eyes locked on hers. His breath was pushing harder against her lips as she knew his pulse was racing.

Sabena adored the effect she had on him.

Eventually, the doctor picked up enough strength to reply. "Thank you for the offer, Dr. Sanantoni, but I have a heavy schedule of work."

Sabena smirked on hearing the doctor's refusal, and her eyes widened, flashing darkly.

"Me too! Pity. I think you'd have been quite an actor."

The doctor's pale-blue eyes looked away from Sabena's.

"Anyway, she's ok to…play with?" murmured Sabena, biting her lip and looking coyly at the doctor.

"Dr. Sanantoni, she's ok. Just don't put too much force in your…activities. You don't want to rip her apart."

"Not until she's ready," said a new voice.

Sabena swung her head back, grinning broadly as she heard Russo's deep, sexy voice, and she pulled her hand away from the doctor's pants.

"You said it, Russo!"

Russo smiled, standing at the doorway, and Sabena giggled like a school girl.

"Come on. Let's go and check on our new toy," said Sabena, and she left with Russo.

But she flicked a glance back to suck up the true horror that floated in the doctor's eyes.

Chapter 4

The plane touched down at 7:40 a.m. Within minutes, Quentin was whisked through security with his other peers, and he quickly found himself in the back of the Audi SUV provided by UN security.

The car gunned down the road out of the airport and Quentin watched the scenery of the beautiful Maltese island. Shrines to the Virgin Mary popped up at regular intervals, dotted between the ochre block walls that lined the roads. Quentin could see the yellowing fields beyond arranged in graduated steps to support better irrigation. Low-level shrubs and spiky, oval cactuses interspersed the stark plains, demonstrating their hardiness to the scorching Maltese sun. Quentin had heard that local farmers used water from the ground brought up through artesian wells, whereas domestic and business water uses relied on the large desalination plants around the edges of the island.

As they approached the town of Marsa, Quentin peered through the darkened windows of the SUV at Maltese life erupting into the early morning around him. Cafés started to put out their tables, road cleaners sluiced the cobbled stone pavements in front of their shops, and small children held onto their pale blue satchels, their eyes wide as they waited for their mothers to take them to school.

The Peace Summit was a two-day affair starting at 10:00 a.m. that day and finishing the next day at noon. Quentin was due to speak at 9:00 a.m. the following day so he had time to relax a little before then. His secretary had hurriedly found him a hotel. It was the Hilton St Julian overlooking the exclusive Portomaso Marina in the north and the beautiful, crystal waters of the Mediterranean in the west. He'd viewed the meeting notes and rapidly loaded a HoloVid of the Hilton in his apartment near Westminster before he'd been collected for his flight out.

The sprawling sandstone palace stood proudly with a line of coconut and date palms outside erect like sentries protecting the holidaying inhabitants within. On such formal occasions, Quentin usually stayed with the rest of the delegation, but such had been the haste of the trip, he'd had to take whatever accommodation was available. The port of St Julian was only a fifteen-minute run from Valletta, and if he was honest, he much preferred to be somewhere less hostilc than amongst his sniping, sneering peers.

As he settled into the journey from Luqa International Airport to the island's capital, the glistening waters and luxurious surroundings of Portomaso slipped into his mind. He smiled, looking forward to relaxing later around the hotel's pool. He may even be able to catch one of those local pretty lovelies he'd spied in Pieta Florentina fretting around their tables and arranging their shop wares. Quentin licked his lips with amorous intention.

He brought out his phone and flicked up the schedule for the day. Perhaps he could even sneak out once the UN secretary general and the US foreign secretary had done their spiel, and the little countries reliant on Al Nadir's financial bolstering started to issue their pathetic defense pleas. Quentin smirked thinking about those countries. They would soon get a taste of what happens for being loyal to the wrong players.

Around him flashed sandstone buildings, a subtle mix of the old and the new. Unlike so many other countries whose main industrial sector was tourism, Malta's construction placed emphasis on keeping new designs sympathetic with the old in style, height, and texture of the stone. The SUV shot down the dusty road, and colonial facades adorning sandstone residences whizzed past his eye line. Valletta was less than five miles away, straight down the number one dual carriageway. As he looked out, a sign pointed to Hamrun. He clicked on the interactive update app and was told in his earpiece that Parliament House in Valletta was about four minutes away.

Quentin stared through the heavily tinted glass. They'd stopped to allow a priest the opportunity to cross the road. On his right, a café served the Maltese breakfast staple of imqaret. They were diamond shaped date parcels in filo pastry, a throwback to when the Arabs governed the island from 870 AD to the 11th Century. The café served them together with pastizzi, a rolled filo shell filled with ricotta cheese. Watching the locals chomp into the delicious looking meal, Quentin became hungry. The food on the plane had been adequate, typical BA fare, but he'd been served way too early in the morning and hadn't been ready for it. All he'd wanted was a strong, black coffee to kickstart his naturally lethargic system. But now his stomach rumbled, impatient to be fed.

He leaned forward and tapped on the UN security guard's shoulder in the front seat.

"Don't suppose there's any chance of stopping for a quick bite?"

"No chance at all, Foreign Secretary," said the bodyguard with clipped, officious authority. "Didn't you eat on the plane?"

Quentin harrumphed. "Food wasn't up to snuff!"

The guard stared non-plussed at him. His cold, bored eyes screamed out, 'Not my problem!'

Quentin scowled. "Look, I'm the minister here. I'm the one paying your bloody wages. So if I say stop at a café so I can grab a bite to eat, that's what you'll bloody well do!"

He fixed a hard stare at the security guard that screamed 'I'll cause you big trouble if you don't!'

Clearly, the guard got Quentin's non-verbal threat.

He nodded reluctantly and muttered in Maltese to the driver, "Twaqqaf il-karozza meta tara dak li jmiss kafetterija! Dan Ingliż idjota irid jittieħed tiegħu xaħam wiċċ!" *Stop the car when you see the next cafe. This English idiot wants to stuff his fat face!*

Quentin detected what he thought was 'English' and maybe 'cafeteria' but couldn't get the rest.

He glared at the guard and said sharply, "In English please!"

"Apologies, Minister. I only explained that we need to stop at a café as you need to eat something."

Quentin eyed the guard suspiciously, and then smirked. Refusing eye contact, he looked out the window and said, "About bloody time!"

The driver raised a conspiratorial eyebrow at the security guard.

Quentin clocked the look, and hissed, "Stop. Now!"

The driver shrugged, drove down Girolamo Cassar Street, and pulled in by the Auberge De Castille. Although carrying diplomatic plates on his car, he also shoved his 'On diplomatic business' dual language sign up on the dashboard. Then he released the internal locks for Quentin and his UN bodyguard to alight.

"Sir, if you follow me, I'll help you locate a suitable café for your needs."

Chapter 5

Ashton lay in bed. Alone.

His trophy wife, Natasha, hadn't yet arrived back from wherever the hell she was the night before. Mariella, his younger daughter, had been carted off to spend time with her grandparents. As for his older daughter, Abigail, like her mother, Ashton had no idea where she was. She'd muttered something about a party in Belgravia and she'd kip with friends. Security services had inserted a locator chip in her phone so they could keep track. Same with Natasha. They were never too far away from being pinged by some spotty-faced analyst in Thames House.

Ashton's mind drifted back to his brief tryst with Katzy. Or, as she was known to her loving public, Miss Judy Katzenberger, number one political correspondent at the BBC and mouthpiece for Westminster's media soundbites.

Her luscious body there on his desk, legs open, wanton…God almighty. He needed her now.

Ashton picked up his phone. To hell with convention. And doing the right thing.

Clicking on her name, he typed in a quick coded message.

'Fancy building up your muscles at my gym?'

The moment Ashton hit send, the message instantly deleted from his sent file. Ashton waited for Katzy's response with the phone nestled beside him. One loud ping. Less than a minute. Such speed signified Katzy's intentions.

He grabbed the phone and read the text.

'I'll be at the gym at 9 a.m. Ready for a REAL workout.'

Ashton smirked. He liked the emphasis. She obviously harbored guilty feelings about yesterday. He knew he'd pushed back despite wanting her.

She'd been upset. Maybe it was time to be true to his feelings. He didn't love Natasha and the feeling was mutual. It was nothing more than a show marriage. Something that looked good in the celebrity mags and photo opps.

But with Katzy, just recalling her beautiful, cheeky face and enchanting, deep, brown eyes, his loins enflamed, and his member twitched. Thinking of his wife, despite her stunning face and groomed, model body, sex with her was like being dunked in ice cubes made of shit.

A cold, revolting experience.

Ashton shivered, and typed back, 'Enjoy your workout. See you soon.'

Ashton clicked on send, and the message sent and then deleted.

Imbued with a sense of passion and fun, he relished a state of mind that, as the prime minister, he rarely enjoyed. Ashton flung off the duvet and headed for his bathroom. In the mirror, Ashton stared at his naked frame. Smiling, he preened, flexing his body. He admired his taut, toned musculature won by hours on the weights. The total package housed in a tall body was quite a change from previous PMs. They had all either widened through middle-age and good living or become gaunt through stress and burning the midnight oil.

After seeing his predecessor with his blonde, unruly mop and paunch-laden body, Ashton vowed not to fall into the unhealthy trap of bad eating and little exercise. His naturally attractive if slightly effeminate looks had streams of women vying to work for him. These women, named 'Ashton's Angels' by members of the opposition and even those in his own party, became media staples throughout his premiership.

Ashton picked up his *Clive Christian* fragrance, and then looked at Dolce Gabbana's *The One*. Katzy had bought it for him, saying it made her horny just smelling it.

Ashton smirked and sprayed his naked body with the scent. He selected an understated Tom Ford grey suit that made the most of his physique and headed outside. His primary bodyguard accompanied him to the car and opened the door. Ashton slipped inside. The bodyguard got in the front.

Ashton took out his phone. With Cumberford, his parliamentary private secretary (PPS) on the line, Ashton called off his 9:00 a.m. meeting with the health secretary. At that moment, Ashton really wasn't interested in the health secretary's bleating, repetitive stance.

More money. No cuts. More money.

Goodness, couldn't the man see throwing money at the problem would only make matters worse? The whole damn National Health Service (NHS) needed a root and branch overhaul, but he wasn't going to be the PM to suggest one. He wasn't suicidal.

Ping!

Ashton stared at his phone, smiling as he read the message.

'Started without you but need your help with the heavy lifting.'

Rapidly, Ashton typed back, 'More than happy to lend a hand.'

His grin spread, and his driver clocked his expression and forced down a smirk of his own. Ashton noticed and raised an eyebrow.

"Eyes front!" he said abruptly.

The driver got the message.

On hitting send, the message deleted instantly after reaching its target. Ashton sneered.

No one would know.

Chapter 6

Russo heard the short ping and turned back to Sabena; his eyebrow arched.

"Hold on, Pedro. I've just got to send this."

Russo watched Sabena tap hurriedly on her phone. As a text came back, she smirked and licked her lips. Russo questioned her behavior but didn't dare ask. He slipped his hand into Sabena's and he gripped her strong fingers. Her eyes drilled into his. Russo could see unmitigated want within her, but sadly, not for him.

"We need to be heading off to Malta, Sabena. She'll be here for you when you get back," he said, pressing down his irritation.

"I know. I just have to see her again."

"What's so special about her?"

Russo couldn't quite understand Sabena's fascination with Ellie. He'd seen her obsessed before, but never like this. It was as if her every cell was attracted unconditionally to their captive.

"She never broke. She never told me to stop," said Sabena finally.

They finished their walk and stopped outside the medical lab that held Ellie.

"She did, didn't she?" Russo thought back to her torture, and realized Sabena was right. Sam had broken. Sam had yelled at Sabena to stop.

Ellie had remained silent.

"I need to break her, Pedro. I need to hear her screams stop. She can't be unbreakable. She just can't. That's not possible. She has to have a breaking point. And I'm going to do absolutely everything I can to find it."

"Then the floor show should be the perfect vehicle to achieve that goal," said Russo, gradually appreciating why Sabena was so fixated with Ellie.

She was a personification of Sabena's weakness. If she couldn't break her, it might cause others, especially Salim, to cast doubt on Sabena's abilities. Russo knew Sabena was outwardly strong. She was a vicious, psychopathic monster housed in a tall, beautiful, sultry skin. But she walked a line of insanity. And that insanity brought her insecurity.

Russo knew Sabena had to control and dominate everything and everyone. She had to be the one making people tremble with fear.

If news filtered through Al Nadir's grapevine that she couldn't break one simple woman, a captive who hadn't been trained in the art of resisting torture, just a normal woman with no intelligence background, who happened to be the wife of the infamous and much hated Dr. Sam Noor, she'd be finished.

It would cripple her standing in the terrorist collective forever.

Now Russo understood Sabena's manic obsession.

It was an anxious need to prove her worth.

And, most of all, a need to demonstrate that she still had what it took to be Salim's number two.

Chapter 7

At the penthouse, aka the gym, Ashton stared at the clock. It was 8:54 a.m. His Katzy wouldn't be long. One thing he knew about Katzy was that she was always punctual.

He busied himself making a double espresso while he waited for his media goddess to arrive. The internal phone rang. Ashton picked it up expecting security to inform him on Katzy's arrival. He'd arranged complete secrecy and discretion with the security company managing the building. Through his usual blend of intimidation and threats of treason, Ashton ensured the guards' mouths remained shut to gutter-press gossip.

"Sir, a Fortnum and Mason's hamper has arrived for you from Miss Katzenberger. It's been completely scanned, sir, and it's all clear. Shall I proceed to bring it up to you?"

Ashton thought for a second. Why was Katzy sending him a present from Fortnum's? It was a bit strange even for her kinky ways. What did she expect him to do? Feed her with salted caramel cookies while he fucked her brains out?

An interesting notion.

Ashton smirked, licking his lips and suddenly getting into the whole food and sex vibe.

"Yes, of course. Bring it up," responded Ashton finally.

The doorbell rang and he opened it wide for the security guard to bring in his hamper. Ashton pointed to the table in the living room. With the hamper deposited, the guard vacated. Ashton heard the front door close. He glanced at his watch. 9:10 a.m. Where was Katzy?

Ashton lifted the lid on the luxurious looking hamper and found a note.

'Time to play with our food! Love Katzy xxx.'

Ashton grinned. She was getting naughtier every day.

Inside the hamper were exotic fruits, champagne and caviar, Turkish delight, clotted cream, and a rainbow selection of various interestingly shaped root vegetables. The collection was eclectic but also deeply erotic. Staring at the food, Ashton began to summon up a range of scenarios in his mind where all items would be enjoyed and fully utilized.

His dick pinged to attention as the naughtiest of scenes rolled through his mind. He wanted to start playing…But where the hell was she?

Ashton poked around the hamper as he tried to take his mind off his Katzy's glorious body and her clutching Kegels. As he picked up each item, he noticed something was buried underneath the straw.

Another card. Ashton smirked at first.

'The look of love. Katzy only had eyes for you, Prime Minister! S x.'

Reading to the end, Ashton stiffened, and a slick of cold dread dripped down his back. His fingers tightened around the card, and he looked back into the hamper. He started to throw the packing straw and food items out, his movements quickening as the dread grew. It threaded persistently through him, stitching into his muscles and making him shiver.

Having made room for his investigations, Ashton dove into the straw packing. Then he felt something. His hands touched a box and his fingers froze.

Slowly, he pulled the box out. It had a see-through cover like a Christmas gift box, the type Boots sold, the type his dreadful in-laws seemed obsessed with buying him every festive season.

Free of the straw, Ashton could now see the contents. It almost made him drop the box.

Packaged inside, clearly visible through the plastic, transparent cover was an intact human heart. But despite its gruesome display, it wasn't the heart that forced Ashton to bring back and use every ounce of his training as a MI6 agent, surging through him, a force of strength and ultimate resolve that kept him from breaking down completely.

For on the human heart were a pair of human eyeballs.

They'd been pushed into the meaty top part of the organ. They stared at Ashton like forlorn creatures searching for meaning.

Ashton turned away, holding down the bile that flew up his throat.

In the eyes, it was all there. Those orbs had borne witness to a horrific sudden slaughter.

He didn't want to, but he couldn't stop himself. He gazed deeply into those grotesque eyes. Like a tractor beam searing out of those eyeballs, Ashton was compelled to return back to them. And it hit him.

Thundered into him. Real hard.

Those eyes. Mischievous, enchanting, and of the deepest brown.

Oh my God! Katzy!

The realization and the tremor it brought on made Ashton drop the box.

The vomit rose in his throat. His previous training was now forgotten as Katzy's demise stormed his psyche. Unable to pull back, shaking with shock and pain, he hurled up his breakfast until his throat was raw and burning.

Chapter 8

Quentin maneuvered himself out of the car and looked around. The security guard motioned towards the Triq il Merkanti (Merchant Street), but Quentin ignored him and stared at Auberge de Castille. It was a strong, square building that seemed to represent the forthright strength and solid reliability of the Maltese people. The two canons pointing out from the entrance were both imposing and balanced in their innate fearsomeness.

The security guard coughed subtly and Quentin finally acknowledged him.

"Ah, yes. Of course. The café," he mumbled with haughty superiority, and the security guard nodded.

Quentin noticed how the guard stood close to him and his hand fluttered by his gun holster in case of any action. Quentin swallowed heavily, suddenly uncomfortable about getting out of the car, but he couldn't recant his decision as it would have shown weakness. He moved a little closer to the guard and the two proceeded to walk down Merchant Street.

Quentin could see, as he walked, that Malta was a country loaded with history. A large, sandstone building with impressive carved stone work and curved black iron grills covering the lower windows took up his right-hand side. Quentin clocked the name. Palazzo Parisio. The gold plaque on the wall signified that Napoleon had lived there from June 12 to June 18, 1798. As Quentin ambled along with the security guard, it seemed that every corner held a historical nugget of gold. But to protect its past, Malta had to look to its future. Quentin recognized this approach ingrained in their current economic drive. Gaunt cranes striding up over the skyline towards the brilliant, blue skies demonstrated the numerous construction projects across the island and the high levels of foreign direct investment that were being sought to fund such projects.

A little way down Merchant Street, the guard stopped, indicating to a café that offered the pastry delights Quentin sought. Quentin seated himself and observed as the guard gave a swift instruction to a young, pretty waitress with flawless, bronze skin and silky, brunette hair tied back in a pony tail that bounced back and forth as she ran around the tables. Quentin licked his lips subconsciously. The guard eyed him disdainfully. Quentin shrugged, not caring for social commentary or political correctness on how he saw or treated women.

As his father had said: "Women. Any are fair game, my boy. Never forget that!"

He never did.

The guard pushed his chair outward, angling his body so that he covered Quentin. He kept his gun in his hand. His eyes searched everyone that passed. Although he didn't like the man's attitude, the UK foreign secretary felt safe under his protection.

The pretty waitress deposited the imqaret and pastizzi pastries along with a frothy cappuccino in front of Quentin and smiled. Quentin smirked. Eyeing the waitress, he lingered on her full, pointy breasts pressing against her navy t-shirt, which was definitely a size too small, thought Quentin, considering how he'd like to liberate her poor, suppressed bosoms as he bit into the delicious Maltese pastry.

Chapter 9

Ellie heard talking far away.

From her dream world of Sam encasing her body in his love, Ellie was wrenched back into a reality of Sabena and a strange man staring at her with lust-filled eyes. She flicked her head away from the door and bit back her fear.

Sabena moved into the room with the man.

"Hello, Ellie. How are you feeling?" chirped Sabena, moving in to stand close to the stainless steel medical trolley.

Ellie didn't answer. She attempted to contract her body away from Sabena's consuming stare. With just a light medical gown covering her nakedness, her vulnerability was evident, and Ellie knew Sabena and the guy with her recognized it.

Ellie sneaked a look at the man with Sabena as he walked around to the other side of the trolley. He was dark haired, very tall, and muscular, just like Sam. But that's where their similarities stopped. The guy, although startlingly handsome, held a glacial, sadistic glint in his eyes. A telling indication that pain was his pleasure. He bent in and touched Ellie's neck. She squirmed and pulled her head back into the soft pillow. He sneered and dropped his hand down to rest on the collar of her gown. He closed his fingers around the flimsy material and yanked the gown upward. Under the force, Ellie's body lifted up and the tie backs came loose, exposing her sculptured collar bone and shoulder.

Sabena watched, and moistened her lips on seeing Ellie's flesh.

Ellie remained still, taking in the man holding her gown. If he pulled any harder the tie backs would come apart, thought Ellie. And then...

She swallowed hard, staring with wide eyes at the man. But she refused to show how terrified she was. Something inside her emitted a resonance of calm, but she couldn't understand how or why.

With his face close to Ellie's, the man growled, "Dr. Sanantoni asked you a question, you little bitch. Have the common courtesy to answer her!"

"Tut, tut, Pedro. Don't be so hard on our guest. I'm sure she's just a bit sleepy. Doc give you a drug, did he? Well, don't worry, babes. When we're back from our little crusade, we'll give you something to perk you right up. Won't we, darling?"

Sabena glanced up at the man Ellie now knew as Pedro and the two of them grinned with conspiratorial and lascivious mischievousness. The man nodded and released his grip on Ellie's gown. She slumped back into the pillow.

"Good boy," said Sabena, sliding around to the other side of the trolley.

She sidled up against the man, who reached out and kissed her passionately. Sabena then detached herself, leant across Ellie, and gazed into her eyes. Ellie could sense Sabena penetrating her soul. She swept a glance down at Ellie's gown. Ellie could see her captor seem to steel herself, wrestling internally with a decision she was burning to make. She moved in and sunk her lips hard onto Ellie's, forcing her mouth to open and receive her invading tongue. Ellie couldn't push away. Sabena gripped the sides of Ellie's face, driving her fingers against her nose. Trapping her tight. Sabena pushed, cutting off Ellie's airways. She couldn't breathe. Sabena's eyes homed in on hers. In them, Ellie could see Sabena's enjoyment of Ellie's desperation and fear.

"Tick tock, Sabena. We gotta go!" said the man, interrupting Sabena's moment of intimidation.

Sabena drew back from Ellie's lips. A line of spittle followed her, and Sabena knocked it away as she continued to stare entranced at her captive. Released, Ellie took a deep, long breath, and then coughed.

"Nice work, darling," snarled Sabena, annoyed by the man's intervention. Then she turned back to Ellie. "Don't worry, babes. I'll be back soon, and at the floor show, we can pick up right where we left off."

The man laughed as he made his way through the door. Sabena joined him.

"That's something I ain't gonna miss," said the man, leering at Ellie.

Sabena took his arm. "Come on, darling. We've got to put a dent in some international policies!"

Ellie heard their raucous laughing gradually disappear as they walked further away. Alone again, Ellie had nothing but her thoughts. She tried to think of something else, but all she could see was the doctor's shocked face when she'd mentioned the floor show.

She could taste Sabena's minty saliva in her mouth, and her understanding of what the floor show really was grew like a cancer to infest her fractured mind.

Chapter 10

The box holding its gruesome wares fell to the floor. The force opened the plastic cover. The human heart flopped out, and the eyeballs dislodged and rolled away from Ashton.

Their trajectory was a proxy for Katzy's state.

Away from him.

Forever.

His sick feeling had now subsided, but in its place was an obsidian rage. A blood-thirsty need for revenge.

Al Nadir had made it personal with the wrong person.

Ashton glanced down at the heart and shuddered.

Now it was just a lump of dead muscle. But it had once brought to life a love that he barely dared himself to feel. He cursed his fixation on conformity. He should have been true to Katzy. She was his love.

One of the eyeballs caught his gaze and he tried not to imagine what they'd done to her. Had she still been alive when they'd taken her eyes? Oh God. No! Ashton shut out the thought.

He gripped the sofa he'd fallen upon. A sack of despair. He felt the material tightening in his fists. He clenched, taking more of the material, and in his mind, it was Sabena's slender neck in his hold, his fingers pushing into her flesh, powered by the raging force that flooded him. He broke through her soft, supple skin. Her blood soaked into his nails as he clawed through her epidermis to the slippery, subcutaneous tissue beneath.

That darkness within gave him the strength to rip away her throat. All the time, he was watching Sabena's eyes. The sadistic light in them slowly fading.

He tore into her until nothing of her vicious soul existed.

Ashton stood shaking over Sabena's bloody remains, but the steady thump of vengeance hadn't been abated.

A resonance built. Stronger. Shaking him. And a dizziness-inducing darkness swept over Ashton. Something within him screamed.

Love taken.

Only hate remained.

And a burning need for retribution.

His Balance shifted.

Opening his eyes, Ashton knew something had changed. Gone was any shred of goodness he may have had.

That steady thump. The resonance of darkness. He settled into its rhythm.

He allowed it to align with the remnants of his heart.

And then take over his soul.

Chapter 11

The tunnel was built from a strange, reflective composite material reminiscent of something found in a 1960's sci-fi B-movie. Sabena often thought that as she walked down the tunnel to the hanger. But today, her thoughts weren't on her surroundings. Holding Russo's hand, she virtually skipped down the tunnel like a dizzy school girl. Every inch of her body frazzled with an energy.

How does First Lady of the world sound to you?

When Salim had said those words, she'd wanted to believe it could be true.

Marching down the tunnel, she knew she was hours away from achieving that insanely ambitious goal. Insane, of course, to a normal person. But not to Sabena.

With absolute certainty rippling through her and causing the buzz of electrifying energy, Sabena knew she would soon be the most powerful woman on Earth.

Russo picked up her vibe and tightened his grip on her hand.

"Won't be long!"

Sabena shot him a broad smile framed by shimmering, scarlet lips, her dinner-plate eyes sparkling with power, lust, and dark ambition.

"Oh, I know that. Come on. Race you to the Runner!"

And with that childish challenge, Sabena shot off down the tunnel, laughing manically as Russo ran dutifully after her. As she ran, Sabena felt the energy within her grow. It was like she was suddenly superhuman. She could do anything. Presidents, kings, queens, all would bow to her and Salim.

Salim and she would be the new gods.

No one could stop them.

The thought propelled her forward at a speed she doubted she could ever have reached before that moment. Her arms shot out either side of her as she did an impression of a plane.

She laughed, screaming, "I can fly."

Russo reached her. He slipped his hands around her trim waist.

"You certainly can. Want to take me into orbit?" Russo grinned with a sexy gleam.

"No time, babes. We gotta get some heat in Malta. Show those fuckers who rules the world."

"Gonna be interesting to see old Treetrunk's face when he finds out we've got his bomb!"

Sabena stopped and turned sharply. All the laughter and merriment was gone. Her face was a glacial mask of chilling, murderous intention.

"It was never *his* bomb. We brought it home to its rightful place. It belongs to us. And it always did."

Sabena whipped her head back toward the end of the tunnel and strode forward, determination in every step. She heard Russo just behind. But this time, she didn't try to clasp his hand or show any crazy joviality.

Sabena reached the end of the tunnel and looked out at the Stealth Runner housed in the hanger. The Stealth Runner was an incredible blend of the best technology from the F35 Lightning Two or, as the pilots called it, 'Panther'. It had Al Nadir's redesigned, sleeker, and more aerodynamic body, featuring a smaller group of collapsible wings to increase velocity. It was a biomimetic design filched directly from the insect world. But the feature that stole the show and demonstrated Al Nadir's lethal leading edge on the world's military was its ability to literally vanish, not just on radar like stealth tech offered, but it could vanish from an observer's sight. Through the use of a unique outer coating of reflective nano-cells that resonated at a frequency range matching a range of specific frequencies within the white light spectrum, the craft was rendered completely invisible.

Sabena flicked her head back to Russo who still trailed behind.

"Tick tock, Pedro. Tick tock!" snapped Sabena, repeating Russo's earlier retort.

She watched Russo run toward her, concern erupting across his handsome face.

Annoying Sabena had mortal consequences.

Ice glazed over her dark brown eyes as Sabena grabbed her helmet from the shelf, climbed into the Stealth Runner, flicked switches, and started to power up the engines. Russo followed suit.

"Ready?"

Sabena smirked, and Russo breathed a little easier. "Absolutely!"

"Alright!" yelled Sabena, suddenly slipping into a manic manner. "Let's go and gatecrash the UN's party!"

Chapter 12

The sojourn at the local café was unfortunately all too brief, and Quentin was hurried back by his security into the waiting SUV. Quentin discerned that the guard didn't like him. Well the feeling's mutual, thought Quentin. In silence, they travelled to the Triq il Reppublica (Republic Street). The SUV approached Parliament House, a new building constructed just two years earlier and designed in limestone, concrete, and steel by Renzo Piano. It was an incredible geometric feat, balanced on stilts, an echo of cubism, but still reflective of the sturdy ancient walls that surrounded the city. The SUV stopped and lined up behind rows of other SUVs and saloon cars that had arrived with more ministers and officials from around the globe.

Quentin stared at his fellow peers and breathed deeply.

This was the summit that could change everything.

The end of Al Nadir.

Nervousness gripped him as he strode forward through the entrance, now ensconced in a bigger group of his peers. Would he ever be found out for colluding with Al Nadir?

He pulled his legs under the table. US Foreign Secretary, Dick Cowl, sat beside him. Quentin was uncomfortable; he loathed the rapid set-ups. He tried to exchange a few light words and cheerful banter with his American counterpart whilst waiting for the summit to commence, but his ankle hurt. He recalled Sam's unbridled attack on him and winced. His earlier feelings of guilt and self-hatred at becoming a killer when he'd heard the news from Godley of Sam's capture had long since dispersed. Now he hoped Sam was getting the treatment he'd dished out to him in that underground garage.

Or maybe even worse.

A tall, imposing man with a long face and strong, square chin stood up.

Quentin recognized him as the UN secretary general. He started to deliver his opening address.

"Al Nadir is an invading cancer in our body of world peace. There is not one representative in this room whose country has not, in some way, been affected by their actions. They are a scourge on humanity. Their activities have ravaged our world for too long."

At this point, the secretary general brought up hideous images of terror for which Al Nadir had been responsible. Biological and chemical attacks, assassinations, executions, bombings. Every known atrocity conceivable was laid bare. The secretary general allowed the representatives time to absorb the full horror before continuing his speech.

"Our institution here is carved out of the stone of diplomacy. We strive for peace at every juncture. We search for the non-aggressive solution to every dispute and conflict. But I ask you, honorable members, how can we hope to achieve peace with an organization like Al Nadir? They are an extraordinary threat, one that calls for extraordinary means to counter their opposition.

"I am cognizant of the fact that there are members here with economic embargoes and sanctions against them. Such measures are in direct response to their country's collusion with Al Nadir. I also realize that, as a result of these sanctions, some member states face a humanitarian crisis. Their situations only serve to contribute to the overpowering need to approve the tabled resolution to employ *extreme force* to remove Al Nadir's stranglehold on the world. I would like now to open the floor and hear from our honorable representative from the United States of America."

Quentin looked on as big-boned, sly-faced Cowl rose, swung a sneer at Quentin, and nodded approval to the secretary general, as he took over the floor.

"I thank the secretary general and join in supporting his commitment to finding a solution to rid the world of Al Nadir. We know the countries where Al Nadir has entrenched operations. The countries where governments are subservient to their activities. The countries that have turned a blind eye to Al Nadir in order that their regimes be given more power to terrorize and dictate. So pervasive and powerful is Al Nadir that the once brutal terror states inside the axis of evil have turned compliant, acquiescing to Al Nadir's hostile takeovers. They have agreed to be connected under the banner of Al Nadir, realizing it is better to be part of a world terror organization than just a regional one. Regimes have agreed to do this because Al Nadir allows them to continue their despicable acts on domestic soil and Al Nadir protects them from outside aggression. It really is a case of the devil looks after his own.

"But the days of plausible denial are over. These leaders must be held accountable. For it is their acts of complicity that have made Al Nadir into the global threat it is today. Concerted force must be applied to ensure these countries uphold international law and expunge Al Nadir from their turf completely."

Sudden shouts from the floor dissected Cowl's speech. Several honorable members had taken serious umbrage at the insinuation that their countries were willingly colluding with Al Nadir.

Quentin could see Cowl was holding down his frustration and his need to continue. Clearly, he didn't want to lose his floor and the momentum he'd so far generated. As expected, he replied with equal vigor.

"We have significant evidence that documents the special relationship some honorable member states have with Al Nadir. Although examples to cooperate with allied forces have been made, it is obvious from reports that these have been token gestures. Their alliances are still very much with Al Nadir."

At this moment, the representatives that were annoyed all stood up as if to leave. Security guards positioned themselves at the end of the aisles, patting the air and indicating for them to sit down. Muttering and cursing in their own languages, the representatives reluctantly returned to their seats.

Quentin stared at Cowl, secretly pleased that the US secretary was getting a hard time. His counterpart eyed the disturbance with simmering anger before continuing.

"Now the gloves are off. The days of softly, softly are long gone. It's time for us to act. In the interests of regaining world peace, under the authority vested in this congress, I would like to put forth tabled Resolution 8091 to use 'extreme unreserved force' to remove Al Nadir from all the countries where they have substantial power bases."

Quentin was hit by Cowl's cunning smirk as he entered the final stage of his address.

"The burgeoning weight of Al Nadir is suffocating world peace. Such is the frequency of their horrific attacks that we have become desensitized to their impact. But we must not. We must look. Every time they target a school, a hospital, a theatre, we must look each time the bloody bodies are brought out. We must remember that Al Nadir is causeless. Their purpose is not of liberation. It is of chaos. They wantonly extinguish lives to cause absolute terror, to disrupt business, and to destabilize global economies. They engage in every crime known to man. Some crimes, they have even created themselves. Their nano-bomb has given new meaning to the term 'suicide bomber'. Al Nadir is the new virus of the twenty-first century. The only antidote we have against them is extreme unreserved force."

"Could the honorable member for the United States clarify the term extreme unreserved force? The tabled documents are quite vague and do not clearly identify just what kind of force will be used. If we are to judge whether to pass a resolution sanctioning this, I would like to know just what kind of force will be used."

Quentin checked where that question originated from, and found it had come from the German UN ambassador. Quentin had been watching him. He'd been listening, head down, nodding intently, seemingly agreeing on the common threat of Al Nadir. But Quentin noticed his movements becoming more agitated, moving around on his seat, uncomfortable at the vague terminology of what 'extreme unreserved force' actually meant.

Quentin smiled inwardly at Cowl as he bit back his irritation like a petulant child at the further disruption to his delivery. Cowl's tempo increased and he projected the words he said with an undeniable force of conviction.

"In answer to the honorable member's question, extreme unreserved force is a term that allows us the right to deploy weapons of significant magnitude required to rid the world of Al Nadir. If we fail to act now, countless millions will continue to lose their lives and we will not be worthy of holding the responsibility or the authority that this institution vests in us.

"I ask you, honorable members, for your serious consideration. We will be no better than Al Nadir if we do not invoke the powers of this congress and make the resolution to sanction the use of extreme unreserved force. In doing so, we will provide a foundation to build a great world for our peoples. For the sake of our great, diverse, and beautiful world, we cannot afford to deliberate further on *whether* to use extreme unreserved force but agree upon *when* we use it. Every second spent in deliberation is another second lost in the war against Al Nadir and the reclamation of peace for our great world nation."

It couldn't be denied, thought Quentin, despite the cat-calling, Cowl finished his speech with the passion and intensity reflective of an actor in an Oscar-winning film.

Taking his seat, Cowl's address was met with clapping and applause. It seemed to Quentin that even the wayward representatives couldn't help but be moved by such a persuasive, powerful speech.

During a brief, midmorning recess, Quentin cornered Cowl in the men's room.

"Dick, you're talking about America's right to use nuclear weapons to oust Al Nadir, aren't you?"

Dick zipped up his flies and turned slowly to face Quentin, his face sage and solemn.

"We're gonna use whatever it takes to annihilate those fuckers. But you didn't hear it from me."

Dick looked harshly at Quentin. His expression to Quentin was clear. 'If this information gets leaked, you'll never live another day'. Cowl then put on a smile of geniality to clear the air.

"Come on, sonny. We've got a resolution to pass."

Quentin followed Cowl like a scared lapdog back into the room.

Chapter 13

The Stealth Runner shot through the clouds just skirting fifty thousand feet, running at Mach 1.8. In her helmet, the Heads-Up Display (HUD) AR panel shuddered, and Salim's face appeared.

"Morning, Sabena. All on track?"

Sabena pushed forward on the throttle and flicked a switch pulling in the retractable set of wings to a sharper degree, making the jet resemble more of a spear than a plane. The plane surged forward, leaping in speed to Mach 1.9 and climbed in altitude. She pressed another button and felt a shimmer of electricity as the nano-cells initiated and started to rise to their target resonance.

"Absolutely, babes. All on track. Can you hold for a sec, darling? We're just counting down to invisibility. Pedro, you there?"

"Yes," answered Russo. "In five, four, three, two, one."

Russo hit the camouflage button. The jet shook and a line appeared on the engineering display panel in front of Russo. It showed a line with one hundred per cent in the center.

"Sabena, we are one hundred per cent invisible, and holding."

"Salim, we're holding invisibility. It's steady and running at Mach 1.9. ETA 10:30 hours."

Salim smiled widely. His dark eyes glinted and he licked his lips, staring hard at Sabena. "I'm delighted, darling. You're changing the world. You know that?"

Sabena recognized his gratitude, and what that would mean for her. "Of course. This is for you, Salim. Your destiny."

"*Our* destiny," he corrected, to Sabena's joy.

She sensed he'd say that. All the references to making her First Lady of the world were just a precursor to this announcement.

"From the moment I saw you in that seminar in Cambridge, everything's been leading to this, Sabena. You felt it. Within the very coals of hell. That's where we were created. And hell is what we'll rain down on our enemies."

"Before the day is done, Salim, the world will quake at your name. I promise you."

Salim nodded. "I wouldn't expect anything less. You are here to deliver. The moment you stop, I stop you."

His mouth took on a sinister smirk that made Sabena shiver. But not in a good way. Despite what he'd said about their destiny, he was still playing her. Twisting her inside out.

Sabena felt Russo's eyes on her in the seat behind. The AR comms link didn't allow for cockpit comms to be split from the engineering deck behind her. Russo had heard every word. And Salim knew that would be the case.

He was using Russo to keep her on point. Sabena breathed hard. She was going to show Salim she was his rightful number two. After Malta, she'd break Ellie, and then no one would question her place.

Not even Salim.

Chapter 14

Treeborne listened as Dick spoke hurriedly on a secure line.

"Mr. President, it's going swell. Resolution is in the can. We're going back to pass the vote. Some of the usual suspects got hot and bothered, but they soon came around. Hey, you'll love this, sir. The Germans wanted to know what we meant by 'extreme unreserved force'. I thought it was a little ironic."

"It's not like *we're* after world domination," replied the president, laughing.

It was Wednesday at 4:00 a.m. in Washington, DC. Treeborne had set his alarm. Cursing time zones, he had knocked the alarm off and dialed. But hearing Cowl's ebullient voice made him pleased that he'd called.

They needed that resolution. Well, in truth, they didn't need a goddamn thing. They could strike when and where they wanted. But the for sake of 'international law', and to keep the bureaucrats happy, it was better to have the use of extreme unreserved force sanctioned by the UN.

Treeborne rubbed his face. He could feel his skin was cold and heavy. He was tired. He wanted to get this over with and go back to sleep.

"Did you use the speech I gave you?" asked Treeborne

He remembered how he had penned the perfect speech. After removing the stone tablet from its hidden safe, he'd taken it reverently over to his desk. He'd placed the tablet in the center of his writing board, sat down in his captain's chair, and taken out some paper from the drawer. Just as his god had told him, the room was kept as dark as possible with only a dim stream from his table lamp. With his left hand wrapped tightly around the cold, hard and resonating tablet, he'd picked up his pen and started to write the speech. In his head, the mantra his god had told him to say rolled through him, filling every cell in his body.

"Trust me. Trust every word I say is true. Fix the belief. Don't let it leave you."

As a result, every word of the speech Treeborne wrote was imbued with the qualities of persuasion, manipulation, and, most of all, trust.

"Straight from the page like I told you?"

Treeborne had given Dick the handwritten document minutes before he'd left for Malta with explicit instructions.

'Use these *exact* words. Don't get it retyped. Don't add anything, nor try and improvise it. Just read straight from the paper'.

The president knew that perhaps Dick might think the request to be a bit weird. But then most in his Cabinet had learnt not to question his little quirks, but instead trust him implicitly

"Yes, Mr. President. I used the speech straight from the paper. It worked like a dream. Yeah, we'll soon have the authority. We're on the home run, sir. You'll soon be able to take the necessary action."

Treeborne heard this and his heart grew hard and cold, as hard and cold as his sacred tablet. Victory was close, just like his god had told him.

"Good work, Dick. Call me when it's passed. I'm going back to sleep now."

Replacing the receiver, Treeborne smiled.

Salim, you little motherfucker, your ass is mine.

Chapter 15

A tall security guard in the corner looked around the space. The representatives were meandering their way back into the assembly hall in Parliament House. He glanced at the clock. He'd held out for an hour. But now he was desperate. The packet was inside his pocket. His hand had wandered to it three times in the last five minutes. It was like an itch that demanded to be scratched. He couldn't hold out any longer. He knew his job description forbade him from leaving his post, but all the suits were back in the hall. A quick puff wasn't going to hurt.

His colleagues, who were positioned at the other corners, were looking in different directions. He saw his opportunity. Swiftly and silently, he slipped through the corridor leading to the back entrance. He passed other people milling around, secretaries, interpreters, and other stuck-up officials, praying he wouldn't be noticed. He needed the job. He needed the money. His wife would go crazy if he was sacked. They were expecting their third child any day now.

The guard slipped through the door. The security guard at the exit checkpoint took his ID and gun. He passed through the detection arch. The checkpoint guard swiped the ID and gave it back to him with his gun. He didn't bother to look up at him. He'd clocked the guy was UN security from his ID. Anyway, he was too deeply engrossed in a particularly gripping film on his phone and didn't want to be disturbed.

The security guard made his way into the back alley behind the state building. He leant against the wall. His hand grasped the packet. At last. He took one out. His hand was shaking. He really would have to give up his habit. He sucked hungrily on the cigarette, inhaling the nicotine fast to give him the required hit.

He closed his eyes, pleased to have a moment's respite from his constant surveillance. The warm Maltese sun beat down, gently heating his face.

A sound of a car engine approached. The moment of quietness vanished. Instantly alert, he snapped open his eyes. Looking up and down the alley, he could see something coming nearer.

He stubbed out the cigarette and walked quickly towards the on-coming car. As he neared it, he reached into his holster and pulled out his gun. The car continued to proceed. Its speed increased. The security guard held the gun in his sweaty palm and ran towards the car.

A pretty blonde woman with stunning, sea-blue eyes pushed her head out of the car's window. She smiled at the UN security guard.

"Excuse me. Can you tell me the way to Mdina? We are lost."

The security guard smiled. The woman's accent was clearly Sicilian. She was nothing more than a tourist. He sighed, relieved, and walked over to the car that had now stopped in front of him. He quickly replaced the gun in his holster. He certainly did not want to frighten the pretty, little thing.

He arrived at the driver's window. The woman had a disarming, sweet smile. If he wasn't married, he thought wistfully, and poked his head through her half-open window.

"Hello, miss. How can I help you?"

"You can die!" replied the woman in a rasping, foreign tongue as she fired point-blank.

His last vision was the blue-eyed babe's luscious, silky thighs, and his last thought was of torrid infidelity.

The hit threw him back, but the impact was made with a minute dart rather than a bullet. Fast-acting histrionicotoxin raced through his blood system. By the time the guard hit the ground, he was already dead.

Chapter 16

Sabena smiled at her handiwork. Bloodless execution was her forte. She knew how to kill a thousand ways without spilling a drop.

With the help of Russo, Sabena stripped the guard and concealed his body in the boot of the car. Russo dressed in the guard's clothes, took his ID, and made his way to the back entrance. He'd watched the checkpoint guy for at least fifteen minutes. He had not checked an ID once. If he checked, Russo would just take him out and proceed as planned.

Taking a beat, Russo gave the guard his ID and gun. He needn't have been worried. The checkpoint guard didn't as much as glance at Russo. Sweeping his ID through, the guard was glued to his phone screen like an ant in a Venus flytrap.

Walking through the detection arch, Russo's heart pumped, hard. Would the quantum bomb be detected? Was it really invisible to all sensors?

Reaching the other side without incident, Russo knew all the reports were true.

The checkpoint guard, still engrossed in his film, muttered a gruff thanks and returned the ID and gun. Russo entered the corridor and headed for the gents toilet. He checked the cubicles for inhabitants. Once satisfied no one was around, he dug his hand into his pocket and brought out the bubble gum package. Russo couldn't help an involuntary smile. He was still amazed by the technology.

In the midst of unravelling the packet, the restroom door swung open. A US Secret Service agent strode in. They were easy to spot with all their posturing and cocksure confidence like they had 'I am an important person' stamped across their forehead. Russo despised them.

The agent urinated swiftly and looked casually at Russo, eyeing his local

UN security attire with a derogatory glance. Leaning forward to wash his hands, he noticed Russo was holding some gum.

"Hey, great, man. BubblyFruit! I love that. Give us one."

The Secret Service officer shoved out his hand expectantly to Russo.

Russo froze. What was he going to do? No way could he give the Secret Service guy the bubble gum. The juicy confectionery that the agent so rightfully identified wasn't bubblegum at all. It was a strawberry-colored, super-advanced explosive quantum compound borne out of superior weapons technology of questionable origin.

Not the type of stuff you'd want to chew on.

The Secret Service officer stared impatiently at Russo, his eyes narrowing as he wondered why the prick with gum wasn't forthcoming.

Russo began to size him up, deciding where to attack first.

Then the Secret Service guy's eyes widened as he touched his earpiece, listening to the instruction.

"On my way."

He turned to Russo.

"Catch you later. Don't blow all that gum." Then he was gone, running through the door.

Russo wasted no time ripping open the camouflage covering the quantum bomb. He reached into his jacket and pulled out a pen. Except, like the bubble gum that wasn't gum, this pen-shaped object wasn't a pen. Following Sabena's instructions, he turned the bottom half of the pen's barrel. The nib glowed pale orange. He positioned the nib in the center of the quantum compound and pressed the top end of the pen. A brief, incredibly bright orange flash jumped from the nib to the center of the compound. For a second, Russo was blinded by the intensity. As his vision restored, he watched the quantum bomb glow internally. Russo had no idea what he had done, but he hoped he'd done it right. Otherwise, he'd end up the way of the guard, courtesy of Sabena's sweet touch.

Staring at the quantum compound bomb, he willed it to work. Nothing happened at first. Then, slowly, little flickers of light appeared inside the object. The light flickers began to move in a sluggish way. Russo could easily trace their trajectory across the compound. Little by little, the movement accelerated until the light paths could not be seen, only the instant flickers from one point to the next. With the rapid movement came vibration.

Russo smiled with cruel fascination. Something was working.

Sabena had told him, 'When you see the lights and it starts to shake, it's activated. Leave immediately'.

Russo had been amazed and somewhat skeptical about the success of the mission. He wasn't a scientist. He didn't get quantum mechanics. He was used to sizable munitions, guns, missiles, mobile rocket launchers, C4, and not small bits of something that looked like the plasticine he used to play with when he was a kid. He found it almost inconceivable that such a small package would be able to create such absolute devastation.

He fixed the quantum bomb underneath the vanity basin bench, between the pipes and hidden out of view from the most rigorous search. Not that anyone, of course, would be searching.

Russo understood the meaning of quantum bomb's position. If it was true what they'd told him about the quantum compound, he could have stuck it anywhere, even on the outside wall of Parliament House, and it would have still worked. The positioning was the ultimate 'fuck you' to the UN, delivering Al Nadir's quantum shit to the people who dared to try to bring them down.

Russo smiled as he made his exit calmly, snaking through the corridors, past the faceless bureaucrats and diplomats, past their AAs, their pretty girls and preppy boys, all the way to the back door.

Russo gave his ID and gun to the film addict. The checkpoint guard took the ID and swiped it. Still glued. Russo couldn't resist. He had to say something. Collecting his ID quickly, he sneered, "Looking at that too much could damage your health."

"Yeah, yeah. What do you know?" muttered the guard, unable to tear his eyes from the gratuitous sex scene on the screen.

Russo smiled at the pathetic guard.

"I know enough."

Chapter 17

Russo slipped into the alley. Sabena was waiting for him. He climbed into the car. Sabena drove away. Not fast. Not slow. Just very controlled and carefully. Then, after passing the threshold of the city gates, she pressed down on the accelerator. Sabena headed for the field where they had left their Stealth Runner.

Sabena turned into the field. It was empty. She glanced at Russo, who jumped to attention, grabbing the small key pad from the glove compartment and pressing in a sequence of numbers.

The air in front of the car suddenly started to oscillate like it was superheated. The atmosphere seemed to slip and slide as if it were liquid mercury, and an outline gradually formed in the growing haze. The form solidified to reveal the Stealth Runner. The ability to cloak the Stealth Runner on the ground was even easier than when it was in flight mode. As Russo had punched in the numbers, the signal was sent to the central energy unit to switch off the resonance. It was the same unit that had powered up the nano-cells to invoke invisibility just under an hour ago.

Sabena parked and jumped out the car. She climbed into the cockpit and Russo slid in behind her. She strapped herself in and pulled on her helmet. Russo did the same. Sabena pulled a panel out from in front of her. It flashed numbers, counting down in seconds. Less than two minutes remained. The size of the quantum compound denoted the amount of time delay that the bomb experienced in progressing to final impact. Smaller amounts, such as those used in tests that had been described in Treeborne's documents that she'd stolen from his own laptop, offered an almost instantaneous impact as their size was miniscule. Larger amounts took a longer time for reality to shatter and for the curled up quantum world particles to connect with the linker and explode. From the calculations Sabena had made back at the quantum labs in Baba Heydar in the Zagros Mountains, the duration of time for the amount of the compound she'd shaved was two minutes. However, the cut had been aligned to the landmass of the UK, not Malta. Time had been against her, and she couldn't change the amount. She knew that the explosion would go far beyond Malta, into the Mediterranean and maybe even hit southern parts of Italy. Nothing could be done about that. Al Nadir's message to the world would once again be delivered, and it didn't matter now on specs or compound sizes.

Sabena powered up the Runner, blasting the engines like a supernova, and radioed Al Nadir air command HQ in Taman Negara in the Malaysian jungle. They gave her the flight codes and path. She took off and headed the Runner out towards the Mediterranean through the Sicilian Canal.

As the Runner sped away, Sabena felt the air electrify. She knew reality at Ground Zero had shattered. Even from the air, she could feel the Earth shake.

And then she heard the screaming. The torturous sound of the thunder strikes. Such a weird sound. It made her shiver, not through fear but excitement. For that sound made everything possible. The ultimate sound of domination.

Sabena listened as the final massive crack of thunder exploded and the shock wave burst out from the compound bomb tucked inside the men's restroom, breaking free of its quantum prison.

She looked at the counter. It had gone to 00. The shock wave rippled rapidly towards the Runner. Sabena flicked a switch and the collapsible wings sleeked back turning the Runner into its shooting spear persona. She pushed down hard on the throttle, increasing the Runner to Mach 1.5, and the spear rose quickly in altitude. Sabena pressed with vehemence on the throttle, her anxiety erupting as she suddenly saw the shockwave on her tail, and the Runner leaped to Mach 1.6.

With just seconds until the shockwave touched the Runner, Sabena flipped a switch and a second level of super-charged jet propulsion hurtled the Runner forward through the sky. The second level energy burst was part of the acquired aerospace technologies originating from 'an undisclosed source' and had been provided by a faithful Al Nadir spy embedded in the very heart of DARPA.

Sabena, thankful to the second level energy burst doing its job, watched as the Runner maintained a decent distance from the wave. She climbed and knew she had to hit the turn if she was to get away over south-west Europe.

The Mach indicator read 2.2. Her turn was approaching fast. On the readout, she could see it almost upon her. She turned a sharp left and dipped hard. The shockwave was miles behind the Runner now. Russo initiated invisibility mode. Sabena whooped excitedly, dove down, and shot off in the direction of mainland Europe.

Sabena smiled, visualizing the carnage behind her. The skies above Malta would be dust-laden, shutting off the brilliant sunshine, turning the comforting blue sky to an angry blood-red. A trained physicist, Sabena knew the force had levelled Parliament House, Republic Square, Valletta, and all of Malta. A ferocious tsunami generated by the quantum blast would have engulfed Gozo and other surrounding islands. The wave would eventually travel to her home, the nearby island of Sicily. She had no problem with that. She had hated her childhood there.

Sabena spoke into her helmet to Russo, "That gum blew one hell of a bubble."

Both laughed, impervious to the destruction, blind to the death they had caused, and high as kites on the chilling power they now wielded.

Chapter 18

The representatives in the UN returned from their brief recess. The final deliverances of key member states were being put forth.

The UN secretary general stood.

"Will all members of this council please issue their vote on Resolution 8091, 'Use of Extreme Unreserved Force in the War against Al Nadir?'"

Dick Cowl slung a look at Quentin who pressed the button for a 'Yes' vote. He nodded, his top lip pulled up in an obscure gesture of a smile showing his immaculate teeth. Then he turned his head around the Council Room in Parliament House, staring hard with a cold, uncompromising vehemence at each member who was near enough to reach his eye line. The members voted.

The results flashed up on the UN secretary general's podium.

It was unanimous.

Not one dissenting voice.

"Members of the council, I hereby advise that Resolution 8091, 'Use of Extreme Unreserved Force in the War against Al Nadir' has been passed unanimously. Secretary Cowl, under the powers of this congress, the United States has the full right to use whatever it deems necessary to expunge Al Nadir, and-"

The words of UN secretary general were never finished.

At the moment the vote was passed, the shock wave connected with the linker. Everyone at Ground Zero was annihilated instantaneously. The ambassadors, the foreign secretaries, their aides, officials, guards, administrators, caterers, cleaners...

Everyone.

Across Malta, the lives of the people were held for a second caught in time.

The little girl painting animals and birds on stones in Marsaxlokk by the harborside. The fishermen bringing in their hoard from the morning trip. The market-goers trying to find a bargain. Tourists checking out the laces and fine-threadwork on the stalls. Teenagers laughing and making faces; the girls coy but enticing, the boys hoping to get lucky. Couples eating ice-creams sauntering along the coastal walk to Sliema. Others having coffee and pastries in little cafés on street corners. Morning bathers enjoying the crystal-blue waters of Mellieha Bay. Unsuspecting holiday-makers in their rentals navigating the tiny roads that mirrored the complex catacombs beneath the ancient city of Mdina. Four kids preparing in their back garden for their musical society's performance of Maltese folk songs in St Julian that evening. Finches and sparrows singing sweetly, high in a church bell tower. Their chirps and calls touching the heart of a bride waiting below on the red carpet, resplendent in white and replete with matrimonial jitters. Fascinated visitors wandering around the Hypogeum in Tarxien, with its multilevel burial chambers and paintings from beyond 4000 BC. Taxi drivers ferrying their passengers across Malta, past the vineyards and little shrines to the Virgin Mary embedded in the sandstone walls, and the short date palms that lined so many streets on the island nation, and on to their destinations to meet up with family, attend a business meeting, or just escape and enjoy a day out.

All the chaos, the busyness, the loudness of people.

Agreeing, arguing, eating, drinking, laughing, crying.

Living.

Thunder boomed all around. The ground shook. And as the shock wave hit the fractured particles of reality around Parliament House, everything in the wave's path was obliterated. Windows blew outwards. Ancient and modern structures crumbled. Everything exploded. The Earth rippled and tore apart. Cracks swallowed everything.

People screamed, running frantically out of their shops, their houses, their offices.

Their lives.

But there was no refuge. There was no place of retreat from the all-encompassing, accursed, and invincible force that rocked their world and took their lives in the second that it hit.

The tidal wave hit the south coast of Sicily.

Suddenly, reporters started to flock like vultures. As devastating as the scene was, it was not a threat to international security. The threat had already been made and executed. The media were free from restriction to cover the story.

Across the world, live news feeds broadcast the unspeakable images of obliteration, showing the ravages of a country that used to be Malta. Programs were interrupted to bring breaking news. People stared at their televisions in hushed silence, horrified that such an atrocity could happen. The broadcasts encroached further, disrupting the entire day's TV schedule and delivering the harrowing sights to more stunned eyes around the globe.

A mother in Spain came in from her orange grove and saw the images. A science teacher in Russia turned on the television during his lunch break and saw the images. A politician in the UK flicked on his smartphone and saw the images.

One country after another awoke to the sight of utter destruction, suffering, and death. The images circled the world. And lives were changed.

Insinuations and recriminations began. Why hadn't the security been better? How had such a weapon of mass destruction gotten into the summit? Who had revealed the location? What kind of weapon could cause such devastation?

Chapter 19

Before Sabena had handed the compound to Russo, she'd held it in her palm, marveling at how something so small could be so mighty. The beauty of quantum engineering. Sabena remembered the disguise. She'd created an inconspicuous Bubbly Fruit gum wrapper for the quantum bomb. A brilliant and perfectly executed cover.

After enduring the savage attentions of President Treeborne to steal the intel about the quantum bomb, Sabena felt justified in blowing up Malta, if only to see that smug smile wiped off the president's pathetic face.

"So, how is this thing really going to obliterate an island?" questioned Russo, holding up the compound a few hours earlier.

Sabena read his mystified and cynical face. She'd laughed at his ignorance. He was clever in many ways. But at Russo's heart, he was a soldier, not a scientist.

Taking the compound from Russo's hand, she'd tried to enlighten him on the mechanics of the quantum world.

"Okay, Pedro. You know the quantum world is real small?"

"Yeah," muttered Russo, staring with wonder at Sabena.

"And do you know what that means for ordnance?"

Russo shrugged. "Bigger explosive capacity in a smaller packet."

"Exactly, darling. Well done. You're learning," said Sabena, beaming as she started her lecture.

"I've got a good teacher," murmured Russo, sliding his hand up Sabena's thigh.

She swiped his hand away. "Concentrate, Pedro! Time for games later. This is important."

Sabena's snapping brought Russo back to focus. "So how does it all work?

I mean, it looks like a lump of plasticine. Is it really that powerful?"

Sabena picked up her tablet, swiped it, and chose the HoloTab app. Folders bobbed in front of Russo for a mere second. Sabena tapped on the folder with the quantum bomb operational schematics files. A stream of files popped up. Sabena pressed on one of them. A broad schematic appeared in the air.

"Okay, Pedro, listen up!"

Russo pulled his back straight in his seat and stopped slouching. Sabena pointed at the detailed schematic.

"What you can see here is the quantum level of reality. Beyond the atomic plane. Through using quantum engineering, all the explosive mass could be densely packed at the quantum level enabling the actual package in the 'physical world' to be extremely small in comparison to the power it generated."

"I know that. I said that. But what is the explosive mass? Where does it come from?"

Sabena nodded, understanding his confusion. "This pen-looking device…" Sabena put the compound down on her desk, and picked up the pen. "This has a variety of different roles to play. One is as a separator, and I used it to shave off the amount of the compound we needed. But it also acts as a detonator, somehow, using an ultra-high harmonic frequency. I don't really understand how it's being generated. So don't ask about this. I'm only telling you what the tech spec outlines. But it would appear that this pen generates a multi-million watt blast of energy. This energy spikes down into the quantum realm and interacts with quantum particles that allow its transfer deep into the extra spatial, curled up dimensions, such as Calabi-Yau manifolds, which current superstring and compactification theory believes exists."

"Dimensions?" said Russo, and his handsome face screwed up into crinkles of bemusement. "Are we in Star Trek territory now?" He grinned.

Sabena shook her head. "No, babes. This is real science. Not the stuff on TV."

"But dimensions, Sabena? I mean, I only know of three dimensions. How many more are there?"

"Actually, Pedro, there's four confirmed dimensions if you include time. But string theory purports eleven dimensions, and latest research in compacted dimensions suggests as many as twenty six dimensions."

"So why can't we see them?" growled Pedro, getting irritated.

Sabena could see he just wasn't grasping her science lesson.

"We can't see them because of a number of reasons, like our angle on this plane of reality. What we perceive as 2D becomes 3D if we change the angle of viewing. If we had the ability to change our angle and depth of observation, we'd see these curled up dimensions within the quantum world. That's where the power is. Between the curled up dimensions is dark matter and this stuff is volatile and super-charged, but it's contained within those curled up dimensions. The energy from the detonator activates the dark matter. A fusion of energies, harmonic and dark matter, takes place. The energy, in shooting into the quantum world, creates a conduit. A pathway for this fused harmonic and dark matter energy to travel through. As it goes through those curled up dimensions, it grows in intensity and magnitude. But that would all be for nothing. That immense energy would still remain within the quantum world if the linker hadn't been provided."

"The linker?"

"Yep. And that's where I don't believe the DoD developed this at all. I think it's from somewhere else." Sabena raised her eyebrows as she looked at Russo.

"Somewhere else? Where what you mean? Area 51 shit?" Russo's eyes grew wide like saucers.

Sabena remained quiet and unusually reserved. "Just somewhere else, Pedro. Let's leave it at that."

Russo nodded but his face became more intent and fixed on every word she said.

"The linker is a bridging device inside the compound that connects the physical world around us to the quantum world. The energy force that hits the linker can be likened to a tightly-coiled spring suddenly releasing after being under great, constant pressure. The energy is essentially a wave of immense power. From that point, an unmitigated blast is delivered by the curled up energies' dark matter and harmonic energy fusion, and that blast is released instantly into the physical universe. And...well, we take over the world. Got it?"

Sabena laughed at Russo as he shook his head. He'd stared at her. Now his expression had not only become confused, but his eyes showed genuine fear.

"Don't worry, Pedro. You're safe with it!" She slammed the compound into his hand. He flinched. "You only need lab suits if you're shaving it. And keep that pen away from it!"

She watched as Pedro held the compound in his hand, puzzlement still rife across his features.

Despite her teachings, Sabena had left the room less than satisfied that Russo had understood one iota of what she'd told him. She thought again about the bomb's origins. Russo's reference to Area 51 had held more credence than she'd wanted to dwell on. The quantum bomb had been kept at a black site run by DARPA in Blacksburg, Virginia by a top weapons scientist called Dr. Ross Whyte. Al Nadir had persuaded Whyte to steal the quantum bomb after they'd taken his family and used them as a bargaining chip. Once Al Nadir had been in possession of the bomb, the scientist with his family had been neutralized as per their usual mission specs.

Despite knowledge that the US DoD funded and developed the quantum bomb, rumors on the wire suggested the compound's origin was 'otherworldly'. Sabena, after working with the DoD for years before being recruited to Al Nadir, had a deep understanding of their portfolio of key weapons technology domains, and certainly the technology she held in her hands was far, far beyond their current capability.

It was weird. Nothing scanned right.

Deep down, she knew the compound was borne of alien tech.

But she didn't care. They had it. That's all that mattered.

Against the compound, a nuclear weapon was a peashooter, a remnant of an era long gone. Al Nadir had the supreme power now. Nothing overshadowed their awesome capability for mass destruction.

The Runner shot over Switzerland. Sabena followed the course coordinates just received from air command HQ in Taman Negara, blissfully aware that another course was also soon to change. History. They had changed it today. Through their compound, they had forced a balance shift firmly away from the mighty, all-powerful America. They knew the world was now their plaything, and they would do with it whatever they wanted.

Chapter 20

Watching the wreckage on his wall screen in the satcomm room, Salim cried tears like everyone else across the world who saw the images. But instead of feelings of repulsion and fear, Salim was awash with jubilance and determination.

Organized crime was now old news. He was after bigger targets.

With the power of the compound as leverage, he could hold any country hostage that he desired. And with the world's media undertaking a global advertising campaign on his behalf, he didn't foresee 'refusal to cooperate with his demands' as an option that any leader could risk taking.

Salim flicked open his comms device and instructed Sam to be brought to the satcomm room immediately.

The guards opened the door to the cell. Sam sat on the cement floor, knees drawn up to his chin, his eyes closed. His boxers were soaked with urine. Unable to move his hands in his welded bonds, Sam suffered the indignity of urinating freely without control. The guard threw ice-cold water over him as a form of a wash. The second guard pulled Sam up from the floor and rammed a needle in his arm. Sam realized they didn't take him anywhere without being totally drugged up. Even in his captive state, they were still afraid of him.

Sam saw a third guard carrying a pair of army fatigues. The second guard placed his hand on Sam's boxers. He pulled at the elastic, cutting it with his knife. The sodden boxers fell to the floor. Sam had endured so much degradation at their hands that his sudden nakedness meant nothing. He stood still. The third guard pushed Sam to step into the fatigues, but his focus slipped to a blur as the drugs hit his system full force. The guard yanked each foot inside and roughly pulled the trousers up.

The two guards pushed Sam in front of them, their arms locked with his. Their automatics stayed trained on him as they walked down the corridor. Sam could feel the barrel of third guard's automatic in the middle of his spine. They weren't taking any chances. With haste, they frog-marched Sam to the satcomm room where Salim waited impatiently.

Chapter 21

The president awoke again for the second time that morning. He looked at the clock: 4:50 a.m. Why hadn't Dick phoned from the summit? As he thought it, the phone suddenly leapt into life. *Good ole Dick. Never on time.*

Treeborne picked up the phone. "Hiya, Dick. What's the score?"

But the caller wasn't Dick Cowl. Instead, Chairman to the Joint Chiefs, Dave Reiner, was on the line. His voice, hollow and tense, instructed the president to turn on his TV. Treeborne laid the receiver on the bedside cabinet, grabbed the remote, and pressed the on button.

He had no premonition, no way of knowing what to expect. Only the sound of Reiner's voice suggested foreboding. In his heart, he prayed it would be just another bombing. The screen winked on.

Treeborne stared. He never expected to come head on to such carnage.

"What in God's name..."

He looked at the screen, his eyes mesmerized by the graphic display of mankind's evil.

"Dave, tell me what the ..."

But Treeborne stopped again. He read the constantly revolving ticker tape of breaking news at the bottom of the screen. His temperature plummeted. His body shook. Fear had already gripped him by the time he read, 'Bomb hits UN Summit: No survivors...Malta flattened...over 550,000 dead...tidal wave hits Sicily...thousands feared drowned'.

The press helicopters circled the sight, giving aerial evidence of the power of the blast. The black, scorched Earth held a crater tens of miles in diameter, raised at the edge like a cankerous abscess on the once smooth, beautiful face of Malta. The ground was strewn with grey-white dust. No structure remained even partially intact. Nothing moved. No signs of life. Treeborne could just as well have been staring at the Sea of Tranquility on the moon. The potential for life was higher there than on the hideously scarred and barren land he saw before him.

Treeborne was aware Reiner had been speaking to him, but he'd left the receiver on the bed. In shock, he had shut out everything except the images.

"Mr. President? Mr. President? Sir, are you ok? Sir?" Reiner's voice was anxious. "Mr. President!" Reiner yelled down the phone, his frustration at no reply giving way to rising panic.

Tearing his mortified eyes away from the television for a second, the president finally answered. "It's ok, Dave. I'm here." His voice was jagged and broken.

Treeborne's passionate rage had been gradually superseding his numbed state and had reached the surface. He seethed. His face was violent red.

His fist was clenched as he thundered at Reiner, "Who the fuck's responsible?"

Reiner answered in almost a whisper, "We don't know, sir. We don't know how it happened."

"You don't know-"

"Mr. President, sir, the data gathered from Ground Zero hasn't told us anything. There were no energy readings or blast wave residues. It was as if something had hit and then vanished. No radiation. No gamma rays. Nothing at all. Our boys are still analyzing the data from the site. We should have answers very soon."

Staring at the blast site, Treeborne slowly began to recognize the crater's formation from test runs of the quantum compound.

"I don't want fucking answers. I want fucking bodies. I want those fuckers' heads on sticks. I want them fucking dead!" screamed Treeborne, venting his fury.

Reiner shivered, silently accepting the full brunt of Treeborne's vilified delivery. "Mr. President, we don't know who-"

Treeborne lacerated Reiner's words. "Of course we know who. Al fucking Nadir. That's who did it. They've got my quantum bomb."

The president stopped to allow Reiner time to grasp the implications.

"Oh my God," replied Reiner. "What are we going to do?"

"Do? What are we going to do?" Treeborne breathed in, trying to control his rage. "Al Nadir has already made the decision for me. I'll see you in my office in fifteen minutes."

The president replaced the receiver. He turned back to the television. A helicopter zoomed in to identify any semblance of life. The landscape was cracked with enormous smoking fissures and mile upon mile of grey-white, lifeless dust. It was all that was left of an island steeped in culture and history. Treeborne closed his eyes from the holocaust. The words of his god rang in his ears.

"Impending doom will take over the Earth. This will be your time to take your stand against the relentless evil. You will stand defiant against their darkness. And you will win. You will rise to reign over all."

Treeborne knew his moment was coming. He would not fail his people or his god.

Chapter 22

Tossed at Salim's feet, a slave in front of his pharaoh god, Sam's will held on strong, vehemently fighting, as he fell on his knees with his eyes fixed like guided lasers on Salim.

Not rising from his chair, Salim kicked at Sam's head, toying with him like he was a wild animal needing to be broken in. Sam grunted and spat black blood on Salim's church shoes.

Immediately, one of his guards bent down and wiped the blood away. But it had stained his expensive loafers. Salim grabbed Sam viciously, his slender fingers pressing hard against the nape of his neck, forcing Sam's head up in the direction of the wall screen.

Sam stared through bruised and bloody eyes. A broadcast from CNN showed scenes of shocking devastation. At first, Sam was unsure what he was watching. Were the images live? Or had Salim computer-generated them? Sam scanned the screen for further evidence of its origin.

A ticker tape popped up at the bottom of the screen. 550,000 dead. Malta.

He shut his eyes. Explanation was not required. Oh dear God. What had he done?

Salim released his grip and Sam fell back to the floor.

"Magnificent, isn't it, Sam?" Salim turned towards the screen, smiling. "Thank you."

Salim's gratification penetrated Sam like bullets. His implication was obvious. By breaking, Sam had helped this monster. He hung his head, shaking.

But dear God, he could not have known that Salim would do this.

"It's all worked better than I ever anticipated. Tell me. What does it feel like to know that you've caused the death of five hundred and fifty thousand people?"

Salim's lion bite of spiteful, cruel words gnawed ruthlessly at Sam. Still on his knees, Sam brought his head up, glaring at Salim.

"You evil fucking bastard."

His shock, sadness, and insane fury threw self-preservation to the wind.

The guards moved in, their automatics trained on Sam. A hard boot struck his side. Then another. And another. No longer on his knees but sprawled flat on the stone floor, Sam tried to assume a fetal position. But the brick boots rammed him from all sides like raw steak tenderized by a chef's continuous pummeling. He bled, his bones shattering like crystalline ginger.

"You know, Sam, you should keep your mouth shut until you learn better manners."

Salim motioned for the guards to stop. They moved away and slowly Sam dragged himself up onto his knees.

"Malta was an example." Crouching down close, Salim continued. "They had to see I meant business. Terms are non-negotiable. Think of it as a trailer, a prelude to the blockbuster."

Sam heard Salim was choosing his words carefully. But Sam did not react. He did not rise to Salim's bait.

"What's it like to know your selfishness caused so many people to die?"

Salim was turning the emotional screw and wasn't letting go. Sam knew he hadn't forgiven him for his cousin Rasheed, nor the missions Sam had sabotaged. Salim was determined to make him to suffer.

Sam listened but he could say nothing. Looking at the horror, the total destruction, on screen, his eyes filled with tears. Could he have prevented it? Had he really killed those innocent people?

He knew the answer. His breaking had written their fate. His decision to stop Sabena from slicing Ellie to death had signed their death warrants. But what other choice did he have? He couldn't have let Sabena continue. No man alive could see his wife suffer in such a barbaric way.

One life against 550,000. But the one life was one he loved.

Sam dropped his head in disgrace.

Without looking, Sam sensed Salim's sardonic smile widen as he gloated over his pain.

Chapter 23

The sound of his phone ringing insistently brought back Ashton to reality.

Dazed, trying to shake the fog of confusion that had infiltrated his mind, he pulled out the phone and stared at the caller. It was Cumberford, his PPS. Ashton noticed the time on the screen. 10:10 a.m.

Had he been sitting there for over an hour?

On the floor, at his feet, the human heart sat like a faithful creature close to its master. The eyeballs had trundled away. One was underneath his cream, leather recliner, and the other stared up through the glass coffee table.

Ashton shook his head and centered himself. Cold hatred flooded through him. Katzy's life was over, but avenging her death was just beginning.

His phone whined again. He looked at it and viewed its inconvenient existence with contempt.

He had only one thought. One action that he needed to do.

Destroy Sabena Sanantoni.

But his phone wouldn't shut up. He breathed through his nostrils, infuriated, and swiped the screen to connect to Cumberford.

Before Ashton could speak, his PPS yelled at full blast, "Sir, Prime Minister, we've been trying to contact you. Have you seen?"

"Seen what?" snapped Ashton. He could hear voices and sounds of feverish disarray in the background.

"Malta!" screamed Cumberford, close to sounding apoplectic.

"Malta…what?" responded Ashton, rapidly remembering his conversation with Sam Noor, and how the agent had stressed the need to find a country free of terrorism for the summit. Agent Noor had done his homework. Across the world, one country stood out.

Malta.

Either because it was too small to be considered, or else it had never posed any direct threat to Al Nadir, but somehow, so far, Malta had been ignored by the terrorist collective.

Not any longer.

"It's gone!" said his PPS, with a hysterical sob.

Ashton fumbled with the TV remote. The screen popped on. Devastation greeted him.

It was like a switch had flicked inside Ashton. Thoughts of his Katzy vanished. The power of compartmentalization, through years of The Firm's training, flowed back to him. He straightened his back, breathed in, and returned to his distraught PPS with graveyard coldness and icy determination.

"I'm coming back."

Chapter 24

A deep, sonorous boom sounded in the halls of the high council across Kudamun. Aby-od's face fell on hearing the sound. A knot of apprehension grew in his stomach as he remembered the last time he'd heard the noise. A planet under his care had fallen past the Zone of Great Risk into the Dark Zone, and as a result the planet had been singled out for immediate, unconditional dispatch, with no redress to recall the Protector of that planet.

Complete planetary annihilation.

That cataclysmic reverberation now penetrated him and suffocated the very essence that made him Kudamaz. For it was the sound of death.

The Observation Room formed around him. He didn't need to look at the display to know that it was Earth on death row.

The dark crystal had dipped dramatically down. On the readout, there was a further balance shift of two per cent from the equilibrium.

Aby-od looked at the readout. *Two per cent.* Balance shifts of this nature hardly ever happened. Global wars and famines caused such balance shifts, but they had not happened for decades. What was happening on Earth?

Aby-od stared horrified at the dark crystal. It pulsed hard in an angry resonance fueled by acute hatred, suffering, and tragedy.

Moving his hands over the light-crystal controls, Aby-od displayed the south-west coast of Sicily. Dark energies snaked across the island, but they were not the cause of the balance shift.

Looking lower down, he breathed heavily. Slowly, he raised his hand up, attempting to touch the dark, oppressive mass that floated in the air above where Malta had been. His hand slipped through the air, and in that second, he witnessed the devastation. He could feel their pain, their sudden shock of dying long before their time. A total of 558,119 lives in a single second ceased to exist. In the same time it took for Aby-od to lower his shivering hand, a population had been wiped out.

Aby-od's usual calmness failed him.

Now he understood the origin of the balance shift, and it crushed his white heart.

Chapter 25

Ellie was alone. The doctor had left hours earlier. And she'd seen no sign of Sabena or Pedro, the other guy she was with. No one had cared enough to even check on her.

Ellie stared at the ceiling. She could see it was made out of tiny cubes, white with a dull sheen like brushed steel. Some of the cubes looked darker as if they were holes.

They're cameras. That's why no one's bothered to check on me. I'm already under constant surveillance.

Arriving at her conclusion, she gazed sadly around her living tomb.

On the counter, she could see her clothes, or what was left of them, still dripping with her own blood. Ellie closed her eyes, shivering, remembering.

How did all this happen? How did Sam get captured? After ten fucking years, why now? The drugs were wearing off and Ellie was thinking coherently. But with coherence came panic. She had to get out. She had to survive.

Ellie flicked her head from side to side, looking for anything that could help her escape. Glass cabinets and stainless-steel worktops surrounded her. Her glance fell on instruments on a medical tray.

The scalpel. Sabena's tool of torture.

Then it all came back, flooding her mind in graphic high definition. The blinding, hot pain as the knife carved into her skin. The horror of seeing her own blood flowing. Ellie closed her eyes but the memories could not be suppressed. Constantly, they streamed, relentlessly forcing her to relive the moment. That moment when she really believed Sabena was going to slice her *there*. Oh God. Ellie shivered, breathing hard, vomit rising in her throat as she remembered the unimaginable terror of that moment.

How could one woman do that to another woman? What kind of animal was she?

If Sam hadn't talked, she would have been dead by now. But they knew he couldn't let his own wife die like that. She had been the security they needed to get him to talk. But what were they going to do with them now? Salim had the location. They could have just shot them.

Through a distant haze in her mind, Ellie recalled Sabena's promise of 'the floorshow'. Oh dear God. No!

Fear overwhelmed her, suffocating her, making her want to throw up again. Ellie choked back on the feeling. She had to get out, somehow.

She pulled her left wrist, hard, and as she did, the rough metal sides of the cuff grazed her skin. Unperturbed, Ellie focused her energy on getting her hand through the tiny cuff. Her brow furrowed into deep chasms as she strained. Her body shook and veins stood out like prominent ridges against her taut, pale skin.

On every tug, the sharp metal dug in, rippling her skin, changing the color from pale, almost translucent ivory to dusky rose. She held the cuff again and tugged desperately, watching dusky rose turn to red. Ignoring the pain, Ellie pulled. The rough metal tore into her soft skin, splitting it open. Ellie swallowed down the nausea. She'd grown tougher over the past few hours. Funny how sadistic torture could do that. A little blood was immaterial. Escape was everything. Nothing else mattered.

She wrenched furiously back and forth. As the metal cuff slipped against her bloody skin, Ellie realized something. She could use her blood as a lubricant.

Millimeter by millimeter, her hand started to move out of the cuff on its way to freedom. Almost there. Encouraged, Ellie yanked harder with renewed strength.

Then suddenly progress stopped. She looked at the obstacle. Her thumb. She tugged, pulling her hand back with such a force that she was breathless. Her heart pumped, hard. But still no release. The problem was anatomical.

With utter dejection, Ellie stared at her hand, half in and half out of the cuff, scraped and bleeding.

If I could only break my thumb…

A pointless thought, as it was far beyond Ellie's capability, much less her stamina.

She looked down despondently and slowly slipped her hand back into the cuff.

All for nothing. No way out.

She turned her head, closed her eyes, and cried into her pillow.

Chapter 26

In the car, almost flying towards Downing Street, Ashton's mind turned over. Sam Noor had suggested Malta, and now he was missing. Had he gone to the other side? Could their best agent have flipped? Ashton recalled the somber words of Sam after they'd concluded the meeting about the quantum bomb retrieval mission, codenamed Operation Wren.

"Prime Minister, may I suggest something?"

"Of course, Sam. What is it?"

"The summit, I think you should…"

Ashton watched patiently as Sam removed a lighter from inside his trouser pocket. He pressed two claws at the side of the lighter, and a small keyboard popped out. A scanning bar oscillated between red and green, and stuck in the green zone. Sam nodded, pressed a button, and the keyboard and scanning bar merged back into the body of the lighter. Ashton smirked, pleased by the agent's fastidiousness to security, even though the room had been swept moments before the meeting.

"Change the location to Malta. According to intel, this is the only place we know Al Nadir has no interest in."

"I'm not sure what President Treeborne will have to say about the change. Do you really think it's essential at this late stage?"

"Essential, Prime Minister? It's more than that. It's a case of survival. We've kept the summit under wraps, but you can bet, somehow, Al Nadir will have found someone to turn to get to the truth. You know so many people, sir. So many people traipse in and out of this building. Opportunities to bug, they're enormous. You can't have eyes and ears everywhere. Even your nearest and dearest."

Ashton narrowed his eyes, not liking the implication.

"You may think I'm stepping over the mark here. But, quite frankly, sir, I really don't give a fuck about how you feel. I just want to keep the UK safe."

Ashton sucked in his cheeks, annoyed by Sam's brash, insolent attitude. But he couldn't help but see himself in the agent. He knew Sam only cared about one thing.

The security of the nation.

He nodded. "Okay, Sam. I'll speak to President Treeborne and get the transfer in motion."

In the car, Ashton wrenched himself back to the present, aware of his satcomm receiver buzzing. He swiped his tablet to see who was calling. US President Jonathan D Treeborne, White House, illuminated on his screen. He sighed. That guy was the last person he wanted to speak to. But allies had to stick together. He invoked HoloLink and connected the call.

"Richie, you seen the news? We gotta take action. You with me?"

Treeborne glared at Ashton, a mass of vilification hovering in 3D in his private lounge with his pretentious bookcase filled with classics behind him.

"Yes, I have, Jonathan," retorted Ashton, dismissing completely with the usual engagement protocol.

"And you with me?"

"Depends upon what action you're talking about," said Ashton, his face purposefully deadpan. He watched Treeborne snarl, lift his bulk up like he was gearing himself for a fight, and harrumph loudly.

"Fucking payback, Richie. What do you wanna do? They fucked the UN. Took out Dick Cowl and your man, Quentin Ludlow. We gotta go in hard and fast. I'm not hanging around anymore." Treeborne's skin flushed a deep red as he spoke to Ashton.

"Jonathan, I want payback too. You don't think I'm just going to sit around here and talk, do you?"

"I dunno, Richie. Talking is about all you Brits are good for."

Ashton bristled with fury. "Now, look here, Jon-"

"No, Richie. You look! Your fucking Noor is AWOL. And he was the one you said suggested the move to Malta. My guys in Langley came up with the same intel. That's why we changed plans. Only Ted and Morgan knew besides Dick. We even used UN security rather than a US appointed detail. We kept our cards close. Besides Noor and Quentin, who else knew on your side?"

Ashton tried to avoid Treeborne's accusative eye. He didn't like what the president was insinuating. He took a beat and breathed calmly. At this juncture, he really didn't want the US to turn their backs on the UK. But he wasn't going to take what the president was dishing either.

"Only Cartwright and I. And what you're implying about Agent Sam Noor is farcical. He's the most loyal, dedicated agent British Intelligence has ever had, and-"

"He's missing. Convenient, huh?" interjected Treeborne, talking with bluster over the top of Ashton. The prime minister's lips became a line of utter determination. He stared at the president and his hazel eyes turned to stone.

"Stop the fuck now, Jonathan! Your CIA man Lydell is also missing. Check your own backyard before starting to hurl unfounded accusations around like fucking confetti!"

Treeborne's eyes almost popped out of his head as he heard Ashton's bite back. He jostled around in his chair, looked away from the camera as if he was talking to someone, got up, and walked out of shot. Ashton waited, inwardly forcing his feathers to stay unruffled.

Treeborne returned to the camera, half smirking.

"Richie, come on. Let's not get off on the wrong foot. The world's faced a terrible disaster today. All I'm saying is we gotta look everywhere for how they got their intel on Malta. Your boy came up top of the list of suspects as he gave you the idea of changing the venue in the first place."

"But he would never do that. I know Sam Noor. He made the suggestion to protect the UK and the UN summit."

"Got half of that right, didn't he?" Treeborne arched his eyebrow in a distasteful, knowing way.

Ashton, determined not to be riled, delivered a retaliatory strike. "What the hell do you mean? He recommended moving the summit so that some other poor country could take the hit? That's preposterous."

"Well, you sure would've been up shit creek if he'd not advocated a move. Your little island would have been blasted to kingdom come. And Noor knew that. Survival kid. That was your boy's play. Admit it."

Ashton breathed deeply through his nostrils. Remembering Six's training, he eased his heart rate down and, with it, his pulse. The cortisol that swamped his system dropped in unison.

"I won't. There's nothing to admit. Agent Noor has probably been captured with Lydell. They're more than likely both dead by now."

"Or sunning themselves somewhere on Al Douri's money."

That was it. Ashton had had enough of Treeborne's snide innuendos. He knew that if Sam could have made it back, he would have. For Ellie's sake.

"Agent Noor has a wife he's devoted to. If he's not captured or dead, he would've returned." Ashton sent a blast of vitriol from his eyes towards the president.

Treeborne appeared to shrug it off. "Yeah, well, we all know what spies are like. Lying's their game. Could have another tasty number somewhere. Or else, he's got her out of the country with him. Anyone seen the wife?"

Ashton listened. He suddenly felt inclined to agree with Treeborne. His cognitive ability seemed to be wavering, and coherent thought eluded him. Just like the time he'd let the president browbeat him into signing up Noor for Operation Wren.

"The wife…" started Ashton. He thought he saw a glimmer of satisfaction slip across Treeborne's face as he faltered with his words.

"Yeah," ranted Treeborne, "that fucking wife's caused me more trouble than I care to imagine. If Al Nadir hadn't attacked her, I'd still have a functioning prisoner. That Noor is a hot head."

"Then why did you want him so bad?" asked Ashton, desperately trying to combat the foggy heaviness in his brain. It was as though someone had drugged him.

"Because he's a ruthless hot head that gets the job done!" answered Treeborne. Then he added with ire, "But this time that hot head of his probably fucked the entire mission."

"Listen, Jonathan, everything you say is supposition. And Ellie's either at her home in London or Winchester. I'll get Six to ping her phone and check her location."

Ashton picked up his phone, hit a single number, and waited. It rang once, and then Nathan Cartwright, MI6's new chief, took the call.

"Prime Minister?" said Cartwright, his voice jarred to attention, awaiting a call to action.

"Nathan, any word from Agent Noor yet?"

"No, Prime Minister. We lost his signal and his CIA co-op, Richard Lydell, at 0400 hours Tehran time. No contact has been made since." There was not a single touch of sentiment in Cartwright's voice as he spoke about his fellow colleague.

Ashton swung a glance back to Treeborne, still on hold. He was busying himself with reading some document. He didn't look up once to check on Ashton's holographic presence.

"Has anyone checked on the wife, Ellie Noor?"

"The wife? Why?" asked Cartwright, and Ashton could almost hear the

MI6 chief's brain processes sparking up.

"Get a fix on her location. Now please," said Ashton without further elucidation.

He could hear Cartwright instructing someone to locate Ellie Noor.

"Prime Minister, sir, it seems she's on the M11 near Duxford, Cambridgeshire."

Ashton listened and swallowed. Cambridgeshire. Home of the suspected and as yet undiscovered Al Nadir cell. It didn't bode well.

"When was she last seen?"

Ashton waited. Treeborne looked up from signing some document.

"Well, Richie? Anything to report?"

"Hold on, Jonathan. I'm working on it. Seems she hasn't been seen for a while." Ashton stopped himself. Why the hell was he telling this to Treeborne? It was as though he was unwittingly trusting him. He couldn't let go of the feeling. "Six are checking on when she was last sighted."

"Keep me posted," growled Treeborne, turning back to his signing.

"Prime Minister, sir," said Cartwright, "Mrs. Noor was last sighted outside the Hotel Du Vin, Southgate Street in Winchester getting into a cab with another woman, thought to be her long-time school friend Verity Harrington. The taxi reg was later clocked on the Worthy Road. Her friend lives in nearby Abbotts Road. We've just spoken to Miss Harrington, and apparently Mrs. Noor left this morning in another cab. There's a possible cab sighting around the same time back on the Worthy Road. We're still looking into this, sir."

"This is top priority. You understand? We must find Ellie Noor. It's a matter of national security."

"Yes, sir. I understand," answered Cartwright. "You think Agent Noor's AWOL status and Mrs. Noor's disappearance are connected?"

Ashton looked at Treeborne. His mind was getting heavier. Perhaps the shock of Katzy's death still lay upon him. He couldn't figure it out, but something inside him was wrong.

"I don't know, Cartwright. It looks that way. Call me the instant you have further intel."

Cartwright rang off with an assurance to do just that.

"And? Where is she?" yelled Treeborne, barely waiting for Ashton to finish his call.

"She's, erm…missing," stuttered Ashton. He shook his head, trying to get his thoughts straight. "My people are searching."

"Any response to pinging her phone?"

Ashton screwed up his face. *Don't tell him. Don't tell him.* He could hear his inner voice, but something rose above that voice.

Trust him.

It was a clear and pure directive that made Ashton feel safe and fuzzy inside. He submerged himself in the sensation. It washed away the pain of Katzy, the failure of Operation Wren, and the aftermath of having to deal with Malta's obliteration.

"Yes. It says she's on the M11 near Duxford."

Treeborne narrowed his eyes. "Where in the hell is Duxford?"

Ashton stared down at the car's floor, and then rose his eyes, meeting Treeborne's with solid resolve.

"Cambridgeshire."

Chapter 27

"What *have* you been doing?"

Ellie flicked open her eyes and turned her head towards the rasping voice. Sabena was back, standing at the foot of the trolley, her eyes running up and down Ellie's body like a farmer in a cattle market weighing up the goods.

An insane smile was fixed on her face. Khaki canvas shorts and white cotton T-shirt accentuated her strong, toned legs and firm, round breasts. Sabena walked over and lifted Ellie's bloody hand. She tutted loudly and shook her head slowly. Locks of long, dark brown hair knocked gently against her sculptured, high cheekbones.

Ellie looked away. Angry and frustrated.

Sabena held onto the metal bar and edged her way up the trolley. Ellie continued to look in the opposite direction. Sabena sighed but kept quiet. Reaching the top of the trolley, Sabena leant in. Ellie could smell her perfume. Spices and sandalwood. Ellie didn't recognize the fragrance. It smelled more like the aftershave Sam would wear than perfume.

Sabena's bare elbow brushed against Ellie's forearm. Skin to skin. Sabena looked down, aware of her proximity to Ellie. Her dark eyes dilated, and she breathed uneasily. Ellie trembled. Sabena's face was close, almost touching her. Grabbing Ellie's face, she turned it to her direction.

"Not trying to leave me, are you, darling?"

Ellie remained silent. Sabena moved back and looked down at her hand again.

"Want something on that? We don't want it going septic. I'll get the doc."

Sabena skirted around the trolley and hurried out. Ellie was amazed. Was Sabena the animal actually showing compassion?

Sabena returned in a beat with the doctor.

"Get that bandaged up," she said with her typical abruptness, and pointed to Ellie's hand.

Ellie watched the doctor. He grimaced as he took in the painful, self-inflicted mess she'd made of her escape attempt. The doctor tipped a bottle of antiseptic onto a medical sponge and applied it to the deep cuts.

Ellie snatched his attention with her stare. She could see his guilt. The moment he placed the medical sponge on her open, raw cuts, her wound burned like acid was being applied instead of antiseptic, but Ellie took the pain, ignoring it, and kept her beautiful blue eyes fixed hard with abject defiance. She wouldn't even allow a tear to form.

Ellie noticed Sabena watching, with keen perception, her interplay with the doctor. She smirked.

"Quite pathetic, Ellie, and obviously quite painful. You silly girl!"

Ellie glanced away from Sabena and stared at the doctor. As he looked into her eyes shame surfaced rapidly.

Yes, you bastard, thought Ellie, you wouldn't help me, so I had to help myself.

The doctor shivered a little under Ellie piercing glare, and silently placed a cotton pad on top of her hand. Hungrily, it absorbed her blood. Removing it, he placed on another to make sure, and then he bandaged her hand tightly.

Ellie recognized Sabena's inherent impatience as she hovered around the bed like a hawk, and then drummed her fingers on the stainless-steel counter in a clear indication she wanted the doctor to finish quickly. The doctor nodded, clearly aware of Sabena's fractious attitude. He fixed the adhesive tape, keeping the bandage tightly around Ellie's hand, and turned around to face Sabena.

"All done," the doctor murmured.

Sabena nodded and waved her hand in the air. The gesture Ellie recognized was a dismissive 'get lost'. The doctor bowed his head, eyes on the floor, and left.

Alone with Sabena once again, Ellie averted her gaze, too terrified of the signals that she would read in her mad eyes.

Sabena suddenly started to laugh wildly. Hurrying over, she bent down, her face up close to Ellie again.

"It was fantastic, Ellie. One hit and pow! No more Malta!"

Sabena's voice was excited, her face ecstatic. She gushed hideous details with joyful enthusiasm, sharing them with a conspiratorial intimacy, like Ellie was her best friend and she had just come back from a hot date.

Ellie stared, horrified, at Sabena's display. She was insane. No question.

Then it struck her. She could use her madness, and use it against her. Sabena's insanity could just be the leverage she needed for escape.

A plan emerged in Ellie's mind. It was a dangerous plan. But she could see no other alternative. She had the power to do it. She always had the ability to act. And she knew how to lie convincingly. At times in her business life, she'd had to lie to save a contract or to save jobs. But this time it was different. It wasn't just a white lie to keep the customer sweet. This was going to be a big black lie. She wasn't lying to save face. She was lying to save her life.

If she could make Sabena think she had changed, if Ellie could sink to her depths and unleash her dark side, the side that every normal person kept in check, then maybe she'd have a chance.

Ellie focused. She remembered the guy in the taxi. The killer she'd killed. Amongst the fear, she remembered the fleeting feeling of triumph. She had killed the bastard. She *enjoyed* killing the bastard. Hold that thought. She *enjoyed* killing. She was evil. She was a killer.

Sabena still jabbered on. "It was like that movie. You know, Independence Day. The wave just tore through the island, ripping it apart."

Ellie watched her, and slowly, she brought on the act. She focused on the lies she'd been told by Sam. How the government had forced him to keep the truth from his own wife. The way she'd been treated by the security services, the bugging of their apartment, seeing her personal moments. Like sick perverts. Ellie could feel the hatred rising within her. She targeted it and used it to make her lie a reality.

Breathing in, she feigned pleasure.

"They deserved to die. Those governments, security services, officials, they're all fucking liars. They cheat their countries. They let their people suffer when they should be protecting them. They don't give a shit about the person in the street. They work to serve themselves and the big businesses that'll give them lucrative directorships long after they're no longer in government. They all belong in hell, and I wish I'd been there with you to see you send them there!"

Ellie pushed the words from her mouth. They were vile. But Ellie hoped they sounded convincing.

Sabena's back was to Ellie as she animatedly explained the explosion. On hearing Ellie's vindictive diatribe, she spun round. Her rasping, snarling voice returned.

"You *what*?"

"I said, I wish I'd been there with you to see them all blasted to hell."

Ellie stared at Sabena, and she took in her body with lascivious delight.

Chapter 28

The British PM was a hell of a hard guy to manipulate, persuade, and trigger trust. Over the decades, so many of Treeborne's subjects had been like putty in his hands. He'd only needed to concentrate the energy in his mind and connect himself with the strange, resonating tablet his god, Aswa-da, had given him. Then anyone he'd targeted had been caught within his trinity of abilities, a willing victim that Treeborne could do anything to.

Except Ashton.

With him, Treeborne had always sensed incredibly strong resistance. Ashton's mind seemed as if it were a fortress, solid and impenetrable. Treeborne knew he couldn't instantly immerse the PM with overriding thoughts of trust and belief. He had to take things much slower, whittling away at his tough, resilient mind, and breaking down the defenses around his powerfully-focused belief in himself.

Through his engagements with Ashton since he'd been president, Treeborne had discovered the PM's triggers. Some words generated certain feelings, and once Ashton was in that state of mind, it made manipulation considerably easier. It was as though Treeborne had drilled a tunnel into Ashton's psyche and then marched through, planted a flag, and taken over the territory.

As Treeborne spoke to Ashton, he used subliminal triggers couched within his words.

"Or sunning themselves somewhere on Al Douri's money." *Sam Noor has turned. He's been bought and is now siding with the enemy.*

"Yeah, well, we all know what spies are like. Lying's their game. Could have another tasty number somewhere else. Or else, he's got her out of the country with him. Anyone seen the wife?" *Sam lies for a living. He cannot be trusted. The wife is either with him or being used as leverage against him.*

The final thought embedded within Treeborne's loaded words was that British Intelligence's secrets were now in Al Douri's hands. Treeborne discerned deep patriotism in Ashton. So he targeted his inner fear that Sam could be a traitor. Then he used that dark fear against Ashton.

In his private lounge, as Ashton sat in his car, Treeborne had noticed a greater pliability within the British PM. Something had happened to make him more susceptible to Treeborne's trinity of abilities. The obduracy he'd felt when he'd manipulated the prime minister into putting Noor on Operation Wren with the CIA had all but vanished. Ashton now seemed much more accepting of the thought that those around him could be traitors.

When Treeborne had persuaded Ashton to reveal Ellie's last whereabouts, some place called Duxford in Cambridgeshire, the PM appeared to submit totally to his dominating force of manipulation. In his eyes, Treeborne had seen a momentary release of duty. In that second, he'd relinquished all the pressures of his job. Ashton had allowed the president to do his thinking for him, and take responsibility on his behalf.

The lifting of the weight from Ashton's shoulders had been almost visible to Treeborne, and he'd loved every moment. He watched as his power of trust thundered into Ashton, and every subsequent word he'd said was met with absolute acquiesce and blind faith in the US president.

Chapter 29

Cruel eyes bore into Ellie. Feeling them tear into her, Ellie was petrified. But she couldn't let it show in her face. She concentrated. *You're a killer.* Bringing back the memory again of the driver she'd killed, she focused even harder. *You're evil. You're a killer. You've taken a human life. You're no better than Sabena. You go well together.* These thoughts she repeated, abandoning all others, until the feeling was total, and encapsulated her soul.

Composed, Ellie continued her act. She knew Sabena had a weakness. She was Sabena's weakness. But could she do it? *You're evil. You're a killer. You've taken a human life. You're no better than Sabena. You go well together.* Her mantra circled and her confidence grew. Ellie could do it. Survival was the goal.

Ellie smiled wickedly. Her tongue flitted out. The tip gently followed the line of her top lip. The effect on Sabena was immediate. Her feral instincts detected sexual invitation. But Ellie could also detect extreme caution.

Moving forward, she stared at Ellie in silence. Her conversational manner dried up the moment Ellie responded in a similar tone. The look she gave Ellie seared into her psyche. Ellie got Sabena's message: *if this is a game you're playing, it's a bad one.*

"What was it like when you exploded the island? Was there a crater? Oh, Sabena, I want you…to tell me…everything," Ellie persisted, forcing Sabena to respond.

Sabena stopped in the middle of the trolley. Ellie saw her hands tightened around the bar. Still her lips remained closed, but her eyes never left Ellie. Under inspection. Every minute detail scrutinized. Ellie felt it. She must have been crazy to believe she could ever fool Sabena, a woman who'd been trained to know deception instantly. But she couldn't stop now. She had to play it out and pray it worked.

"Tell me, Sabena. Tell me everything. Oh, I wish I'd have been with you, sharing that moment of those bastards destruction. Together."

Sabena bent over and gripped Ellie's face, pursing her lips, preventing her from speaking. Sabena's sharp nails dug into her face. She moved in close, her peppermint breath on Ellie's cheek.

"Would you *really* have wanted to be with me?"

Sabena's intimidation left Ellie in no doubt. This had to be the best acting she'd ever done. And whatever she did, she mustn't bring down the curtain on the final act.

Sabena removed her hand, allowing Ellie to answer.

"Yes, I would. I would have loved to have been there with you."

Ellie watched Sabena move back and stare at her. Ellie could see she was picking up on something. Perhaps, a change in her? Ellie recalled again how she'd killed the taxi driver without a moment's thought. That darkness she'd felt. And all the anger she harbored about MI6 and the British government. It surged within her. She used it, focused it and channeled her dark persona. Forcing her eyes to turn into cold, piercing, grey-blue ice, she urged herself to succumb to a darkness within her that felt all-consuming. The rush made Ellie feel light-headed, as if she was free, and could do anything she wanted. The sudden almost uncontrollable dark power made her shiver with a fear.

Ellie glanced at Sabena body with unashamed lust. Sabena nodded. She was almost satisfied, and a slither of a smile formed.

"What happened to Miss Goody-Two-Shoes?"

"You killed her. I was trapped inside her body, always doing the right thing. I could never give in to my temptations. But that's changed. You liberated me. You set me free!"

Sabena tilted her head. Just one last test.

"What do you want me to do, Ellie?" Sabena's voice was pure cold seduction.

"Anything," Ellie replied.

Sabena shook slightly. Unable to contain her excitement. Not delaying a second more, she thrust her hand underneath Ellie's medical gown. On contact, Ellie's eyes flashed with desire. Sabena ran her hand with haste up Ellie's smooth leg, scanning all the time in Ellie's face for a flicker of any other emotion. But she saw only wanton lust. Her hand inched into the curve of Ellie's crotch, her fingers outstretched, searching. Recognizing what was slipping though her touch, Sabena sighed heavily. Ellie mirrored her deep sighs.

"Get me out of these things. We can have a good time." Ellie breathed deeply, pulling against her clamps.

"Oh babes," growled Sabena, moistening her lips, "Aren't you having a good time now?"

Sabena edged her index finger downwards. Ellie moaned in response.

"Oh, God, yes! But I could give you a good time too." Ellie flicked her tongue out and licked her lips, leaving no room for wrong interpretation.

Sabena smiled widely, removing her other hand from the trolley bar, and Ellie watched as she nestled it between her own legs.

"Bet you've never felt like this with Sam," Sabena whispered, as Ellie writhed with pleasure under her expert touch.

Don't bet on it, bitch.

"I can see you've wanted this," Sabena continued as Ellie arched her back again, closing her eyes, gasping.

Yeah, right!

"You're a natural, Ellie. You're going to be my protégé. I'm going to teach you."

Teach me what?

Ellie tried her best to suppress the revulsion. But her inner voice was too overpowering.

Come on, Ellie. You're a killer. You're evil, debased, and corrupt. Just like her.

I'm nothing like her.

You enjoy this. *I want to throw up.*

You want this. *Like hell I do.*

You can do it. *I can't. Oh God, Sabena's touching me, touching me.*

Imagine it's Sam and not some psychopathic super-bitch. *Oh, Sam, help me.*

Enjoy it! *I just can't.*

Fucking enjoy it, you bitch. *I'm sorry, it's all too much.*

Sabena paused. Her hand remained where it was. Ellie opened her eyes, looking straight at Sabena. Why had she stopped? Sabena smiled knowingly. Ellie tensed, sensing something. Sabena bent down and kissed her hard, her tongue intertwining with Ellie's. Ellie forced herself, despite the encroaching nausea, to return the kiss. Then Sabena pulled her hand back from underneath Ellie's gown, smiling, her grin an expression of sadism. She held her hand up.

"Nice try, darling." Sabena's rasping voice had returned full force. "But I wouldn't even give you a C for effort."

Ellie was numb. Her last chance at escape had been dashed. Her own body had betrayed her.

"If you really wanted me, like I want you, you'd have been a fucking waterfall, babe."

Moving forward up the trolley, Sabena tugged hard at Ellie's hair, pulling her head up. With eyes flashing angrily at how Ellie had so nearly tricked her, she leant in.

"Still the repressed Miss Goody-Two-Shoes, bitch."

Ellie opened her mouth to say Sabena was wrong, that she needed more time. But it was too late. Sabena had seen through her act.

Twisting her rings around so that the stones were palm-side facing, Sabena struck Ellie viciously across the face. The sharp-cut diamonds and sapphires tore into Ellie's cheek as her punishment for attempting to con Sabena.

"I'm going to show you, my sweet Ellie, exactly what I do with liars."

Refraining from elucidating further, Sabena left the room, bitter and furious at herself for believing Ellie.

At the door, Sabena halted, turning around to look at Ellie. She licked her lips, and then she beckoned the guards. They joined her and, laughing ensued amongst the group as Sabena described in lewd, loud detail exactly what was going to happen to Ellie during the floorshow.

It was, of course, all intentional. Ellie was expected to hear, to make her mind conjure visions, to imagine what was to come. Listening, Ellie shivered. Bile rose and her stomach flipped. Now she understood the doctor's reaction.

Oh God! Why hadn't it worked? It should have worked. For a while, Sabena had been convinced. She would have given herself to Sabena. If it meant freedom, Ellie was ready to do anything. But that alley was now closed.

Sabena had been smart, and Ellie's own body had been a lumbering, repressed idiot.

Ellie prayed her death would be swift. But as Sabena's words assailed her, their contents suggested otherwise. Swiftness was a luxury she would not be afforded.

Suddenly, Ellie shook uncontrollably as the true horror of Sabena's words sunk deeper into her tortured mind.

Chapter 30

Ashton took the tirade of innuendo and supposition from President Treeborne, and tried to deflect his hypothesis about Ellie. Ashton didn't want to dwell on what his mind was now inferring after his conversation with Treeborne had ended.

Those around him couldn't be trusted.

Ashton had tasked his Mr. Fix-it, Defence Secretary Charles Godley, to deal with the problem of Maide and his treasonous activities. Godley's showdown in Whitehall led to the capture of Maide and other perpetrators who'd abducted and tortured Ellie Noor, as well as staged a false flag Al Nadir attack on Silent Waters, an event that had placed British civilian lives at severe risk. The attack had not only almost killed Ellie, but it had injured the security door man and countless other residents of the swish London apartment complex.

Ashton had requested for Maide, a man who should have known better, to undergo a psyche evaluation. The reports came back that Maide was an alcoholic suffering from delusional traumas and extreme distrust. Considering the secrets Maide held, he was now a liability. As a result of his alcohol-induced paranoia, Maide had orchestrated acts of terror on UK soil and severely tortured an innocent woman. With no other option open, Ashton knew Maide must be silenced, and thus, he instructed incoming MI6 Chief Nathan Cartwright to remove the threat that Maide had become to national security.

Cartwright had confirmed the threat had been neutralized. Maide's tech and other files had subsequently been seized. Under Ashton's instructions to bury everything, the clean-up team had raised the residence to the ground. Any secrets therein were incinerated, and the truth behind what had really happened to Ellie and the residents of Silent Waters would stay hidden forever.

After Cartwright's tech team had swiftly hacked the password to Maide's laptop, Cartwright passed the contents of it, as instructed by Ashton, to Godley for review. Godley then passed the contents on to Ashton.

Ashton had reviewed the surveillance footage, taking a brief moment to admire the stamina of the Noor couple. Then he'd swiftly forwarded the footage to the moments in the kitchen. Ellie was pensive, her face clearly waiting for something.

Ashton noticed she didn't touch her ear, to confirm evidence of an earpiece. She just spoke to an empty kitchen. The place must have been wired. Or else, she could have had the comms as a subdermal implant. But nothing had shown on Dr. Davison's medical report when Ellie had mysteriously died. Perhaps the comms device had dissolved? As Ashton considered Ellie's weird kitchen behavior, he became more concerned that, despite Maide suffering from paranoia brought on by excessive drinking, his instincts about Ellie may still have been right on the button.

Ashton ran the clip of Ellie in the kitchen in his mind.

"I'm listening."

Ashton recalled Ellie scrunching up her face in painful concentration. Then her prod to whoever she was speaking to.

"Tell me what you want."

Ashton had played the scene again and again. There was no denying it. Ellie was worried by the caller. There was desperation in her voice. She'd wanted to know what was expected of her. Those two responses signaled that Ellie was on someone's payroll.

But then, the last of Ellie's responses didn't make any sense.

"What is too far gone?"

A good question, thought Ashton, as he replayed the moment. The first two responses, Ashton would've expected to be said from an asset to their handler. But the third was plain weird. It just didn't sit right.

Too far gone? What was too far gone?

On the surveillance, Ellie's face had contorted. She was definitely unhappy. Desolation sounded in her voice. Someone was telling her something she didn't want to hear.

Ashton shook his head in dismal acceptance of the facts. As mad as Maide had been, there was no getting away from the visual proof. Ellie had been talking to someone. Perhaps Maide's unlawful surveillance had snatched something real. His sense to check out the Noor household had been borne of his thirty-eight years in intelligence. It was not just a side effect of the DTs brought on by his constant whisky tangoing.

If Ellie was Al Nadir, it would explain why she'd gone to ground, and Sam had vanished. It also explained how Al Nadir knew to target Malta.

The car rounded the corner into the tiny but world famous Downing Street, and the driver stopped. Ashton's bodyguard stepped out of the car and opened the door.

Ashton, barely cognizant of his surroundings, strode through the threshold into Number 10. Only one thought resonated within his mothball-like mind.

Sam and Ellie Noor were Al Nadir spies and traitors.

Chapter 31

After witnessing the devastation, Aby-od knew he could wait no longer. Mourning the dead would not bring them back. He had to act to prevent more lives being lost.

He shimmered into the adjacent Hall of Umray. He had to re-awaken the Protector now. There was no time to lose. Reconstitution was an immediate necessity.

Aby-od found the seven-sided formation of small, colored crystals embedded into the side of the wall. Similar to a key pad, the crystals had characters on them. Although he'd used the locator device many times before, he was nervous. His hands drifted over the small crystals, and he pressed them in a certain sequence, one that had been pre-programed a long time ago and belonged only to Earth.

Turning around, he expected to see a 3D transparent globe. But nothing happened. Thinking that, in haste, he may have inputted the wrong combination, Aby-od tried the sequence again. Still nothing.

Fear started to rise in Aby-od. This was wrong. This was very wrong.

With anxiety building, Aby-od walked farther down the same side of the translucent wall. He smoothed his hand over the wall. It instantly melted away to reveal a light-crystal circuit. Rows of pulsating crystals and arcing lights: the heart of the locator device's control panel.

Peering inside the circuitry, Aby-od tried to understand why the locator device was malfunctioning. He stared, blinking hard. A barren, cold recess met his eyes. He'd found the reason for the locator device's failure. It wasn't that the crystal was malfunctioning. It was that the crystal wasn't there. Someone had deliberately removed it.

Sabotage. He'd heard of it before on other planets. But never in Kudamun.

He had never witnessed anything criminal firsthand. They were the guardians, the overseers. They didn't involve themselves in such matters. They had protocol and practice. They had laws and legislation. Aby-od glared at the empty recess and his piety crumbled.

After all their heritage, all their history, someone had stooped. Someone had broken the law. Who could do such a destructive act?

It had to be someone from the opposition, the House of Etima. He couldn't believe anyone from his own house could undertake such a heinous crime.

Aby-od's contemplation was interrupted abruptly. A high-pitched whine assaulted his senses. The second alarm. It indicated that a planet had gone past the Zone of Great Risk and was near to entering the Dark Zone. Instinctively, Aby-od knew it had to be Earth. He realized the time to ratify the obliteration of Earth was fast approaching.

His only recourse was to construct a new locator crystal. It was a procedure that was not only lengthy but prone to errors leading to energy conflicts if it was hurried, thus making the crystal useless.

Aby-od moved his hand over another part of the translucent wall. Once again, it disintegrated at his touch. Inside were rows of palm-sized, misty, beige crystals. Aby-od selected one. He walked across the hall. His hand brushed against the wall. Instantly, another crystalline control panel appeared. Aby-od had used this panel earlier to raise the Preparation Tower, used to 'tune' the reconstitution crystals.

Aby-od frowned with deep worry. He had the tuned crystals ready for reconstitution, but he had no Protector's life-force to reconstitute. What kind of maniac would do this? Who would want to condemn an entire planet to death? Who would sabotage their only chance left? Aby-od's thoughts whirled in kaleidoscope of confusion.

He quickly turned the pale red crystal in the center of the crystalline panel. The hall began to shake slightly. The Kudamun emblem in the center of the room vibrated. Aby-od looked at the emblem. Hands cradling a planet like a babe in arms. Protecting. His heart beat faster. He had a duty to Earth. He was a planetary guardian. He couldn't let the high council dispatch Earth without giving it a fighting chance. Aby-od glared at the floor. Where was the Tower? Why was it taking time?

In answer to his thoughts, the Preparation Tower began to appear, rising through the mosaic floor. Eagerly, but through disturbed eyes, Aby-od watched the Preparation Tower ascend to its full height. It stood a few inches higher than Aby-od, who was seven feet tall. He barely allowed time for the black and white crystals on the Tower to flash, signifying it had been locked, before he commenced the process.

Aby-od placed the misty, beige crystal into the crescent holder at the center of the Preparation Tower. From the data banks of the Preparation Tower, he brought up the Protector's life-force frequency.

Aby-od worked deftly at the controls, aligning the Protector's life-force energy frequency to the locating algorithm embedded in the crystal. Put simply, Aby-od was entering the energy frequency of the Protector's life-force into the crystal thereby enabling its inherent search and locate program to seek out the same life-force energy frequency on Earth. Once an energy frequency match was made, the Protector's Holder could then be transferred immediately to Kudamun.

It appeared to be a straightforward process. However, Aby-od understood that the smallest error in the frequency's alignment would result in failure.

The alarm shrieked persistently in his ears to alert Kudamun that Earth was almost beyond redemption and dispatch would be called for soon.

Aby-od tried not to notice. Blocking out the sound by focusing on his work, his actions accelerated, each movement reaffirming Earth's chance of survival. He prayed he would have sufficient time before protocol and politics plunged Earth, the universe, and even Kudamun into utter, unforgiving darkness.

Chapter 32

Silence.

A sea of eyes drowned in the images on screen, and no one came up for air.

Time stopped. No one moved. No shuffling. No fidgeting. The images turned them to stone. Like a petrified forest, they stood, stock-still, transfixed and gripped in absolute fear.

A silent nod from the president's communications aide towards the AV operator in the control room snapped off the images. The spell was broken. Release had been granted.

The president wasted no time to capitalize and manipulate the effect of the shocking images to achieve his end game.

"What you have seen is the result of a next-generation weapon of mass destruction. This weapon is in the hands of Al Nadir. The ravaged, barren landscape you saw used to be the island of Malta, the venue of the UN Peace Summit. Present reports show few survivors on the island. The State building where the summit was being held has been confirmed as Ground Zero. Our dear friend and colleague, Foreign Secretary Dick Cowl, was among the many dead. And, senators, there were many, many dead. The present count is over 550,000."

The president halted his monologue to allow his senators to grasp the gravitas of the appalling event. The faces on the senators showed an emotional mix of fear, terror, anger, and hate. But one feeling, like consciousness itself, united them all: a thirst for quick and brutal revenge.

Treeborne continued, his voice powerful and strong. This was his time to prove his worth in the face of all dissenters who believed his hard line stance on terrorism fueled the war rather than promoted peace.

"This unspeakably evil act is yet another chapter in Al Nadir's unending willingness to destroy our world. And this is only the beginning, senators. This morning, the NSA received this transmission."

The communications aide indicated again for the AV operator to play the broadcast from Salim Al Douri. Heads turned back to the screen, hardly bearing to consider what they might see.

A happy, smiling, maniacal face gorged up the screen area like a troublesome teenager up too close to the lens, trying to recreate the art-house genre in his bedroom.

"Hi, everyone, especially you, Mr. President. I'd like to tell you about my new hobby. It's cartography. But doing it on paper is boring, so I'm doing it for real."

Salim moved back from the lens to reveal the huge map of the world behind him. The cameraman panned across from left to right, then back to Salim. Still smiling, he picked up a big, black marker pen and waved it in the air.

"I'm giving the world its first real makeover."

The camera zoomed in on Europe then panned down towards Italy.

"I'm taking off the excess fat here."

Salim thumped the map. The camera focused in on Malta.

"Think about it. Malta had to go. It weighed far too heavily on my life and constricted my movements. It had an infestation, a disease that threatened my very existence. So I removed it."

Salim's smiling, satanic face was replaced by his hand. Hurriedly, he drew a big, black X through Malta. The senators watched. Beads of sweat erupted on their foreheads like daisies on a summer lawn.

"So that's a little bit of fat gone. But oh, we're still no nearer to those beauty queen stakes. We still gotta lotta fat to lose."

Salim purposefully scratched X's on a number of countries known to be allies with the United States including the United Kingdom. Angling his face towards the camera, his eyes glinted with mischievous intention.

"But even taking out these guys, I'm still going have to radically diet if I'm to win that beauty contest."

Salim moved across the map, across the Atlantic.

"And I don't like to diet!"

Treeborne watched as the senators swallowed hard. It was as if they had second-guessed Salim's destination.

"So hell, I say, if I'm gonna win, I gotta lose me some significant pounds. Know what I'm a-saying, boy?"

Salim's impersonation of an American from Houston was exacting and disturbing. Salim looked face on directly into the lens. Treeborne stared back. The effect was unnerving. Salim was staring directly at him like he was there in the Senate in the flesh.

"Gotta lose me the weight that's dragging me down. Get my drift, Mr. President?"

Salim pronounced 'Mr. President' with such pure hatred, Treeborne could feel his own hands trembling. A few of the senators close to the president turned to see his reaction. Treeborne caught their eyes. He looked away. He had to keep it together.

Once again, the camera zoomed in on Salim's hand. From Washington State to Alabama, he drew a line. From California to Massachusetts, he drew another line. The cross intersected at Kansas. Salim pulled away to allow the camera to show the huge X he'd placed across the US continent. Salim replaced the lid on the marker pen. He pointed with it at the camera as he spoke. His tone was mocking and theatrical.

"That kind of fat reduction will make me the winner!"

The camera zoomed back in on his manic but handsome features.

"A real prom queen. Don't you think, Mr. President?"

Salim walked to the screen and did a 'ta dah' pose, camping it up to the hilt.

Treeborne was quiet, taking it all in. Maybe Salim was bluffing. Maybe he was just playing a game of poker. He couldn't possibly, really possibly, believe he could destroy America.

Salim stared hard at the screen. Slowly, he grinned, and through the electronic frequencies that delivered the broadcast, he sought to read Treeborne's mind. Or that was what the president believed, for Salim's next words offered no other meaning.

"Think I won't do it?"

A shiver ran through the president. He knew that Salim was connected directly to him. That somehow, through the broadcast, an inexplicable psychic bond had suddenly been created, enabling each to read the other's thoughts.

In a bid to break the supernatural link, Treeborne looked away from the screen.

The senators watched Salim start to toss his marker back and forth between his hands. The movement suggested time passing. He was giving the president time to consider that he wouldn't go through with his threat.

"Why don't you ask the people of Malta what they think I'm going to do?"

Shocked whispers rippled through the Senate. Treeborne did not react. He stared at the screen.

"Or better still, ask Dick Cowl!"

Salim's laughter penetrated the silent Senate, a hyena's howl in an empty church.

"And it's no good getting your 'intel guys' onto this." Salim smirked in a deeply patronizing way. His condescension of the intelligence community was obvious as he made speech marks with his fingers.

He threw the marker into his left hand.

"The quantum bomb has already been deposited." Tossing the marker into his right hand, he looked at the camera, smiling, and raised his right eyebrow. "Or has it?"

Salim was playing them, and it was obvious from his face that he loved every moment of the panic-filled uncertainty. Treeborne found that both he and the senators were subconsciously focusing on the pen as Salim tossed it from one hand to the other. The movement was infuriating, but the pen was symbolic. It represented Salim's decision-making. The left hand: annihilation. The right hand: safety.

The pen passed into the left hand.

"Who knows? Maybe countdown's already started."

Salim tossed the pen back into his right hand.

"Or we may be hours away."

Finally, the pen remained in his left hand, leaving the president and his Senate confused and dizzy with the distinct feeling they had been watching a street magician with superior sleight of hand.

"I'll leave you to wonder whilst you expedite my demands."

Chapter 33

Inside Number 10, Ashton was bombarded by strained, shocked faces. All had seen Malta's demise. He clocked Martyn Redfern, his cabinet secretary, and Godley walking his way.

"Prime Minister, did you speak to President Treeborne?" asked Redfern. "His chief of staff, Nate Van Der Maart, called at least a dozen times wanting to get hold of you."

"Yes. I've spoken to the president," snapped Ashton, pushing through the throng of advisors and ministers.

"We need to hold a COBRA meeting, Prime Minister," suggested Godley, walking fast with the PM.

"Why COBRA? We didn't get attacked," said Ashton, staring, confused, at Godley.

"We did, sir. Quentin Ludlow, he died. Al Nadir took out a member of your Cabinet. And, sir, it could have been us if you hadn't changed the summit. It still might be. We don't know their intentions. I mean, with that kind of destructive power, anyone can be a target."

Ashton took a beat. Poor Quentin. He hadn't really given the man a moment's thought. First Katzy, and then Malta, he was overwhelmed by events. And that fogginess since he'd spoken to the president still hadn't left him. Coherent thought evaded him.

God almighty, Ashton, he berated himself, concentrate man!

In the confines of Number 10, he felt his clarity of thought filtering back. Was the UK now under threat? Malta had been obliterated. Wasn't his first course of action to make a live stream broadcast giving his sympathies and condolences to the Maltese people, and reassuring the UK of his government's commitment to keeping them safe? Ashton thought again. Oh, that angle sounded a bit crass. It was like a poke at the Maltese government for not keeping their country safe. No, just a reassurance that the perpetrators would be brought to justice. Something over-arching and non-specific.

"Dawes," said Ashton, walking rapidly into his office, "we need a live broadcast. Shock, horror, and sympathy with a commitment to eradicate terrorism. Scribe it up. Make sure I'm ready for a live stream in half an hour."

Paul Dawes, Ashton's director of communications, nodded his round, tubby head, and started writing on his tablet within seconds of Ashton speaking.

"Okay. COBRA. Yes. Good call, Godley. We have been hit. Quentin Ludlow, our Cabinet colleague was murdered by Al Nadir. We have to make a concerted effort to locate and remove Al Nadir from our home soil. Redfern, set it up to be in two hours."

Redfern gave a somber sweep of his head and vacated to set up the meeting with police and security chiefs in Cabinet Room A.

"Shelagh?"

At the sound of her name, Ashton's private secretary, Shelagh Murray, a dark-skinned woman in her late fifties with a broad bust and backside, and kind, loyal eyes, jumped to attention.

"Yes, sir."

"Get me Mark Thornburg on the phone."

Godley raised an eyebrow. "Chief of police, Prime Minister? May I ask why?"

"No. You may not," barked Ashton, uncharacteristically closed to his Mr. Fix-it, who bit back the smarting annoyance with an upturned pout of his lips. Ashton looked to his private secretary. "Shelagh, just do it! I'll be in my private office. Put the call through to me."

Ashton marched into his private office and shut the door. He sat heavily in his chair and dropped his face into his hands. Tears were pressing behind his eyes. He let them come. He gave into the feelings of wretchedness wracking his body.

He sobbed.

Everything was too much.

Katzy was dead.

Malta was obliterated.

United Nations was gone

Sam was AWOL.

Ellie was missing.

He'd had hardly any time to process one disaster before another one hit. His phone rang out. With a sigh, Ashton breathed deeply, wiped the water from his eyes, and picked up the receiver.

"Prime Minister, Commissioner of Police Mark Thornburg for you, sir."

"Thank you, Shelagh," said Ashton, purposefully sharp, and he waited for his private secretary to put the call through. "Mark, hello there."

"Prime Minister. Terrible times." It sounded like Thornburg was on speaker. "Redfern has just requested me to a COBRA meeting in a couple of hours. My condolences on your Cabinet colleague Quentin Ludlow's demise."

Ashton would normally have let Thornburg ramble, but not today. His cognitive ability was growing stronger again. He was becoming more decisive with every second that passed. He didn't want the fog to return, and so he targeted his mind on action.

"Yes. Terrible, devastating times."

Ashton lowered his voice an octave, indicating to the commissioner the need for secrecy. Ashton had known Thornburg for quite a while. They'd been sparring partners in karate and taekwondo at a local club. But their sparring had eventually slipped beyond the sports mat and into the bedroom, and they'd shared a few intimate moments together in the past.

"Mark, I need you to handle something for me." Ashton's voice came out breathy and intense. He knew Thornburg had picked up the receiver as the line lost its faint echo.

"Yes, Rich?"

"At my penthouse, you'll find remnants of what I believe to be Judith Katzenberger."

Mark took a sharp intake of breath. "Oh God, Rich. I'm sorry."

"Yeah, yeah. Listen," continued Ashton, wanting to concentrate on what he had to say. He didn't want the tears to start. Not when he was on the line to Thornburg. "They were delivered in a Fortnum and Mason's food hamper. There's a note from Sabena Sanantoni."

"Fucking bitch!" hissed Thornburg.

"Everything is as I left it. I'm doing a live stream on TV about Malta and keeping the positive vibe for the people in the UK. But I want this handled immediately. Get your best on this. I want answers. The hamper may have clues to those fuckers' whereabouts in Cambridgeshire. I'm not sure whether Sabena killed Katzy herself, but knowing her MO, she most probably did, which means she was in London yesterday. I want every piece of CCTV scanned for her. Katzy was still alive yesterday. I saw her here." Ashton remembered their brief but blisteringly hot encounter on his desk. He swallowed, forcing his compartmentalization training to kick in. "Liaise with Five and Six. Gibbs and Cartwright will give you access to anything you need," finished Ashton with harsh authority.

"Rich, I'll throw everything I have on this. I'm really, really sorry about-"

"Save it!" whipped out Ashton. "Just get her. And I'm not running this through the CPS. Understand, Mark? So keep this tight. I'll deliver justice my way."

"Rich, you think she's still in the UK?"

"Could be. We have to locate that fucking Cambridgeshire cell. This may just be our chance."

Chapter 34

The broadcast abruptly halted. Stunned to silence by Salim's vituperative transmission, only Senator Dougall had sufficient composure to speak. Made from hard, Scottish stock, Dougall was a fighter, and big mouth bullies like Salim didn't intimidate him.

"Was there more, Mr. President? Did Al Douri state his demands?"

The president looked down, breathed gently, and then raised his eyes to the heavens. He realized he couldn't keep the demands from the Senate. They would have to know. The first two of Salim's demands, although difficult, could be undertaken. But the third…

How could he tell Senate that America's survival was contingent on him surrendering himself and his entire family to Al Nadir? His family, he couldn't care less about. There wasn't much love amongst all those fickle, money-grabbing off-spring and his beautiful but vacuous wife, who shagged anything and everything the moment his back was turned. She could take her chances with Al Nadir's thugs. She didn't matter. His kids didn't matter.

He could make another family. He could find another wife.

What really mattered to Treeborne was the demand to surrender himself.

It was a cruel, vicious requirement. And, most of all, it was personal.

He was damned if he'd acquiesce to his own death.

"Senator Dougall, there were three demands made at the end of the transmission. It is demanded that we withdraw our troops from the seven war zones we are currently in with immediate effect. It is demanded that one hundred billion dollars be deposited into a Cayman Isles account under the name of Grant Browne. And finally, it is demanded that I surrender my wife, my two daughters, my son, and myself to Al Nadir.

"We have until 12:00 a.m. tonight Eastern Standard Time. Failure to comply in full with all three demands by the deadline, Salim Al Douri has confirmed that he will destroy the United States of America using the same technology he employed to annihilate Malta. I have no doubt in my mind that he will carry out this action."

The president's delivery was clipped, precise, and free of emotion. The senators had no such emotional shield. They turned to look at one another, visibly horrified and deeply shaken by the revelation of Salim's unbelievable demands.

"I want it to be known, here and now, that I have no intention of acquiescing to *any* of Salim Al Douri's demands. America does not negotiate with terrorists."

"Mr. President, I understand that the US has a hard 'no negotiate' policy when it comes to terrorists. But this is an exception. We're talking about our survival, the continuation of our great lands. You must have some kind of plan. What do you intend to do? They are threatening to destroy America with a weapon of immense destructive capability. We have seen what it can do. How can you place the lives of all American people at risk?"

"Senator Dougall, the lives of the people of America is my responsibility. And they will not be put at risk. We intend to fight. We have located fourteen of Al Nadir's training and research bases. We are presently taking steps to remove those bases by unconventional means."

A collective shudder rippled through the senators. 'Unconventional means' was soft speak for nuclear attack.

A past supporter of unilateral disarmament, Dougall was again the first to speak.

"Mr. President, by what authority do you have to launch our nuclear capability against Al Nadir? If that is what you intend to do."

Hearing the impudence from Dougall's lips, the president's previously controlled anger hit Dougall head on. "The authority I have is the authority that was conveyed to me by the UN before it was blasted to oblivion. Dick Cowl, in his last words, confirmed that the UN had sanctioned the use of 'extreme unreserved force' to remove Al Nadir, and by God, I shall do just that."

The tablet in his jacket pocket vibrated as Treeborne spoke. In his head, whilst he delivered his address, the mantra given by his god rang clearly, meaningful and true.

Trust me. Trust every word I say is true. Fix the belief. Don't let it leave you.

The resonance ran through Treeborne's body. Touching every cell. Giving him the power he needed to align the minds around him to his end game.

Imbued with the tablet's power, the president launched his closing tirade with unstoppable fury.

"Al Nadir is evil. Salim Al Douri is the devil incarnate. I intend to use whatever means necessary to protect my people and this great nation from the cancer that has infected our Mother Earth. My friends, the day of reckoning is approaching. I know you are all frightened by what you have seen. But believe me when I say we will win. We will reign victorious. Yes, lives will be lost. That is unavoidable. But we will, on that glorious day, soon to come, be soaked in victory. Al Nadir cannot be allowed to fester. They must be removed, and we must put a stop to their torturing, terrorizing, and killing once and for all. They cannot be allowed to hold the world to ransom. We have the power to act. We have the right to act. And by my God, we *will* act. You bet we're gonna act. Al Nadir will be brought down. Salim Al Douri will die. Those inhuman animals will meet the same fate they have delivered to so many innocent victims. Have courage in this moment. Believe in me. Believe in what I say. We *will* win this war. We will achieve our victory."

Leaping up, every senator, moved by the president's powerfully persuasive and uplifting words, cheered and clapped. They could feel victory in their hearts and Al Nadir blood dripping through their hands.

Treeborne viewed his disciples. They were enthralled, the blood lust evident in their eyes. Their souls were burning for revenge.

He would not disappoint them.

He would deliver his righteousness to the world.

And they would be grateful.

Chapter 35

Aby-od had finished his preparations of the new locator crystal. Shaking with anticipation, he quickly placed the locator crystal into its control panel. Whilst he worked diligently, the balance shift in total numbers appeared within the translucent wall in front of him. The numbers flashed in red continuously, showing Earth had experienced a ten per cent balance shift from the equilibrium and was about to enter the Dark Zone.

Shimmering into the Observation Room to identify the cause of the sudden balance shift, Aby-od saw thick, ebony masses of utter hatred erupting across the planet. Reading data streams, Aby-od acknowledged the unthinkable: Earth had started down the road to global war.

He shimmered back to the Hall of Umray. Dark sorrow filled him totally. If the locator crystal did not perform, and the Protector could not be found, everything would be lost. The balance of the universe would change forever.

Fighting back the dark thoughts that enshrouded him, Aby-od watched anxiously as the light matrix hunted through the 3D transparent Earth suspended in the center of the hall. The arrow of light was erratic, almost chaotic, in its technique, shooting through country after country on its search.

Holding his hands together tightly, Aby-od continued to stare at the super-fast light crisscross through the world, and he willed the light to find the truth it sought.

Suddenly, Aby-od heard his name bellowed throughout Kudamun. The high council was requesting his return immediately.

He knew, as leader of Kudamun, it was his duty to return without question. By now, the council would have seen Earth's dramatic balance shift, its persistent and unrelenting move towards the Dark Zone, and they would soon be requiring a remedy. The Protector, so far, had not been delivered to them, and if Aby-od didn't locate the Protector soon, their next course of action would be calling for the dispatch of Earth.

In answer to his desperation, the light arrow converged on an island in the Northern Hemisphere. Aby-od flicked the controls to bring up the visuals and noticed he was still shaking. He'd brought back so many Protectors from other planets, but none had affected him like this.

Adjusting the observation visuals, Aby-od remembered that this Protector had always been special, such a wonderful example of everything that was good, honest, true, intelligent, and so very, very brave.

The 3D visuals came into final, clear focus around him, and Aby-od stared. Taking in the scene, his heart twisted painfully. The Protector's Holder was incarcerated, life signs were very low, and the Holder was in excruciating pain.

Aby-od watched as someone hit the Holder's face. Aby-od was fuming. How dare anyone touch the Protector's Holder in this way!

And then, like a blow from a lethal Harmon wave, Aby-od was hit with a realization. The entire situation that had befallen the Earth was no accident. The Protector's Holder's incarceration was no accident. Someone on Kudamun had deliberately sabotaged the locator crystal, knowing that the Protector's Holder was in mortal danger.

Aby-od turned the controls, frantic to pinpoint the exact location of where the Holder was being kept. Only then would full body transference be enabled to him.

The calling of his name became more persistent and the tone was angrier. Aby-od ignored the pounding voice and concentrated on the transference process.

Having identified the exact location, Aby-od completed the final routine for transference. Touching a crystal to lock the location, Aby-od's hand gripped hard, and he realized he'd been a fool. A trusting imbecile. He was determined to uncover who was behind this treachery.

Abruptly, his mind flipped back to three Earth days earlier. Aby-od knew that's when the betrayal had started.

He recalled how the shrieking alarm denoting a Protector Emergency had disturbed his observations of another set of planets in another galaxy under his care. Such a sound chilled a Kudamaz elder for it signaled a Protector on a planet was in a life or death situation.

On the Observation Screen, the Protector's human life-force Holder was being threatened. Aby-od had no alternative but to take evasive action to prevent any further harm being done to the body of the Holder.

He shimmered into the Hall of Umray where a transparent, holographic globe made out of a shell structure of intricate golden crisscrossing light rays turned slowly in the center of the Hall. A bright light flashed towards the top hemisphere of the globe. The locator crystal had then been in situ and it had done its job. The crystal had been specifically programed to detect the Holder's resonance and thus their location.

Aby-od moved his hand into the shimmering globe of gold light and touched the shining star that lit up a small island. The moment his hand cut through the bright star, a real time visual appeared in front of him. Like a holographic running film. Aby-od could see everything in high-def detail.

The Protector's earthly Holder was glaring, wide-eyed, with a crazed expression. It was obvious the Holder was terrified about something, but Aby-od could only see a man standing in front of the Holder with an amused grin on his face. He didn't touch the Holder's body at all. His arms were crossed into his chest and he seemed to be watching the Holder. On his face was a growing state of expectancy.

Aby-od frowned, unable to reconcile the two emotional states. He called out in his mind to the sentient crystals around him to furnish background intelligence on the scene he was observing. Information streamed into him, delivering the torturous truth behind what he was witnessing, and horror spread across Aby-od's face.

The sentient crystals analysis predicted the end state for the Holder and thus the Protector. The shrieking alarm increased in volume, tearing into him. Aby-od had to act. The influence the Holder had been put under was affecting the heart organ. Trauma was setting in, disrupting the electrical current and halting blood flow.

The Holder would soon extinguish if he did not act immediately. He stared at the visual of the Holder going into shock. He had to initiate transference of the Holder's soul force. As the temporary transference started, Aby-od was aware he'd suspended the Holder's oncoming death. Although first level ascendance had commenced, he'd interrupted the flow when he hauled the Holder's soul force into Kudamun.

Aby-od had contained the Holder's soul force within a light energy construct replicating the Hall of Umray. On transfer, Aby-od knew the Holder would have experienced a world of crystal, light, and rainbows, but it had all been a light-energy-generated simulation. The Holder hadn't actually been in Kudamun. That wouldn't have been possible in non-corporeal state.

The soul force transference had given Aby-od the time he'd needed to address the injury caused to the Holder's body. He'd touched the visual and entered into the Earth's timeline through the image. As he stood over the body of the Holder, he blasted its fragile frame with targeted energy to re-engage the heart and get the blood flowing again.

Inside the energy construct, the Holder had questioned Aby-od's simulated persona. Aby-od smiled watching a replay of the simulation after the event. The Holder had been strong and tenacious but equally curious of Kudamun.

Most of all, Aby-od had recognized, the Holder had been unafraid.

With the Holder's body alive again, Aby-od had propelled the soul force back down, shooting it through a tunnel out of the energy construct, through the Reality Gap, and back into the universal plane where it could reconnect with its corporeal body.

Reading the analysis, as the Holder's soul force dropped through the Reality Gap, Aby-od had noticed a distinct change. A formidable strength flowed inside the Holder, an intense sense of purpose he'd not seen in humans before. Unable to determine why this had happened, Aby-od assumed it was an effect of the soul force transference.

Retrospectively, Aby-od could see it was the inner calling of the Protector's own life-force bestowing a level of courage and fearlessness the Holder hadn't demonstrated earlier. In the flash before soul force transference, he'd scanned the Holder's life patterns.

The level of selflessness was extraordinary, more akin to the need to save than survive. That was, at least, what he thought he'd scanned. But such was the speed and his need to preserve the Protector's Holder's life, he really could not be sure. So much about this Protector was different. His great knowledge, which had never failed him, was tested to its very limits.

Soul force transference had been the only option open to him as the Earth had not suffered a serious Balance Shift, and the decision had not been formally made to bring back the Protector. It would have been against antediluvian law to employ full-body transference and would have had consequences for him politically.

Nevertheless, he should have been more sensitive to the dangers. He should have realized that the very fact the Protector's Holder was in peril signaled that something dark was afoot.

But he had been blind, caught up in bureaucracy, believing without question in the antediluvian laws, and upholding the rules of nonintervention until a critical situation decreed no alternative.

Aby-od jolted out of his reverie and back to the terrible situation he was now faced with.

Flicking back to the visual, the Holder's agony stabbed through him. If only he'd opened his myopic eyes and removed the Protector's Holder via full-body transference three days ago when he'd had the chance. He could have saved the Holder from so much suffering. He chastised himself for his incompetence, stupidity, and ignorance, and for caring more about his political life than a human life.

Aby-od vowed to put right the wrongs that had been done in front of his unseeing eyes.

Chapter 36

The forensic team entered the luxurious penthouse followed by a tall, auburn-haired guy with a thick-set jaw, big chin, and striking, light brown eyes. The guy was Chief of Police Mark Thornburg of the Metropolitan Police, and the man who had been personally instructed by the PM to handle the investigation into Judith Katzenberger's death.

Thornburg glanced around the apartment watching his forensic team take photos of everything.

A human heart sat on the floor. An eye ball stared up at him through the glass coffee table, and he could just about see another eye ball underneath a cream recliner. A plastic-fronted box containing streaks of blood in its molding was also on the floor. Thornburg surmised that was how the heart and eyes had been presented to Ashton.

God, what a thing to get delivered. Poor guy!

He moved his attention towards the dining table. Stepping judiciously around the heart, he arrived at the table with the hamper on it. Thornburg couldn't imagine how Rich had felt on the receiving end of something so utterly gruesome. But evidence of his friend's insane fury was all around him, in the way the foodstuffs had been hurled around and the packing straw scattered to make a bizarre halo around the hamper.

But there was nothing heavenly about what had happened.

Thornburg reached a gloved hand inside the hamper and pulled out a card.

'The look of love. Katzy only had eyes for you, Prime Minister! S x.'

He swung a look behind him at the eye underneath the coffee table. One of the forensic team was removing it and placing it gingerly into an evidence pack. Those Al Nadir fuckers were sick, cruel bastards.

Thornburg noticed another card to the side of the hamper where Rich had obviously chucked it.

'Time to play with our food! Love Katzy xxx.'

Scratch cruel and sick, thought Thornburg, Sabena was totally depraved and twisted. She knew that Rich would have been so happy getting that message. He would have been totally unsuspecting of the contents, and the shock would have been immense, the emotional equivalent of twisting the knife once it was inside the victim.

His forensic lead stood in front of him.

"Sir, all is bagged, tagged, and ready."

Thornburg nodded. "That's good. Get them back and start analysis ASAP."

The forensic team departed, leaving Thornburg alone in the apartment. His phone rang. A video call was coming through via HoloLink on a secure transmission. He sat down on the sofa and invoked the call with a swish through the air. He placed his phone down on the coffee table and allowed the HoloLink to broadcast. In front of him, Dudley Gibbs, MI5 chief, sat with Nathan Cartwright, his opposite in MI6. The HoloLink transmission just about captured the two of them in Gibbs' office in Thames House.

"Commissioner, Miss Judy Katzenberger was caught on a number of cams coming out of her apartment on Millbank, and walking down Abingdon Street, Parliament Square, down Westminster Bridge Road, and onto the Embankment," started Cartwright.

Then Gibbs followed. "There was a flurry of activity at 11:52. A paramedic estate car collected someone from an alley. We couldn't ID the face, but the form is female, dressed in that trendy leisure wear women like these days."

Gibbs smirked. Cartwright did the same. Thornburg watched. He didn't join with the chauvinistic jibe. It seemed pretty pointless in an audience consisting only of men.

"Right," said Thornburg slowly. "Which medical unit is the paramedic car licensed to?"

"It isn't. DVLA couldn't locate the registration to a paramedic outfit. The plates are registered to the owner of a Maserati not an estate car. The owner, a Mr. Peter Amfield, is a retired stock broker. He lives in Egham in Surrey. We've got a local questioning him, but it would appear to be a straight clone job."

"Al Nadir. Is that what we think?"

"Has to be," said Gibbs. "Someone who looked like Katzenberger was caught on cams, after the paramedic car had left, getting into a cab. She looked absolutely fine. But it could have been an Al Nadir operative wearing a nano-mask."

"Most likely Sabena. Are you running probabilities on the AI analyzer at GCHQ?" retorted Thornburg.

"Still running. Al Nadir's abilities have got much better in nano-masking. Stein-Muller has clearly earnt his crust. Tracking vectors are harder to determine than they used to be."

"Yeah, I know. Makes spotting those bastards more difficult." Thornburgh and all three men looked solemn. "You think that was Katzenberger taken out on the stretcher?"

"Would make sense."

"Did you track the cab carrying Katzenberger?"

"Yeah. It ended up just outside Downing Street. She had a lunchtime appointment with the PM."

Thornburg's face paled. "You know what this means?"

Gibbs and Cartwright nodded in unison with Cartwright taking control. "If that wasn't Katzenberger, but an Al Nadir imposter..."

"Jesus Christ!" yelled Gibbs.

"Fucking hell!" replied Thornburg. "Al Nadir have penetrated Number 10. They've gained access to the prime minister."

The three men suddenly lost their voices. What did that mean for national security? Had the PM been compromised? After Malta, how bad was life going to get?

"Ok. Put a call through to Number 10 security. Get the place swept completely."

"Already done. Nothing," said Gibbs.

"Right. Specifics. Any sign of the car?" asked Thornburg, homing back in on the investigation. He tried to avoid believing that Al Nadir had penetrated Number 10.

"The paramedic estate was caught on cams at Northumberland Avenue, Pall Mall, Piccadilly, and then on the A4 heading out of the city onto the M4," answered Cartwright. "The cams had the paramedics car turning off to Heston services. But no sign of the estate car returning to the M4. I've got local at the service station checking right now."

Thornburg wasn't pleased.

"Okay. Where does all that leave us? An unidentified woman on a stretcher who may or may not be Katzenberger, a missing cloned car with fake paramedics, and a perfectly healthy Miss Katzenberger who may or may not be Sabena Sanantoni, who minutes later had a one to one with the PM."

"Sounds like that's about it," muttered Gibbs.

Cartwright stayed quiet. He just narrowed his eyes at Thornburg. The commissioner recognized the look as being the eye equivalent of 'we're really in the shit!'

"I'm going to inform the prime minister immediately. I need that probability report on Katzenberger. If that was Sabena, I need to know. You know the PM and Miss Katzenberger shared a strong working relationship." Thornburg stared back at Gibbs and Cartwright. They didn't so much as blink. "And that car needs to be found. The moment local report back, I want to know."

Thornburg rang off with a hurried goodbye, pocketed his phone, and vacated the penthouse. Heading back to New Scotland Yard, Thornburg stared at the phone nestling in his hand. He knew he should call the PM, but until evidence stated unequivocally that Sabena was Katzenberger in disguise, he didn't want to place more undue pressure on his old friend.

Watching more footage on Malta's annihilation, Thornburg tried but couldn't get away from the nagging, incessant doubt that maybe Rich had been more than indiscreet with Katzy, and that pillow talk had resulted in over half a million people losing their precious lives.

Chapter 37

Never-ending.

Dante's Inferno on a loop.

Like barbecue skewers, the pictures penetrated Sam's broken heart. Taken from the retreating Stealth Runner, the images showed Malta literally blow apart, taking the full brunt of released energies as the quantum world connected with the linker and unleashed its surging pressures onto the physical world.

Dots appeared to mass together then vanish as the island succumbed to the quantum bomb. The dots were people. The dots had lives, homes, loves. Did they deserve to die?

Sam turned his head away from the screen, the pain of their deaths too difficult to withstand. He stood, immobile. Automatics were trained on him, ready to shoot if he tried anything, not that Sam could. After the drugs they'd shoved into him, he could just about stand.

"Five hundred and fifty thousand instead of little Ellie?" Salim smiled, raising his eyebrow. "Oh, she *must* be worth it, eh, Sam?" His sordid innuendo made clear, Salim continued. "We'll know soon enough. By the time Sabena is through with her, Ellie will wish she'd been on that island too."

Sam stared at the floor, his body shaking and his mind racing. He'd heard about Al Nadir's floorshows from agents who'd escaped. Sam's stomach churned as he recalled what he'd read on those mission reports. The floorshow victims weren't just raped, they were savagely humiliated, degraded and destroyed. When he'd listened to Salim's suggestion of the floorshow, he'd prayed they would shoot her. He actually *prayed* they would shoot her, that they wouldn't go through with what they had planned. But it seemed his prayers went unheard. Travelling to the upper reaches of the heavens, his divine message must have been intercepted by Satan.

Where had his good luck gone? Why had all this happened? What had he done to deserve this treatment?

Condemning 550,000 innocent lives to death might have something to do with it. Sam's conscience kicked in, screaming the thoughts he tried to bury.

No, that wasn't my fault. I was only a receptacle of information. I didn't make or plant the bomb. I should not feel guilty.

"Want to know who betrayed you?" asked Salim, circling Sam.

"I know this whole fucking mission was a set-up from the start."

"Yes. But why?"

Salim picked up a stainless-steel baseball bat and whacked it hard into Sam's stomach. Sam doubled for a second as his guts exploded internally. But Salim pulled him upright again. Salim swiped the bat to the side of his face, and Sam could just see red. Salim watched as Sam dropped to the floor, his eyes bleeding, his face mangled by the bat's weight crashing into him. Salim smashed the bat into Sam's tired body and grinned as he fell. He motioned to his thugs to drag Sam back up.

"Maybe because you don't conform, you don't follow the rules. Maybe because you like to make others suffer. You're a maverick, Sam. A loose cannon. Someone saw you as a liability. They wanted you out. Want to know who?"

"Do you really think I give a shit?"

"Yes, Sam. I think you do."

"Then you don't know me."

"That's where you're wrong. I know everything about you, your family and, of course, dearest Ellie. Amazing what you can buy on the open market if you've got connections."

"And you have connections?"

"Oh, yes. I'm well connected."

"How well?"

"Very well."

"And?"

"My connections got me what I wanted."

"Which was?"

"You."

"So you're saying you bought someone off to get to me?"

"Not just anyone."

"No?"

"No."

Sam refused to ask who betrayed him. It was what Salim wanted. He wanted Sam to beg for the truth. Sam still had his dignity.

Annoyed, that Sam didn't plead to know who'd sold him, Salim took a hefty swipe with his bat to the small of Sam's back. Before Sam fell, Salim gripped Sam's hair, yanking him back, and spoke through gritted teeth.

"If I was in your position, I'd want to know who'd fucked me."

"I told you I don't give a shit."

Salim stepped aside and stared at Sam, his arms crossed, his face tilting to one side. "You really don't care who's responsible for betraying you? Who's brought all this onto you? Onto Ellie? You don't want to know, considering the way she's gonna die? You really don't care who's behind all this?"

"I don't give a fucking shit if it was the Queen. I don't care if it was the Pope. I don't even care if it was the President of the United States. *I don't fucking care!*" Sam screamed through torment and pain, through tiredness, acute worry, and unimaginable stress. He found that he really didn't care. What good would knowing do him? He couldn't seek retribution. Knowing was only self-serving to Salim. It was just another instrument to make Sam suffer.

"Would you care if it was Quentin Ludlow?"

The name tore through Sam like bullets from a .38. Ellie's old words flooded through him, echoing and resonant. 'What goes around comes around. Everything's connected'. It was her saying. It was one she'd always used to explain away coincidences in life. And now Sam understood how prescient she was. Indirectly, Sam was to blame. He'd caused their incarceration the moment he lit up that flame. Sam shut his eyes hard. He didn't want Salim to see his tears.

Oh, God, if only I hadn't been so reckless.

'An eye for an eye'. That had been Quentin's adage. Sam's entrapped state was an indictment of Quentin's conviction in this axiom. But he failed to believe that Quentin had wanted Ellie to suffer. She didn't know him. She hadn't done anything to him. Ellie's suffering was purely a consequence of his own actions.

"Strange though," continued Salim, moving around to the other side of Sam. "I'd always taken Quentin for an effete, subservient, little twat. It makes you wonder who was pulling his strings."

The insinuation was clear. Quentin had not been alone. Only three other people had access to Sam's personal files: Charles Godley, Nathan Cartwright and Richard Ashton. After their kind words and sincerity, had they really sold him?

"I wouldn't feel too bad about Quentin. He got his dues at the summit. Ironic, really. If he'd never given us the means to capture you, we wouldn't have located the summit in time and wouldn't have exploded the bomb, killing him. Fucking you fucked him. What goes around comes around. Eh, Sam. Everything's connected?"

Hearing Ellie's words repeated, Sam shuddered. Could the bastard read his mind as well?

"And so here we are…and what a merry web…and so forth, and so forth."

Salim waved his hand in a circle like a Shakespearian actor. On waving, he glanced at his watch.

"Oh! The floorshow," said Salim. "Sabena should be ready. I trust you will be joining us. Light refreshments will be served."

It hit Sam. They were going to do it. Sam found himself begging. He couldn't help it. He couldn't hold back. His dignity was gone.

"Please, Salim. You can do anything to me. Anything. But don't hurt her."

"Oh, I don't think she'll get hurt. I know from your file she likes it 'rough and hard'. She'll have the time of her life. Don't worry, Sam. Just sit back and enjoy the performance."

Suddenly and unexpectedly, Sam began to hyperventilate. So many missions, and he'd never experienced anything like this panic.

Salim watched with tremendous amusement.

"Please, Salim. I beg you. Don't do this to her."

"I'm afraid it's out of my hands, old boy."

"Please, don't."

"It's Sabena. She rules the roost. You know, wearing the trousers and such. Hell to pay if I get involved. You know what women are like. I can't possibly interfere. Sorry, old boy!"

And that was it. Sam turned to the screen. In a few moments, he knew he'd see his wife up there debased, defiled, and destroyed.

With nothing but a deep-seated faith that this was not how each of their lives was meant to end, Sam steeled himself in preparation for the broadcast from hell. And he prayed silently for a miracle to release them both.

Chapter 38

Sabena entered the room with the guy who'd manhandled Ellie earlier. Pedro, thought Ellie, as she remembered his lascivious manner and sensed him fixing his eyes on her body, which was barely covered by the flimsy medical gown.

Sabena circled the trolley, a hideous smile growing across her chiseled face.

"Time for the floorshow, darling. We mustn't keep Salim waiting."

Ellie stared motionless at the ceiling. Sabena moved in, grabbing her chin and turning it towards her.

"This is a wonderful time! We have so much to celebrate. Did you know we're taking over the world? Thanks to that little quantum bomb and your sweet Sam. So, my darling Ellie, we need to celebrate."

Sabena stepped in closer and lowered her gaze, and Ellie felt her eyes dancing across her body, and her lips licked with salacious desire.

"And you are the bottle we're going to pop!"

She heard Pedro laugh. A deep, aggressive growl of a laugh. "Oh yeah. We're gonna pop that cork good."

Ellie trained her eyes on the little cubes in the ceiling. She could not face Sabena or Pedro. She did not want to reveal her unmitigated fear at what was going to happen to her.

"Oh, look, Pedro. She's shy. How very sweet."

"Soon change that!"

Pedro slithered in towards Ellie. His hands reached out and, for a second, Ellie believed he would tear off her gown. She froze. But he grinned, enjoying his twisted game, and his hand descended onto her body and drifted towards her left breast. Sabena smirked, watching its path. His hand rested over her breast. Ellie breathed in sharply. He stared at her, his eyes hard and brutal, and then he cupped her bosom, sneering, as if it was his property.

"Seems a shame, Sabena, not to enjoy a little pre-show taster."

Ellie squirmed. Although clamped by her wrists and ankles to the medical trolley, she tried to pull herself in, making herself smaller, as if, somehow, such a movement would make her disappear.

Sabena laughed at Ellie's maneuvers.

"Ellie, darling, I didn't take you as shrinking violet. You certainly weren't a few days ago with Sam. I love that blue, satin robe by the way!"

Ellie shivered, not quite believing what she was hearing. The surveillance Sam hadn't found but knew MI6 had taken had clearly landed in Sabena's hands. Suddenly, Ellie wanted to vomit.

"So, Ellie, you can see why we're all looking forward to your starring role!"

Ellie swallowed hard and kept her eyes firmly down.

Sabena leaned in, snatching her chin and yanking Ellie's head up to face her and Pedro.

"No need to be shy, darling. We're all one big family."

Sabena glared fiercely at her. Ellie could see, deep down, beyond the smiling, she was still viciously annoyed at Ellie's almost successful attempt in fooling her.

"Yes. We're just one big family. All friends together. You, me, Pedro, and a few others. It's going to be great. Sam's going to love the performance. It's something he's never going to forget for as long as he lives." Sabena flashed her evil eyes at Ellie. "And that won't be long."

Ellie tried to control herself, but her body shook involuntarily. Noticing the movement, Sabena bent in towards her trembling body, moving up to her ear. Lightly, she brushed against Ellie's lobe.

"It's going to be the ride of your life," she whispered.

As a keepsake, Sabena bit Ellie's earlobe, hard. Tasting Ellie's blood in her mouth, she gasped, instantly aroused. Pulling away, she licked her lips. Ellie stared at her with utter revulsion.

"We'll see *all* of you real soon, darling," called Sabena, as she exited the room with Pedro, who blew a kiss back to Ellie in a display of mock affection. Her final words left Ellie in no doubt as to the unbridled horror she'd be forced to endure.

Ellie lay in the room alone, stared at the cubed ceiling, and prayed to die. She prayed so hard, at that second, for her life to end. Only instant death would save her.

Although Ellie knew the reality facing her, she still had a strong, optimistic streak. She forced herself to imagine the impossible, that she would be saved from the death that awaited her. She imagined succumbing to a pure, beautiful, peaceful death. Her stunning belief in all that is good gave her strength. Closing her eyes, she prayed hard, whispering her chant over and over.

"Dear God, let me die now. Dear God, let me die now."

Ellie had gone beyond terror, beyond fear. Her tears no longer came. She was a husk. Her life had already been hollowed out. Emotion had gone. She had nothing. She was alone in every way, except for her continuous words of searching salvation.

"Dear God, let me die now. Dear God, let me die now."

Then a tingling feeling.

Ellie's eyes flicked open.

Tingling.

That electrified sensation on the tracks before a train arrives. She remembered the time before. Her kitchen. The sounds. The voice. *The call.*

It all flooded back. Everything. Being on that cliff, the darkness and his voice. His voice. Suddenly, every nerve in Ellie was alert. All her synapses in absolute unison sparked, communicating a sensation, an overwhelming emotion she couldn't interpret.

Ellie looked down at her hand. It was bathed in light. She turned. Her injured arm was also absorbed in the same brilliant white light. She looked down as her body dissolved into shining, spinning particles of rainbow light. All around her, the cold, disconcerting metal surroundings started to fade from view.

She closed her eyes.

Maybe this is death. Maybe my prayers have been answered.

Despite how terrifying the spectacle seemed, Ellie was unafraid.

Something is happening. Something good is happening.

In a blink, Ellie materialized in the Hall of Umray.

Chapter 39

Thornburg hadn't been at his desk more than five minutes when Gibbs called.

"It's ninety-four point eight per cent probability the woman we thought was Katzenberger was Sabena Sanantoni."

"Ah shit!"

"I know, Commissioner, that's not what you wanted to hear. But, unfortunately, AI analysis gives a positive probability. And it's way higher than the accepted risk parameter of eighty-five point zero per cent probability used to greenlight our missions."

"I have to tell the prime minister now."

"Yes, and you'll have to tell him Katzenberger's body was found at the back of Heston services in the boot of that estate car. And it wasn't a pretty sight. I hope to God she was dead before they did that."

"Did what?"

"You'll see. I'm sending you the images."

Thornburg clicked on the image file as it came in, and he instantly heaved. The BBC correspondent's body had been stripped. Her chest had been hacked open, like an autopsy had been performed, and her heart had been removed. He steeled himself to look at her face. Her once beautiful, brown eyes had been torn out. The optic nerve and arteries dangled underneath black holes of congealed blood.

"See what I mean?" said Gibbs, swallowing.

"Yeah, I do," said Thornburg. "I can't show these to the PM. It would be too traumatic for him."

"But he needs to know the truth."

"Any evidence in the car besides the body?" asked Thornburg, clicking close on the gruesome images.

"No. Forensics said it was clean. Not just wiped clean. All the surfaces were coated in a fine, smooth veneer of something. Our tech guys believe it to be some kind of nanotech cleaner. It eats dust, dirt, sweat, even fingerprints."

"You're kidding?" said Thornburg. But Gibbs' stern expression stated that no jokes were passing his lips.

"Forensics couldn't lift a single print off anything. If this becomes their MO going forward, we're going to be in for a tough time. They're using nanotech on scenes of crime to do what they did with suicide bombers and upgrade the whole fucking thing. We're going to have to do something radical if we want to stay in the game."

"I agree. But right now, we need to find Sabena. And I need to speak to the PM."

But after Thornburg hung up on Gibbs, he didn't have time to call the PM. Another call came through from the pathologist. He was a gruff man in his fifties who'd just about seen any type of atrocity one could name in a pub quiz. Witnessing such horrors hadn't dented his compassion or his humanity. Thornburg trusted the man and his unwavering medical capabilities.

"Commissioner, the tissue of the eyes and the heart match Miss Katzenberger's DNA on file. We're waiting on the body arriving, but it's safe to say these remains are definitely Katzenberger's."

Thornburg hesitated before asking his question.

"Erm, the remains, her eyes…was she still alive when they were taken?"

"Thankfully, Commissioner, the body was mutilated post-mortem. No blood flow. No signs of oxygenation. She was dead before they started carving her up."

Thank God, thought Thornburg. At least he wasn't going to have to tell Rich that his friend was tortured.

"Cause of death?"

The pathologist's tone held a slightly fortunate inference. "The tox report showed traces of a tetrodotoxin in the heart. It would have been virtually instantaneous. She wouldn't have suffered."

"That's at least something. Time of death?"

"Between 11:45 and 12:00."

Thornburg recalled the timestamp on the clip of the cab as it dropped Katzenberger off at Downing Street security. 12:07. It was final. It was confirmed.

British Prime Minister Richard Ashton had 'entertained' Al Nadir's second in command: The Slayer, Dr. Sabena Sanantoni.

Thornburg gave his thanks to the pathologist rapidly, requesting a further update once the rest of Katzenberger's body arrived.

He picked up the receiver and then stopped.

He knew Katzy and Rich were lovers. What that implied was rather unpalatable. He didn't really want to be the one to tell his friend the truth. But, then again, he was a friend. Maybe he could find a way to soften the blow.

He dialed and waited until he heard the gently effeminate timbre of Ashton, a tone that belied how ruthless and hard Thornburg knew his friend could be, and had been in the past. With that in mind, he centered on his delivery tactic.

"Rich, you know how you're always saying how you'd like to fuck Al Nadir?"

"Yes," murmured Ashton.

"I think you might well have done."

Chapter 40

Ashton trembled. The conversation with Thornburg had long finished but the message his friend had delivered stayed with him. Like indigestion. Something lodged inside him.

Ashton closed his eyes. He could still feel her luscious body encased around him. Moving faster and faster.

Squeezing the life out of him.

He'd been caught in the moments of that last tryst. He'd used the memory as a way to stabilize himself against the avalanche of pain.

But now that moment had been ripped from him, just like Katzy had been, and he was plagued with shattering shame for sinking into a false memory.

Sabena was a taker.

She'd taken Katzy. She'd taken him. She'd taken that moment.

Ashton cursed his stupidity. Why didn't he recognize what was in front of him? All that training. His antennae permanently primed, aware of every situation. Reading everyone. Analyzing constantly.

Still, he allowed himself to be tricked.

Thinking back, so many aspects became clear. Katzy's sudden reticence to spend more time with him. Her reluctance to go with him to the penthouse. Her subtle but persistent questioning on the summit's location.

It all made complete sense. But how could he possibly have seen? The lens he'd looked through then was one filled with lustful need. With the lies laid bare, that lens had been refracted, jarring his view and displaying a different projection of reality.

A version of reality that had Al Nadir breach the inner sanctum of British politics. And he had been the fool to allow it to happen.

Ashton pulled a drawer, took out a bottle of Jack Daniels, and unscrewed the cap. He rooted around for his glass but couldn't find it. He sneered, recognizing the symbolism of the missing glass, reflecting the gap in his life now Katzy wasn't in it.

He shrugged, grasping the neck, and brought the bottle to his lips. He let the drink pour, unrestricted, down his throat. He didn't stop for a while. He swallowed the whisky in gulps, and allowed it to warm him.

Giving heat to dull the savage coldness within him.

He lost himself in the action and became subsumed within the smooth, liquid gold.

A shuffling outside his office kicked in Ashton's senses. He swiftly removed the whisky bottle, screwed back on the cap, and hid it in the drawer, just seconds before he heard rapping outside the door.

"Yes. Come in," yelled Ashton, pushing a stern intonation in his voice.

His compartmentalization processes started taking over. Katzy was gone. He had to move on. As brutal as it sounded, Ashton knew it was the only way he was going to survive and cope with the next few hours.

Dawes stepped into the room, looking concerned. "Prime Minister, sir, your speech for your broadcast to the nation is ready."

Ashton pushed back his chair and stood up.

"Show me," Ashton said roughly.

Dawes thrust the speech into the PM's hands. Ashton scanned down the page and raised an eyebrow once or twice, indicating to Dawes that he'd nailed the tone and sentiment exactly.

"Excellent, Dawes. Are we set then?" said Ashton, as Redfern walked in.

"Sir, everything is ready for you. Your public awaits, Prime Minister," confirmed Dawes, issuing a slight smile of satisfaction. Ashton could see he was actively searching for recognition. Ashton nodded. It was a sign of gratitude directed at Dawes, who received the message with humility.

"Well, we'd better go then. Hate to keep them waiting," said Ashton, and he smirked. Then he looked at his cabinet secretary. "Redfern, something you need?"

"Prime Minister, just to let you know, COBRA meeting will be at 1200 hours. All parties have been duly instructed."

"Thank you, Redfern. I'll be there straight after the public broadcast."

Ashton headed out with Dawes. Stepping through the door to the outside, he could see the podium Dawes had set up. In front, crowds of reporters from across the world huddled around, pointing cameras, shoving microphones, and calling out to Ashton.

Ashton strode forward, his face somber, his eyes hooded.

"Today the world has been rocked by the destruction of Malta and, in unison, the obliteration of the United Nations. Amongst the dead was my honorable Cabinet colleague and friend, Foreign Secretary Quentin Ludlow. I would like to express my condolences and deepest sympathy to Mr. Ludlow's family. I hope they can find comfort in the thought that Quentin Ludlow was in Malta on a peace mission. Malta was targeted because it was staging the UN Summit, a summit that was trying to bring peace to the world.

"We have seen, over the years, the heinous and horrific crimes of Al Nadir. But this morning's blast has escalated their terrorist attacks to genocide. For centuries, Malta has had a strong bond with the UK. English was the official language of Malta. And although, since 1964, it hasn't been part of the UK, Malta holds a special place in the hearts of the British people. Over half a million British people visited the country as tourists every year and there are at least twelve thousand British people who made their home on Malta. Our thoughts and prayers are with those who had family and friends on the islands of Malta, Gozo, and Comino. The last act the Maltese people did was to offer a platform for the United Nations to discuss peace. But that intention was blasted to hell this morning by Al Nadir. In the destruction of an entire country, these terrorists now believe they are unstoppable. But hear this..." Ashton stared, eyes like coals, into the camera, and his voice took on a flint-sharp inflection as he supplemented Dawes' words with his own. "Salim Al Douri, you are not unstoppable. You will be brought down. You will not hold the world to ransom. We have technologies and capabilities that will annihilate you, your lieutenants, and your second in command, Sabena Sanantoni."

Ashton took a beat as he centered himself. Knowing what she'd done to him already, he gritted his teeth, hard, and scowled, full of venom, as he delivered the last part of his speech.

"All of you Al Nadir lieutenants, hear this. We are now after you. Your days of drifting around thinking you're untouchable are over. By what you did to Malta, you've lost any advantage you had."

Ashton glared into the camera, hoping that Salim and Sabena were watching. He was directly referring to 'the agreement', that unwritten rule between Salim, Sabena, and the intelligence agencies around the world that the couple couldn't be touched, and, in return, top command would hold back from raining down true hell. But through what they'd done to Malta, they'd forfeited that agreement. It was now open season on Salim and Sabena, and Ashton was making sure everyone across defense and security knew it.

"We will not sit by and watch your evil continue to fester. I make this solemn vow to the great peoples of the UK that Al Nadir will be removed from this country and obliterated from the world, the way they obliterated Malta. Take this, Salim and Sabena..." Ashton noticed the camera man came in closer as if he could tell Ashton was making this address personal. Ashton paused, narrowed his eyes, and growled his words, not holding back on his vicious undertone. "Take this as your final warning. You won't see us coming. But you will feel our wrath. Your time is coming. Your day of reckoning is approaching. We will destroy you!"

Ashton fixed a rock-hard glare into the camera. He'd placed all his vulnerabilities and sensitivities aside. What the public now were seeing was a formidable fighter, someone who had the balls to take on and defeat Al Nadir. They saw a man of power, courage, and stone hard conviction.

At a time of great sorrow, Ashton had shown the British public he could be the nation's backbone. He could hold up against the mighty Al Nadir. By referring to the terrorists on a first name basis, it had brought a personal edge to the PM's announcement. Ashton had successfully disassociated the behemoth of Al Nadir and made the broadcast about Salim and Sabena. Two people who were just fallible humans. He'd stripped them of their super-humanness that the celebrity mags and TV shows had bestowed on them. They were diabolical, evil murderers, plain and simple.

And their days were numbered.

Chapter 41

Ellie opened her eyes and immediately remembered the translucent walls, the grand ostentatious mosaic flooring and of course, the rainbow crystals. She was in Kudamun.

Just like the time before, three days ago, when she'd been there.

The memory flooded into her…

The flames around her built faster. Her end was coming at a velocity Ellie could never have anticipated. Closing her eyes, she sent her love to Sam forever. The flames engulfed her. Intolerable pain raged through her body. Death. She wasn't afraid.

Flames vanished. Body, ice cold.

Opening her eyes, a dark cavern took her gaze.

"Step forward, Ellie."

The voice was peaceful, calm, and kind. Ellie trusted it. She stepped forward and fell through the darkness. The fall seemed endless. On and on, she fell. Disoriented, she closed her eyes.

"Do not be afraid, Ellie."

At the sound of the voice, Ellie snapped open her eyes and took in a building of stunning crystal. The architecture was so impressive and opulent, she was reminded of ancient civilizations. Ellie stared in sheer wonder at the ceiling. Except, it wasn't. The ceiling moved. It was a strange undulating sky of deep blues with sudden bursts of vibrant orange and silver streaks like lightening. It was everywhere above her.

As Ellie watched, all around her, details seemed to shimmer into view. She couldn't decide whether it was her eyesight refocusing or the walls, arches, and steps literally materializing in front of her.

How did she get there? She couldn't recall. It was like everything was somehow in the middle. No beginning. No ending. Only a constant feeling that Ellie had been there, standing in that magnificent hall, forever.

Emotions took over and Ellie arrived at the only conclusion possible. This magnificent place was heaven. And she was dead. The tears flooded from her in the instant she realized she would never see Sam again.

"Ellie, why do you cry?"

"I'm dead. This is heaven," Ellie cried to the disembodied voice.

"Oh, Ellie, you're not dead. And this isn't heaven."

"Then where am I?" she murmured quietly.

"A distance from your place," he answered kindly but enigmatically, his voice reverberating inside the hall.

"Who are you? Where are you?" Ellie questioned.

Strangely, her boldness had increased. She felt familiar with her surroundings. They should have been alien to her, but she was comfortable and felt relaxed. And she couldn't understand why.

"My name is Aby-od. I am here."

On his last word, Aby-od moved from behind a crystal pillar Ellie was sure hadn't been in the hall a second before. Aby-od smiled and his black eyes shone with a gracious, regal quality.

"Ellie, you have been kept in darkness. Welcome to the light!"

Ellie found it strange why she only remembered her time in Kudamun at that moment. But hadn't recalled anything whilst she'd been on Earth. Looking at Aby-od, she smiled for the first time since her capture.

"You're safe now." Aby-od held her close to him, feeling her shaking, terrified frame gradually restore to calm and peace. "We're all safe now."

Chapter 42

Sabena scowled at the screen as the prime minister finished his address to the nation.

"Fucking bastard!" she yelled, and stormed in the direction of the satcomm room. She flicked on the controls and called up Salim.

He appeared, sneering. "Time for the floor show?"

"Almost. But that's not why I'm calling. Did you see that fucker Ashton? Did you see him reneging completely on the agreement? He's put open season on us, Salim. It was a blanket-wide kill order couched in patriotism. We're gonna have to watch our backs."

Sabena regarded Salim. His posture was unmoved. His face was unsurprised. He pushed back some stray strands of his silky, dark hair, and shot a look back at her from his smoldering, sinister, black eyes.

"Sabena, we're taking over the world. Do you really think I give a fuck about what that stupid prick Ashton is saying? I can take out the USA tonight. Do you understand that, Sabena? I can wipe out hundreds of millions of people in a blink. We don't have to play to any of their tunes anymore. We write the symphonies and we make the arrangements. They play to our tune only. If they want to live, and I'm sure they do, they're gonna have to submit to us. There is no one stronger. We, Al Nadir, we are the dominant."

Sabena nodded, feeling the power of Salim's words. She knew he spoke sense but couldn't avoid the sensation that Ashton was going to cause them trouble.

"I suggest you focus on enjoying yourself and showing us all what a good time Al Nadir is gonna give to Mrs. Ellie Noor. Stop all these concerns about Ashton. He's small fry."

"Salim, I will do just that. I can't wait to entertain you. But I really don't think Ashton is small fry. He's dangerous. An unknown variable that could screw the whole equation for us. When I was within him…" Sabena unconsciously licked her lips, recalling the thrusting power that overpowered her as Ashton thundered into her without a precursor. He didn't ask. He just took her. The darkness she sensed within him turned her on even more. Every movement he did was unexpected and vicious. She knew he hid everything. What he really was. And anyone who hid themselves that well unnerved her. "He was brutal, almost raging in his intensity."

"You must have reveled in that," remarked Salim, smirking, and he raised an eyebrow.

Sabena grinned. "Of course I did. But, Salim, don't get me wrong, I know we have a great power in the quantum bomb, but he really scares me."

"Sabena, a preoccupied man is no longer a dangerous man. Give him something else to fret about. His Katzy. He obviously wants to keep her murder quiet. Why don't you drop a few breadcrumbs to the UK press and blast his relationship wide open? Then see how scary he's gonna be when his caring, family man facade crumbles before his eyes."

Moments after her broadcast with Salim, Sabena started posting out to various news channels the fact that Katzenberger hadn't been seen since her meeting with the PM yesterday. She then gave little indications that Katzenberger's relationship with Ashton was much more than just professional. Perhaps there was more to her disappearance than meets the eye.

Sabena smiled as reporters and net hacks started to bite, flinging back cries for more intel, which Sabena duly furnished. She had no visual proof. Katzy had been ultra-careful of taking inappropriate pictures. But all Sabena needed was to poke holes in Ashton's unwavering, charismatic, and family-loving persona, in order to light the fires of suspicion. Any hack sniffing around would do the rest.

It would certainly disrupt Ashton's psyche even more than it had been already. And that's all she needed.

Sabena knew that a little disruption goes a long, long way.

Chapter 43

Greeted on his return to the Great Hall by an agitated array of elders, Aby-od knew his delay in ratifying the dispatch of Earth was the primary cause of their distress. They didn't know he'd located the Protector. Now they just wanted to get on with dispatching Earth and moving their interests to another planet on their balance shift radar.

"Honorable elders, I bring great news. The Protector of Ki has finally been located."

Aby-od stared out at the high council, examining each expression. Aswa-da's face was openly caustic, but this was no different to any other time. His scowl matched the other elders in the House of Etima. They were not recognized for joyous dispositions. Dispatching Earth would have given success to the House of Etima. So much so that procedures to replace Aby-od with Aswa-da as leader of the high council would certainly have commenced. It would have been Aswa-da's finest hour. He would have had the most to gain.

Although Aby-od had no evidence to directly point a finger at Aswa-da, intuition told him that his nemesis was, in some way or another, involved. But this suspicion could only remain inside the corridors of Aby-od's mind. Under Kudamun's legal system, no senior elder, even the leader himself, could make such a claim. If Aby-od disputed the reasons behind the balance shift, he would need solid evidence that placed Aswa-da at the heart of a criminal act. Confronting a senior elder with allegations of sabotage and manipulation of a planet, without fully corroborated evidence, was an event as momentous as dispatching a planet in their care.

The law was absolute and brutally uncompromising. Failure to provide a completely substantiated case would lead to the plaintiff being charged with high treason against the order of Kudamun. The plaintiff would then face summary execution. The accused would go free.

Aby-od knew only too well the law, and although perverse in its construct, it was established to prevent senior elders from making false allegations against their opposing counterparts, thus seeking supremacy through illegal maneuvers.

The protocols laid down by the order of Kudamun had to be respected and adhered to, for it was not just Kudamun who could be affected if they were contravened. The balance shift of an individual planet or even an entire galaxy could create such dire consequences, the very nature of Kudamun could be called into question.

Aby-od understood, as every senior elder did, the implicit need to remain within Kudamun law. The ramifications of drifting were too devastating to contemplate. But now, despite his knowledge to the contrary, he hated the laws. They confined his investigations, if one could call them that, and certainly prevented him from unveiling the truth.

The only play he had was to 'reconstitute' the Protector and finish the task he'd started.

After delivering his address, Aby-od excused himself from further high council deliberations, stating that he would return once the reconstitution process was complete. Grudgingly, the high council nodded their approval.

Wasting no time, Aby-od shimmered back to the Hall of Umray.

He looked at Ellie sitting down and talking to his female assistants. Wrapped in a long, metallic, gold gown, she looked almost Kudamaz. One could be forgiven for not believing the girl had endured a living hell. But he knew what the flowing robes hid so well.

Chapter 44

Ellie raised her head when she noticed the air shimmer in front of her. From the moment she was transferred, Ellie had not felt a sense of panic.

Every instinct told her she should be terrified. Every vision defied the laws of the physical world. She was in a place that her brain could never comprehend. She was in the company of beings of great power, ageless and commanding. Sweat should have been building on her palms, as it did when she drove home late at night. Her pulse should have been racing like a Formula One driver on his last lap. And her throat should have gone as dry as the crisp breads she used to eat to keep her figure trim. She should have felt a sick, twisting fear bubble up in her stomach.

She should have been afraid.

Instead, she felt only peace and calm. But it was not just surface calm, the kind you show when you know you're worried, but you put on a brave face. Ellie's calm was deep. It penetrated her. The feeling was overpowering. It was as though every atom in her body was being stroked and soothed with luscious, relaxing oils. She felt light-headed and dizzy. Ellie swallowed slightly to curb her dizziness and was hit by a euphoric high. She fell back, laughing.

Aby-od walked towards her, concern rippling through his erudite face. "Has this happened before?"

His assistants shook their heads. "No, she has been very stable, but she has been asking a lot of questions."

"Ellie, how do you feel?" Aby-od sat down next to Ellie and stared into her eyes. Her pupils had dilated, and her skin had turned pearly pink. She was shining from the inside.

"I feel wonderful. Like I'm having a never-ending massage. Everything in me feels alive."

Aby-od knew she was allowing herself to be absorbed by feelings of incredible exhilaration. If she continued, she would be absorbed totally. Ultimate euphoria would flood her brain at levels a human just could not imagine or handle, and plunge her into a fatal coma. He had to get her to stop the absorption.

"We haven't got much time." Aby-od stood up. "Ellie, I need you to listen to me. I need you to let go of that feeling you have and concentrate on my voice. Can you do that?"

Ellie looked into Aby-od's face. The power of his apparent worry broke through her ecstatic feeling, and she focused. Almost immediately, she came crashing down from the high.

"What's happening?" whispered Ellie, frightened for the first time since her arrival in Kudamun.

"Ellie, you're having an adverse reaction to Kudamun. Every being that comes here is affected. This is why beings that come here only come here for a reason."

"A reason?" muttered Ellie, feeling suddenly unsettled.

"Yes, Ellie, and there's a good reason you were brought here. But the way Kudamun is affecting you so quickly means I don't have much time to explain."

Ellie stared back, confused. But Aby-od continued, undaunted by his task.

"There is a life-force inside you that has the power to save Earth from certain obliteration."

Aby-od waited and watched Ellie. She stayed mute. Words were meaningless. What she was being told was beyond understanding. She couldn't even string a sentence to frame up a response. All she could do was continue to gaze at Aby-od and pray that, somehow, in some way, she would reach a point of comprehension. However, the more Aby-od continued, the deeper Ellie's abject confusion became.

"That power needs to be set free."

"Power? How? How do I have a power inside me, but I can't feel it?"

But as Ellie repeated the words, she knew that Aby-od was absolutely right. Three days before, she had felt that feeling of detachment in her hand, that tingling electricity at its base, and everything she did had been just that bit out of synch like she couldn't catch up. And reality, real reality had seemed deeply hidden from her view.

She felt Aby-od watching her as her comprehension started to dawn slowly.

"Recently, I've felt it," she said. "I knew I was different. Maybe I've always known but hated to admit it. Most of all to myself." Ellie was quiet and thoughtful for a moment. Then she turned to stare hard at Aby-od. "How will the power inside me be set free?"

"We have an ancient process. Everything is ready." Aby-od made to stand up, but Ellie pulled at his heavy, silk sleeve, forcing him to remain seated.

"What's this process? What will happen to me?" Ellie's voice was small. She knew but didn't want to acknowledge what her perceptive mind told her. At that moment, she wanted to feel the calm she'd felt a few minutes before.

"You'll be different."

Ellie's eyes flashed with fright as she caught the look he tried to hide away. His shame and embarrassment.

"How will I be different?" Ellie's eyes searched Aby-od's for explanation. Aby-od noticed her eyes shining. The whites of them were glowing, luminescent as if illuminated from the inside. Time was running out. He had to get on with reconstituting Ellie while she was still lucid.

"You will not be the Ellie you are now. You won't be human. But you will retain Ellie's memories, amongst many others. And you'll be incredibly powerful."

"Will I still look the same?" asked Ellie, touching her face, trying not to dwell on the words 'you won't be human'.

"I cannot say. It depends upon the reconstitution process."

"Sorry? What did you say?" said Ellie. Her psychic wanderings had been right on the button. "For there to be a reconstitution process, something needs to be deconstituted first."

Aby-od shook his head. He didn't want to have this conversation.

"Is that something going to be me?" asked Ellie.

"Ellie, you'll be perfectly safe. Do not concern yourself with the process. We'll handle that." Aby-od hated adopting his dismissive attitude, but there wasn't time to elaborate, and if he did, she'd never agree. The less Ellie knew, the better for everyone.

"But what is this process? You've told me nothing. If I'm not human, what will I be? What will I look like? Aby-od, I need to know just what the hell I'm going to become."

Ellie was fiercely alert and ready, but her bravery didn't equal stupidity. If Aby-od wasn't going to tell her, she wouldn't play ball. Ten years Sam had kept her in the dark. The day she learned the truth, she vowed no one would do that to her again.

"Ellie, you'll still have the physical appearance of a human, but internally you will be a surging power designed to protect Earth. You may not change appearance at all. It depends upon the final physical construction program. Sometimes it's the originator's form, and other times, it's the host's. In either case, you'll remain as beautiful and gracious as you are right now. Your originator was a wonderful Kudamaz. If you take her form, be proud. She was a truly special."

"I won't look the same. That's what you're saying. Oh God, no. I can't do this. Aby-od, take me home. You've got the wrong person. I'm not special. I just want to stay me."

Tears welled up in her shining eyes. Aby-od could see behind her the numbers of the balance shift increasing rapidly as Earth plunged farther into the Dark Zone. He looked back at Ellie. Her skin had a sparkling outline. Absorption was happening by stealth. Although Ellie was focused and unaware of the euphoria, she was still in grave danger. Aby-od had no choice.

"Ellie, I'm sorry. There is no alternative. You either go through the process or die through euphoric absorption. I can't stop what's happening to you. I tried but you're reacting too fast. You must always have had empathic tendencies, and this openness to connect with others is speeding up the absorption. We can't wait any longer. We have to start now."

"I don't understand. I don't know."

Her head felt like it was full of cotton wool covered in bubble wrap. All the clever thoughts that once used to race around her brain had vanished. Her synapses, previously shooting in all directions, had stopped firing, and everything was slowing down. Ellie stared blankly at Aby-od as his words came out at the wrong speed.

"Ellie, once you are reconstituted, you will know everything. Telling you will take too long. We have to start the process now."

"Is there another way?" asked Ellie, shaken and desperately trying to maintain focus.

"I wish there was. But there isn't. It's reconstitution or death."

Chapter 45

Thornburg picked up the call. The gruff but compassionate pathologist came on the line.

"Commissioner, the rest of the body arrived."

"And? Did you find out how the poison was administered?"

"Well, she was in a bit of mess. A real hack job. Made my investigations harder. But I can confirm the tetrodotoxin was administered transdermally."

"No injection marks then?" asked Thornburg.

"I checked the body thoroughly. The only residue of the poison was on her lips. And there was something else. A bit odd. There are two hues of color on the lips. One color is underneath and is clearly Katzenberger's lipstick. But there are traces of another deeper pigment on her lips. And the particles of the tetrodotoxin are locked within the particles of deeper pigmented lipstick."

"What?" responded Thornburg, realizing what the pathologist was saying. "So someone kissed her and administered the poison at the same time?"

"Yep. That's more than likely what happened."

"Any other evidence of torture or rape?"

"Nothing, Commissioner. She was clean. She wasn't touched. Just poisoned. Clean and precise. Just a bit strange with the kissing thing, but at least it was immediate and painless."

Thornburg rang off and stared into space. This was getting more and more crazy. Sabena was obviously the killer. She'd used a nano-mask to shield from the poison and administered it by kissing Katzenberger.

How Ashton was going to take this news, he didn't know.

Ashton was on his way to his private office when his phone rang. Thornburg had more news. After his victorious powerhouse of a speech, he had to maintain his semblance of calm. Everyone had praised his delivery and his brutal, uncompromising stance on terrorism. He refused questions from reporters, stating enigmatically that enough had been said. Now it was a time for real action.

Ashton took a beat and answered the commissioner's call.

"Yes?"

"Rich, path report is in."

"Ok. Wait," said Ashton, moving to the side of the main hall. Redfern turned and looked over his shoulder, but Ashton flicked his fingers forward signaling for Redfern to head on to the Cabinet Office.

Redfern turned back, shrugging, and then stiffened and walked away.

"Tell me," added Ashton, as he made sure he was out of earshot of everyone. Advisors, assistants, ministers, and Number 10 staff continued to look at Ashton, so he turned his face to the wall and spoke brusquely. "Be quick, Mark."

"Rich, the tetrodotoxin was administered transdermally."

"Through the skin?"

"Through the lips."

"How do you know that?"

Ashton listened. What the hell had Sabena done to Katzy?

"Different pigment of lipsticks. The darker one had poison particles embedded."

"Right," said Ashton, absorbing the intel. "Anything else?"

"No signs of torture, rape, or assault. Her heart and eyes were definitely removed post-mortem, as I said before."

Ashton went silent. He could hear his own breathing. His training took over and he found himself falling again into the steady, defined rhythm of his heartbeat. It calmed him. It stopped the fury from breaking out and destroying his logic. Cognitive command was his weapon and he fired round after round until the balance of his energies were in a form of equilibrium.

"Rich, I know it seems a bit kinky, how she was killed, Sabena kissing her and everything, but she didn't suffer. We know what The Slayer is capable of. Katzy was one of the lucky ones."

Ashton heard the word luck, recalling the eyes that had stared forlorn and desperate at him. He quipped sharply, "I don't think I'd quite use that turn of phrase."

"No, sorry, Rich. Perhaps not lucky. That was unthinking of me. But you know what I mean. She could have done much worse to Katzy. But she didn't."

"No. She didn't. She tortured me instead," responded Ashton quietly, eyeing the people gathered behind him. "Look, I've got to go, and you need to head on over to Room A. Remember, Mark. Not a word."

"Of course, Rich. You can rely on me."

His friend's gentle reassurancc carried with it a declaration that the confidence Ashton had entrusted to him would never be compromised.

"Thank you, Mark."

Ashton paused. Katzy's death had left a void within him. He needed something to pull him away from that grasping abyss that had taken root the moment he'd opened the hamper.

"Care to have a deeper discussion about this later tonight over a single malt?"

He listened as Thornburg breathed slowly, understanding the invitation.

"Love to," he responded finally.

Ashton couldn't suppress the faint tingle of exhilaration as the pain he'd been beset with finally yielded to thoughts of pleasure.

Chapter 46

Ellie had struggled to grasp the information that Aby-od had imparted. *Save Earth.* Ellie slowly smiled, not through euphoric absorption but through memory. She had always felt there was something special about her, that she was born for a purpose. Staring ahead at the balance shift numbers in free fall, Aby-od didn't see her smile.

"I can really *save* Earth?" whispered Ellie. Her lips trembled as the incredulous words left her mouth.

"I know you're frightened. I understand how you must be feeling right now. But I cannot say this any clearer. If you refuse to go through the reconstitution process, billions of your people will die. You will die. And Earth will no longer exist."

Aby-od was aware that his delivery was psychologically monstrous and shattering for Ellie, but the time had passed for carefully structured emotive speeches. Looking back at her, he saw her smile. Believing the euphoria had broken through completely, he stood up abruptly and pulled Ellie to her feet.

"No more talk. We must start now."

"Aby-od, I am ready. Do whatever you must."

Ellie's words were strong and brave. She had a duty to perform. Hearing Aby-od and the responsibility he'd placed on her slender shoulders, her fear took second place.

Aby-od could see an echo of Selema's resilience and determination in Ellie's shining eyes, a shadow of her courage in Ellie's valiant attitude. Undoubtedly, over the centuries, Selema's powerful traits had infiltrated the human Holder's genetic make-up, and now Ellie's personality was built on the foundation of Selema's fearless, daring character. The smile he was observing was not an effect of the euphoria. It was Ellie's own, and he was pleased to see it.

"Thank you, Ellie. Earth and Kudamun will be forever in your debt." Aby-od lowered his eyes in respect. "Now we must get on."

Taking Ellie's hand, he led her to the center of the Hall of Umray. Ellie looked down at the decorative flooring: a huge, intricate mosaic that depicted two massive hands encasing an orb at the center. When she'd asked the assistants about it earlier, they'd told her it was the symbol of Kudamun, the planetary guardians. *Some guardians, needing my help.*

"Ellie, stay there. Do not move," instructed Aby-od.

Ellie complied without question. She watched silently whilst Aby-od worked on something flashing with crystals for keys. *Must be a computer of some kind.*

Standing there, her mind drifted. Suddenly, she felt a crushing blow. *Sam!*

Like a major news event superseded by an even greater story, her arrival on Kudamun had made her forget about her husband. Ellie did not know it was the effects of the euphoria that had destabilized her memory patterns and had wiped her mind of recent events. Now, in the center of the hall, with the reconstitution process commencing, Ellie was shielded from the euphoric effect. All she could feel was overwhelming guilt. How could she have forgotten her beloved Sam? Tears streamed down her shining face.

"Aby-od!" she yelled. "What about Sam? I have to save him!"

A huge crystal began to lower towards Ellie. She looked up as the exquisitely faceted chunk of gleaming ice descended upon her, but she did not move. Instead, she screamed back at Aby-od.

"I must save Sam! Al Nadir has him."

Aby-od heard 'Al Nadir' and remembered how Ellie had been after she'd transferred to Kudamun. Broken, shivering, and showing signs of significant blood loss and extreme traumatic shock. Aby-od didn't think she would survive. After being clothed in her robes, Aby-od had taken her bloodied medical gown, a testament to Al Nadir's abuse, and placed it on the ground in a darkened room on the other side of the hall. Shaking with an uncustomary rage, with tears streaming down his face, Aby-od had taken out a small, oval device known as a Harmon gun and trained it on the ground. Pressing a button, a high-pitched harmonic, well above the human sound scale, emitted from the device. The instant the Harmon wave hit the gown, it blasted into millions of sparkling particles and was gone. Aby-od had dried his tears, his fury vented, and returned to his duties in the Hall of Umray.

The recent memory swayed Aby-od's focus. No Protector had moved him to tears before. He collected himself. What was it about Ellie that moved him so?

“Aby-od, did you hear me?” Ellie hollered hysterically. “Al Nadir have Sam. I love him so much. I must save him.”

Aby-od nodded calmly, indicating acknowledgement. “Ellie, the power is inside you. You will do what needs to be done.”

The massive crystal continued to lower. *Please, don’t crush me.* Her eyes flashed in fear at Aby-od.

He smiled gently. “Close your eyes. No harm will come to you. Trust me, Ellie.”

Satisfied by the kindness she read in his face, Ellie nodded her head. Somehow, she knew Aby-od spoke the truth.

“I do,” Ellie whispered bravely, closing her eyes.

Chapter 47

On his way to Cabinet Room A for the COBRA meeting, Dawes suddenly pulled Ashton to one side.

"Excuse me, Prime Minister, but we have a very big problem."

Dawes' pudgy face was sallow and stricken. He handed Ashton his tablet. The prime minister scanned the intel that had come in from a political hack wanting to verify with Dawes a story that was about to break on the web.

Ashton glared. Hardly taking the time to consider the facts, he screamed, "Put an immediate injunction on this. Claim national security reasons. If they go live, they will be liable for treason and will be held and tried with the full power of the law against them."

"What about freedom of the press?"

"Fuck freedom of the press," snarled Ashton. "Get an injunction or else you're fired. Got it?"

Dawes swallowed. "Yes, sir, Prime Minister. So there is no validity in the story at all?"

Ashton swung around to face Dawes. The Number 10's director of communications' nose was almost touching the PM's. Ashton grabbed him by the lapels.

"Did you hear me? I have given you a direct order. File the injunction. Bury this fake news. And do your fucking job."

Ashton was aware of people turning to stare, but he didn't give a damn.

Redfern sidled up to him. "Everything alright, Prime Minister?"

"Yes. Fine. Let's get on with this. I'm in the mood for fucking annihilating Al Nadir from history."

Ashton marched forward into Cabinet Room A, leaving behind a bewildered cabinet secretary and a somewhat confused and shaken director of communications.

Chapter 48

Gently, Sabena stroked the satin, letting her hand follow the undulations, the little valleys created by the buttons. Downwards, her fingers travelled into the groove and slowly encased the button between her thumb and forefinger. Sighing, she twisted and tweaked it. In her mind, it was something much different.

Closing her eyes, she thought back. How she'd loathed to clothe her. How she'd wanted her, wanted to take her, there and then, on the grass, amongst the briars. And then her ineffectual and rather risible attempt to trick her. But Sabena had still been enticed. That moment, even though she'd suspected it to be a trick was too much to refuse. If there'd been a flicker of truth in Ellie's act, she couldn't let that opportunity pass her by. For a few short minutes, it had been so wonderful. Ellie had submitted totally to her. And yet although tied to the stainless steel trolley, naked beneath that thin medical gown, Ellie had seemed vulnerable yet invincible. Sabena had felt her dark energy. That pulse of the forbidden. An inner determination to take even that which was withheld to her. Denial was just a prelude to conquering what she wanted.

Salim had it. Kinley had it. Ashton had it.

Ellie had it.

Her incarceration had unleashed something deep within Ellie, and despite it being all an act of deception on the conscious level, subconsciously, inside her mind, her lust had been insatiable.

Sabena could again have taken her on that trolley, but it wasn't the time. It wasn't what Sabena really wanted. Ellie deserved much more than just a heated moment of vicious passion.

Ellie deserved an audience.

Ellie deserved a floorshow.

Sabena pressed hard against the corner of the divan, forcing it, tongue and groove like, to nestle between her legs. The zenith rammed deeply in. Slowly, she rubbed up and down, her arousal growing on each rise and fall. Soon Ellie would be here. Finally, her hunger would be satisfied, her position reaffirmed.

Sabena pulled away from the divan and inspected her landscape of sexual torture. Everything was there. Her contraptions and devices were lined up in front of the huge satcomm screen just as she had demanded. All for her sadistic, hcdonistic pleasure.

Looking around, Sabena breathed hard. Her skin flushed and eyes dilated like dinner plates as she imagined what the next hours were to hold.

The floorshow was supposed to be fifteen minutes later. But, thinking about Ellie, Sabena couldn't contain her desperation. With her leather trench coat flapping open to reveal bronze, well-toned and muscular legs, Sabena pelted down the corridor, eager to start the show early. Underneath her coat, Sabena had inched herself into the smallest leather-studded G-string and nothing else. The leather of the coat slid against her tight, firm buttocks, and Sabena felt more aroused than she'd ever been before.

She'd had so many, men and women. She didn't really care. Whatever captured her passion at that moment, she took. But with Ellie, it was different. Ellie was special.

All through the torture, Ellie had never begged her to stop. She'd screamed, sure. Who wouldn't? But she'd been strong. So incredibly strong. Even at the point where Sam had broken, Ellie had stayed resolute and silent. That resilience was an aphrodisiac to Sabena. It drove her crazy, fueling her burning need to break her completely.

Reaching the door to the medical room, Sabena stared, eyes widening, not out of insatiable desire, but from confused amazement.

The metal binds holding Ellie were still there. But Ellie had disappeared.

Thinking maybe Russo or one of the other floorshow players had taken her, Sabena charged down the other side of the corridor. Maybe one of them was trying to get a *head* start.

I'll show him.

Outside the door to the satcomm room, Sabena listened. Nothing. With her frustration growing, Sabena flung open the door, half-expecting to see one of the players with Ellie in flagrante.

To her utter disappointment, the room was empty. Where the fuck was the bitch?

"OK, who has her?"

At the sound of Sabena's irritated voice screaming through the intercom, her minions came rushing into the room. Sabena glared at Peter and Marcel, the two thugs she'd stopped from raping Ellie.

"What have you done with her? You couldn't wait, could you? You knew she was mine. But you had to fuck her first, didn't you? To keep up your macho fucking ego. Led by your pathetic little dicks. So where is she? What have you done with her?"

The thugs stared back bemused like children being explained Einstein's theory of general relativity. Sabena examined their faces. From their expressions of sheer bewilderment, their up turned mouths, their arching eyebrows and startled eyes, it was obvious to Sabena they didn't have a clue as to how Ellie had vanished.

Marcel was the first to summon up the courage to address Sabena, who eyed him with a doubtful stare and a skeptical sneer.

"Miss Sanantoni, we don't know where she is. We last saw her on the trolley in the medical room. Of course we wanted her. You know that. But we'd never touch someone you had chosen."

"So where is she?" screamed Sabena, the veins on her neck prominently popping up as her frustration shot to anger.

"I don't know," answered Marcel.

Sabena stepped forward. She recognized the change in speech pattern. Marcel's use of we had slithered into I at a hefty speed. So much for looking out for each other.

Sabena bored into him ruthlessly. "I don't believe you."

Lowering her eyes to Marcel's crotch, Sabena thrust her hand out and gripped his genitals with a white-knuckle force. Marcel screamed. His eyes begged for mercy as instant pain struck him. Sabena twisted his testicles like she was twisting tomatoes off the vine.

"Where is she?" screamed Sabena, continuing to twist, her teeth gritting hard with vengeance.

"Believe me. I…don't…know!" gasped Marcel, his face contorting in agony.

"Liar!"

"Please! Oh, God, please stop. I don't know where she is. Ah!"

"So if you don't have her, where is she?"

"Maybe she's escaped."

The voice from behind Sabena made her swing around and let go of Marcel, who cupped his bruised balls through his jeans, panting.

"Escaped?"

Sabena could barely believe it, let alone say it. Her dark eyes burned with incensed fury. Peter swallowed, taking a step back.

Hammering the intercom so hard the plastic button shattered, Sabena yelled, an insane banshee erupting inside her, "Ellie Noor has escaped. Find her!"

Would the floorshow ever happen now? Sabena, like a lioness whose catch had been snatched by another, was flooded with unbridled rage. She'd longed for Ellie from that first glance. If she was to be denied her moment with her...

Sabena's hand slipped deeply in her pocket, fingering the metal of her Desert Eagle .50 caliber pistol.

"I wanted her!" she screamed. "Consider this your termination."

Sabena took just a second a piece to fire straight into Marcel's mashed-up groin, and then into Peter's. Both thugs fell to the floor, doubled up in eye-watering pain. Gaping bloody holes sat where their family jewels had shone. Their jeans soaked up their juices of life. Sabena stepped coldly over the thugs and left them to bleed out.

Chapter 49

Warm bodies started to drift into Cabinet Room A. On their faces were signs of extreme shock. Ashton regarded each one who entered and sat down. They were hardly a fearless bunch ready to take on a terrorist collective. These were pen-pushers. Bureaucrats. Even his military and security chiefs. They had little fight in them. It was all about getting enough things done to be thought of as achieving something. An exercise in checking boxes. Toeing the line.

And if it all went pear-shaped, well, that's a lesson learnt, folks.

Ashton smirked as it hit him: that was the nature of politics. Defense was no different. It was just part of the machine.

Gibbs and Cartwright took their seats next to one another. Ashton thought they looked like the odd couple. Gibbs with his massive, rugby-built, forty-two-inch chest, his sturdy, short, tree-trunk legs, and boisterous, sergeant major manner alongside Cartwright's tall but muscular frame, slender legs, and clipped, arrogant demeanor, always made Ashton want to grin. He also thought it was humorous how they consistently tried to outplay and outsmart each other in the presence of the PM. Cartwright didn't have the experience of his predecessor Sir Justin Maide, and in matters such as the one that threatened the UK with potential oblivion, he was running a paint-by-numbers playbook.

Ashton knew that approach was never going to work.

He waited for Defence Secretary Charles Godley to take his seat, with Mark Thornburg, who rushed in at the last minute before proceedings commenced. Ashton declined any immediate eye contact with Thornburg, but he felt his old friend's eyes on him before the meeting started.

"Right, well, we've all seen what happened this morning. It's devastating. Our hearts go out to those who died. But now we need to move on from sentiments of sorrow and sympathy and take real action against these bastards. We've got to find that fucking cell in Cambridgeshire."

Ashton glared with vehemence at Gibbs. As head of MI5, it was his responsibility to locate the cell and neutralize it after actionable intel had been secured. Gibbs shuffled in his seat, and Cartwright moved a little to the left giving distance between himself and Gibbs.

So much for camaraderie, boys.

"We're not talking about a huge land mass. It's only 1,309 square miles. We even had intel from Rickard Allan about the cell. I just can't understand how your people, Gibbs, haven't located it."

His name had now been placed on the table. Gibbs couldn't shirk away from the PM's blatant inquisition.

"Prime Minister, we have a possible indication that-"

"What about our spy satellites? Can't they find it?" shouted Ashton over the top of Gibbs' faltering response.

"Al Nadir has some kind of cloaking technology. We've still not been able to crack it. From the satellite footage we take, it shows nothing. Just a field. And there are many fields in Cambridgeshire."

"Isn't there a heat signature? Surely they're running some hefty tech. They must be burning wattage. It should show up on the grid," stated Ashton, slipping into his old MI6 shoes. Then he pulled back. He wasn't an agent anymore. He had others to do the thinking.

"No, Prime Minister. There's no immediately traceable heat signature. They run off their own generators. They never link to a national grid infrastructure. They're self-sufficient. Same method across the world. We know from agents who had gone undercover that's their operational MO."

Ashton couldn't help but remember the brave, handsome face of Matt Kinley, the MI6 agent who had lasted four years in Al Nadir under Operation Snowdrop, but who had been massacred with his young daughter and beautiful wife just four days before.

"But since Allan gave us the indication there was a cell in Cambridgeshire, has Five managed to narrow it at all?"

Gibbs nodded and chimed in, "We are getting closer. Finding Ellie Noor's phone in Duxford and knowing that she's in some way connected to Al Nadir is helping pin-point a different region to the one we were concentrating on before. Although Allan gave us the existence of the cell, he didn't help in its specific location. In fact, his intel led us down a blind alley."

Ashton scowled and moved forward, his expression a growing storm. "Ellie

Noor. What do we think about her disappearance? Siding with or taken by the enemy?"

The men around the table looked at one another, exchanging hesitant shrugs.

"Well?" snapped Ashton. "She's gone missing. Her husband, agent Sam Noor, is also AWOL. Richard Lydell, his CIA co-op, has vanished. The president has already stated his doubts about Noor's loyalty. He believes that Noor's been flipped and is working for Al Douri, and his wife's been extracted by Al Nadir to meet him in another country. He doesn't want to doubt the trustworthiness of Lydell. The president is of the opinion he is beyond reproach."

"No one's beyond reproach in this business," said Cartwright harshly.

"Quite," continued Ashton, "but the president, as we all know, isn't one that handles listening to others too well."

Around the table, men nodded and smirked.

"Has the Noor's residences been searched?" asked Ashton to Gibbs.

"Both the apartment in Chelsea and their home in Winchester have had teams searching through everything since we lost contact with Agent Noor. Nothing suspicious in either residence."

"Cartwright, latest intel on the ground?"

Cartwright moved forward, scanning down his tablet. "No further update from Agent Noor since 0400 hours Tehran time. CIA, likewise, haven't had any contact from Agent Lydell at the exact same time. Both fell off the grid. We have assets in Baba Heydar, but they have seen nothing. Of course, they may have been flipped. The state of play at the moment in the field is very duplicitous. Al Douri flashes his cash and agents and assets fold. No one seems to have a shred of decency and loyalty anymore."

The room seemed to issue a sigh of despondency at Cartwright's announcement. Ashton recognized the burning sensation of hopelessness that singed the air of the room. He brought back the tone to one of potential promise.

"Cartwright, I don't believe that all the good men and women out there are being acquired. There is still such a thing as integrity and faith to the flag. Isn't there?"

Cartwright shrugged. "One hopes so, Prime Minister. But Al Nadir aren't just freedom fighters scratching for donations like so many terrorists have been in the past. They're a structured, powerful, trillion dollar operation. They buy people, governments, countries. Nothing about our old playbook exists. They've rewritten it completely. Whatever is happening with Lydell and the Noors, we can't rule out the possibility that both agents have been bought."

"So, the wife, what's the latest on her?" said Ashton, deflecting the discussion from being bogged down in deceit and treachery.

"His wife hasn't been seen since 0120 hours this morning. Her phone was found dumped on the hard shoulder near junction 10 on the M11. Unfortunately, around that area of the motorway, there are no cams. We found evidence of tire marks in the middle and outside lanes. It looks like a car skidded around in a circle and then stopped. No sign of crashing into the central reservation. No remnants of front or tail lights, or bits of metal. Just the skid marks. It's unknown at this point whether the marks are related to Mrs. Noor's disappearance or not."

Ashton listened intently to the new intel from Cartwright, and then looked at Gibbs, signaling the need for him to continue updating his investigations by Five on home soil.

"We're working with the local Cambridgeshire police in Huntingdon to widen the search. We have helicopters now scouring the area. A fifty mile perimeter around Duxford has been set up and officers on the ground are searching. We're running AI scans across SocMed platforms, interrogating Facebook, Twitter, and Instagram accounts of all residents in Cambridgeshire region to establish any possible correlations, sightings, anything that looks anomalous and suspect. Nothing has emerged. But we're putting everything on this to try and find Ellie Noor."

"Good," said Ashton. He turned to Thornburg, "Commissioner, anything to report on Miss Katzenberger's murder?"

He was aware of Thornburg staring at him, but Ashton didn't flinch.

"Prime Minister, the estate car was coated in a nanotech film that eats dust, dirt, sweat, essentially the things that leave fingerprints at scenes of a crime. We've got nothing. Al Nadir parked in a blind spot area of Heston services. We didn't pick up any further movement. We're liaising with Five to AI analyze everyone caught on cams from Embankment through to Heston services. We're accessing and interrogating SocMed accounts of pedestrians, drivers, anyone and everyone. Someone will have something. I feel sure of it. We will find them."

Ashton gritted down and swallowed. He tried to grasp Thornburg's wonderful positivity, but he clocked Godley's ashen face, and that feeling of futility started to wash through him once more.

"Defence Secretary, your update please."

Godley shuffled in his seat and eyed the table slowly.

"As terrible as the outcome was, the UK was most definitely saved from obliteration by Agent Noor's quick thinking."

All around the table nodded solemnly. Ashton tilted his head, taking in Godley's stance. Back curved, slightly ingratiating, his lips trembled, and spittle bunched in the corners of his mouth.

"However, his ability to deflect the impact of the bomb on the UK does not necessarily exonerate him from blame. He may have chosen Malta as a location to take the hit rather than his home. It would weigh a little less on his conscience that way. Perhaps. This is only conjecture."

Godley stared at his colleagues, and then at the prime minister. Ashton felt a shiver. His words were very logical, but it didn't align. Sam Noor, the man he'd entrusted to deliver Operation Snowdrop, probably the most devastating undercover mission ever devised, would never have turned. Ashton just couldn't find it in his heart to believe it.

"If he has been taken, it is safe to assume Agent Noor broke under torture and revealed the location of the summit. Either way, Agent Noor now should be considered a liability, and his wife, the same."

Thornburg shook his head. Ashton recognized his friend's thoughtful expression descending into annoyance. "Hold on, Defence Secretary, why should we consider Ellie Noor to be a liability? There's nothing to allude to her being a hostile or working for Al Nadir."

Ashton glanced at Godley, who placed both hands on the table, palms facing down. Then he turned them over. It was a clear signal to Ashton to open the locked file, codenamed Phoenix.

Ashton scanned the table and knew there was no avoiding it. The truth, it seemed, was always going to find a way out.

Chapter 50

In the security room, Sabena selected the surveillance systems monitoring the medical room and ran through the recordings. On all monitors, views of Ellie from multiple angles were displayed. Sabena paused and then flicked forward, staring intently at each monitor. She could see Ellie was terrified. Her clamps were secure. Sabena had tightened them so that in the end she could hardly move.

Pushing the recording forward, Sabena tried to ascertain whether Ellie had been assisted in her escape. But Ellie was just there, looking as scared as Sabena knew she should be.

Then something happened. Ellie, from looking terrified a moment before, had a face of pure serenity and peace. She smiled, her eyes sparkled, and she was gone!

Sabena stared incredulously at the screen. She wasn't easily shocked, but Ellie's vanishing trick left her dumbstruck.

Slowly, she skipped back frame by frame, looking for any intervention at all. Nothing. Sabena swallowed again, trying to get a mental handle on what she was witnessing. She took the film forward frame by frame. And still nothing. No help. No intervention. Just the same sequence on the last three frames: frightened, serene, and gone.

"No…no. No!" yelled Sabena, as she forwarded the recording frame by frame for what seemed the hundredth time, her thumb aching from the pressure of pushing the button with such ferocious force.

"This is not happening!" she shrieked. "This is not fucking happening!"

She blasted the monitors with her remaining bullets. They exploded and glass flew in all directions, narrowly missing Sabena's colleagues as they stormed into the security room.

"She's fucking escaped!" growled Sabena, pushing past her stunned colleagues.

Back in the satcomm room, dead thugs in the background, Sabena flicked on the screen.

"Salim, she's gone." Sabena rasped her words with vitriolic anger.

Salim had been surprised to receive the signal transmission from Sabena but thought that she was too sexed up and wanted to start the floorshow early. Grinning broadly at Sam, he rubbed his hands together, excited that the floorshow was about to start. Sam closed his eyes and prayed Ellie would survive, though he doubted that would be Sabena's goal.

But as Salim listened to Sabena's ranting, the smile froze on his face.

"The bitch has gone. Fuck knows how. But she's escaped."

Listening to Sabena's shrill, rapier voice sounding more insane than ever, it was Sam's turn to smile. Ellie had escaped. Such words as they met his ears were couched in sheer, unadulterated joy. He was enraptured as he watched his captors trying to understand desperately how it had happened. But Sam knew. He knew one of his little prayers must have been smarter than the rest. And it only takes one to get Heaven to make the miracles happen.

"How did she fucking get out?" screamed Salim, equally as inflamed by this disastrous turning point.

"I've gone through the surveillance, Salim. She just disappears."

"Disappears? What the fuck does that mean?" Salim stormed back at the screen.

Sam watched and smiled as Sabena jumped back instinctively despite their conversation being over transmission. Her face was now wary. Her movements were involuntary and defensive.

Sam's smile had turned into a laugh. Incensed, Salim whipped around, hitting Sam hard in the face to stop his laughing.

"Get that fucker out of here."

Salim's thugs dragged Sam away from the screen.

All the way back to his cell, the smile of elation never left his face.

Even when the guards threw Sam hard against the wall. His jaw cracked painfully. But amidst the blood streaming down his face, his smile remained. She was free. Sitting on the urine-soaked floor, he sent another prayer thanking God for Ellie's deliverance.

With Sam out of earshot, Salim let rip on Sabena. His jaw line hardened, his eyes turned to black coals, and his mouth pulled back into an animalistic snarl.

"This is fucking disastrous, Sabena."

"I know that."

"Your security wasn't tight enough!"

Salim was livid with his second in command, a position he vowed, as he stared at her squirming in sycophantic discomfort, would be re-evaluated soon. Demotion, Al Nadir-style, was now definitely on the cards for Sabena.

"Salim, it was," Sabena pleaded. "She was chained to a trolley in a locked room, in a factory with hundreds of armed guards."

"I don't want excuses. Just find her, Sabena. Find her now."

Salim's face stated he would be merciless with Sabena if she failed. He observed her shuddering and smirked, knowing too well how accomplished he was in such matters. Indeed, she had schooled him in methods of unthinkable evil.

"You know what will happen to you if you don't."

Salim watched Sabena swallow. Her lip trembled, and then anger took over her face as she whirled around to her colleagues and delivered her command.

"Find that bitch!" she screamed. "Find her now!"

Chapter 51

The room waited on Ashton's word. Godley looked towards the prime minister and arched an eyebrow. Ashton breathed deeply. He knew Phoenix contained 'eyes only' (EO) intel on the Noor home's surveillance, Ellie's enhanced interrogation, and the false flag attack that eventually caused the downfall of former MI6 Chief Sir Justin Maide.

The file was a damning indictment to Maide's alcohol-induced insanity, but it also contained unanswered questions about who Ellie Noor really was and if she worked for, or was an asset for, anyone else. The illegal surveillance had captured the possibility that despite being the loving wife of Agent Sam Noor, she could also be an Al Nadir asset. Her strange, unaccountable behavior in the kitchen might have been some kind of trigger making her ready to do Al Nadir's bidding.

Ashton was aware that the file held extremely sensitive intel on Ellie's apparent death and resurrection, and MI6's part in her death. If Sam really had discovered the truth behind Ellie's attack, as Maide surmised he had, that knowledge alone would have given him sufficient motivation to flip sides and turn against MI6, the establishment that had sat by and watched impassively as his wife had been tortured.

Could the truth possibly be filtered?

Cartwright knew Maide had committed treason, but the specifics had never been revealed. He'd accepted his position with gusto and never pressed the PM on the reasons for his sudden appointment and Maide's removal. Only Godley knew the full story. He'd been the PM's confidant. He'd seen everything. And he'd acted on the PM's instruction to 'deal with the problem'.

Now the problem was resurfacing. Ashton stared at Godley, and nodded

"Actually, there is," Godley confirmed, and allowed the sighs and gasps of astonishment time to subside. "There is reason to believe that Ellie Noor could be an Al Nadir asset. Further investigations have produced ambivalent outcomes. The case is inconclusive, but doubt still rests over her."

Ashton noticed Cartwright watching his non-verbal interplay with Godley and saw he was gearing up to speak. He leapt in to avoid confrontation.

"This intel is in a locked EO file. It will not be opened as its contents are a matter of national security and any leak of the information will be damaging for the UK." Ashton stared, leveling his hard, uncompromising eyes at everyone around the table. "So forget trying to gain any clearance on opening that file. Just remember. There is reasonable doubt over both Sam and Ellie Noor, which swings both ways and can't be forgotten in all of this."

The room fell silent. Ashton sensed uneasiness. Gibbs and Cartwright were both scowling, infuriated by what they'd heard. Thornburg shook his head, inwardly maddened. Only Godley appeared unaffected by the intel just delivered.

"Our top priority is locating Ellie Noor," stated Ashton, cutting through the tension. "That is your main objective. Understand?"

"I'm not happy about intel rationing," muttered Cartwright.

"No one is asking you to be happy," retorted Ashton. "Just do your job and find Ellie Noor."

The security chiefs puffed themselves up with indignance. Their mouths remained downturned, expressions full of vexation.

"When did this intel come to light about Ellie Noor?" said Gibbs, not wanting to drop the questions quite so easily.

"Recently," admitted Ashton.

"You know it's not right," said Cartwright, sucking in his cheeks and stroking his chin. Those two actions Ashton had already recognized as indications of Cartwright's insecurities when things didn't quite transpire the way they should. Despite his arrogant, brash demeanor, Cartwright suffered from an overblown ego that, Ashton knew, when pricked, exploded like a balloon, reducing his shallow confidence to little pieces.

"What isn't?" snapped Ashton, glaring at Cartwright. "The fact I locked a file? Are you questioning my judgement?"

Ashton shot a barrage of vitriol at Cartwright, who couldn't meet the PM's eye.

"No Prime Minister. Of course not."

A heaviness permeated, and Godley coughed uncomfortably. Ashton caught Thornburg's eye, and raised his brow as a signal for the commissioner to chip in.

"Look. I believe we need to widen the search for Ellie Noor. I mean, she may not be in Cambridgeshire at all. She could be in another part of the UK. Maybe it's time to put out an announcement on TV," suggested Thornburg, glancing at all assembled. Finally, he rested upon Ashton, who nodded, agreeing.

"Excellent idea, Commissioner. We need to up the pressure on where she is. If she's been abducted, they may realize the situation is getting hotter. Put out a reward. Fifty thousand pounds to anyone who provides information that leads to finding Ellie and making an arrest. Let's get those bastards agitated. When they're under pressure, that's when they'll make mistakes. They may try to move her. We may get lucky if they do something stupid."

"The way it sounds, we're still believing she's innocent and that she's been abducted," said Gibbs. "Or am I wrong?"

Ashton shook his head. "No. You're not wrong. The skid marks where her phone was found indicate that she has been taken, and probably not of her own freewill. But, as I said, nothing is conclusive, and in your investigations you need to be cognizant that she may be working with Al Nadir alongside her husband. Or she may be the one who betrayed him."

"She may, of course, already be dead. And Sam too," said Godley softly, but his slow burning negativity ignited their fears.

"Let's hope she isn't," stated Thornburg, pushing his optimistic streak.

Ashton was grateful of his faith in this whole episode having a good outcome. The thought of seeing Thornburg later enthused Ashton, and although absorbed in the meeting, he could still discern a faint tingle of anticipation fluttering through him.

"So now we rest on the matter of the quantum bomb. Al Nadir have this weapon of mass destruction and aren't afraid to use it, as we've seen, to devastating effect. I don't believe that Malta will be their one and only target. As the defence secretary rightly acknowledged, it could very well have been the UK that had been annihilated. This is why I have my doubts about the loyalty of Sam Noor. My experience of the agent suggests he's always been sound. He suggested the change of location in good faith. He had no ultimatum other than to keep the UN Summit safe. His case files show no evidence of disloyalty."

"No, but he's gone rogue enough, and he's a maverick, and he doesn't conform to authority," said Godley.

Ashton didn't agree. "Name me any agent who hasn't had to go rogue just to get a job done. Nature of the beast. Isn't that right?"

Ashton's confidence, borne from his own background as an MI6 agent, shone through as he looked between Gibbs and Cartwright to vindicate his conclusion.

"Yes, Prime Minister. Often situations change in the field. In this time we live in, with Al Nadir, positions flip and loyalties swap. An agent needs to know when to toe the line and when to cross it. Agent Noor is definitely one of those agents. He's one of the best," said Cartwright.

"Good to know," said Ashton. "But Sam Noor's gone now, and Operation Wren is incomplete. We still have the quantum bomb as a very serious threat. Gibbs, Cartwright, you need to step up surveillance on Al Nadir activities across all channels. Use the nanomotes where you can and maximize the autonomous AI capabilities at GCHQ. Any signs that they could be mobilizing for a hit on the UK, I want to know."

"Of course, Prime Minister."

Ashton finished the security meeting in his usual brisk manner. Before Godley had a chance to vacate the room, Ashton pulled him over.

"Godley, could you write an epitaph for Ludlow? I know you and he were quite close. It would seem fitting."

Godley turned his head slyly and bobbed it in front of Ashton. The prime minister thought for a second he seemed a touch too elusive. But then, as Godley's body language opened up to show willingness, Ashton acknowledged that the defence secretary was only too pleased to do something for his fellow colleague.

"Of course, Prime Minister. It would be an honor. Quentin Ludlow was a good man who was struck down too soon in his life. I'll write something tonight for him."

"Thank you, Godley."

"You know, Prime Minister, you acted well in your handling of Phoenix. You know you can never allow that information to come out wholesale."

Ashton nodded. "Of course I do."

"But the truth is safe with me, sir."

Godley fixed the PM with an intense, steadfast stare that echoed trust and conviction.

"Godley, why were you so negative about Sam Noor?" asked Ashton. It grated on him that his confidant didn't feel the same about the agent as he did.

"Sir, I know that you have a special connection with Sam Noor, and I think, in the beginning, he was a good agent."

"But not anymore?"

"No, Prime Minister. My intuition tells me he's turned. We know what happened with Ellie Noor, how she was mistreated and almost died. Considering everything that had been done to her, I think something inside Noor snapped. I think Maide was right, that he really did find out that Six was behind everything. Even that attack. He's taken his retribution on us. He changed the location to Malta to make himself feel better. But I assure you, Prime Minister, Sam Noor has definitely turned. He's working with Al Nadir. We'll never see him or Ellie again."

Ashton held the words of Godley. They seemed plausible. In fact, more than that, with the intel from the Phoenix file, the words Godley said depicted a truth that Ashton really didn't want to face.

"Thank you for your honesty, Godley."

"I can only speak what I feel, Prime Minister."

"You know, I shouldn't say this to your face, but I really do wish I could believe in everyone else the way I believe in you, my friend." Ashton touched Godley's elbow as he shook his hand.

"Prime Minister, I'm here for you. Always have been. Always will be. My words are my actions. You know that, sir."

"I do know that, Godley."

Ashton left Cabinet Room A with an uncharacteristically buoyant feeling. Men like Godley and Thornburg were exactly what the country needed. Perhaps guys like them would get them through the encroaching darkness to a lighter, happier future.

Chapter 52

The floor shook gently. At the movement, Ellie opened her eyes, not knowing or comprehending what she would see.

A ring of translucent metal rose up from a seemingly solid, decorative floor. Its movement with every millimeter of elevation defied gravity. Remaining motionless, Ellie watched the ring continue to rise.

Aby-od collected the tuned crystals from the satin-lined casket. Slowly, and with great reverence, he placed each crystal in the crescent-shaped dishes that were positioned at seven points around the ring's circumference.

On placing the final crystal in the seventh crescent dish, the huge crystal above Ellie's head began to glow. Ellie could feel radiance on her face like the sun's rays. She knew an immense energy was just a few inches above her.

With his hand inside the translucent wall, Ellie could see Aby-od was working on something, but his body prevented her from gaining clarity on his actions.

A light hum reverberated from the massive crystal above her. The sound made her feel scared again. Although Aby-od's assurance had calmed her initially, the crystal's sudden audio explosion, like the nerve-wracking sound of a dentist's drill, had driven her fear to return. She'd never realized until now how sounds created such feelings. But it wasn't the same abject terror she'd felt when she'd been in Sabena's hold. The feeling she had was akin to being afraid to let go, to step into an unknown place, of simply not knowing what was going to happen.

Aby-od smiled softly at her as he read the fear in Ellie's face. His soft reassurance filtered through, making her strong again. She had nothing to fear.

Ellie couldn't understand why she felt so at peace. The massive crystal glowed like a supernova above her. The low pitch humming escalated to a shrill harmonic, and the smaller, previously innocuous crystals in the ring around her suddenly started to pulse. Each crystal lit up with incredible internal energy and displayed on each pulse a specific color from the white-light spectrum.

Ellie shut her eyes instinctively as the light above her became too bright and the painful pitch threatened to blast her eardrums.

"I know it is bright and loud. But do not move," instructed Aby-od.

Ellie suppressed the feeling that she needed to block out the deafening inhuman noise, holding her arms tight and straight like a bamboo cane. She wanted darkness in front of her eyes, to give her transcendental calm, but burning white light seared through her eyelids, the flimsy skin membranes no match for the supernova sight surrounding her.

Ellie imagined for a moment she could see through her lids, that she could see the smaller colored crystals aligning their sporadic pulsing to throb their respective colors in parallel. She felt their internal energies multiplying on every burst of light. A crescendo was building.

Aby-od turned a crystal in the wall, and all the smaller pulsing crystals around Ellie burst forth energy beams like brightly colored streamers. All seven beams simultaneously arced over Ellie and hit the huge crystal.

Ellie couldn't discern any outlines. Brilliant white light was everywhere. Without warning, the massive crystal released its accumulated energy straight down onto Ellie, turning her into a torch of white light. Ellie was one with the light. It was like the light and she were together. There was no distinction between her body and the energy that pounded through her. Despite the cacophony, Ellie had a sense of deep quietness, a gentle peace that carried on and on, connecting and encapsulating the white energy to deliver her forward. She couldn't think. She didn't want to. Didn't need to. The strength of connection, of understanding, of knowing the things not meant to be understood, they flooded into Ellie.

The white light changed, due to a deconstruction at the granular level, into sparkling rainbow-colored particles. The particles entered and absorbed into Ellie's form completely. Aby-od watched, still and proud.

Ellie remembered how she smiled. She would smile again, only stronger and more radiantly than before.

The hall blazed with light and vibrated with sound. Harmonies rang out, reaching their aligned powerful configuration.

One specific instant was caught and suspended. *When we met.* All the joy.

All the love. In one single look. *Sam.* Forever connected.

At the exact same moment, the particles that had completely taken over Ellie exploded into a mass of rainbow light.

Ellie, the confused, bruised, and broken human, was gone.

Aby-od dropped his eyelids in respect at her human death.

Gradually, the rainbow particles began to reform. Each particle zoomed into place, following the alignment program that Aby-od had pre-set when he'd tuned the crystals earlier.

Slowly, a form came into focus. Aby-od breathed hard. Would it be Selema or Ellie? Even he did not know the way that side of the program would go.

The form sharpened. Although tall, it was not the towering presence that he would've expected to see if the Protector had taken Selema's form.

Ellie's form stood in the center, eyes still closed, as the last flickering particle sped to its designated point on the Protector's body, making her whole.

Opening her eyes, Ellie could feel the change. She could feel her body pulsing with immeasurable power. She looked down. The flowing, silken robes had been replaced by a white, short-sleeved top and white, hip-hugging trousers. Both garments were designed to accentuate her fabulous figure.

She raised her arm, already aware of a difference. Her hideous injuries inflicted by Sabena had disappeared. Her skin was now smooth and flawless.

She smiled at Aby-od. That strong radiant smile she knew she'd smile.

"Let's go!"

Ellie stepped out from the center.

She was reborn, renewed, and ready to return the balance back to her world.

Chapter 53

A skeletal woman in her mid-forties flitted around the lounge within Number 10's private living quarters. The woman had long, blonde hair, an angular face, high forehead, and eyes that shouted no sign of life. Although she was human, her bony physique, impossibly small waist, pumped-up, pert breasts, and firm, curved ass made her resemble a Barbie doll.

The woman was Natasha Ashton, wife of the prime minister. She scooted up her Hermes handbag and Burberry mackintosh, and opened the door leading from the personal quarters into the main operational office area. Sheelagh, her husband's personal secretary, looked up from her desk.

"Mrs. Ashton, can I help you?"

"Yes. Has he finished yet?" said Natasha, nodding in the direction of the connecting door to the Cabinet Office.

Sheelagh shook her head. "No, Mrs. Ashton. The meeting's longer than usual due to current events."

"Oh, what events?" murmured Natasha nonchalantly, staring at her phone and checking out her Instagram likes. She frowned as her likes hadn't increased much.

"Malta, Mrs. Ashton," said Sheelagh, staring with shock at Natasha.

Ashton's wife clocked the expression, and asked, confused, "What about Malta?"

"Mrs. Ashton, it's gone. Blown to smithereens by Al Nadir terrorists. Didn't you watch the prime minister's broadcast?"

Natasha pursed her lips and shrugged. "No. Had a bit of a headache. I've been lying down. Haven't seen a thing. So Malta's gone, eh? Bit of a blow to holiday makers. They'll have to find somewhere else to go."

Oblivious to how crass and insensitive she sounded, Natasha half smirked, thinking her remark was amusing. Sheelagh tightened the sides of her mouth and held her lips tightly closed. She fixed her attention to her screen, and ignored the PM's wife.

But Natasha was aware that Sheelagh had squeezed her eyes into small, blackened peas. She sensed an acute awkwardness in Sheelagh, and she really didn't want to get involved. So she wandered a little way from the open office and Sheelagh's reproachful glare. A door to one of the offices was ajar and she could hear raised voices as she listened.

"No. There is absolutely no validity to the absurd claim that Miss Judith Katzenberger had anything more but a professional relationship with Prime Minister Ashton."

Natasha stopped and pretended to be searching for something in her sizable Hermes bag. She kept the bag in the crook of her arm and rooted around inside the luxurious satin lining. But all the time, she kept her attention on the conversation within.

"If you try to say that or print it, Prime Minister Ashton will slap a high court injunction on you. He's not holding back. And he'll see you be arrested for treason."

The caller was a woman, and she was so loud and vocal that Natasha could hear her yelling. Natasha peeked through the door, careful not to be seen on either side. Dawes, Number 10's director of communications sat at his desk. His face was a mass of sweat, and his delivery was becoming more agitated.

"Yes, that's what I said. Treason. Yes. I do know what that means. The prime minister will not back down on this. And he will go through with it. He has the Lord Chancellor behind him on this one. We are not standing for anymore fake news. This story is a complete fabrication. So lose it."

Tubby-faced Dawes had gotten redder and his eyes bulged. Natasha thought his blood pressure must be stratospheric as his veins were popping up along his neck and around his temples.

Interesting news though, considered Natasha. She'd always had her suspicions about that Katzenberger woman. She always wore very short skirts, low-cut, silk blouses, or tight-fitting tunic dresses when she'd been around her husband. But on TV she'd been much more conservative in her dress sense.

Natasha recalled meeting her once. She'd been interviewing her husband in the private lounge. Very breathy and girlish. Perhaps her husband had a school girl fetish. She could easily picture Katzenberger in pig tails, a pleated, short skirt, blazer, and ankle socks, sucking on a lollipop and bending over ready to be caned. Just the kind of shit that got her Rich off.

Natasha hung around the door, but Dawes had slammed down the phone. He was now in conversation with the legal department, and the discussion wasn't anywhere near as juicy. Obviously it was the truth, realized Natasha, otherwise her Rich wouldn't be making a big scene, calling for high court injunctions to block publication and threatening treason. How in God's name could a story about an extra-marital affair with a journalist and the prime minister be construed as treason? It was absurd, and it showed how desperate Rich was to kill the story.

She placed her bag into her hand and was about to turn away when she heard a door open. Hurried voices emanated. The clipped, hard voice with an effeminate undertone, she recognized.

"Natasha, what brings you here?"

Natasha smiled with a breezy air at Ashton. "Just needed to talk to you about Abigail. But I can see you're busy. Terrible business about Malta."

She felt Ashton stare at her. She pushed her hair back over her small, delicate ear and looked demurely at her husband.

Ashton furrowed his brow. "Yes, terrible. I'm going to be caught up until late tonight."

"I understand. What I had to say about Abigail, don't worry. It can wait. I understand the obliteration of Malta takes precedence."

Ashton glared at his wife again. He was trying to read her, and with his visual analysis, Natasha could feel his wariness growing.

"By the way, is Judy Katzenberger covering the Malta bombing? Is she coming later?"

Natasha left the inference to hang in the air. Her vacant eyes locked with her husband's. His anger was rising. She swung a glance at Redfern, her husband's cabinet secretary, who couldn't look at her. Another man next to Redfern had a face of stone. A man to the right of her husband, who Natasha remembered as Godley, the defence secretary, looked at his shoes, clearly embarrassed by the situation.

She watched as Ashton paced forward, his face darkening in mood with every step. He stood in front of her and glowered, just, but only just, quelling the rage that packed every cell in his body.

"Natasha, Judith Katzenberger was found dead today."

Natasha's jaw fell slack with shock. As Ashton continued, his manner was controlled and precise, but Natasha sensed his amusement from her sudden discomfort.

"Apparently, Al Nadir didn't like the way she reported about them. It would appear that her words had consequences. A case of be careful what you say as you never know if, one day, those words may come back and bite you."

Chapter 54

Sitting in the room adjacent to the Hall of Umray, Aby-od was nervous. The Protector sat beside him. She waited with great eagerness, ready to begin her mission to save Earth. But Aby-od was unsure. Her insistence for him to still call her Ellie and not the Protector gave him cause for concern.

"I know I'm not Ellie anymore. It's just I don't want to sound like I've just stepped out of a Marvel movie!"

Aby-od smiled by this reference, but something didn't feel right. In quiet contemplation, he examined the Protector's outward behavior, painfully aware that any anomaly in her personality would signal a breakdown in the reconstitution process. At this stage, there was no margin for error. She *had* to be ready or return to face oblivion with the rest of her race.

Aby-od took in every inch of Ellie with his stare. Deep, intense, and utterly focused, she exuded a regal elegance. The gentle tilt of her head carried in its angle a grace and subtlety not visible whilst Ellie was human. She had the faint wisp of a smile, almost smug, but not supercilious, reflective of someone of great power who could still feel the humility. But human examples could never capture Ellie's expression now she was the Protector. An energy no human could possibly conceive was part of her very being. Every movement she made declared this state was not possession. It was control. The power was unquestionably under her full control.

Beholding to nothing, wanting for nothing, she was complete.

Aby-od recognized that look of sheer enlightenment, the moment when all the questions you've ever asked, or ever wanted to ask, were in an instantaneous moment answered, leaving behind the philosophers and the scientists to wander wearily down their never-ending paths of wonder and hypothesis.

Aby-od stared into Ellie's brilliant blue eyes, so much more vivid and alive than her tired slate-grey windows. These eyes now seemed to reflect the deepness of the cobalt skies on Earth and the bottomless azure oceans below. Encapsulated in her was a power far from alien. It was fundamental to her origin: the primal power that had helped create life on Earth.

Aby-od was pleased. He had to be certain that reconstitution had worked. Humans were so different from other species he'd reconstituted before. He had no benchmark, no guideline. No other species in the entire universe came close to being like a human. They were unique, a sometimes wonderful, sometimes terrifying, race. They had never ceased to intrigue, horrify, and enchant Aby-od.

Aby-od smiled by what Ellie said, as the Protector reached out and gently stroked his hand.

"It's all clear to me, Aby-od. I understand why you tried to contact Ellie."

The Protector recalled Ellie's memories, her startled and fearful confusion on hearing the words 'too far gone' and 'balance shifted' in the domestic setting of her kitchen. The space-time displacement Ellie had experienced for a mere micro-second turning her world to darkness, before plunging her into the sea-cliff manifestation, came flooding back. Standing on that cliff, feeling someone behind her, believing she would be pushed, in that moment, Ellie had stared death in the face. With no frame of reference, the trauma on Ellie had been unimaginable. The howling voice, reality shattering, it had all been too much for human Ellie. Her brain had acted in protect mode and had shielded her, blocking out the experience.

The Protector understood why all these things had happened to Ellie. Aby-od had tried to contact her but communication had been jammed. Something on Kudamun had prevented Aby-od from making contact telepathically. Forced with no other option, Aby-od had pulled Ellie one degree out of reality to enable clearer contact. The space-time displacement, as Ellie entered a reality one degree from her own, had created such fear in her that all she could do was scream. On seeing the distress he'd caused Ellie, Aby-od had abandoned communication.

Just playing that memory caused the Protector great pain. For that memory signified a decisive moment that reshaped Ellie's life, a turning point that netted together all future events. The inevitability of a life pre-defined. It made Ellie shudder, a brutal realization that nothing could have been changed. Even if the book of her life had been spread before her that very morning, nothing could have changed the future. What had to be, had to be. It chilled her. But it was her destiny.

"There's one thing I still don't understand. Why did you call me *before* I was the Protector? You must have known the fragile, human frame could not withstand such contact."

The Protector's eyes, although full of energy, were sad. Aby-od's ill-timed contact had resulted in so much pain and suffering for Ellie, and she couldn't, at the moment, hide her severe disappointment in Aby-od.

Alongside the Protector, Aby-od shook his head. She turned around and stared into his confused eyes. He was clearly at a loss to understand why contact with her had been so disastrous.

"My observations showed that Ellie was already receiving signals from your life-force code. The triggers of balance shift had enacted changes in Ellie's physiology, and therefore, according to my assessment, I believed contacting her would help to speed her understanding of the dire situation that faced Earth. Other species that had received the same signals from their Protectors' life-force code and had experienced physiological changes had welcomed my contact."

"But you got it wrong, didn't you?" Ellie's voice was soft but tinged with a razor-sharp edge.

"I must have miscalculated. The physiological changes were less than what I first thought I had observed. The human framework confounded my assessments. I broke transmission the moment I recognized the effect I was having on Ellie."

Aby-od looked down, and the Protector recognized how embarrassed he was by his inadequacy.

Ellie nodded. Although it was awful to realize that even the Great Ensi, Lord Aby-od of Kudamun was not beyond making mistakes, his incompetence and the subsequent fallout from it was in the past.

It was her duty to focus on the future.

Ellie felt Aby-od's watchful eyes upon her as suddenly, her body started to tremble.

Chapter 55

"Ellie? Protector?"

But as Ellie tried to speak, her mind jammed full of visions, images of people, their faces etched out like countless sculptures, motionless, trapped in time. Families sat on sofas watching TV. Young children huddling around a cooking pot in a mud hut. Commuters squeezing together on a tube. A nervous woman settling into a plane seat. A man smiling at his new wife. An angry woman raising her fists.

Her mind filled with indelible, undeniable images of humankind from across Earth. On screening each image, it was instantly catalogued and stored in her mind. Ellie didn't know how she could do this, only that she could.

"They're in your mind, aren't they? It's SearchSight," explained Aby-od quickly.

"SearchSight. Yes, yes, I know. Amazing. So many people. I can see them so clearly."

"And you will see more," stated Aby-od. "Can you feel them?"

"Feel them? How?"

"Just concentrate on one of them. You'll know what to do."

The svelte, brunette woman in her mid-forties raising her fists. Ellie brought back the vision and focused. With the force of an orange hit by a mallet, anger, hurt, and pain burst into her. Gasping, Ellie clutched at her chest, the suddenness of raw emotions forcing unexpected tears to well up. In an instant, she knew the woman would kill.

The vision changed, the color drained, and everything went creamy white. The woman rose off the white screen surface like a raised letterhead on expensive writing paper. Slowly, a darker tone took hold, defining the woman's three-dimensional features and outlining her being. Ellie could feel the woman's pain increasing in parallel with the darkening mass that filled her body. Ellie knew the woman was experiencing a balance shift to the dark. Ellie concentrated on reversing the shift. But the woman was too far gone.

Appearing back in color, the woman held a kitchen knife. As tears snaked down her mascara-streaked face, the woman thrust the knife into something. Her pretty face was distorted by anger and hatred.

Color seeped away to show the balance rapidly shifting, her form becoming darker against the creamy white from whence she'd originated.

Focusing on the destination of the knife, Ellie could see it was lodged into a man's back. Ellie shuddered, detecting his last ebb of life. A life of regret. He couldn't help his infidelity. He loved her so much. He forgave her.

Like a ricocheting bullet, Ellie sent his forgiveness back to the woman. She fell to the floor, her face a landscape of sorrow and guilt. Bending down, she touched him and felt his life slip away like the warmth on an autumn evening. He forgave her.

Gently, she withdrew the knife and smiled. From color, the vision flashed to dark and light. Ellie could see light gradually encroaching back into the dark areas. Back to color, the woman, still smiling, calmly pushed the knife deep into her heart. All at once, the dark to light balanced.

Ellie closed her eyes, the traumatic crimes of passion exhausting her for a second.

"There is much more. SearchSight is but one of the gifts you have."

"Why am I seeing them? Are they real?" asked Ellie, but as she uttered the words, she knew the truth. She had SearchSight, the power to search out, see, and feel every living organism on planet Earth.

"Why couldn't I change the woman's shift?"

"I didn't see what you did, Protector, but I know SearchSight is the first power of every Protector. Please don't be alarmed. You can't help everyone. Sometimes, they have to change. You can only influence those that want to. Lower-level organisms can be changed by you, but higher-level beings like humans can only be influenced. They have to make the final decision to change themselves."

"It's very sad."

"What is?"

"A person's vengeance, their darkness. It made me feel sad."

"That's to be expected. It lasts only momentarily. You have incredible emotional strength to feel for anyone on Earth but not be affected by their emotions. I could not even handle this. You have to be a Protector to be able to take such raw, unfettered emotion streams."

Ellie smiled. As a human, she always had been a little empathic. She knew Aby-od had recognized that earlier when she'd almost succumbed to the euphoric absorption. But now she had the power to really feel for everyone and everything that lived and breathed on Earth.

"Aby-od, you said there was more."

"You wanted to change the person, the woman you saw, but you couldn't. Her shift was too far to the dark. You can only change someone if their shift is within a five per cent range."

Ellie nodded. It all made sense. The woman had already shifted too far before she 'felt' her. Her only path to redemption, to return her white-light balance, was to take her own life.

"Why only five per cent?"

"It is decreed by the Ancient Ones. We never ask. It is just accepted that five per cent is the limit."

"And if the person's beyond five per cent shift?"

"You have to employ your power of light. Do you feel this yet?"

Ellie searched inside herself. She could feel something. Looking at the palms of her hands, she could see speckles of rainbow starlight flickering just underneath her skin.

Aby-od too noticed the light.

"When you return to Earth and find someone who has a balance shift that shows they are borderline dark, with just a shift of five per cent, you can make them good. You can increase their light energies to bring them out of balance shift."

"And if I can't?"

"If you can't, you have to employ your power of light. It is your duty to remove evil from Earth, and to do that, you have to obliterate it from the people where the dark side has taken hold."

Neither stunned nor shocked, Ellie nodded. She already could feel these capabilities waiting to be unleashed inside of her.

"You have the Kudamaz elders' ability to shimmer. This is how we all travel. The ability was given to the Kudamaz elders by the Ancient Ones. My understanding is that it uses a principle similar to what humans call 'quantum entanglement', which is the ability to be in two different states at the same time. But the mechanics of shimmering are much more complex, involving eleventh-dimensional space-time and a total knowledge of every place in the entire universe. You need only to think of a location, the place where you want to be, focus your mind, and you will be in that location."

"The pull to shimmer is great. Ellie's memories of her home keep flashing in my mind, and I feel like I want to go there."

Hearing Ellie refer to herself in the third person was reassuring for Aby-od. It was, however, also somewhat unnerving. He knew that she was the Protector, that her human side was effectively dead. But hearing her insistence to be called Ellie and looking at her, some part of him wanted to believe 'old Ellie' still existed in a greater form than just a strong, hard-wired memory for the Protector. But her last words suggested otherwise.

"Just resist the feeling and it will sink back."

The coolness in Aby-od rose, aware with some sadness that the woman before him was not, and never would be, the Ellie that he rescued from the death grip of Al Nadir.

"You said I could change things apart from humans. I don't sense that power yet. Please, Aby-od, explain further."

"Your SearchSight can be pinpointed to a single elemental formation."

"You mean a wave or particle?"

"Yes. Everything on Earth is made up from string. Each string has an energy resonance, or rather, a vibration that you are connected to. You will be able to manipulate and change these vibrations and create different structures that will assist you in your mission."

Absorbing like a kitchen towel soaking up spilt red wine on a marble worktop, Ellie soaked up the information. Ellie had been a jigsaw with the pieces missing. But now, as the Protector, she could see the whole picture. She had a clear purpose.

"Before you leave, there is something else you need to know," began Aby-od, speaking in a secretive whisper.

Chapter 56

Deep in the bowels of the Pentagon, anxious glances were exchanged. The vice president, chairman to the joint chiefs, and secretary of defense engaged in a heated discourse about Al Nadir. Following Al Douri's mind-blowing broadcast at the Senate, Treeborne called upon his 'men of honor' and departed for the Pentagon. His objective was simple: to set in motion the steps needed to annihilate Al Nadir once and for all.

The senators' faces had been stricken with the fear of death. Al Douri had made his position clear. He would destroy America if his unforgiving demands were not met. He had the power to do so, and unlike other dictators in the past, there would be no warning, forty-five minute or otherwise. One second they would be alive. The next, they would be in line, awaiting Lucifer's deliberations. For their shady deals, and all the collateral damage they'd caused to cushion their retirement coffers, none expected to meet St Peter at the pearly gates on their demise.

The senators knew the power of the US was mighty, but both time and ethical considerations were against them.

Unlike his senators, the president had no such trifling concerns about ethical consideration. To him, the solution was obvious: take out Al Nadir before Al Nadir took out them. Just like when he was a boy in the marshes, hunting boar, one wrong move, one indecisive action, and the hunter became the hunted. And Al Nadir was one big, ugly boar he was going to stick until they squealed for mercy.

He had intimated his intention to the Senate, but he had not elucidated further on when and how. Only the term 'unconventional weapons' had been used, but again, Treeborne had been economic with the facts, diverting to his 'save the world' speech to rally enthusiasm for the actions he was about to take. Supported by the confirmation from the late Dick Cowl that the UN had granted Resolution 8091, 'the use of unreserved extreme force against Al Nadir', the Senate had risen like bloodthirsty savages, ready to avenge the deaths of their comrades, and most importantly, ready to ratify the president's actions.

Of course, all the words flowing from Treeborne's lips were hearsay. No paperwork remained about the UN ratifying the resolution. No one remained to say anything to the contrary. There was no way to counter his argument, and the president knew this. He had free reign to do anything he wished.

Allowing himself a little time to feel the flow of righteousness, Treeborne remembered his god's words.

"When impending doom takes over the Earth, this will be your time. To take your stand against their relentless evil, you will stand defiant against the darkness. And you will win. You will rise. To reign over them all."

In the back of the car, on the way to the Pentagon, Treeborne felt a quiet calm, a reassurance that he had his god by his side. The feeling soaked into him, remaining with him, as he walked with purpose into the Pentagon.

The lift seemed to take an age to descend. Weaker men would have used these precious moments to reconsider, but not Treeborne. For he had a force for righteousness inside him. His actions were the work of his god. He could not fail.

The president's colleagues were already seated around a large titanium table in a goldfish-bowl room. Waiting with growing impatience, they looked out beyond the sound and bulletproof glass that flanked all five sides of the room. On the other side, monitors and equipment hummed, confirming that they were in the heart of US national security. The power to destroy was concealed behind innocuous glowing panels and LCD screens. People worked with order and precision, their hushed demeanor a reflective reverence of the tremendous power they controlled.

Treeborne walked into the goldfish bowl and sat down with a thud at the head of the table. Dave Reiner had been in a heated discussion with Frank Weitz, but all conversation silenced on the president's entry. Immediately, the men rose to their feet like they had all been yanked up simultaneously by invisible strings. The puppets of the president.

"Easy does it, boys." Treeborne shot a comfortable smile.

His homespun attitude disturbed Al Hutchinson. They were facing a moment of severe international conflict, and the president was greeting them as if he'd asked them to his ranch for fudge brownies and mint juleps.

Hutchinson moved uneasily in his seat. Something was different about the president, but he couldn't place exactly what it was.

Treeborne sensed Hutchinson's reticence. Staring hard, he launched a scathing address at his colleague.

"Hey, Al, you got some misgivings about my desire to protect our country? To rid the world of the evil power of Al Nadir and to restore world peace?"

Hutchinson looked on, aghast, feeling unpatriotic and small. He couldn't begin to comprehend how the president had picked up on the virtually invisible nuance that he was not in favor of his actions. And the insinuation that he didn't want to cooperate to secure world peace was insufferable. He wanted to retaliate, but the look in the president's eye told him he dare not.

"With less than twelve hours to go before Al Nadir's ultimatum expires, we have no alternative but to act in self-defense," said Treeborne. "We have to use our nuclear capability to protect our great nation."

The president scanned the faces of his men for shock or dissention. Their expressions were blank, drained, empty slates awaiting their emotions to be written on.

Pleased with their strategic impotence, Treeborne continued, unencumbered by emotional sensibilities, his plan of attack. Pressing a button in front of him, one of the glass panels frosted over, turning the shiny surface to matte. The lights in the goldfish bowl darkened and images flashed up inside the panel, projected by a tiny camera embedded in the ceiling.

"What you see in front of you are live sat recon images of what we believe are Al Nadir's command and control labs and training camps. Fourteen in all. It's suspected there's more, but somehow, they're hidden to us. We gotta aim at what we can find."

The president flicked through the images. Sat recon of China, Colombia, Southern Asia, and North Korea flashed up like a rapid-fire trailer of a new film.

"It is proposed that we use precision-guided nuclear missiles to take out each of these bases. Although we believe the compound to be in the Middle East, removing all fourteen bases will lessen the risk of us missing the base where it is being kept."

Dave Reiner stared in horror at the president.

"Mr. President, sir, we have our forces in at least seven of these regions. Other special forces' campaigns are ongoing in many others you've stated as targets. They're all engaged in deep fighting. Pulling out troops in less than twelve hours is a logistical impossibility. There's half a million soldiers out there. What are we going to do about them?"

Reiner squared up to the president. He wasn't one to shirk a battle or run from the enemy, but as chairman of the joint chiefs, he had a responsibility to all the men and women fighting Al Nadir across the world, and he wasn't going to just accept their deaths as part of the president's pre-emptive strike.

"Dave, my good friend, I'm sure you would be the first to realize that war brings casualties in many forms. Our brave fighting force knew the dangers when they signed up. Like many that have gone before, they will become casualties of war. Naturally, we'll do everything in our power to pull them back. But, as you said, it is logistically impossible to save all. Lives will be lost. It is a terrible but unavoidable consequence that we face in our quest to remove Salim Al Douri and Al Nadir. Gentlemen, I want you to understand that this war is against all the evil and oppressive forces suffocating this world. I intend to use everything in my power, as leader of the free world, to ensure Al Nadir's horrific hold on our beautiful planet is relinquished."

Treeborne again examined the postures and expressions of his team. Their body language indicated agreement. Then, almost in a whisper, Hutchinson broke through the subservient air.

"Collateral damage will be monumental."

Whipping his head round, Treeborne faced him, his face a twisted mass of vilification, furious at being questioned. Seething with rage, he spat his vitriol at Hutchinson.

"There are 374 million in the US today. What do you want me to do? Sit around and watch them die?"

Treeborne's acerbic voice burned like hydrochloride into Al Hutchinson, without mercy.

Hutchinson gulped louder than he intended. Weitz watched, thoroughly startled as his colleague committed career suicide.

"Al Nadir may not carry out their threat," began Hutchinson, making a feeble countermove against the president. "Maybe they're bluffing. Maybe they used all of the compound to take out Malta and they're hoping fear will make us capitulate."

His argument was sensible. His delivery was reasoned. His putdown was brutal.

"I wish I could be as naïve as you to believe that there was still hope. I wish I had that luxury for a moment." Treeborne glared at Hutchinson.

The room was silent. All the men knew what was to come.

"But I've seen the analysis. The scientists have analyzed the data, and correlated the amount used to destroy Malta. They've discovered that Al Nadir only used ten per cent of the total compound's mass. They have enough of the compound to carry out their threat and still wipe out the UK as well. We have no option but take out all of their labs in a pre-emptive strike. I know civilian deaths will be great across all locations, but the threat Al Nadir poses is worth the risk. Our precision-guided missiles will keep collateral damage to a minimum. But we must strike quickly and take out this evil before it grows and devours us all."

Chapter 57

Aby-od hunched over, his majestic frame caved in, and he took Ellie's hands in his. He looked at her straight in the face. What he wanted to say required absolute disclosure. There could be no more hiding from the truth. That was what Ellie read in his face, but she could see more: the pain in his eyes. Staring deep, she knew it was more than pain. It was abhorrence. A disgust took over his body, a shadow of shame that lined his long, immutable features.

"Long before Earth was born, my ancestors created a powerful artefact called the Therab. They thought they knew what they were doing. They thought they could control the power it generated. But they couldn't. The first time it was activated on Kudamun, it almost brought our destruction. Naïve stupidity had driven them. They wanted to hide what they had done, and so they banished the Therab to a new world just formed. Encased inside a dimensional lapse field, the Therab has remained hidden inside a ziggurat in Ur, Iraq. But now Earth's balance shift to the Dark Zone will activate the Therab. For you see, Ellie, my ancestors were not as brilliant as they thought. The Therab has a design flaw. It automatically activates on a ten per cent balance shift, and Earth has gone beyond that. This is the first time ever that Earth has gone that far into the Dark Zone."

"Aby-od, I don't know what the Therab is."

A little piece of Ellie's customary irritation broke through the Protector's cool reserve. With all her powers and great knowledge, she had no pre-programed intelligence to explain this mysterious Therab, and it annoyed her.

"It's a multiplier and chain-reactor of dark and light energies. It takes the planet's balance shift that it's on, in this case, Earth, and multiplies the level at least ten-fold. Instantly, it forces this multiplied level of balance shift onto each planet throughout the universe. If it activates whilst Earth is in the Light

Zone, that is a ten per cent shift too far to the light side, the level of shift will multiply and everything on Earth and everything on every planet in the universe will immediately lose the ability and the drive to want to do anything. This will force a downturn in the evolutionary spiral, upsetting the fragile balance of life itself. You see, a swing too much to the light is just as devastating as a swing too far to the dark."

"But a swing to the dark-"

Aby-od finished her words.

"Is what will happen if you don't succeed. Yes, I'm sorry, Ellie. That is what you're faced with. Earth and the universe's only chance at survival is for you to remove the Therab's ability to chain-react. You will then need to activate the multiplier effect of the Therab just enough to bring the shift back to balanced equilibrium again on Earth."

"Why don't you reverse this Therab thing?"

Aby-od shook his head. "I cannot touch it. The Therab is connected now to the dark energies. I am of the House of Giznu. If I were to touch it, I would be obliterated, and all of the members of the House of Giznu in Kudamun would suffer the same fate. Only you and those of the House of Etima can touch the Therab when it is activated by a ten per cent shift."

"But how do I do that? You've told me nothing!"

Hearing Ellie's irritated voice, Aby-od searched into her blue eyes for a flicker of her former self. "I do not know how. All I know is you are the conduit. You will find a way. The power is in you."

Ellie opened her mouth to speak. But suddenly, on hearing the deep, sonorous boom, Aby-od pulled her to stand up with him.

"We must hurry. I have already used up precious time. Now you must go. Cast out as much evil as you can. Then go to the ziggurat in Ur. Use this to shut down the dimensional lapse field."

Aby-od handed Ellie a tiny oval device with a small crystal in the center. Holding the device in her strong, elegant fingers, Ellie could feel it vibrate gently. It should have been alien to her, but she knew naturally how to operate it. Such in-built knowledge remained latent until Ellie concentrated and suddenly the knowledge was brought back like film on demand.

"I know what I have to do. I sense Sam's pain very strongly. I need to save him."

"You must leave now. No more talking." Aby-od took Ellie's elbow to emphasize the need for haste, but something suddenly struck him, halting his movement. "You are seeing him through SearchSight?"

Ellie concentrated. She could feel his terrible, shattering pain, but she had no vision in her mind like she'd had with complete strangers. She focused hard on the pain, but nothing appeared in her mind. She focused again. No contact. She could not be sure, but she felt as if something in her mind was blocking her SearchSight capability.

"No, I'm not. I don't understand this. Why can I see complete strangers, but I can't see Sam? I can only feel his pain." Ellie's strong, solid voice started to crack like a floorboard carrying an immense weight. "Aby-od, why is this?"

Aby-od looked past Ellie, not answering. He didn't understand it himself. But somehow, he sensed it, which is why he'd asked. Perhaps the emotional bond that Sam and Ellie had was causing the block. He'd never experienced anything like the current situation, so he had no reference point. He had no knowledge, inherent or acquired. He had no hope of comprehending why the Protector couldn't SearchSight Sam. He could not lie, so he delivered truthfully the crushing blow of, once again, his own incompetence.

"I don't know."

"You don't know? What do you mean you don't know? You're Lord Aby-od. You know everything."

It was as much as Aby-od could do not to smile. The words were Ellie's words. Her indignant inflection was a joy and a revelation for Aby-od to behold.

"Maybe it's Ellie's connectedness to her husband, maybe this is causing the block. But I really do not know. It is only conjecture."

Ellie eyes, like ice water on a winter day, extinguished his temptation to smile. Her stony, stoic expression penetrated Aby-od as she spoke.

"Before I leave, answer me one final question. If you can!"

Aby-od raised his eyebrows, a shadow of hurt drifted across his noble features. Not being able to provide a reason for her lack of SearchSight on Sam was no reason for her disrespectful tone. He was still leader of Kudamun, after all. It seemed that manifesting the Protector in a human's body brought out all kinds of personality traits he was not aware of. In many ways, humans were very similar to Kudamaz. Perhaps this was the reason behind the Protector's current fallibility.

"What will happen when it's all over? When I've brought Earth back to equilibrium? What will happen to me? Will I remain as I am? Or is there another process to turn me back again to being human?"

Ellie's question gave Aby-od cause to be remorseful. He had told Ellie so very little. He had explained she wouldn't be human after reconstitution, but he hadn't told her that those effects were lasting. She had been denied the truth. Ashamed, he faced her.

"You should have been told, but therewas, there still is, so little time. Your human form, the genetic framework that made you human, has gone. It's dead, overwritten completely by the Protector's framework. After your mission is complete, you will return to Kudamun and live out your long life as an elder of the high council."

Stunned for the first time since reconstitution, Ellie ventured another question. "And if the Earth takes a nosedive again?"

"Then we obliterate it. The Earth has only one chance at redemption."

With her deep knowledge as the Protector, Ellie already knew the answer, but she was buying time for her final question.

"Can I bring Sam here? Can he live on Kudamun?"

Her question was one Aby-od was pleased to hear but saddened to respond to.

"Oh, Ellie, you should know that euphoric absorption would kill him. It almost killed you when you were human."

Aby-od saw the Protector stiffen.

"So that is it? All questions asked. Time for me to go."

"Ellie, I'm sorry," Aby-od's kindly eyes looked at Ellie. This was not fair. She should have been told so much more before reconstitution. He hated himself for not telling her.

"No need to be sorry. I understand, as Sam will understand. Now I have to go."

"Ellie, even though you're now the Protector, you still love Sam, don't you?"

"Of course. Love spans time and space. The love I feel for Sam is immortal. Forever connected."

Ellie's voice was pragmatic, her face restrained, but she could not meet Aby-od's eyes for fear that her strength, great as it was, would crumble. In respect, Aby-od lowered his head. Somehow, Ellie's love for Sam had lived on inside the Protector. This made him feel even more ashamed.

Feeling a vibration, Aby-od looked up to see Ellie shimmer out of view, gone to deliver salvation to man but leave the man she had been destined to love.

Chapter 58

The room hushed to silence. Weitz, feeling like he was in a church rather than a Pentagon war room, coughed uncomfortably and shuffled his feet.

"Something you wanna say, Weitz?" thundered the president.

"Erm…allied forces…" muttered Weitz, reaching a level of unintelligible communication even he didn't think possible.

"What?" Treeborne glared at Weitz's pathetic face.

Weitz straightened his back like a puppeteer had again pulled his strings. Placing his hands on the table, he tried again to make a more erudite response.

"Mr. President, there are allied forces in deep with our troops. What are we going to do about them?"

"Prime Minister Ashton will be joining us shortly via HoloLink satcomm. We can discuss this matter directly with him then."

As the president finished speaking, a red light illuminated in the center of the table and a screen that had been frosted, went transparent, and then holographically displayed the prime minister's warm, if slightly effete, features.

"Good afternoon, Mr. President," intoned Ashton affably, and smiled.

"Afternoon, Prime Minster. I won't, as you guys say, beat around the bush. We have a serious problem with Al Nadir. They're threatening to take us out the way they took out Malta. Their capability for utter destruction has already been demonstrated, and we know they have more than enough of the compound to carry out their threats. They've given us…Well, they've given *me* until 12:00 a.m. EST to acquiesce to their demands. We have less than twelve hours to resolve this situation."

"And how do you intend to resolve it?" Ashton asked the question for formality's sake. He already knew, given the president's gung-ho attitude to war, exactly how it was going to be resolved.

"Fourteen bases have been confirmed. The base in the Zagros Mountains, on the Iraq/Iran border, is believed to hold the compound. However, latest intel from Langley suggests that the compound that wiped out Malta may have come from one of their bases in Europe, maybe even the UK."

Treeborne stopped to gauge Ashton's reaction. All he got back was a steely stare and a cold, "Really?"

The president, piqued by the PM's nonplussed performance, continued. "A resonance signal coming off one of their Stealth Runner's was detected shooting over the channel by US Navy reconnaissance. Of course, it was cloaked, so they couldn't fix a track on it."

Ashton didn't know whether to feel more shocked at the insinuation that the UK was harboring Al Nadir operatives with weapons of mass destruction or that he, as the prime minister, was not informed immediately of the incident by the US Navy. Each feeling made him realize, with utter dismay, the total lack of power he had in his own country.

"Why wasn't I told of this business with the US Navy before now? I should have been-"

The president interjected, waving his hand in the air, signaling, quite candidly, for Ashton to shut up. "Yeah, yeah. Well you're been told now. Anyway, that's old news. We got a new a problem now."

"Sounds like it's your problem," cut in the prime minister, his voice deliberately mocking.

"No, Richie, it's yours. Intel has intercepts confirming they're going to do the same to you."

Caring for his smarted ego took a sudden back seat as he heard the worst news since Piccadilly. "Are you sure?" asked Ashton. "When did you learn of this?"

"It doesn't matter anymore about how, where, and who. It's gone way beyond that. Richard, they're out to fuck us all. It's just a question of when. That's why we gotta strike. We gotta strike 'em hard. We gotta get the job done right. We gotta make it final."

"I agree. What do you suggest?"

The president smiled. Ashton thought it was a strange, almost perverse, reaction to his question.

"Pinpoint missiles with unconventional payloads," said Treeborne.

Ashton's eyes widened and he became aware of clamminess on his hands.

"Unconventional meaning?" began Ashton. But the hairs on his neck had already pricked in a physical premonition to an unsaid response.

"Nuclear, Richie."

This wasn't just final. This was Arma-bloody-geddon.

"Oh God Almighty, Jonathan. You can't!" Suddenly, state protocol seemed irrelevant.

"I can and I must. For the sake of everyone in our countries, I must act now. Fourteen precision missiles with nuclear warheads will be dispatched following this transmission. Locations are being transmitted to MI6 right now."

Ashton was struggling with the speed of events. His aide placed the pages in front of him. Nathan Cartwright had sent them instantly. Ashton picked up the first sheet and then dropped it instantly as if it was coated in sulphuric acid.

"I've troops in seven of these locations. It'll be a massacre. We need more time."

"Richie, we strike now. Preparations are already underway."

"But we can't. They'll die. What right have we to kill innocent people?"

Ashton wasn't averse to killing. But the reason had to be right. Killing on a whim wasn't his style.

"What right? I'll tell you what right we have. The UN, before it was blown to hell by Al Nadir, approved Resolution 8091. The right for us to use unreserved extreme force against Al Nadir. They sanctioned the use of unconventional means. If we don't act, five hundred million people could be wiped out in an instant. You saw Malta. You saw how quick it was. And they will do it again. We have to kill the few to save the many. I know this is hard for you. It's hard for all of us. But we have to eradicate this evil, chop it off at the base, dig out the root, and burn it. You know we have a duty to this world. We are the peacemakers Richard, you and I. We both want peace. And by my actions, I only want to free the world of this encompassing evil. Stand with me, Richard. Be my number two in this moment, this day of reckoning."

Ashton listened. Despite the feeling deep down in his mind that it was not right, he could not help but feel moved. Compassion burned inside him. A dizzy euphoria erupted in his heart and he could feel the faith. His soul sucked up the joyous aura that radiated from the president. It was like absolution. All his many, many sins would be washed away. All he had to do was follow the path the Treeborne had laid.

"I'm with you, Jonathan. By your side. Restore world peace. Make it happen. I'm with you."

Treeborne smiled. He could see in Ashton's eyes the look of an innocent, trusting creature unaware of his fate. It made Treeborne feel stronger. With his roadmap to peace drawn, soon victory would come, and with it, his right to reign at his god's side.

Chapter 59

In the Observation Room, Aswa-da regarded the interplay at the Pentagon with growing pleasure. The holographic image of the Earth showed that the black mass had spread, an indication that now the Earth was on a path of self-destruction.

Dispatch of Earth would soon take place despite the return of the Protector. The high council wouldn't let Earth become a threat to neighboring planets. The energy from the Harmon wave would be sucked up by the Therab making it even more powerful, and giving it the boost he so desperately needed to launch the final stage.

Aswa-da watched the numbers of the balance shift plummet farther into the Dark Zone. He knew the Therab would have already self-activated, ready to multiply every element of evil, taking in both ends of the scale, from the darkness a human needs to kill another to just an envious thought. All acts of dark, no matter how slight, would swell to cataclysmic proportions, creating in their wake a world where two wrongs made a right, where diplomacy was dead and sheer brute force won every argument, where the powerful and corrupt destroyed the meek and kind. Earth would be a place where continual injustice reigned, where double standards defined every procedure and practice, and where goodness and honesty were locked away, far from the hearts and minds of the vacuous inhabitants that would take over the world.

Earth, of course, wouldn't be the only planet to fall. The Therab's chain reaction capability would use the Earth as a catalyst, taking its dark framework as the blueprint for all planets across the universe. Darkness would spread like a super virus, eating the light with the ferocity of rabid, hungry dog. Gutted of goodness, the universe would display a void where benevolence had once lived.

The House of Giznu would not just fall. It would collapse. All that would remain would be the hollow shell of a tired, tautological lie, a husk of an antediluvian yesterday. The demise of the House of Giznu would signal a new dominance, a new dawning of absolute darkness.

As the new leader of Kudamun, the first order Aswa-da would pass would be the former leader's execution. Imagining Aby-od's body ripping into a billion particles, a clandestine smirk shot like a firework across Aswa-da's face then dissipated like a starburst, vanishing as quickly as it came.

And why would all this soon be possible? Aswa-da cast his mind back.

Chapter 60

6,000 Earth Years Earlier

Stupid, pathetic Dimkur. It had all started with him. Aby-od's predecessor did not have the presence or undeniable charisma that Aby-od commanded, but still, he managed to maintain the House of Giznu as the central powerbase on Kudamun.

During his reign as leader, Dimkur's achievements in keeping equilibrium on some of what should have been the darkest planets amazed all of the elders on both sides. Planets that, it seemed, at any moment would plunge into balance shift, unbelievably retained balance. Especially Earth. A torrent of hideous events, famines, plagues, and devastating wars underlined a growing evil in a time of such darkness it was nicknamed in later years by humans as the Dark Ages. But miraculously, Lord Dimkur and the House of Giznu sailed Earth through the most barbaric times with effortless skill. As an elder, Dimkur's mind could not be read, but Aswa-da was scythe sharp. He knew something suspicious was transpiring beneath Kudamun's gracious surface.

He had rounded up his subjects from the House of Etima and made ready to force Lord Dimkur to reveal his secrets, one way or another.

"Lord Aswa-da, what do you want from us?"

The senior elder had spoken for all the subjects standing in Hall of Etima-Si-Sig, also known as the Hall of Dark Silence.

"Watch Lord Dimkur. Watch his every movement, every nuance, and every action. Watch him, be his shadow, walk in time with him, and be one with him. I want to know what has been shielded from our great house. You will know when you see."

With his orders set, Aswa-da just had to wait. He was patient. On Earth, centuries passed, civilizations rose and fell, and still, Aswa-da waited. He knew his subjects were the eyes and ears of a continual, relentless surveillance. The moment would soon come. Lord Dimkur continued his reign of success, unbeknown that his movements were being furnished to Aswa-da in intricate detail.

But nothing untoward was found. And still, Aswa-da continued to wait, confident in the knowledge that his tenacious persistence would be rewarded.

Aswa-da affectionately remembered the day when it was.

Dimkur had entered the Observation Room at great speed, running instead of shimmering, which was uncharacteristic of a senior elder. One of Aswa-da's acolytes lurked in the shadows, still and watching. Earth's equilibrium hung in the air. Massive, translucent numbers flickered as another unseen black act of humankind forced Earth towards a balance shift. Looking at the numbers plunge towards the Dark side, Dimkur muttered a Kudamaz profanity and shimmered into the Hall of Umray. Behind a pillar, sandwiched like a stick insect against the smooth crystal surface, another one of Aswa-da's spies silently observed Dimkur's actions. He watched Dimkur as he entered the security area and removed a dimensional lapse field controller for Earth. The acolyte realized Lord Aswa-da should be informed of the leader's strange behavior. Slipping out of the hall, the acolyte contacted Aswa-da. Not sparing a moment to even finish the communication with his spy, Aswa-da shimmered into the corridor outside the Hall of Umray.

"He took a controller. It was set for Earth, Lord Aswa-da. And it is one that is time fixed. He's going back to specific point in Earth's history. He must be accessing something locked by a dimensional lapse field."

"You have done well. Now leave!" Aswa-da's eyes flashed with cold evil, as he dismissed his servant.

"Of course, Lord Aswa-da." The acolyte bowed deeply and departed, leaving Aswa-da alone.

Aswa-da entered the hall in time to see Dimkur shimmer. Acting quickly, Aswa-da caught the trail of Dimkur's energy pattern and found himself standing in a hot, cavernous chamber with a stream of sunlight flowing in from a sky light high up in a never-ending ceiling.

Dimkur, so engrossed in turning off the dimensional lapse field, failed to notice Aswa-da's presence in the chamber. Aswa-da stayed in the shadows and watched in amazed silence.

Chapter 61

The sandstone walls encasing the chamber started to oscillate. Aswa-da knew that was the sign that something was coming out of a dimensional lapse field. The air sparkled and swirled, and amidst the swirling particles of light and dust, an object began to form. Particles settled into place, revealing a large sandstone block with a sizeable unit standing one and a half meters high on top. The unit appeared to be made of solid-black granite, but as the rays of sunlight touched it, the unit seemed to have an inner dimensional quality like it had great depth. Staring at it, Aswa-da was reminded of the times he'd seen the starlit skies on Earth. A fool would believe it was made from the very fabric of the universe, but Aswa-da was no fool. He knew it was equally as old but infinitely more powerful. Had it been standard Kudamaz technology, it would not have been hidden from knowledge and view. Although it looked vaguely Kudamaz in design, he had never seen anything quite like it before. His sharp eyes could see the carvings were extremely ancient. Their geometries were cruder in their complexity but were still unmistakably Kudamaz.

Whatever this unit was, Aswa-da knew he'd stumbled upon Dimkur's power. Pushing farther into the shadow, he watched with earnest fascination as Dimkur swiftly began to operate the unit.

Dimkur rolled back his heavy, embroidered satin sleeve, placed his right hand on a large white crystal at least ten centimeters in diameter, and turned it a quarter way clockwise. And then he waited.

The unit began to hum slightly, and suddenly the white crystal glowed internally. Dimkur touched the white crystal again, this time turning it halfway counter-clockwise. Things emerged from the base of the unit like bubbles emerging from soapy water. Small, rounded fragments of the same black-granite material slipped out and coalesced, forming larger objects.

Aswa-da watched these objects turn on their side in unison, revealing their structure as intricately carved crystals. Slowly, the crystals formed a ring which started to pulse with light and gradually revolve. Within seconds, the ring of crystals spun so fast each one could not be determined separately. Just a blur, the crystals rose up the unit and headed towards a massive multifaceted crystal that lived on the top part of the unit. Levitating towards the pinnacle of the crystal, the ring of flashing crystals appeared to transfer energies to the large crystal, causing it to glow incandescently with pure, white light. The large crystal pulsed for a second, as if breathing in, then shot forth blinding light from its top. The light leapt through the skylight and vanished into the sky.

Dimkur dug into the deep robes and took out a mobile balance shift counter. All at once, massive holographic numbers bobbed in the air like buoys on an invisible sea. Aswa-da watched as the numbers plunged. Within a few seconds, the balance was back to equilibrium. Aswa-da was astonished. Nothing he knew of could reverse a balance shift so rapidly. This was certainly a find. And it was most definitely the reason for the House of Giznu's continued success in reigning over Kudamun.

Having completed his task, Dimkur quickly turned off the unit, reinstalled the dimensional lapse field, and shimmered back to Kudamun. Aswa-da followed on Dimkur's tail and then returned to the chamber with a lapse field controller.

Slowly, he set about studying the unit. He knew it was powerful. The senior elders had locked the unit not only in a dimensional lapse field out of reality, but also locked it in time at 6,000 years into Earth's past. Time and reality locking meant the senior elders had been scared of its power. They hoped no one would find it. Aswa-da smirked to himself. Of course, they'd been wrong.

The many inscriptions he read denoted the unit was called the 'Therab'. Aswa-da discovered its function was multiplying dark or light energies and activation could be achieved at different levels of intensity. The Therab was designed so its power could be focused on 'Earth or on any other planet in Kudamun's care'. Reading the last inscription, Aswa-da shook with excitement. He gripped hard the sides of the Therab as he re-read the inscription just to make sure he wasn't mistaken. It would seem his ancestors must have possessed true genius. Not only, when focused, could the Therab control the balance shift on any planet, but in full activation, it could create a chain reaction delivering a specific level of balance shift throughout the entire universe. Every planet would immediately be overwritten with the dominant balance shift position prevalent on Earth. The higher the level of balance shift, towards dark or light energies, on Earth, the more devastating the effect throughout the universe.

Although he had no solid evidence, instinct told Aswa-da that Dimkur's predecessors had used the Therab to manipulate the white crystal energies and maintain equilibrium on planets that were experiencing potential balance shift to the dark.

The House of Giznu had cheated. They should not have held onto the leadership of Kudamun. Nor should Earth be still in existence. Had the Therab and his less-than-white ancestors not intervened, Earth would have been dispatched many times over.

But instead of the stunning hurt he knew he should've felt, Aswa-da only smiled. It was a simple but self-assured and deeply satisfied smile of a person who, although still the underdog, had the knowledge that his days of subservience were numbered.

Over the Earth centuries, Aswa-da continued to study the Therab and learned everything he could about its many operations. When Dimkur relinquished his life-force and committed it to the Library of Ummia, his seat as the leader of Kudamun was passed to Aby-od. Aswa-da knew it was time to speed up his plan.

Aswa-da was certain that, although he most certainly knew of the Therab, Aby-od had never used it, nor did he know of the severe breach of the antediluvian laws by his predecessors. He was a by-the-book bureaucrat who tried to restore equilibrium the right way. He was an ignorant, pompous fool whose leadership was an unlawful mistake. And Aswa-da was determined to reverse it.

Many Earth centuries after he'd followed Dimkur, Aswa-da returned to the ziggurat. With Aby-od in situ as leader, Aswa-da initiated the first stage. Softly, as the inscriptions had instructed, he smoothed his hand against the base of the Therab. Atoms in the structure seemed to deconstruct at his touch, revealing a blue crystal the size of a golf ball. Reaching in, Aswa-da removed the blue crystal. He'd discovered through his countless investigations that this blue crystal was central to chain-reacting the balance shift level on Earth throughout the universe. But there was much more to be learned about the crystal itself. The inscriptions had described 'specific reactions in carbon-based life forms'. Aswa-da was intrigued and wanted to understand the effect the crystal could have on humans.

Aswa-da returned to Kudamun with the cobalt-blue crystal and, in secret, ran tests on it. Through fastidious research and analysis, he discovered just how an Earth human's framework was affected, and this knowledge paved the way for Aswa-da's dark plan.

Chapter 62

26 March, 2017

Ellie sensed Sam's torment. Using his shattering pain as a beacon, she slipped through the Reality Gap and navigated her way through space-time, through the spinning, looping sea of quantum particles, to arrive in Baba Heydar.

Shimmering into the cell, Ellie was instantly punched by the pungent stink of despair and death. Cramped, claustrophobic, and barely big enough for a human. Walls daubed in blood and grime telling a story of recent tragic events. On the grey, concrete floor, urine pooled in cracks and cockroaches scuttled freely over human feces.

Ellie retched and closed her eyes. In the beautiful, charmed life Ellie had had, she could never have conceived such places existed. Naivety was her sanctuary.

Ellie turned her head away from the disgusting surroundings and saw her beloved Sam. Her mouth leapt open as if to scream, but her newly assigned powers kicked in and immobilized any human emotions. She dropped to the stinking floor where he'd been thrown. Ellie could see he'd been tortured so viciously and completely that, even in sleep, his body shook with pain and he bled from every orifice.

Kneeling in the filth, she pulled Sam to her. On contact, he awoke with a judder. Believing he was being manhandled for another session of pain, he braced himself for the worse. Then he looked up and saw Ellie.

His bloodied, dazed eyes focused, and then fear registered and he edged out of her arms into the corner of his cell. Having been shot with so many different drugs, Sam didn't know what was real and what was an illusion?

So many times, had he imagined Ellie, only to be confronted with her transmogrifying into a creature so utterly evil and terrifying that his darkest nightmares could not produce.

Ellie watched his response and lowered her voice.

"It's ok, sweetness, it's me. It's Ellie." She braved a smile and moved in to caress his torn face.

"Ellie?" Sam's voice was weak. "I'm sorry. I'm sorry."

Sam repeated his apologies again and again. Her piercing screams had tormented him. Constantly, he'd blamed himself for the pain she'd suffered. He should never have let them hurt her. He should have given them the location sooner. He shouldn't have listened to her, brave or not, when she'd screamed out for him to hold back on Salim. He should have just told them. Time may have spared her the sheer agony she'd endured. As it was, the end result was still the same. He couldn't have changed that.

No, Sam knew he was the one to blame. He held himself and only himself responsible for what Ellie had gone through. He'd said his forgiveness to her in his head a million times but never expected to see her again. To tell her face-to-face. His words of sorrow couldn't come out fast enough.

"Please, forgive me. Please." He placed his hand out to touch her arm, recalling again the moment when Sabena ripped into her flesh. Tears of guilt flowed. "Your arm..." Through blood-filled eyes, Sam had expected to see an ugly, jagged wound, but he saw only gossamer-soft skin. "Where..." Sam couldn't finish his sentence. The strength he'd summoned on seeing Ellie failed him.

Confused, he searched Ellie for an explanation.

Ellie shook her head, not wanting to enlighten him further at that moment. Her main concern was stabilizing Sam's frayed frame of mind.

"Oh God, Sam. You have nothing to be sorry for." She moved towards him. Each slow step calculated not to alarm her husband. "I'm getting you out."

Sam could feel a sensation of calm and peace around his wife. It was quite strange. Staring at her perfectly healed arm, he remembered what his mother said to him as a boy when he'd asked if people who were blown up were put together again in Heaven.

"When we meet our maker, we are complete. What has been taken is returned. We face the Lord as he has made us."

Sam knew her flawless, beautiful skin could only mean one thing. They were both dead.

Ellie, now an angel, was taking his broken body to a better place. Grateful of the release, he welcomed the ever after.

Through blurred vision, he watched as Ellie took his welded metal binds in her soft, elegant hands and wordlessly rubbed them with her thumbs.

Ellie could feel the resonance in the atoms that made up the steel structure of the binds. In her mind, she could 'see' the atoms. They were vibrating in a set pattern, maintaining a solid structure. With a brusque, swift command, she instructed the atoms to change their vibration. Within seconds, the atoms vibrated more violently. Their increased oscillation pushed their temperature up and their molecular structure broke down. Sam watched as the binds, no longer holding together under the increased stress, shattered to dust.

Free, he flexed his fingers, as the blood rushed to his tips.

"How?" he started, as deep wonderment and confusion built in his eyes.

Ellie touched his face again. This time he didn't back away. Slowly, she moved in to kiss him. Their lips met. Time stopped.

When she had been a prisoner of Al Nadir, she truly thought that this moment would never be. That she would never again hold the man she loved. Never smell his warm, comforting body. Never look into his beautiful, brown eyes.

The sacrifice she'd made had been great, but to be in her darling Sam's arms again. To hold him. Kiss him just one more time. So be it. Her sacrifice, however great, had ultimate, undeniable reason.

Ellie's kisses became more hurried, more overpowering. Gasping for air, Sam started again. "How, how did this happen?"

Even after all he'd gone through, the words of Quentin Ludlow rolled back to him. 'She's different, Sam'. Looking at Ellie, her ethereal, almost glowing body devoid of injury, with no shadow of pain, he knew that Quentin had been right.

"Sam, we have no time for explanation. Just take it from me: I'm a little bit different from the Ellie you married."

Smiling enigmatically, Ellie pulled Sam to his feet. Feeling the incredible force behind her strength, Sam thought that his wife's last sentence was perhaps the most understated comment he'd ever heard.

"Been working out?" Sam remarked, his flippancy surfacing more than he intended. He was still deeply confused and somewhat afraid of Ellie. What the hell was she?

But above the fear, Sam had an overwhelming aura of peace he couldn't quite fathom. A comfort that made him certain everything would turn out well. He had no reason to be afraid. It was then that Sam acknowledged something was happening to his face. Tension pulled at the corners of his mouth. His cracked lips were smiling.

Ellie dropped down and kissed Sam again, but this time, their moment of intimacy was broken. Two guards, on hearing the voices in Sam's cell, stormed in. Their intention was to mete out another dose of inhuman misery. Seeing Ellie and Sam out of his binds, the guard hit the alarm. Raising their guns, they shot directly at Sam.

With a speed Sam could hardly perceive with his own eyes, Ellie moved in front of him and calmly took the bullets full on.

"Get out the way!" cried Sam

Ignoring Sam's scream, Ellie remained steadfast.

Closing her eyes, her mind pictured the oncoming bullet. A simple object, its energies were instantly revealed. In a blink, she increased the vibration, and the atoms heated. Their structure unable to function, broke down, and the bullets dropped, disintegrating on impact with the cold, concrete floor.

Wide-eyed, the guards could not believe what they were seeing. Believing the woman had some kind of secret weapon, they carried on firing. They intended to test the new weapon to its limits. One bullet after another suffered the same fate as the first, shattering to dust on impact.

Sam was just as amazed as the guards. He couldn't see any weapon on Ellie, but she was destroying the bullets at the same rate as they flew out of the barrel. A fug of dust particles and a faint metallic smell hung in the air, the only evidence of the ballistic massacre.

Throughout, Ellie remained still, only her eyes blinked in parallel with each bullet's descent.

Realizing the odds were stacked against them, the guards stopped firing.

Ellie snapped her eyes open, turned her head towards the guards, and focused her attention on their guns. The structure was a little more complex than the bullets, but the moment Ellie connected with the gun's atomic structure, the deconstruction had already started. Maybe five blinks instead of one, but the result remained the same. Unable to take the massive internal vibrations Ellie created, the bonds between the molecules heated and disintegrated, rendering the firing arms to dust in seconds.

The guards were at first transfixed by Ellie's display, and then reality dawned. Real danger stood in front of them in the shape of someone beyond their understanding, they backed away.

Ellie stared at them, reviewing their balance shifts. Ellie looked at the first guard, and in her mind, his form flashed to white, and then black started to encroach, defining the guard's form. The balance of light to dark shifted rapidly. Ellie could see his shift was just on the borderline of five per cent. He was redeemable. She concentrated on increasing his white-light energies. Light from Ellie's palms poured into the first guard. Smiling, as the cloud he'd carried since his father took his own life and that of his sister's lifted, the rage of injustice, hurt, and pain drifted from his body. He could see through clear eyes, no longer holding a red mist of anger. The immediacy of absolution overcame him, and he cried tears of pure joy. Edging forward, his first thought was to fling his arms around the woman who had freed him from a life of living hell.

But his colleague had other ideas. Seizing the moment, he lunged at Sam, pointing the knife at his throat.

"Let him go," Ellie stated with firmness. But her tone was soft. She had no wish to use her lethal energy on such a misguided creature.

"Fuck you," spat the second guard as he pulled Sam's head back, ready to slice him.

Rainbow light streamed out of Ellie's palms, enveloping the second guard. Still holding the knife, he looked down, terrified at the shining light taking over his body. The light intensified, absorbing his form into just a ball of glowing energy. The light shone and pulsed out a sun-radiant brilliance for a second. Sam and the first guard instinctively closed their eyes, unable to take such intensity. In that second, the light shattered into a billion particles, instantly evaporating in the air. On opening their eyes, Sam and the first guard saw the second guard had vanished.

Sam, still unsure of whether to run from Ellie or hide underneath her arm, was completely confused and confounded by her powers.

"Where's the compound?" Ellie asked hurriedly.

She could see the confusion in her husband's eyes but wasn't going to elaborate. Her tone was hard, pragmatic. She recalled Sam and his compartmentalizing of emotions. Now she knew it was the only way to get the job done.

"Salim has it. In the lead box he carries. He won't let it out of his sight."

Ellie grabbed Sam's hand.

"Stay good!" she shouted at the first guard.

With the fate of his colleague indelibly printed on his mind, he shuddered and replied, "Yes, strange lady, I will."

Chapter 63

Sabena was incensed. Her team had searched the base several times, but each time they came no closer to discovering any more about Ellie's sudden disappearance. The more Sabena searched the base, the more enraged she became. Her instructions to her subordinates had descended from "Find the bitch now!" to "I'll kill you if you don't find her!" to finally a sharp blast from her machine gun.

Rapidly aware that all she was doing was rationalizing her staff, Sabena decided on a stay of execution on the next shivering slave she pointed her gun at. A swift slap around the face was the only act of retaliation she delivered.

With her blood turning to magma in her veins, she slammed past her stunned staff into the medical room where Ellie had been imprisoned and where she'd last been seen. Sabena scanned the room, a bird of prey searching for a harvest mouse in the corn. Her interrogative stare took in the cupboards, floor, and ceiling. She could see the tiny aerial cameras nestling between the stainless-steel cube blocks. They knew what happened to Ellie.

"Tell me your secrets," snarled Sabena in a hoarse whisper, looking deep into the camera. "Where did she go?"

But no answer was forthcoming.

The suffocating silence erupted panic in Sabena. She had failed Salim. Failed him big time. This was the worst thing she'd ever done, far more devastating than second-level nano-bomb deployment. She had lost Ellie, his vital trump card, and the means by which he would make Sam suffer.

Even if she could escape, Salim would track her down, slaughter her, gut her alive, and take her innards as a trophy of conquest. That is, of course, if she was lucky.

But she knew her death wouldn't be quick or painless.

Feeling the futility of her life, Sabena let forth her Heckler and Koch into the medical room. Sparks flew as bullets ricocheted off the stainless-steel surfaces. Whizzing past her cheek, Sabena hoped that at least one would hit her and finish her off before Salim could get his hands on her. But her hopes were not fulfilled. The cartridge exhausted, Sabena remained untouched and very much alive.

Across the entrance, shadows formed. Sabena looked up and swallowed hard. Guards had arrived for her already. Their expressions were no longer subservient. Their machine guns, midway from their bodies and pointing straight in her direction, told Sabena her reign was over. Grim eyes took her in, slowly, salaciously from head to foot. Sabena felt uncomfortable. Sexual torment was fine, as long as she was the tormentor, but this was different. No longer in control, she was now at their mercy, the people that she, not five minutes before, had been blasting to death for their ineptitude at failing to find Ellie.

"Dr. Sanantoni, your presence in the satcomm room is requested by Dr. Al Douri."

Sabena did not move. The words had frozen her.

"Immediately," added the guard, advancing. He grabbed her arm tightly and pulled her towards the door.

"Get your hands off me," hissed Sabena indignantly, struggling out of the guard's grip.

"Hey, when Dr. Al Douri says he wants you in the satcomm room, it's not an invitation. It's an order. Understand, bitch?"

A heavy hand slapped hard across Sabena's face, making the point clear. A second guard grabbed hold of Sabena's arms, forcing them back. The first guard locked his hand around Sabena's throat while a third thrust his hand through her long, flowing, dark hair and tugged it back viciously.

"Do you understand?" repeated the first guard.

"Yes," gasped Sabena, no longer struggling. Whatever they were going to do, she would have to see Salim first, and that could buy her time to concoct some form of defense.

People lined doorways watching her walk, their hate radiating openly. Each face was filled with contemptuous anger at the way they'd been treated by her. They just wanted to see her dead.

With a savage shove, Sabena was hurled in front of the satcomm screen. Salim was already in broadcast mode.

"I'm bitterly disappointed in you, Sabena. Despite your best intentions to keep Ellie incarcerated, it seems that she has escaped. This has angered me greatly." Salim's evil, glaring eyes filled the screen, his wrath about to descend upon Sabena. "But as you know, I am a reasonable man. A case of such a sudden and unexplained disappearancedeserves investigation I therefore want to hear your side. A plane is being sent for you now. Unfortunately, this failure has voided your contractual terms as deputy commander of Al Nadir. From this moment, you will relinquish your command to Pedro Russo. Reinstatement may be an option once we meet and I am satisfied by your account of Ellie's disappearance."

Sabena tried to explain that she had followed all the correct procedures for such a high-profile hostage, that she had never been left alone, that she was always tied up, but her escape was completely beyond human understanding. She must have had insider help, but Sabena couldn't find any evidence of this so far.

"Salim, if you just let me do my job, I'm sure a further interrogation of the staff will prove fruitful. Help from this base. It's the only answer to her escape."

"I have already been informed of your 'interrogation methods," and I'm sorry, Sabena, but I can't allow more wastage to take place. Face it, Sabena. You're no longer in command." Salim grinned at the screen, amused by Sabena's predicament.

"Salim, darling, I've done everything for you. Please, don't let it end like this," pleaded Sabena, aware that she had to try one last effort to persuade Salim to keep her on.

"Remember Malta. I brought you that power. Salim, I've done it all for you. Remember. Please, remember everything I've done. It was always for you."

"All I remember, Sabena, is you've gotten very powerful and very, very rich, and you've been able to act out your sordid little fantasies on whomever you chose."

"That's not-"

"It's always been about you, Sabena, and all the time you succeeded, I wasn't bothered. But I vowed that the moment you fucked up, I'd have you. So the plane's on its way. Goodbye, Sabena."

Salim went to turn off the broadcast, but Sabena screamed back, "So where do you think she is?"

Salim, poised to turn off the unit, let a sour, sadistic smile sneak across his face.

"I haven't the foggiest, darling. Unfortunately, neither do you."

Chapter 64

The subject of Salim and Sabena's conversation stood patiently outside the satcomm room. Ellie had focused her mind to detect Salim. Such an overpowering, dark, fury-filled resonance wasn't hard to find.

"In here." Ellie pulled Sam into the room.

Hearing a noise behind him, Salim turned his head from the screen. He stared in absolute disbelief at Ellie.

One glance told him that this was not the same person he'd seen hours earlier. That fragile, abused woman covered in blood, trauma, and shock was not the bold, strong creature standing before him now. Maybe Sabena had been right. Maybe Ellie's departure had been beyond human understanding. Because right now he was struggling to comprehend the vision of Ellie: her curved, beautiful body encased in tight-fitting, pure-white clothes free of any visible wounds. Salim flicked back to the screen to face Sabena.

"She's here," was all he could say.

Sabena's eyes flashed with confusion.

"What the hell are you talking…" Sabena stopped midsentence, staring at the screen.

Ellie stood to the right side of Salim, and her husband Sam to his left. Sabena's gaze dropped to Ellie's arm. The short-sleeve top Ellie wore etched out every toned muscle, but Sabena wasn't taking in her glorious musculature; she was incredulous at the lack of any sign of her torturous attack. No scar, no injury, no evidence that Ellie had been subjected to anything more horrific than three weeks nonstop in a gym.

Ellie had somehow morphed like a caterpillar into a butterfly. She had turned into…Sabena was unsure even how to finish her thought. What she was watching defied any reality she understood.

Her stupefied gaze widened as Ellie suddenly appeared to have a lead box in her hand. Sabena was sure she'd seen it on the table just a second before. She certainly never saw Ellie move, but now she was holding the box, and thrusting it into Sam's grateful hands. Sabena blinked. Who was she looking at? More importantly, what was she looking at?

Ellie turned to confront Salim, who'd been so amazed by her entrance he'd failed to call for his guards.

"I'd like to know what you're thinking right now." Ellic's voice was urbane, her face stoic.

Sabena stepped back. Until that moment, Ellie had been like a mirage, an angry spirit seeking retribution. But hearing her voice, that unmistakable strength, made Sabena shiver. On hearing her enunciate every word, Sabena knew that yes, Ellie was real, but she was definitely not of this world. Sabena was fully cognizant of the fact that aliens existed. The upgraded tech they'd fused with the Panther jet to make it the Stealth Runner was testament to that. The superior technological complexity of the quantum bomb was yet a further example of alien technology. She was one hundred per cent certain the US president was not its creator. However, knowing of alien's existence and coming face-to-face with one, if that's what Ellie was, were two very different things.

Common sense told Sabena she should leave before Ellie got to her, but she was totally mesmerized, like a moth to the flame, to events as they played out on screen.

Salim couldn't help himself. Seeing Ellie looking so stunning, he licked his lips, salivating gently. "I'm disappointed the floorshow was cancelled. I'm sure you'd have given some performance!"

Sam gritted his teeth and strode forward with as much energy as his broken body could muster. He'd teach that perverted bastard.

Ellie put her arm out to stop him.

"No, no, leave him to me," she whispered.

Sam shook his head. It seemed that Ellie's voice was in his mind, not his ears. He pulled back and allowed Ellie to continue.

She smiled broadly and advanced, sashaying her way to Salim. Moving with unbelievable seduction, Salim could feel himself immediately hardening. The mysterious danger of the situation was only an aphrodisiac.

"Oh Salim," purred Ellie, rubbing herself close to him. "The floorshow's not cancelled. I can still put in a mouth-watering performance. Isn't that what you wanted? We're all here: you, me, Sam, all friends together. Isn't that what you said, Sabena?" Ellie whirled around to face the screen, smirking with inner menace.

Sabena jumped back, terrified at what she was witnessing.

"So why cancel?" Ellie continued, her voice booming and magnificent. "But first, before we get down and dirty, a question to you, dear Salim."

Salim rested his hand on his gun. This game, whatever it was, was too weird for him. He didn't want to play anymore.

Ellie focused, heated, and disintegrated Salim's gun before he had a chance to fire. Sabena's hand flew to her mouth. She felt sick.

"No, Salim. No more games. Sam, lock the door."

Sam obediently obliged. He remained just as staggered by his wife's powers as Salim.

"Now back to that question."

Salim stared at Ellie, searching for any sign of weakness.

"Have you deposited the quantum bomb anywhere else yet?"

Ellie waited. No response. Salim's cold eyes flickered with dark arrogance. Whatever she did, he wasn't going to break.

Chapter 65

All eyes stared at the small blocks moving gradually towards their respective targets. The president had commenced the launch sequence the moment he'd finished speaking to Ashton. In the cavernous, dark room of dazzling monitors, clicking switches and flashing lights, organized chaos ensued, preparing for the launch.

Dave Reiner opened a satcomm channel, his duty was to instruct the warrior chiefs to commence the retreat of their forces from each war zone. Five-star generals' complaints blistered the airwaves, but Reiner hid behind the 'these are the president's orders' shield. As commander in chief, Treeborne's orders had to be obeyed.

Each general swallowed down their abhorrence and disgust at the president's actions. They knew these were exceptional times. Treeborne was faced with challenges like no other President before him, and as such, they all knew whatever methods he employed, he was only doing what he believed to be right. As much as they hated these actions, all the generals understood the president's rationale for them.

Reiner could see the dismay in their eyes, mingling with the hurt that they were not finishing the job they'd started. Reiner could see something else in their eyes: the fear that tens of thousands of their people would die in the impact, and they wouldn't be able to do anything but watch as summary sacrifice took place.

The generals were fighters. Scenes of Malta's demise chilled their war-torn bones. To imagine such a power hitting America was unthinkable. The president had taken the only move available, but the orders to fall back and return to base camp still stung on their tongues.

Reiner could only visualize the immense logistical nightmare that now faced leaders on the ground in the theatre. Troop maneuvers were the hardest part of military action because of the many variables that needed to be controlled. Reiner was skeptical of their ability to pull out all the troops safely in time before the missiles struck. But he prayed that his doubting demeanor was misplaced.

In parallel, whilst Reiner dealt with the military retreat, Weitz gave orders to initiate the launch of fourteen precision-guided missiles with nuclear payloads. A glowing bank of lights and switches housed the nexus of command and control for the fourteen weapons.

Slowly and accurately, the launch codes were entered, locked, and held for each missile. Across the globe, on receiving the launch sequences, secret US military bases sprung to life and missiles were primed for their designated targets.

Weitz noticed he was sweating as the final launch code was entered, locked, and held. He turned, visibly shaking, to Treeborne. "Mr. President, all fourteen missiles are armed, locked, and ready to fire."

The president had been aloof and quiet, basking in his own hubris. Sitting back in his chair, he watched the military machine, like a high-performance car, well-oiled and well maintained, accelerate into top gear.

He was just an observer, an ethnographic researcher impassively viewing the interpersonal communications and practices of his team.

Heads swung like pendulums to look at the president as Weitz spoke.

"Ready, sir, on your command."

Weitz shook. They'd be retaliatory strikes. Maybe not the total obliteration that Al Nadir threatened, but there would still be destruction on their home soil. Why was he doing this? Why was he agreeing with the president? Weitz knew he had no option: total annihilation against partial destruction. He knew what would get his survival vote.

Treeborne stepped forward, his eyes scanning the room. Everyone was numb. Their faces petrified. Unlike before, when they'd continued with their duties oblivious of the president and his officials in the 'glasshouse', all were now immobile, waiting, their actions caught and frozen in time. The president's inner circle was the same. Reiner, frightened for his troops. Weitz, frightened for everyone.

The president looked at Hutchinson. The man who had been so taciturn in his speech now followed his actions with complete understanding. Fear was in his eyes, but truth was in his heart. Treeborne issued a warm, gentle smile that signified his appreciation to his subjects for their loyalty and following.

"My friends, the decision I now make will change the world for good. For too long, this great place has been home to evil. I am the landlord, and from this day, evil is evicted. It will no longer find refuge on our planet. A new beginning is coming. A new hope for our great nation. Rise up, ye who follow me and tread in my footsteps, and thou shalt know who has blessed thee with a new tomorrow."

On hearing the president's words, Weitz, Reiner, and Hutchinson shot bemused looks at each other, but no one made any move. Treeborne was the president. He had to be believed.

"The meek shall inherit the Earth. The injured shall be healed, and a new world shall be born. The day of reckoning is upon us, friends. We are the creators of this new peace.

With these arrows I employ.

Dark evils I will destroy.

Rain fire by my hand.

And bring peace across this land.

My children, let the Earth be free."

Treeborne's voice was an incessant, hate-filled chant.

Reaching his crescendo, he announced almost in a whisper, "Fire the weapons."

Treeborne closed his eyes.

For you, my god.

On opening them, his face glowed with power. His beady eyes watched the screen with the rest of the room. Slowly, the fourteen blocks moved towards their assigned targets.

Soon, it would be all done, and Earth would be his to reign over.

Chapter 66

Heat. Salim's right arm started to feel hot. Glancing at his shoulder, he saw his right arm was floating a few centimeters away from his armpit. Somehow, his arm had been sawn clean through from the shoulder. The sight made Salim instantly scream. Over the satcomm channel, Sabena, observing developments, screamed in unison. But there was no blood, no pain. No natural warning had sounded in his mind to tell Salim his arm was disconnected. It was only when he actually looked at his arm that he recognized what had happened. *How could this be? Was it magic? An illusion?* Salim's mind started to flip. Watching his arm floating helpless in space, with each blood cell tightly packed inside the recess at his shoulder and in the arm joint, Salim tried and failed to understand. Staring at his cells caught in some form of suspended animation that defied gravity and every other natural law he'd ever learned about, Salim realized he must be suffering from a drug-induced trompe l'oeil. A vision. It must be a new form of NMS. *But how had it been administered?*

Ellie stared at Salim, her brilliant blue eyes glowing with supreme power.

"I ask again, Salim. Have you deposited the quantum bomb anywhere else on this planet?"

Silence.

Ellie stood in front of Salim, her warm breath touching his skin. It was certainly a very real illusion.

"Refuse to answer me and I'll turn the pain control off. Believe me Salim, what I can do to you and still keep you alive far exceeds your pathetic attempts at torture. So I suggest you answer me. Is this all the quantum bomb, or is there anymore?"

Salim remained silent. The cock-teasing bitch illusion didn't frighten him.

Whatever stunts she pulled, he could take it.

Ellie's eyes flickered for a second. Screams of utter pain reverberated around the room. Salim's eyes flowed tears. His body shook as the full impact of his severed arm hit him.

Sabena watched on thunderstruck, and sneered, secretly pleased that Salim was going through hell. He'd hardly be a threat to her now.

Salim knew all at once it wasn't an illusion. This terrible, horrific stuff was happening for real.

"It's the entire bomb. Please, stop. Please. For God's sake. Stop!"

"And there's no more anywhere?" asked Ellie calmly.

"No, no. I never had chance to place it anywhere else. Please, stop. Please."

Salim's words erupted from a deep, dark place he'd not visited in years. He had, of course, forced his victims to visit that place again and again. A place of agony, a place of white-hot, eye-watering, toe-curling, unutterable, excruciating pain.

Sam stared at Salim's groveling. He was weak and pathetic, his power driven by the fear he instilled in others. He couldn't believe how fast he'd acceded to Ellie's questions.

Ellie viewed Salim's balance shift. He was almost ninety per cent to the dark side. Hardly any light could be seen. His presence on Earth had caused so much of the planet's balance shift to the dark. His actions acted as a catalyst for the misery, suffering, and inevitable destruction that faced the Earth. Ellie could not stand being bathed in his evil energies. Despite the Protector's inner shield to all emotions, the bottomless evil that engulfed Salim threatened to disrupt her own balance.

She turned, smiling softly to Sam.

'The time has come,' he heard in his mind. But his wife had not uttered a word.

Turning back to Salim, Ellie opened her palms. She unfurled her fingers until her palms faced outward.

"For all the suffering, torture, and death that you have delivered, so be it, the delivery of your own destruction."

Lethal rainbow light shot from Ellie's palms.

Her words were profound. Salim opened his mouth in a last-ditch attempt to protest, to plead his innocence, but his words were swallowed in the shining light that surrounded him.

Ellie, Sam and Sabena through the satcomm watched as the light energies grew. A brilliant white light shone out, the embodiment of all the innocent souls Salim had taken. When Salim's form could no longer be discerned amongst the brilliance, the light shattered him into a billion twinkling, rainbow particles.

His reign of tyranny and terror over the world had ended.

Ellie dropped her hands limply by her side. Dispatching Salim had exhausted her. The moment her fatigue took over, Sam could see a shadow of Ellie, the woman he'd married, standing alone and vulnerable. He wrapped his arms around her, pulling her close.

"I love you, sweetness," he whispered, kissing her forehead.

Ellie closed her eyes and drew strength from the love Sam imparted. She could feel her strength through the empathic bond quickly returning. Renewed, she pulled out of the embrace. Sam stared at Ellie. Her formidable power once again overshadowed the old Ellie he knew. Suddenly, he felt that once again he was holding a stranger. He looked at the floor, embarrassed by their moment of intimacy.

Ellie felt his shyness. Although they had kissed before, it had been raw passion at seeing each other again. Sam was now beginning to see that Ellie wasn't the Ellie he knew, and this confused him, made him uncomfortable by the closeness he was desperate to feel again.

A gentle hand touched his blood-encrusted face. He closed his eyes and held her hand close to him.

"I love you, Sam. Never forget that. I love you. I returned for you. You need not know more than that. Only that I love you and I will always love you."

"Let me out!" screamed Sabena at the guards outside the satcomm room. Her screeching voice emanating from the screen sliced through their loving moment. Breaking apart, Ellie turned to face Sabena. Her lofty expression echoed a superior knowledge. Sabena stood back instinctively recognizing the subtle arrogance that emanated from Ellie. Although just a slight whisper of a smile, the result for Sabena was terrifying. She could see what lay behind the smile. She could see that Ellie had the power to crush humans as easily as if they were ants.

She tried to reason with her anxiety that Ellie was out to destroy Salim, head of Al Nadir, not her. To rebuke her logic, Ellie spoke.

"I hope you enjoyed the floorshow. Your performance will be called for soon."

The owner of those staggered, frightened eyes that had watched Salim's spectacular demise was determined not to go the same way. Sabena shook the door, screaming to be let out.

The door opened, and like a cat with fireworks on its tail, she shot through the opening. Ellie watched her go. Run, girl. Run. But you'll never hide from me.

"Ellie, she's going. We've got to get to her before she escapes."

Motionless, just smiling, Ellie responded.

"Hold onto me, darling, and close your eyes. We're going on a ride."

Ellie placed her arms around Sam. Still gripping the lead box Ellie had given him, Sam slipped his arms around Ellie's waist. Looking straight into her gorgeous blue eyes, he dropped his head to kiss her soft lips. Closing his eyes, Sam was caught in an amazing, beautiful and pure feeling. It was as though he could sense everything across the entire universe, but for a second in time. His head pounded with excitement and energy, but one thought stayed with him: 'I love you.' It was Ellie. Her voice kept him centered. Kept him whole. As she had always done.

As their lips locked, Ellie visualized the satcomm room and shimmered to where Sabena was. She had a mission to fulfil. She knew she couldn't squander time, but at that moment, all she wanted to feel was love. The love of her darling Sam. The kiss seemed to last forever.

Chapter 67

Aby-od glared depressively at the observation screen. The 3D globe showed darkness erupting across the world. In anger, Aby-od switched to the real-time on Earth visual to see what was really happening. The screen displayed weapons shooting through the skies. The data confirmed that fourteen missiles were on trajectories that would reach their target within one Earth hour. The weapons had been cloaked to prevent enemy detection, but Aby-od was sure that reprisals would follow.

"Great Ensi, Lord Aby-od, you are requested to attend the Great Hall forthwith," the booming voice of the speaker rang out, commanding attention.

Aby-od had seen a rapid balance shift to the light when Ellie had first returned to Earth. He'd even ventured prematurely to believe that Ellie had removed Salim Al Douri and was on her way to activating the Therab, bringing Earth back to equilibrium.

Something was wrong.

Earth was now on a path of self-destruction and the shift was dropping farther into the Dark Zone. Time had run out for Earth. Evidence showed it was a threat to other planets in its vicinity. No alternative remained except dispatch.

Aby-od turned off the visuals. The Protector would stay on Earth, her fate signed with the rest of the humans on the planet. Tears welled inside him. Why did this have to happen?

"Great Ensi, Lord Aby-od, you are required to attend the Great Hall, now." The speaker's voice was becoming more irritated. Aby-od knew he'd have to go to the Great Hall before the high council official guards were sent for him.

With disappointment coursing through his body, he shimmered into the Great Hall.

On arriving, Aby-od saw the elders from both houses were in disarray. The elders from Giznu were sniping at the elders of Etima, who had clearly started the altercation that was now ensuing.

"Honorable members, please have a care for where you are!" shouted Aby-od angrily. "For many a millennia, we have faced these situations, and yet it is only now that you chose to descend into anarchistic tendencies. This is a place of decorum. A place of wisdom. As long as I am leader on Kudamun, I will not have this sacred place defaced by such refractory behavior."

The elders turned to face Aby-od, who was quietly seething underneath his calm exterior. Their gabbling and bickering instantly ceased.

"Honorable Speaker, please read the case against Ki." Aby-od tried to remain serene, but the energies in his light-based heart were sparking so hard they hurt him.

He sat down, smoothing his silken robes, and looked to the elder that stood up.

The speaker took to the stand and commenced delivering his case against Earth and the remedy of dispatch. Aby-od listened uncomfortably as mankind's faults were laid bare to the high council.

"And finally, the last act of wanton destruction, something that directly breaches antediluvian law, has been the launch of fourteen nuclear missiles. One of the targets is near one of Ki's most sacred places. The Holy of Holies in Ur, Iraq. The birthplace of civilization and the place where we sowed the first seeds of humanity. This beautiful place is now a target for utter destruction."

The speaker waited as the elders' cries of 'Dispatch the barbarians!' died down.

"In accordance with the powers vested in this council, under the order of Kudamun, it is hereby decreed that the initiation of the Protector has failed and thus, under antediluvian law, the planet of Ki, commonly known as the Earth, should now be dispatched with immediate effect. No cause for appeal is justified. Any appeals put forward to this council will not be viable. Continuance of dispatch is a requirement under the order of Kudamun."

The speaker returned to his throne and seated himself, smugly assured of the course of action he'd communicated.

Aby-od was completely mortified. The elders hadn't given the Protector a chance to achieve her mission. She'd had hardly any Earth time.

Calls for dispatch rang through the Great Hall. Hearing their disgust, the decision was clearly unanimous. Dispatch was the only solution. Aby-od could do little.

A powerful man with no power to change the archaic laws, he was resentful of their decision. The elders were weak, policy-pushing cosmic bureaucrats who were terrified of change. Rage boiled inside him. In his long, long, life, he'd hardly felt any impassioned feelings, but twice now he'd felt such emotions, such burning rage. And both occasions had been because of Ellie Noor. She deserved a chance. She was extraordinary, and she was powerful, and they just had to give her proper time to complete the task she was set to do.

The words sailed around in Aby-od's head, and before he knew what he was saying, he screamed at the high council, "No, this is wrong! You must give the Protector the time she deserves! She will achieve her mission!"

All the elders looked at Aby-od, their heads shook. One elder from the House of Etima shouted scornfully back, "The balance shift is almost at fifteen per cent to the negative and is well within the Dark Zone! Your Protector would need to perform a real Ki miracle to bring it back to equilibrium! The Protector is dead, as Ki is dead!"

"No, I do not agree. If I said she could perform a Ki miracle, would you then give her the rightful time she deserves?"

The elders viewed Aby-od with distrust and cynicism.

Aswa-da spoke. His words of calculated, vehement insinuation punctured Aby-od's pseudo-calm.

"Great Ensi, given your solid assurance in the Protector's success, is there another facet to her mission that you have not revealed to the high council?"

Aswa-da's eyes flashed with mischievous delight as he lit the flames of conspiracy in the minds of the elders.

"My honorable member, Lord Aswa-da is unfounded in his accusation." Aby-od's tone was defensive. Instinct now told him Aswa-da knew more about the Protector's mission.

"Great Ensi, I mean no accusation. I just stated that your belief in the Protector is quite amazing given the seemingly doomed situation she faces. If there was other information regarding her mission that has not been revealed to the high council but could hold such gravitas as to mitigate the call for dispatch, then this information should be brought forth right now and heard by our honorable members."

Aswa-da sat down, his supercilious features breaking into a slow, wry smile. His eyes stared joyfully at the coup d'état he had maneuvered to make Aby-od either reveal the Therab or sit by and watch Earth and his precious Protector blown to oblivion.

Aby-od rose. His legs shook. He smiled nervously at all the elders, their eyes trained on him, watching him for signs of discomfort. Was he concealing something from them? Such a position was, under antediluvian law, a treasonable offence and punishable by death. Aswa-da knew the law. Aby-od knew his game by now. He had to play for his life.

"The only information I have is to tell the high council Ellie Noor as the Protector is an incredible source of power. We have not given her time, nor have we held the faith that she can do the task she was assigned to do. Please, join with me and share in my belief that Ellie Noor will win. That dispatch is not the only action open to us. Please, give the Protector a chance. Join in my belief and have faith."

Aby-od was fervent. His voice was inflamed. His argument was inspired. He searched the eyes of his elders and the opposition. Only cold skepticism greeted him.

The speaker arose. "The honorable members have heard your pleas. A vote will now be taken on the dispatch of Ki under the order of Kudamun. Honorable members, please place your votes now."

The elders moved their hands through the air, either to the left or right, signaling their vote. In the center of the hall, a holographic screen winked into view displaying for and against the motion for dispatch. The elders cast their votes with their sweeping hand gestures. Aby-od watched and then dropped his head in regret. The vote for dispatch was unanimous.

"I am sorry, Great Ensi, but the belief you hold in the Protector is not shared by the rest of the high council. Dispatch of Ki, the Earth, will take place. The final procedures will be undertaken. The Protector has a couple of Ki hours. And then Great Ensi, Lord Aby-od, head of the House of Giznu and leader of Kudamun, you will undertake the dispatch. The case for Ki is over. This session of the high council is now closed."

On the speaker's final words, elders shimmered out of view. Aswa-da smiled slyly at Aby-od and then shimmered rapidly away, leaving Aby-od in a stupor, unable to move. Ellie Noor had so little time. He prayed with all his heart that she could make it within the Earth hours given.

Chapter 68

Horror showed on her tense, stricken face as Sabena ran. In her panic, the guards had slipped her mind.

"Whoa! Dr. Sanantoni, where the fuck do you think you're going?"

The ruthless guard held her tightly, pinning her flailing arms to her side.

"Not trying to leave, are you? I'm sure Dr. Al Douri wouldn't be happy about that."

Lifting Sabena up into the air, the guard threw her back into the satcomm room. Images of Salim's death sped through her brain, making Sabena break, hysteria sounding in every syllable.

"For fuck's sake, you morons. He's dead. Salim's dead, and that's how we'll all end up if we don't get the fuck out of here now."

The second guard looked at Sabena. She certainly seemed scared stiff about something. Her words were touched with verisimilitude. He pulled back to the first guard. "Why don't you ask Dr. Al Douri what we should do about her?"

The first guard nodded.

Sabena heard their words. They still didn't get it. How could they? They hadn't witnessed her awesome power, yet.

"She's coming and we're all dead!" shouted Sabena manically.

The first guard shook his head and moved into the satcomm room to call up the transmission. The broadcast came online but no Salim appeared. The first guard gathered from his absence that he had other issues more important than demotion of Sabena Sanantoni. He whirled around to Sabena and told her to remain in the room until the plane arrived for her.

Sabena ran up to the door, but the guard had already locked it behind him. Looking through the little window, he grinned and extended a single middle finger at Sabena as she screamed to be let out.

After shouting her mouth dry, she knew they wouldn't release her. Slowly, she walked over to the screen. It was devoid of anything, just static. Ellie and Sam had vanished.

Fear crept up, throttling her. She coughed and gasped, clutching her throat. She was going to die. Today, she was going to die. The finality of this conclusion made her sit down heavily in the Temptress chair. Her body had started to perspire, and now her leather garb she'd worn for the floorshow stuck uncomfortably to her like cling-film over a dish that had lingered too long in a microwave.

Glancing at the equipment around her, she shuddered, imagining how Ellie could have been. She'd done it before, splitting open the gates to the hereafter for her victims whilst finding ecstasy herself. And she'd loved doing it. Salim was right about that. Hearing her subjects scream their souls out just turned her on even more. She couldn't help it. She was made that way. She couldn't make any allowances. She hadn't been abused as a child. She hadn't had bad parents. On the contrary, her parents had been fabulous, rich, and always giving to her, their only child. No, she couldn't hide behind any environmental impact, the usual argument of nature versus nurture. She was just born evil. Simple as that.

She didn't know why she was that way. She just was. Why should she be killed because of that? Most of the world's politicians were the same: evil, greedy, and sex-mad. She could certainly vouch for the latter, remembering how thoroughly President Treeborne had seen to her affairs.

Of course, the effete British PM, Ashton, proved to her that his feminine inclinations were just for the camera. Oh yes, she'd had them all: statesmen, business icons, religious leaders from all faiths. They were all just as warped and egotistical as each pretended to the other they weren't.

Lost in memory, Sabena didn't instantly notice the air wavering next to the gyno-bondage chair. Instinct from primitive times told her to move. Like a squirrel crossing an open plain, she ran without looking to the nearest hiding place, behind a super king-sized bed. From the sanctuary of the divan, Sabena watched Ellie shimmer into view, locked in a romantic embrace with Sam. She literally appeared from thin air. Sabena could not believe her eyes. More than ever, she knew that Ellie was an alien.

Scanning the room, taking in the sickening equipment that filled Sabena's pleasure parlor, Ellie's stomach flipped. If Aby-od hadn't saved her when he did...She didn't even want to contemplate what would have happened.

Sam took in the scene and shouted, his vengeance boiling over, "I'm going to fucking kill you, you disgusting little whore!"

Ellie moved in, the words inside her still unspoken.

'I detect her.' Sam could hear Ellie's words in his mind, but outside, she was silent.

Sabena blinked, hardly risking a breath. She kept still. She blinked again. Ellie was nowhere to be seen. She blinked for a third time. Ellie loomed up, towering over her.

Sabena recoiled, unable to compute how Ellie got there.

"Are you afraid of dying?" Ellie's voice cut through the silent room.

Sam dragged Sabena by her coat collar. Sabena didn't struggle. It was meaningless to expend energy. She'd already seen how Ellie had handled Salim.

Ellie, now in the flesh in front of her, with her eyes blazing, skin gleaming, she looked like some kind of warrior goddess from ancient times.

Sabena stared at Ellie through mendacious, wicked eyes. "I'm not afraid of anything."

Ellie circled her, smirking at Sabena.

"Not anything?" echoed Ellie doubtfully as she closed in. "You're obviously a purveyor of pain," Ellie continued, gesturing to the surroundings. "So why should we stop you from enjoying what you like?"

Ellie picked up Sabena with one hand and threw her against the bed. Sabena landed hard on her back. Before she could pull herself up, Ellie had tied her wrists and ankles tightly in the leather straps dangling from the bed. Sabena's lips trembled.

"Feeling aroused now?" whispered Ellie in Sabena's ear, and she glared with dark anticipation at her.

Sabena recognized the look. She'd seen it in the medical room when Ellie tried to trick her. What Sabena didn't know was that Ellie wasn't acting. For now, she was reflecting Sabena's own evil abyss of darkness back onto her.

"You wanted a floorshow, didn't you? I'd hate to disappointment you."

Sabena was speechless and sick with fear. She knew what was to come.

"Any last wishes?" asked Ellie whimsically, walking slowly around the bed.

"Yes!" screamed Sabena, enraged. "I wish I'd fucked you and ripped you apart when I had the chance."

Ellie tutted, stroking Sabena cheek, and then she slapped it hard. A trickle of blood edged out of Sabena's mouth.

"I bet you do," purred Ellie in a quiet, menacing tone. She stared Sabena straight in the eye.

Ellie leant in to Sabena's ear and bit it drawing blood.

"As a keepsake, you understand," whispered Ellie, pulling back and she licked her lips, savoring the blood. All the time, she never broke contact. Keeping Sabena locked in her dangerous glare.

Sabena swallowed and struggled, infuriated by her sudden impotency.

Time was ticking for the planet, and as much as Ellie enjoyed disturbing the seditious Sabena, there were greater tasks to be undertaken. Briskly, Ellie reviewed Sabena's balance shift. It was what she'd expected of such a vile creature: eighty-five per cent to the dark. Like a mad killer dog, she had to be put down.

"Sabena, you are a cruel, despicable, and perverted monster that has sadistically tortured, raped and killed so many innocent people. Their requital is served in your termination."

Sabena watched, aghast, as lethal rainbow light hurtled towards her from Ellie's opened palms. She tried to move her body, but the leather straps held her tightly, right in the middle of the light's onward path. Sabena turned and spat spitefully at Ellie whilst the blinding light engulfed her.

In seconds, the light intensified, and Sabena was but an outline. Ellie could have been mistaken, but she thought she could still see Sabena's venomous smile hanging in the air after her body had burst into flickering dots of Technicolor light. The particles dissipated. Then nothing. The air was still like it was at peace. Sabena was gone.

Catharsis swept through Ellie and Sam. Their mutual nemesis was no more.

Chapter 69

The chamber was dark and forbidding. The ancient walls filled with cuneiform, and logo glyphs gave reference to a once invincible civilization.

In the corner, the air darkened and undulated like the fabric of reality was peeling away, and Aswa-da appeared. Racing over to the sandstone podium, he used his dimensional lapse field controller to switch off the dimensional lapse field. Dust particles on the sandstone block swirled around like a vortex, then sucked into the middle as if a tremendous force was pulling them in. Like a tiny black hole had erupted a meter above the block, matter around the sandstone started to pull into the swirling vortex. Aswa-da watched as pieces of rock were ripped from the wall and hurtled towards the vortex.

It had begun. The Therab wasn't even fully locked in Earth's reality. It was still 0.5 degrees out, but it was still affecting all matter around it. Such was the awesome power of the Therab that the dimensional lapse field could not contain its energies. The time lock that had the Therab trapped 6,000 years into the past didn't even work now the artifact had self-activated. The Therab had pulled itself into the future. Aswa-da, of course knew, having investigated the artifact for so very long, that this would happen. He was depending upon this reaction to deliver his plan.

The air above the sandstone warped and buckled. Aswa-da approached slowly. A thin beam of light burst through the vortex. Instinctively, Aswa-da shielded his eyes. Intense light burned through the air, filling the dark cavern with brilliant red light. As the red light strobed across the cavern, in the center of the sandstone block Aswa-da could see the outline of the Therab.

Materializing quickly, the Therab pulsed like a massive heart, the crystal at its center burning a violent red. The ring of crystals Aswa-da had seen before when Dimkur activated the Therab were now spinning at the uppermost point on the device. No longer did they sparkle with rainbow colors. Their color had turned black. They provided a charcoal halo around the blood-red crystal.

Aswa-da's first feeling was the Therab looked 'angry'. But he knew that was impossible. It was only a device that was advanced and connected to every nuance of good or bad in the entire universe. It couldn't actually have feelings itself. That was just being irrational.

The darkness of the crystals showed him that the Therab was powering up to start multiplying the balance shift to the dark. Aswa-da lowered his head in veneration.

This was the place where it had all begun. The birthplace of civilization would now serve as the genesis point for his new universe. Where darkness would reign, and evil would be the new good.

Unafraid, Aswa-da touched the Therab. Of course, he'd touched it many times before, but this time, the smooth, almost liquid feel of the metal held an inner coldness like the Therab could anticipate its new role.

Aswa-da smiled. Justice would be delivered. The House of Etima would once again take its rightful place, and he would take his seat of reign.

Chapter 70

"I've got to get these back to Ashton."

Sam was amazed by his own ability to remain focused. What he'd seen and been subjected to would have blown apart a weaker man. But not Sam.

Ellie looked at the lead box in Sam's trembling hand.

"You're right. But he can't keep it. The quantum bomb needs to be destroyed. It was never meant for this planet. I don't know how it got here. The people of Earth will continue to abuse its power. It must be destroyed."

Ellie's words vexed Sam. Her use of 'this planet' and 'people of Earth' stated beyond doubt that Ellie was not herself. Events had transpired so quickly that she hadn't had the opportunity to reveal the facts behind her 'change', but Sam guessed her transformation had not happened overnight. Quentin had been right all along. She was different. He'd spoken of her dying. At the time, Sam hadn't wanted to accept Quentin's words, believing he was spinning a yarn to save his skin. But maybe her dying contributed to the transformation he was seeing now. Something incredible had happened to his wife. Sam didn't know, couldn't begin to understand how she'd cheated death and returned two hours later after being proclaimed clinically dead. But maybe it was all part of this change. Or maybe not. Sam's mind was buzzing like he had a hornet's nest for a brain, and each thought stung him with pained perplexity.

"Ellie..." he began.

"I'll tell you everything," replied Ellie, reading his mind.

She expected Sam's ream of questions to begin the moment they could regain their breath from their whirlwind execution of evil. Ellie stared at Sam. Her piercing blue eyes roamed over his dirty, scarred, and broken body. He couldn't see Ashton looking like that.

'Don't worry,' he heard in his head, not in his ears. She was doing that telepathic thing again. 'Hold me. Close your eyes.'

Ellie issued the command with more force than she'd meant to. But Sam obediently followed her instructions, and together they shimmered into familiar surroundings. Silent Waters, their Thames-fronted apartment in Chelsea. Sam could see investigators, probably from Six had been there. Little things had been changed, but they'd been careful, and mostly the place remained as he remembered it.

Sam looked around and grinned, nodding slowly. He never believed his eyes would fall on such mundane items of comfort again. Alone in his cell, his mind had floated back to home. From what he was faced with, the intractable moments of merciless vindictiveness, the savage hell state of Salim's own design, Sam knew that this life of little things, personal luxuries, a normalness that he'd accepted and hardly regarded, would never be returned to him. He was resigned to his fate that he would die never touching Ellie or seeing his home again. For Sam, home became a spiritual place. A sort of Elysium he felt was waiting for him when all the torture was over.

Overcome with an effusion of emotion, Sam sobbed. Ellie held his hand and guided him to the bedroom. He followed, barely able to see out from his streaming tears.

He felt he was trespassing, that this flat was no longer his. So sure had he been in his mind that his life was over, he'd sold the flat to an unseen buyer. Now stepping on the glistening marble tiles, he really believed he was invading someone else's privacy. Someone else called Sam Noor.

Sam turned and looked with great confusion at Ellie.

"We shouldn't be here. We should be dead. This isn't natural. How did it happen? How did you change? What are you, Ellie?"

Sam's disoriented and mixed-up mind wrestled with everything he'd witnessed. Utter confusion beseeched from bemused, black eyes.

"My darling, I'll tell you everything. But you really need to clean up before you meet Ashton. You can't see him looking like that."

Sam caught a glimpse of his reflection in the mirror and gasped. He looked like he'd been a year living rough, not just a day in the custody of Al Nadir. Those bastards had robbed him of his imposing stature, his chiseled good looks. Now just a mess of blood, bruise, and bone, he shook his head, fearing he'd never return to that head-turning gorgeousness he'd had. Ellie detected the despondency. She knew what to do.

"Go, darling. I'll tell you all when you come out." Ellie smiled broadly.

Sam felt comforted by her gentle words. Somehow, he'd see this through. After all, he wasn't fighting for survival anymore, was he? The miracle he'd prayed for happened. All the pain had ceased. He'd been rescued. By love.

Ellie sat on the edge of the bed and watched Sam disappear into the bathroom. She looked around the bedroom but felt nothing. No jubilation, no feelings of ecstasy at having returned to safe surroundings. It had to be the Protector's shield keeping her emotions in check, for Ellie was aware that her return had not affected her in the same way it had Sam. Her torturous experiences, her feelings of desolation at being at the mercy of sadistic, ruthless creatures were undoubtedly the same as Sam's. Deep inside her, a thought grew. The Protector's shield was strong, but maybe this feeling, this natural acceptance to coming home, was grounded in her faith in goodness. Her enormous faith that her life would not end and that she expected to somehow, in some way, be saved.

Listening to the water cascading down, Ellie lowered her eyes. Whatever was to come, this was their moment. She would make it last. Removing her clothes, Ellie slipped into the bathroom.

Through the steam, she viewed Sam. His toned, muscular body ravaged by unspeakable acts of savagery by Salim and his henchmen. Watching the deep lesions open, dripping blood down his body, tears welled up inside her. Feeling her presence, Sam turned. Ellie opened the door and slipped in beside him.

Placing her fingers gently on his back, Sam revolved to face the wall as soothing droplets caressed his tortured frame. He closed his eyes. He could feel Ellie's warmth radiating from her skin. Her touch calmed him. Hands wandered purposefully down his back, stroking each ugly, bleeding tear, connecting with each injury inside and out. Focusing on each wound, within seconds, in her mind, she could see Sam's cells regenerating at their slow, ponderous pace. At that rate, he would take weeks to repair. Biology needed a helping hand. Using her age-old powers, Ellie sped up the regeneration of his cells. Sam's injuries began to heal with unnaturally fast agility. Water still flowed over his body, but the rivers of blood ceased.

Sam could feel the sudden change. Turning to face Ellie, his face softened as the last flickering of pain vanished from his body. He was rejuvenated. Alive again.

He touched her face. Ellie rubbed her cheek against his palm. Reaching up, she kissed him. Unafraid, he returned with passion. His hands smoothed down Ellie's hair and he held her close to him, her head resting on his shoulder.

Nuzzling his neck, Ellie kissed behind his ear. Pulling back her head gently, he held her face in his hands. Her startling blue eyes burned with passionate intensity. Her face was a statement of love. Sam gazed at her, wanting desperately to believe that this was the same Ellie he'd been with all his life.

"I love you, Sam," whispered Ellie, breaking his moment of deep thought. She knew he was still confused and maybe even afraid of her. "I love you, Sam. I always have and I always will."

Her eyes connected with Sam. In that millisecond, he felt Ellie's love. The undying, forever-unto-eternity love that they'd always shared came rushing back.

This was his Ellie. No question could deny this.

He bent his head down and kissed her deeply, each kiss growing in potency. He knew he had his real love back again.

"I love you, Ellie. God, how much I love you." Sam showered her body with soft kisses; like rose petals, they fell on her delicate, warm skin.

Ellie arched her body in pleasure at Sam's caresses. His lips dropped down. She gasped and sighed, closing her eyes as Sam's lips engulfed her.

His touches, his kisses, went everywhere. Like their first time, they were fresh, new lovers again. Exploring and discovering. Tentative at first, and then emboldened by desire, venturing into new territory.

Ellie lovingly returned Sam's voyage of discovery with one of her own. Her kisses were impassioned. No part of Sam's now reborn body was missed in her fervent delivery of her love. Sam's heart raced as he watched his own private goddess on her knees, loving him in the special way only Ellie could. Rolling his eyes with sensual delight, he knew unequivocally that this glorious woman could only be his Ellie.

Sam gripped her body, kissing her neck. With a gentle flurry, he slid into her. Home. It felt so unbelievably wonderful. Overwhelmed, Sam cried into Ellie's soft, sweet-smelling neck. They clung together as each sensory-packed thrust signified a promise that Sam would never, never leave Ellie again.

"I love you, Ellie Noor." Sam kissed Ellie's sculptured back.

"And I love you, Sam Noor," replied Ellie, knowing in her heart that this was the last time they would be together.

"Hold me and love me forever." Ellie fought back her own tears as she kissed him hungrily.

"No one lives forever," returned Sam, recalling Ellie's words from a couple of days ago.

Suppressing the echoes of desperation in her voice, Ellie whispered, "Let's try."

Chapter 71

Ellie would have liked to have been more leisured in their lovemaking, but time was already against them. The brief few moments were a self-indulgence that would have been deemed by the high council as totally irresponsible.

Issuing great restraint and self-control, Ellie disengaged from Sam and dressed quickly.

With his strength restored and skin shining with renewed vigor, Sam found his favorite Armani suit and attired himself with pleasure. Today he wanted to stand out. Wanted to tell the world Sam Noor was back in business. Catching his reflection, he smiled widely, remembering the disgusting shack of a man who had stared back at him before. What a difference an hour made.

"You look gorgeous, stud!" Ellie tapped his shoulder. She could almost feel like it was old times again. Of course, it was nothing more than Ellie's memories playing back, but the feeling made her happy, and steeled her for the sadness to come.

"Before we go, I need to tell you about me." Ellie's voice was strong, hiding the blatant apprehension she felt. The time had come for him to know.

"Ok," replied Sam.

"If I told you it was a long story, you'd say that was an overused cliché. But Sam, it really is a very long story, so long it started six thousand years ago."

Sam sat on the sofa spellbound and listened to Ellie unravel a story of such immense proportions a precipice of delirium beckoned.

"The life-force that created me was locked inside…" Ellie stopped. How could she explain this bit and not devastate Sam completely? "Let's say, Ellie Mark I."

Sam's eyebrows raised on hearing the sudden versioning applied to his wife. With his sci-tech background, Sam had been prepared to hear anything. His mind was open, ready to believe absolutely anything, but somehow 'versions of his wife' didn't quite qualify.

"Ellie Mark I?"

Ellie realized too late that her words were disturbing instead of reassuring Sam.

"Yes, Mark I. Ellie held the life-force blueprint for me, for the Protector. Ellie was a direct descendant of that Sumerian princess six thousand years ago, who was entrusted to carry my life-force on Earth."

"Descendant of a Sumerian princess!" exclaimed Sam, thoroughly bewildered, feeling he'd fallen down a rabbit hole.

"As I've explained Sam…" Ellie tone sharpened. The annoyance at having to repeat herself yet again apparent. "The princess was the first in a long line of humans to carry a specially altered string of DNA that held my life-force. All the way down the line to Ellie."

"But you're Ellie, aren't you?"

"Yes and no."

"What kind of fucking answer is that?"

"Sam, don't be like that."

"Well, tell me. Are you Ellie or not?"

"I am Ellie." She paused and then added, "And I'm not."

"What you're telling me doesn't make any sense. Ellie or not? It's a simple fucking question." Sam, despite his gratitude at being rescued, was getting angry and very embarrassed. Just who the hell had he made love to?

"It's far from simple, darling. Can I finish?" retorted Ellie, showing her typical antagonism when Sam used to annoy her. Sam noticed it and remembered it. He couldn't help but smile dryly.

His hands rose up in resignation and acceptance. He just had to open his mind that bit wider.

"Ellie kept my life-force inside of her, integrated into her very being through the altered DNA sequence. She held it inside of her until the day she was called, and I was reconstituted."

Sam blinked, still utterly confused. "Reconstituted? What's that?"

"Just say it helped me become Ellie Mark II."

"Let me get this straight. Are you Ellie? My Ellie?"

"I am everything Ellie was. All her memories, they are all in me. Everything she experienced, everything she went through, I have in here." Ellie tapped her head. "As if I went through it myself. I am Ellie. And much more."

She knew her answer was ambiguous, but it was all she had to give. Sam was shaking his head, a snarl on his gorgeous face. He'd had enough. What kind of a place was Kudamun, where life-forces could be swapped like sweaters? For all he knew, the person in front of him was an impostor, some creature that'd commandeered his beloved's body for its own gain.

"Tell me the truth!" he shouted, tears of hurt filling his darkening eyes. "Is my Ellie here right now, in front of me?"

"Oh God, Sam. I never wanted it to be like this. I am Ellie. I promise you. It's just my physiology that's changed. I'm no longer human. I'm a Kudamaz/human hybrid attuned to the energy resonance of everything on this planet."

"What!?"

Sam's face showed to Ellie the information she was telling him just wasn't being comprehended. She tried again. "Sam, I am Ellie. It's just my internal make-up that's changed. But I am Ellie. Do you understand? I am Ellie. No one else. Not some weird alien creature that, I know by your face, you think I am. I am your Ellie."

Sam stared at his wife, trying to believe, but the abyss between reality and what Ellie was explaining was too great.

"I'm on a mission, the same as you were when you were captured, but my mission is of universal importance. I have to save Earth from certain obliteration. I can't discuss this any longer. We have to leave now. What I haven't told you, you'll have to pick up along the way. As a spy, you should know that drill by now anyway!"

In a beat, Ellie's voice changed from sensitive and caring to cool and professional, with just a touch of bitterness. His betrayal, he could hear, still hurt her. The voice speaking back to him was his Ellie. Her clipped efficiency. Her hard, uncompromising, 'take no shit' attitude. So Sam swallowed, welcoming back the belief that had been locked out of his heart.

Chapter 72

Sam thought about what Ellie had told him. She had a role as the Protector. This new Kudamaz/human hybrid make-up gave her incredible powers. And she had to bring the light and dark energies back to equilibrium using a device called a 'Therab'. The world had experienced a 'balance shift' to the dark and now Earth was in danger of being destroyed.

A cold shiver ran through him. Those words 'balance shifted', he'd heard them before. His mind racked, he concentrated, but the trauma caused by Salim's insanely sadistic actions had disturbed his mind. He could hardly remember yesterday let alone a time before. Absently, Sam looked down at the table: the dictionary. Semantics. Words. Yes, he remembered where he'd heard 'balance shifted'. It was from his own lips just three days before.

He had used the words in the context of a shift of information, after he'd revealed his true job wasn't at the Foreign Office as a diplomat. At the time, Ellie had been bewitched by the words. She'd persisted in asking whether the words could mean something else. It all started to make sense.

"You were obsessed with the words 'balance shifted'. Did that have anything to do with all this?"

Ellie nodded, grateful that Sam was finally beginning to understand.

"Yes. For some reason, Aby-od, in his desperation, had tried to contact me, to tell me they would soon be recalling me. Although as I had no knowledge of Kudamun, Aby-od, or the Protector, all it did was frighten the hell out of me. One second I was in the kitchen with Aby-od shouting at me, and the next I was on a sheer cliff, experiencing being pushed over a cliff to my death on the rocks in the swirling churl. I've never been so scared in my entire life. That's why I screamed."

Sam was dumbstruck. That incident had caused so, so much. That single, brief moment in time had defined everything else that followed. Absolutely everything. In fury, Sam retaliated at Aby-od's injudicious action.

"That guy Aby-od must be a fucking idiot. Why did he try to contact you before you'd changed, reconstituted, whatever?"

Sam's face was angry and sad. All the pain, all the torture, all the death. Would it all have been caused if some fool called Aby-od hadn't tried to communicate with Ellie?

Maybe he would have been captured. But without Quentin Ludlow's help, they would've never have gotten to Ellie. He sincerely doubted they would've gotten close to him. All because of that fucking Aby-od!

He stared at Ellie, although beautiful, he knew she was not the woman in the wedding photograph on the dresser next to him.

"He totally fucked up our lives!" Sam raged, suddenly incensed. What right did Aby-od possess to change his Ellie? If Aby-od had been standing in the room, he'd probably have killed him. A valid recompense for what they'd both been through.

"He didn't fuck up our lives. He gave our lives back. You know they'd have killed you, and after that *thing* they were planning for me, they would've killed me too. Aby-od did right. He saved us both. Can't you see that?"

All her powers, and yet she still didn't know the real truth.

"I was set up by Ludlow. It was revenge for what I did to him."

"I don't understand." Now Ellie was the confused one. She tried to read his mind, but still that block she'd encountered when she'd tried to SearchSight him remained. She searched Ellie's memories, but nothing came through.

"I interrogated him."

"You interrogated him?"

Sam nodded.

"But that wouldn't make him set-"

"It was brutal," Sam interjected, crashing through Ellie's words. Then he lowered his eyes to the floor.

"But why? Why would you do that, Sam? You're a good man. Why would you hurt someone?"

"Because they hurt you. For Christ's sake, Ellie, don't you fucking remember what they did to you?"

"Who? What did they do?"

Ellie shook. Her total lack of recall delivering to her a very real human emotion. She was scared.

"They took you. Tortured you. Almost killed you. Don't you remember anything?"

Ellie listened, horrified, taking in each word.

"You mean Al Nadir? Of course, I remember." But as she said it, she knew Sam was referring to someone else.

"No, not Al Nadir. My people."

"MI6?"

"Yes, they took you, Ellie. They tried to find out why you screamed. It was captured on their surveillance."

"But why would they be bothered about that?"

"There was a case a while back, a woman, Sarah Masters. She was happily married to an MI6 agent. One day she just flipped and beat him to death. Then she disappeared. Went to ground. We never found her. Our only assumption was that she'd been a plant by Al Nadir. The case haunted us. It haunted Maide, MI6's Chief, more than anyone."

"So why target me?"

"It was that scream. That fucking scream. Maide, in a moment of extreme paranoia, authorized your abduction. When I confided in you, told you what I did, he thought you were a threat to national security. Thought you were Al Nadir. He even thought I'd swapped allegiances. He was looking for answers. He thought he could find them in you."

"I, I don't remember," stuttered Ellie. What had they done to her? Why couldn't she remember?

"I know you don't. They drugged you. Forced you to forget everything they did."

"When did they do this?"

"When I was in the US on Sunday."

"But that was when I was attacked by Al Nadir."

"No, it was my people again initiating a false flag attack. A cover up. We call it an ME9. Masquerade as the Enemy. I know the procedure. I've done it before."

Hearing what Sam was saying, Ellie was struck dumb with desolation.

Awkwardly, Sam continued, "Times in the past, when our government wanted to force through unpalatable foreign policy or impose a bill that smacked at the heart of civil rights, we'd stage an ME9 attack. There wouldn't be much objection after that."

Ellie stared horrified. How little she really knew about Sam. She shook her head, saddened.

"I'm sorry, Ellie. It was my job. I was only following orders."

Only following orders. Sam couldn't believe he was actually hiding behind those words. Everything Al Douri had dished out, he'd warranted. For the life he'd led, he didn't deserve to live.

"How could you? How could you be a part of all that?"

"I'm sorry. I can't say it enough."

Ellie couldn't hear anymore. She was confused, angry, hurt. Too many emotions. The Protector's shield didn't seem to be working. She was feeling everything and was being affected by it. She tried to center her mind, to regain her incredible strength.

"Why me? What did they hope to achieve?"

"Maide wanted to find out why you screamed. He was a man obsessed. Now do you see why I'm saying Aby-od fucked up our lives? If he hadn't tried to contact you that Saturday morning, you would never have screamed and none of this would have happened."

Ellie was silent, analyzing all Sam had told her, and determined not to dwell on the fact that Sam had played the enemy. Ellie thought about Aby-od, his role in their eventual incarceration. Could Aby-od really have been that stupid?

Sam opened his palms outwards towards Ellie. "Don't you see? There would've been no interrogations, no murders, no torture, no…"

Back in the satcomm room, staring at his wife strapped to the chair, his heart ripped open. A cavity of catastrophic despair. An intolerable, bone-shaking ache created by knowing he could do nothing to save her. Sam closed his eyes to shut out the memory, to give a shield to the growing reservoir of tears. Despite what he'd seen in his wife's eyes, the pain and shame, he wanted to believe that somehow, she'd been spared from such vile and heinous a crime.

"Pain," he continued. "We've gone through all of this, because of him."

Sam was exasperated. Couldn't she see? Couldn't she understand?

Ellie knew his words were logical, but she knew much more. Everything was connected. Lives and destinies were written. They couldn't have changed what was meant to be.

"No, Sam. You're wrong," answered Ellie, finally. "Our lives are pre-defined. Whatever paths we could've chosen, we'd still have had the same pain, same torment. But our lives were not destined to end that way. Didn't you feel the faith when you were alone in your cell? Did you really lose all hope?"

Chapter 73

Sam heard her words and knew what Ellie said was true. He knew that he was in the presence of an ancient wisdom. She could see life so clearly. And she was so right. Even in his darkest hour, watching Salim laughing, licking his lips with sordid anticipation at the thought of Ellie's forthcoming performance, he had the 'deep-seated faith' that this was not how each of them should die. His faith and hope had kept him from going completely insane and had given him the strength to stand the humiliation and torture until the release came.

"Ellie, you're right. Every word you've said is right. I'm sorry I've let you down. I've been a terrible person. I didn't deserve for you to save me. I'm so, so sorry." He lowered his head like a disgraced dog, suffused in shame.

Ellie touched him. She knew what a scourge Al Nadir had been, knew only too well. God knows what he'd had to deal with. His past was that. She had no right to judge him. That wasn't why she was there.

"Whatever you've done in your life, I know you're not a terrible person. Maybe you've had some misguided loyalties, but that's not for me to say. I don't know what you've faced. I believe you only did what you thought was right."

Sam lifted his head. His eyes had lost their sparkle, their cheeky playfulness she loved. Revealing to her more of his "activities" had stripped him of his humanity. Sam thought back. He'd been an absolute fool, allowing himself to be used, a political tool. Like a white paper, just fodder to keep the invisible ones in power. It wasn't going to be like that again. This was his last mission. He'd make sure of that.

"I know you hate Aby-od, and you have every right to. That is your choice. But believe me: Aby-od is a good man trying to do good for all the worlds in his care. Understand this, my darling."

On hearing the endearment, Sam shot an involuntary smile. She still loved him.

Ellie continued, "If I fail, there will be no Earth. So Sam, I cannot fail. Not if we want a future together." She smiled.

Sam nodded in agreement, not knowing her joyful expression camouflaged the absolute torment her heart was carrying. She couldn't tell Sam she would leave him after the mission. She wanted to believe they'd find a way to build a life together. She wanted to believe in hope.

"We've delayed too long. We must leave now."

Bringing out a small, silver device from the pocket of her trousers, Ellie pressed the button to gain a reading of the balance shift. Instantly, a bank of red numbers floated in the air like pollen spores on a hot spring day. She watched the numbers accelerate. Her instinct told her the numbers should have been decelerating, but still the blazing angry numbers increased. Why? She'd killed Salim Al Douri and Sabena Sanantoni. They had been responsible for so much evil, so much balance shift. The swing back to equilibrium should have begun by now.

"Sam, we've got to go."

Ellie watched the numbers increase with rapid succession. They now reflected a sixteen per cent balance shift. Earth was now fully in the Dark Zone.

"Where are we going?" Sam asked, staring with curiosity at the gravity defying readout. With Ellie, he'd come to expect anything.

"Ashton. You've got to get that quantum bomb to him."

For a short while, Sam had completely forgotten his mission. But Ellie hadn't.

"I'm SearchSighting him. I need to know his location accurately, so I can calculate the shimmer velocity." Ellie's words came out rapid fire, forgetting Sam had no knowledge of Kudamaz transport ability.

"Huh?" muttered Sam, at a loss to understand. "I know where he'll be." Sam flicked his head around to look at the calendar on the kitchen wall. "It's Wednesday." *My God, still only Wednesday. So much had happened. I've lost track of time.* "After Malta, he'll be with his war cabinet at Whitehall, probably in conference with the president."

"Hold on, and don't forget the compound."

Sam grabbed the lead box and gripped hold of Ellie.

"And close your eyes," whispered Ellie, as the apartment dissolved around them.

Chapter 74

Just as Sam had imagined, Ashton was deep in conversation with his war cabinet. Ellie had sensed Ashton's resonance. Arriving 0.99 per cent out of reality, she checked no one was around at the arrival location. A darkened corner with a column in front proved perfect for an inconspicuous entrance. Reality locked in around them, and Sam took Ellie's hand and walked quickly over to the door that led to where he knew the PM would be.

They entered together, and as if Marilyn Monroe and Elvis had just strolled in, the room fell to shocked silence.

The PM, always feeling he should be the one to break the mold, spoke.

"Dr. Sam Noor. This...is...unexpected. We heard you'd been captured."

Sam listened to Ashton's voice dripping with callous indifference. He felt Ashton's eyes dance over him for signs of interrogation. Sam knew he looked extremely fit and healthy. In response to the visual inspection, Ashton furrowed his brow, pondering hard. If he'd been in the clutches of Al Nadir, he wouldn't be looking like he'd just gotten back from holiday.

"How did you get away? It's almost impossible once Al Nadir catch you." Ashton's words came out glacial sharp. His taciturn face told Sam he believed he was a traitor. Sam shook his head.

"Later, sir." Sam fixed a hard glare back on the PM and, in it, he tried to communicate all the suffering he'd be through. Ashton, however, didn't pick up on a single nuance of Sam's subliminal message. Or he didn't want to, thought Sam bitterly.

"What happened to Lydell?" the PM snapped.

"He flipped and gave me up as a peace offering to Al Douri."

Ashton lips pursed together.

Sam could see he was judging what he'd heard.

"It's true, sir."

Ashton shrugged, non-committal, and turned his attention to the package Sam was cradling.

"What's that?" asked Ashton coldly.

"Prime Minister, it's the quantum bomb." Sam opened the lid and then brought the pen close to the block. It shone bright. The room let out a series of concurrent gasps at the wonder being held by the agent.

"All of it, sir. No more exists. I got that assurance from Salim personally."

Sam's words trailed off. Salim's petrified face at the moment Ellie severed his arm appeared in his mind. The recollection only underpinned what he knew to be true: Salim did not lie.

Ashton looked down at the open box, shining and sparkling, and then into Sam's eyes. Something finally registered.

And the PM seemed to regard Sam with new eyes. He issued a little, customary smirk, and then spluttered, staring at the shining compound block. Instead of distrust and hate, incredulity was written on the PM's face. Then, finally, he broke into a huge smile. Leaping up out of his chair, he flung his arms around Sam in a heart-warming embrace. Sam half expected a kiss to follow.

"Sam…Sam, what can I say? We're indebted to you."

Sam smiled gracefully, slowly observing others around the table. Ashton's unexpurgated show of 'spin-free' raw emotion had sparked his colleagues into their own displays of gratitude.

Nathan Cartwright was cheering. Brownie points for MI6 now. He could dine out on Sam's incredible success for months to come. Godley too was cheering, but his face was reflective. His eyes were less exuberant and seemed distant. Sam noticed it.

"Godley, aren't you pleased?" asked Sam pointedly, his penetrating stare cutting deep.

I'd always taken Ludlow for an effete, subservient little twat. Makes you wonder who's pulled his strings. Salim's words were still fresh in Sam's mind, as were the feelings stabbing through him. Betrayal. Treachery. Duplicity. Sold like a piece of meat. Abused ruthlessly, callously abused.

"Well? Aren't you?" Sam's smile had already gone stale. He tried to mask it, but the coldness came.

His colleagues looked to Godley, and he stiffened in his chair. He couldn't meet Sam's eyes. Keeping them fixed on the lead box, he answered, "Of course, I'm delighted, Sam. Well done. God knows what you been through to get that."

Sam gritted down so hard he could feel blood on his lips. "Quentin Ludlow would know *exactly* what I've been through, being as he was the bastard that set me up in the first place."

The cheering and backslapping abruptly stopped. Looking solemn, the PM stated icily, "Quentin's dead, Sam. He can't defend himself against your accusations. How did you come by this information?"

"Salim told me while I was being tortured. He told me Quentin had sold the access codes to my files to Al Nadir."

Sam stopped. Looks of disbelief surrounded him around the table. How much should he tell them? Sweeping a sideways glance at his wife, shining with radiance and beauty, he knew they'd never believe she'd been tortured. They obviously doubted he'd been through anything, so completely had Ellie's regenerative powers worked to eradicate his injuries. And Ellie's metamorphosis had removed all sign of her wounds and damage. They had no evidence to show what they'd been subjected to.

Only in their minds did the torment of the last twenty-four hours hold any credence.

Sam made a decision. He hoped it was a good one.

Chapter 75

"Prime Minister, may I speak with you alone?"

Sam's request was met with suspicious stares from those gathered.

The prime minister glanced down the table. What was it that Sam needed to say, that he couldn't say in front of his colleagues? Years of political experience told him Sam was sound. A man to be trusted and believed.

Nodding graciously, Ashton asked those around the table to leave the room.

"Richard, I'm going to tell you things that are absolutely unbelievable, but I assure you they are all true."

Sam beckoned his wife to come forward. Until this time, Ellie had been silent, just watching her husband, but now she knew it was time to support him.

"Ellie, could you shimmer for me to the far side of the room?"

Sam was aware that if he started telling the PM anything, he wouldn't believe him. Far simpler to just demonstrate Ellie's capabilities and win Ashton's understanding immediately.

Ashton waited patiently, wondering secretly if Sam had in fact gone mad. Shimmer? What the hell was…?

His thoughts trapped abruptly in time. Sam's wife had disintegrated in front of him into a whirling, swirling vortex of rainbow flecks that vanished and then reappeared at the end of the room. The flickering lights quickly solidified to form Ellie Noor again.

"What the fuck?"

Ashton's expletive showed he was shocked to his soul. Walking over to Ellie, he reached out and touched her arm. It was solid. It was real. She wasn't an illusion, some CGI trickery. She really had done—what was it? "Beam me up, Scotty."

Suddenly, Ashton looked afraid. He stepped back, glaring warily from Sam to Ellie.

"Who are you people? How did she do that?"

Sam smiled. Ashton had the same reaction as he'd had.

"Ellie's a Kudamaz/human hybrid. She's been brought back virtually from the dead to save the Earth."

God, what a line. He couldn't blame Ashton's eyes enlarging and his tired mouth cracking into a curved line. Sam's annoyance only fired his mirth.

"Richard, don't be naïve. We don't live in the public's world. You know aliens exist. The quantum bomb and its true origins, it was never the president's invention. Come on, Richard. You know it, and the president knows it."

Ashton's face went ashen. "Oh my God, the missiles. He's fired them. It was in self-defense. Salim sent a broadcast threatening to do the same to the US and UK as he'd done to Malta. We couldn't wait. We had to act. But if that's all the bomb." The PM pointed to the lead box. "There's no reason for the attack. We've got to stop him." Ashton flicked on the conference controls in the center of the table.

Sam was worried. He never expected revenge strikes so fast.

Quietly, Ellie asked, "These missiles, they're nuclear, aren't they?"

From the degree of balance shift from the equilibrium, she knew they had to be. Nodding in answer to Ellie, Ashton's face paled. His eyes bloodshot with stress. Slowly, he pushed the paper with the strike zones in front of Sam.

"The president has launched fourteen nuclear missiles targeted at key Al Nadir bases throughout the world."

Skimming down the list, Sam stared back at Ashton, horrified.

"Pakistan, Iraq, China, Iran, North Korea. For fuck's sake Richard, they've got the bomb. This'll be World War III. Kudamun doesn't need to obliterate us. We'll do the job for them."

Ashton looked puzzled at the reference to Kudamun.

"Never mind," said Sam tersely. They didn't have time for explanation. "Get on that line. Call the president. Those missiles must be aborted."

Chapter 76

Godley had refrained from looking back at Sam as the PM had requested for the room to be cleared. He moved and was first out of the door.

He needed to get inside the adjoining room. As he turned the handle, he hoped no other meeting was taking place. But, on opening it, he could see the room was empty. Inside, he sidled up to the wall, stuck his ear to the fabric wallpaper, and strained to hear Sam's conversation.

Sweat around his collar and under his arms had built, making him wet and thoroughly uncomfortable. Although his body was clammy, his mouth was dry, a wadi in need of rain.

He'd never expected to see Sam again. At least not alive.

How the hell had he escaped? Al Douri wasn't one to drop his guard. Did Sam know of his collusion and his deep allegiance to Al Nadir?

Godley couldn't understand it. Things were unravelling out of control.

Rich Lydell, Sam's CIA co-op had flipped sides instantly when the money was offered by Salim Al Douri. The CIA pension was never going to get him thirty million dollars. But a quick betrayal certainly would.

Needless to say, Lydell hadn't been happy about sharing his blood money.

"You gotta be outta your fucking mind!" Lydell had yelled at Godley over Al Nadir's cloaked satcomm network.

Godley had stared at the tall, blonde guy with piercing, brown eyes.

"I'm sorry, but Dr. Sanantoni signed off on the split. Without my maneuvers to get Sam detailed on Operation Wren, you'd have had to revert back to opportunistic tracking. I'm delivering Sam Noor where he needs to be."

Lydell scowled. "I still don't see why you're taking half. I'm the one on the ground actually getting the guy. You're just ponsing around. That's not worth fifteen million!"

"On the contrary, the fact that I am ponsing around, as you call it, is exactly why I'm worth fifteen million. I've got access to the prime minister. I've got access to defense. And I've got access to Sam's personal files."

"So what? Al Nadir can hack anything."

"Yes, they can hack digital. But it's not so easy to hack analogue. Bits of paper in a file. Old school, Lydell. Remember it?"

Lydell glared. "But you gave us the memory drive with the access codes to Operation Wren. It had all the mission specs. That's what Al Nadir paid you for."

"No. They paid Quentin, not me. I gave Russo the offline personal files direct from River House. You see, Lydell, being defence secretary gives me that privilege, that level of access, and few question my reasons. I gave Al Nadir something you didn't."

"Yeah? What? What did you give them?" snarled Lydell.

"The wife."

"And why's she so important?" grilled Lydell, still not getting Godley's plan. Godley observed his wild, gung-ho attitude and was quite surprised he was even in the CIA. Intelligence seemed a long way from his natural ability.

"Leverage, Lydell. The thing to break Sam Noor."

He recalled how Lydell had smirked, but hadn't said anything derogatory. He'd simply nodded his head.

"Fair enough," he muttered finally, and switched off the broadcast.

Godley was well aware of Al Nadir's tactics. Ellie Noor should be dead or at least severely messed up. Sabena, after all, had had her paws on her. Not many tend to live after The Slayer touches them.

Godley recalled their entrance. Ellie had looked incredible. Like a thunderstorm had been personified in a woman. He could feel her power.

He couldn't understand what was happening. Sam claimed to be holding the quantum bomb. But Salim would never have given that up. Godley shook with worry as he pressed his ear harder against the wall.

Was that his name? Had Sam said his name?

Oh dear God, he had to get out. Terror rolled through Godley, not just for his political career but now his life. Treason still carried the death penalty.

Not to mention what Sabena and Salim would do to him. His position in the Cabinet had earned him fifteen million dollars for both Sam and Ellie's lives. But now, with the power couple free, he was a liability.

And Godley was well versed in how liabilities were handled in Al Nadir.

Chapter 77

Inside the darkened room of the Pentagon, the gang of four viewed the progress of the missiles. With an unexpected flash, the red HoloLink satcomm light came on, signaling a new conference call was coming through. A short, stocky man swirled around in his chair.

"Mr. President, the British PM is on the line for you, sir. Shall I connect him?"

The president was cautious. Why was Ashton calling again? Action had already been taken. He'd sought and gained his 'approval' for it. What did he want now?

Weitz, on seeing the president's indecision, responded quickly. "Mr. President, he may have news concerning Al Nadir. I think you should take the call."

Weitz hoped secretly that Ashton had found a way to avert the attack the president had sanctioned.

"Ok, ok," muttered the president irritably. "Put him through."

The frosted glass turned into the AR driven HoloLink comms platform and Ashton appeared.

"You must abort the missile strike, Jonathan. Sam Noor's arrived back. He's got the quantum bomb. It's all here." Ashton's voice was strong and commanding as he pointed to the lead box in front of him.

Weitz, Hutchinson, and Reiner breathed a singular sigh of relief. Tightly drawn mouths slowly upturned. Gradually, the tension of the past forty-eight hours dissolved and people around the room started to smile. Only the president remained impervious to the show of gratified emotion by the apparent good news bestowed by Ashton.

His face creased, and distrust flickered over his worn features. His callous eyes stared at Ashton. His self-righteous, relentless tirade struck back without mercy.

"Why do you think that is all the bomb? How did Sam escape so easily when we all know he was captured by Al Nadir? It could all be just a ploy by Salim Al Douri. Give Sam something to take back and trick us into believing that there's no more, and then blow us all into tomorrow like he'd planned."

The president was deeply concerned. No one was allowed to prevent his destiny. He fingered the sacred tablet in his pocket, willing Ashton to trust his judgment and his word. *Trust me. Trust every word I say is true. Fix the belief. Don't let it leave you.* The mantra rang clearly in his head. He could sense the energies flowing out of the tablet, making him stronger. With almost vicious determination, he repeated his question, turning his eyes on Sam.

"So boy, how did you *really* get away? I know Al Nadir. They don't just let people get out that easily. So how'd you do it? What makes you the special one, huh?"

Ashton listened. There was an element of truth in the president's analysis. Turning to face Sam, he abruptly requested him to answer the president.

"Mr. President, sir, we're still on an open channel, secure as it may be. All I can say is that it was down to my wife Ellie, and it was a miracle. If it hadn't happened, Salim would have tortured me to death."

The president raised an eyebrow, clearly doubting Sam's word. Sam stared at Ashton, entreating the PM to believe him. Holding him in his gaze for a second, Sam thought the PM believed him.

But the president, who'd picked up on Sam's last words, shouted, "Tortured you to death? I don't think so, boy. There's not a mark on you. More like you've been on vacation than in Al Nadir's death camp. I think you're full of bullshit and that stuff you got there is nothing more than C4. What did he say? Al Douri? That he'd give you a nice little amount in a Swiss account? Sell your soul and your country for forty pieces of silver?"

The president held firm his argument against Sam. All the time, his hand tightened around the tablet in his pocket. Ashton shivered unexpectedly, turning to look from the president back to Sam. Deep in his mind, the president's words rang true.

Unable to take the president's ridiculous posturing and the PM's sudden reproachful eye, Sam exploded with rage.

"For fuck's sake. I'm no turncoat. Rich Lydell, Quentin Ludlow and others here have been, but not me. Salim Al Douri is dead. Sabena Sanantoni is dead. He never distributed it in the US. This is all the quantum bomb.

There is no more. Salim told me under extreme duress. Now for God's sake, stop this madness and abort those missiles!"

Sam's words shook with anger and frustration. The insinuation he'd joined an alliance with Al Douri was reprehensible. He would have died before disclosing state secrets and would never have told Salim the summit's location, had they not gotten to Ellie.

Aware that his powers from the tablet were having no effect on Sam, the president glanced at the woman by his side. She looked stunning. An air of regal opulence surrounded her. She held tightly to Sam's hand. Who was she? Why wasn't she affected by his powers? Disturbed, Treeborne stared at her. Never in his entire life had he encountered anyone untouched by his powers of persuasion, manipulation, and trust. There was something about her…

He focused on Ashton, but Treeborne was cognizant, in the presence of that strange, beautiful woman, his argument against Sam weakened by the second.

Ripples of excitement and confusion formed behind the president on hearing the simultaneous demise of Al Nadir top man and his vicious number two.

Weitz, standing out of Treeborne's eye line, shouted, "Whoa! Way to go, Sam!" as he made an upward sweep with his arm.

Reiner spluttered incredulously at the amazing information. Hutchinson, standing on the opposite side of Weitz, started a slow clap that increased in speed to an all-out thundering applause. Weitz nodded fast in agreement and started clapping too. Reiner joined in, all three signifying their naked appreciation that Sam had killed two of the evilest creatures in the world.

Treeborne was annoyed. No one seemed to be listening to him. He just couldn't match Sam's powerful presence. He tried a different tact.

"OK, Sam, Salim maybe dead, but how can we really be sure that's all the bomb? He was an evil liar. He could have told you a pack of lies. That's what terrorists do. What guarantees do we really have?"

The president's eyes pierced Sam with such ferocity it made him wonder why the president was so intent on nuking the world.

"What was done to him, to get his confession, Mr. President, you don't want to know. Just believe me. He would not have lied. Not in that situation, no one could."

Sam's tone was arrogant and cold. He painted a picture in their minds of atrocious torture inflicted on Salim, a man who could appreciate the value borne of such terror. Ashton shuddered as Sam spoke. But he was grateful to hear the truth in the words.

Weitz didn't hold back. Balling his fist, he slammed it into his palm, shouting, "You got the little fucker!"

The president was nonplussed. His action stood. Nothing would turn him. He had been given his instructions by his god Aswa-da.

'Impending doom will take over the Earth. This will be your time to take your stand against this relentless evil. You will stand defiant against their darkness. And you will win. You will rise over all.'

He knew his way was right.

With god on his side, he could not fail.

Treeborne glared back at the agent with a flicker of pity for his gullibility.

"Sam, you're a good man, but good men are fools. I cannot risk the lives of my people against the dying words of an accomplished, evil liar. The attack will continue. The missiles will not be aborted. So long, Richard, Sam. Goodbye!"

Abruptly, the president cut the satcomm connection.

Whirling around to stare at Ashton, Sam's face was saturnine.

"Richard, he's mad. He's going to blow up the world."

Chapter 78

Ellie had been quiet, just observing and taking in everyone around her. The moment Ashton connected with the president; she knew the truth.

"He's not just mad. He's like me. He's got a Kudamaz pattern resonating within him. This isn't just a coincidence. Something is very wrong. If he's got a resonance, it means the elders are involved. Sam, he's pushing the world on a path of self-destruction. The very action that would force the high council to obliterate the Earth, without waiting for me to complete my mission. He must be stopped."

Ellie's eyes flashed with understanding. Ashton, however, was completely lost. Kudamaz? Elders? What the hell was going on? He looked with increasing confusion at Sam to provide answers. Sam just shrugged.

Ellie let go of Sam's hand and grabbed Ashton by the shoulders, shaking him softly.

"I'm sorry, but we don't have time to explain. We have to stop the president and the elders involved. If we don't succeed…well, I'll tell you all in the afterlife. If we do succeed, then you don't really need to know." Ellie smiled, an echo of warmth and mystery. Ashton shook his head, not able to comprehend what he'd seen and heard over the last few minutes.

"Ok, ok." Ashton surrendered to the fact that something was going on that was totally beyond his comprehension. He was, however, delighted to hear that his darling Katzy's killer Sabena had been destroyed. He imagined, looking at Ellie and the immense power she obviously possessed, she'd have enjoyed making Sabena suffer. At least, he hoped that bitch Sabena had suffered in her dying moments.

Ashton flipped back into focus after letting his mind drift to the love that had been wrenched from him.

"Just answer me this, Sam. When you told the president you weren't a turncoat, but you said others here were, do you want to elucidate on that remark?"

Sam stared at the PM, recalling Salim's words.

Makes you wonder who was really pulling his strings.

"I know that Quentin wasn't working alone. He'd had help to deliver those access codes to my files. Access to my files meant that they could access my life, every part of it. Richard, I know it's hard to understand, but they took Ellie. Sabena cut her up real bad. She was a shredded mess. I know she looks fine now, but she's been through a regeneration process. Believe me: she was virtually dead. We were both set up. I can't be sure but..."

Sam glared at the chair where Godley had been seated earlier. Ashton turned his head, following Sam's stare.

"I can't be sure," Sam continued. "But I certainly wouldn't leave Godley in charge of defense. In fact, I wouldn't leave Godley in charge of anything."

Ashton looked flabbergasted. "Charles Godley, the cornerstone of the party? The most trustworthy man I've met? Surely not." His eyes wide with disbelief.

"Whoever gave the intel from my personal file knew that Al Nadir would target Ellie," stated Sam stonily.

"But not Charles Godley. He's so sound. He couldn't possibly." Ashton watched as Sam shook his head, defying the PM's ill-placed trust. Siding up to Ashton, out of his wife's earshot, he whispered, "They planned to gang rape and rip her apart alive in the process. Get rid of him!"

Sam's words were unbelievably barbaric. They numbed Ashton. Inside, he felt like ice. He could never have known what Godley was planning. Nor where it would lead. All he wanted, all he ever wanted, was 'zero exposure, utter discretion'. Godley's actions were his own. He could not be held accountable for someone else who had fraternized with the enemy.

Ellie stared at Ashton. He seemed deep in thought, but his balance shift was in equilibrium. Still she sensed something. *Something* she couldn't discern. It perturbed her greatly. She wanted to find out, but glancing at the clock, she knew she had no time. But she wouldn't forget.

"We've got to go, Richard. Pray we succeed. Come on, Sam. You know the drill."

Ellie shot her words with machine-gun speed. Sam immediately slipped his arms around his wife and closed his eyes.

Ellie could feel the president's Kudamaz resonance pulsing with incredible strength. She homed in, pinpointing its origin, and shimmered to the location.

Chapter 79

Ashton watched them dematerialize. He rubbed his eyes, still very unsure of what he'd really witnessed. He didn't understand what Sam had told him, but he did understand traitors. He couldn't do anything about Lydell, but he could handle turncoats nearer to home. Ashton rose from his chair, heading for the door.

In the adjacent room, Godley panicked. His ear had turned purple, such was the force he'd applied to get closer to the wall and closer to the words Sam spoke to Ashton. He could not hear much. Just a word here and there. But towards the end of the conversation, he thought he'd heard Sam mention his name. In a blind fright, Godley vacated the room and ran with haste down the sweeping marble staircase.

Scrambling down the steps, panic misted his vision. He knew Ashton wanted results, but not necessarily the results he'd instituted.

"Godley, where are you?" Godley heard the intonation in Ashton's voice, angry and glacial. Frantic to get away, Godley leapt down two steps at a time.

"Godley, wait!"

Ashton's voice was getting louder. Godley turned around to see Ashton taking to the stairs after him.

"Wait!" called Ashton, putting his hand up to signal Godley to stop running.

Godley jumped forward, not stopping. Looking ahead, he pretended to not hear the PM. If he'd looked down, it may not have happened. Or if he'd had cheap rubber soles instead of expensive handcrafted leather ones, again it may not have happened. But Godley did not look down and he had leather soles. So it happened.

His sole connected and slid across the plush carpet like maple syrup across a pancake. Inertia pushed Godley backwards, the right side of his head hitting the ivory marble ridge on the step. The heavy force of the impact carried through Godley's weight. Blinking through blood-filled eyes, Godley felt the pressure in his head. A million migraines exploding all at once, Godley cried out in pain. Blood surged in his ears, eyes, and nose. The embolism erupted in his brain and sudden darkness took his sight.

Ashton arrived at Godley's side. Dropping down, he could see a stream of blood flowing from his right ear. Ashton picked up Godley's wrist to feel for a pulse. There was nothing.

He looked around as officials gathered.

"It was an accident. He slipped. I think he's dead."

Ashton felt his voice was distant, unconnected, not quite created by his own vocal chords. The experience chilled him.

Paramedics appeared quickly at the scene and strapped Godley to a stretcher. Ashton watched stock-still against the wall. Godley's unmoving body was removed and taken away. Whatever the truth was, it died with him. Perhaps, the way it should always have been, mused Ashton, turning his head from the macabre debacle. For the dead can never confess.

Chapter 80

Treeborne realized his action of snapping off the satcomm connection had been enervated. His voice had descended into a feeble whine. His argument of Sam being a traitor had been desperate and pathetic in its execution. At a time when his power should have been surging, it was waning. *That girl.* Something about that girl unnerved him.

Weitz watched the president. He'd been deeply troubled by the president's willful insistence to pursue the nuclear attack on Al Nadir bases, despite hearing Sam's confirmation he'd taken out Al Douri, his second in command and had all the quantum bomb. Hutchinson was similarly perplexed by the president's fixation on continuing with such extreme force.

Reiner knew that the president was emotionally unstable and, although he was no authority on the area, quite possibly mad too. But locked inside the Pentagon's most secure control room, surrounded by Secret Service agents, he couldn't take any action to remedy the untenable position.

Treeborne was aware his grip was slipping. He held on tightly to the tablet in his pocket and forced eye contact with all three of his compatriots around the table. In his head, the mantra vibrated, a dominating resonance. *Trust me. Trust every word I say is true. Fix the belief. Don't let it leave you.* Little by little, the insecurities and fears that had struck Reiner, Hutchinson, and Weitz diminished. Once again, they pledged their complete support to the president.

Treeborne had barely finished forming absolute trust in their minds, when he noticed the air in front of him sparkle with incandescent light. Reiner, Weitz, and Hutchinson also observed the unusual air spectacle. They pulled away from the president, frightened and unaware of what was happening.

In her panic to get to the president, Ellie had failed to reconnoiter the area

0.99 degrees out of the reality as she had done when she'd arrived at Whitehall to find a suitable location. Coming out of shimmer, she realized instantly her mistake as three sets of eyes widened in unison. Only the president was unaffected. He had seen this sight before. His god had this power. And his god told him others would come wanting to destroy him. False gods. Messengers of Satan who had great powers. But he would be protected. His god would save him.

"Seize these vessels of evil," cried Treeborne, his eyes shining with rage. "They are born from the seeds of the devil. They come to destroy our great lands. My children, stand with me. Embrace the power of God. Embrace the power of me, your new Messiah!"

Treeborne lifted his arms skyward and stretched them out in the form of a cross. Reiner viewed this insanely religious performance with increasing dread. The temporary trust the president had invoked vanished instantly the moment Ellie materialized. Her inner power removed the curtain of deceit that had been drawn across their minds. For the first time, all three men saw the crazed antics of their totally deranged President. With eyes clear and free of Treeborne's powerful influence, they watched in horror as the missiles headed towards their targets. Data streamed in confirming retaliatory strikes across the world were counting down.

"The president's insane! He's gonna nuke the world!" screamed Weitz, unable to contain himself. The sudden realization that they all faced oblivion spurring on his outburst.

The president continued his tirade, unaffected by Weitz's verbal explosion.

"Fear ye not who are blinded by evil. Let me show thee the way. Step thee into my shoes and follow my path of goodness." Having finished his theological verse, the president side-stepped out of the glasshouse and signaled the Secret Service agents waiting immobile with confusion immediately outside.

"These two people are Al Nadir assassins. They've been sent to kill me."

The president's words were strong and coherent, reflecting none of the religious fervor of seconds before.

Instantly, the agents, although still mortified by the fact that Sam and Ellie had entered the Pentagon out of thin air, charged in to aid and protect the president and capture the two strange assailants.

One of the agents attempted to grab Ellie. On touching her, she shimmered to take up position behind Reiner. The other agent, stunned by

Ellie's unique method of evading capture, stood dumbfounded. Sam used the precious moments of bewilderment to render the agent unconscious with a single strategic blow to his neck.

The second agent, watching his colleague fall to the floor, touched his coms device in his ear and shouted, "Code one! Lighthouse under attack. Give me back up, level G. Lighthouse is in danger. Repeat. Code one, Lighthouse is in-"

The second agent was caught mid-sentence by Sam's right leg smashing into his stomach. Like flicking a switch, Sam's extreme martial arts training took over. He spun around with great accuracy, landing a hefty blow to the agent's head. Revolving at speed, Sam's leg shot out and connected with the agent's torso. The force sent the agent crashing into the table. Sam snatched his gun, as another agent charged him. Sam struck out, smashing his fist into the agent's face and torso, and threw him against the glass wall, pelting him hard into the stomach. Puffing out, spitting blood, the agent lumbered forward, his gun in his hand ready to fire. Before Sam could react, Ellie once again employed her mysterious powers, disintegrating the gun in a blink. In answer to the other Secret Service agent's plea, more agents stormed in, only this time, they fired frantically at Sam and Ellie. The bullets barely survived a second from their guns before Ellie smashed them with her mind to dust. Turning her force onto the weapons, she shattered their molecular configuration whilst the agents looked on aghast and powerless.

'Tell them Lighthouse is ok.' Ellie's voice boomed loud in the agent's head as he looked on to see other agents running down the corridor. 'Tell them, or you'll go the way of your guns.' The first agent swallowed. This was one Miss he didn't want to mess with. Way beyond his paygrade! He touched his intercom.

"Lighthouse is not in danger. Repeat. Lighthouse is not in danger. Further assistance is not, repeat, not required."

The agents outside the door turned, nodded, and walked away. They had gotten the message. Other agents inside the glass room remained silent, completely under Ellie's influence.

Witnessing the scene, the president shrieked, "She is in league with Lucifer! She is the devil's whore!"

Treeborne's skin had turned a deep magenta, and he looked like he would explode. His dark, close-set eyes scanned the room for submission, but no one met him. His thin, cruel mouth opened, issuing a command. "Kill them. They're evil. They wish to destroy me. I am the creator of the new world.

Without me, life will not exist. Evil will win. Darkness will spread. Satan will reign. Her kind will destroy us. You saw her power. Kill her now while you still have the chance."

Fury and fear ejected from Treeborne. He had to win. But his men were shaking their heads. Each displayed a look. An expression confined to owners before their pets were put down. Seeing it, Treeborne was incensed.

They didn't trust him. He couldn't persuade them. He couldn't manipulate them.

Oh God, what had happened to his trinity of abilities?

Chapter 81

"That's it! I've had enough!" yelled Ellie, thoroughly riled.

No one in the room really understood the damage the president had caused and was continuing to cause. She'd viewed the president's balance shift. Ninety-eight per cent shift to the dark. So close was he to being totally one hundred per cent evil, she wondered how he could function as a person, let alone run a country.

Everyone turned to stare at Ellie. Even Treeborne ceased his biblical diatribe.

"Can't anyone see this man is completely mad? He's fooled you all. He's the evil one. He wants to start World War III, and right now, he's close to achieving it. By launching those missiles, he's put Earth on a path of self-destruction that will result in the high council in Kudamun obliterating the Earth. For the sake of all life on this planet, he must be stopped. Abort those missiles now!"

Ellie stared at Sam for support. He opened his mouth, but a second too slow. Treeborne jumped right into the gap made by her husband's less than immediate reaction.

"She lies!" screamed the president, gently edging towards the fallen guard. "She is the evil one. I have none of the powers she possesses. Cut me, do I not bleed? I am your Savior. Our new world will be one of peace and hope. Listen to her, and be consumed by darkness."

"We don't have time for this shit!" Ellie shouted, frustrated at how fickle and indecisive humans were. "Can't you see he wants me to fail? He's being controlled by one of the elders. They want to destroy Earth for their own reasons. Hutchinson, you're vice president. You can stop all this madness. He can't continue. Relieve him of his presidential duties and take your stand as a new, sane president. Stop this senseless attack. Ashton has the quantum bomb. All of it. There is no more. Please, Hutchinson, call off the attack. Salim and Sabena are both dead. With them gone, Al Nadir are no longer the threat they used to be. Conventional means will rid the world of Al Nadir. Please believe me, Hutchinson. Save yourself and save the world."

Hutchinson was caught, incredulous and immobile. What should he do?

"And so, like the evil serpent tempted Eve, so she tempts you. And thou shalt seek truth and find only darkness."

More uncoordinated and frenzied had the president's chanting become. He smiled with mad euphoria, his eyes blazing with a fervent hatred.

Ellie could stand it no longer. The president's pious, interminable intonation gnawed at her, provoking an impulsive action more befitting of human Ellie before she was reconstituted.

"Shut…the…fuck up!"

The president, amazed by Ellie's brash audacity, shut up. Using the stunned silence to her advantage, Ellie pressed the device in her hand. At her touch, holographic numbers suddenly appeared and hovered a few inches off the table.

"The numbers here represent a level of balance shift. I can't explain much. It'll take too long. But understand this: the numbers here are counting another act of evil conducted on this planet. Right now, because of this…this fool's actions," she said, indicating to the president, "the shift is accelerating. This is the very same indicator that the elders use to decide whether to obliterate a planet in their care. Earth's on death row. Now do you believe me? Abort those missiles."

Ellie was exhausted, although she knew it was only a phantom feeling, a reminiscent flicker of her human life. Her Kudamaz framework prevented her from ever getting tired.

Hutchinson glared at Ellie, then at the ethereal numbers in front of his face, and then finally back to Ellie again.

"She speaks the truth, sir." Sam fixed eye contact with all the men around the table.

Weitz and Reiner nodded slowly in agreement. Hutchinson knew it was time for him to fulfil his duty. With hope burning inside him, he turned to the control staff at the missile command station.

"Abort all missiles."

The officer, bemused and somewhat terrified by what he'd seen, acknowledged and welcomed the normalness of Hutchinson's soft, confident command.

"Yes, sir," replied the officer. He inputted the abort sequence.

Witnessing the mutiny, Treeborne lurched slyly towards the Secret Service agent who hadn't moved since Sam had so efficiently knocked him to the ground with a sharp hit to his neck. His automatic lay beside his body. It was the one weapon Ellie hadn't disintegrated.

Ellie glanced back at Sam, pleased to have gotten through to the immovable humans. Sam nodded approval, looking at Hutchinson. A second passed in time, and no one watched the president.

The president, the automatic in his hand, rained bullets into the weapons control panel: the heart of command and control for the nuclear missiles.

Forcing their way into the panel, the bullets hit the complex circuitry, shattering it on their impromptu journeys through wires, membranes, and boards. The metal twisted, capacitors crumpled, and the intricate PCBs that made up the panel exploded in a torrent of sparks, smoke and fire. A series of vicious explosions hurled the officer screaming to the floor.

Too late, Ellie whirled around to see the president's manic face jeering at her, in ecstasy at the havoc his actions caused.

"Exalt! Rejoice! The new world is coming, and the meek shall inherit. They shall win against their evil!" shrieked Treeborne, pointing in turn to Ellie, Sam, and finally Hutchinson. "You cannot stop destiny. Let the truth be known, and thy will be done."

Treeborne's insanity, now unshielded, could be seen by all in the room. In utter desperation, knowing his inability to lure any of the observers back under his power, the president lifted the automatic, ready to shoot everyone in his immediate vicinity.

Chapter 82

Ellie stared at the automatic, connected with the atoms, increased their vibrations, and heated the gun. Treeborne's hands reddened as the metal burned deep into his skin. He dropped the weapon, shouting, "Infidels! Disciples of Satan! See how she uses the flames of hell to destroy me!"

Hitting the ground, the gun disintegrated into grey particles and vanished to dust. Without his weapon, Treeborne backed away from Ellie who now advanced upon him.

Thousands of miles away, Aswa-da regarded thoughtfully the empty recess at the base of the Therab. The final ingredient. And he knew where to source it.

Sensing Treeborne's resonance, he focused on the energy pattern and shimmered. Appearing out of thin air, directly in front of Ellie, Aswa-da's presence injected absolute fear into the hearts of all around him. Feelings of a loss of hope and desolation permeated instantly throughout the room. Even Ellie was initially touched, but she recognized and blocked the sensation with her formidable emotional shield.

On seeing Aswa-da, the president fell to his knees. His hand slipped secretly into his pocket. He had to feel it. He had to feel the power resonate to replenish him.

Ellie noticed the president's furtive fumble and sensed the strong Kudamaz resonance emanate from him. Staring at his pocket, Ellie could discern an outline. It was clear Treeborne had taken hold of an object.

Flicking to the side to look at Aswa-da, Ellie tried to check his balance shift, but she couldn't read him at all. He was clearly from Kudamun, and with his shimmer ability, he had to be an elder of the high council.

At an inconceivable speed, impossible for the human eye to track, Aswa-da moved towards the president. Ellie approached Treeborne with equal rapidity.

Aswa-da looked down, sneering, "Arise, my child."

Treeborne rose. Sensing the resonance reverberating from the president, Aswa-da made to grasp at the president. Ellie knew the elder was after whatever the president had in his pocket. The air started to grow denser, an imperceptible sensation for humans to see, but Ellie recognized it as a precursor to the elder shimmering.

In a blink, Ellie shimmered over to the president, her hand sliding safely unnoticed into his pocket. She snatched the item, within a millisecond of Aswa-da and the president disappearing in a swirling dark shadow of glistening ebony particles.

Ellie pulled back and held up the item retrieved. A small, sandstone tablet.

Chapter 83

The leader of Kudamun suffered dejection and remorse. Earth was firmly in the Dark Zone, the Protector still had not activated the Therab, and now he was being summoned to the Great Hall to commence the total obliteration of his beloved planet. By the high council's standards, the Protector had failed, completely. Time had now run out for Earth.

With his head bowed in dismay, Aby-od shimmered into the Great Hall.

All the elders had gathered to witness the dispatch. Except Aswa-da. Aby-od glared at his empty throne, the veil of deception dropping, finally, from his eyes.

What a fool I've been.

Yet again, he'd trusted the Kudamaz protocols. He'd kept faith in the antediluvian laws, only this time, the laws were being manipulated and molded to another design. Aswa-da was responsible for everything that had happened. Aby-od was certain of this, as he was certain that the leader of the opposition was on Earth.

Heads turned towards him and impatient mutters floated through the assembled crowd. His face forced a serenity he did not feel. He nodded, indicating for the procedure of dispatch to commence, and then abruptly shimmered into the Observation Room. He'd barely enough time to bring up the location visuals of the ziggurat in Ur, when the high council guards appeared at the entrance.

"Great Ensi, Lord Aby-od, it is demanded that you return to the Great Hall without further consideration to your current undertaking."

The guards delivered their words of command with brutal respect and honor, but their command didn't stop Aby-od from attempting to home in on the chamber where the Therab was hidden. He moved the dial on the panel to the right, literally zooming in on the visual of the chamber. He could see light coming from deeper inside, just a little bit farther.

"Great Ensi, Lord Aby-od, failure to return on demand to the Great Hall to complete dispatch of Ki will result in your leadership being forfeited and your life extinguished as a saboteur and traitor of the antediluvian laws, under the Order of Kudamun."

The guard's sharp address hit Aby-od. Such irony. To think he could be executed as a traitor. Listening to the coldness of the guard's speech that reflected the icy efficiency of their politics and protocols, Aby-od felt tired. For so very long he'd upheld every law in the book, and what had it gotten him? A masked accusation of him being a traitor. His hand rested over the panel, ready to delve farther into the ziggurat's chamber, and did not move.

Perceiving resistance, the guard charged up his Harmon gun. Aby-od noticed the maneuver. Not wanting to be executed there and then, he removed his hand from the dial. The visuals vanished. Aby-od lowered his head to signify submission. Instantly, the guard halted his charge-up.

Aby-od, flanked by guards on either side, was led out. Denied the right to shimmer, he had to walk like a criminal back to the Great Hall.

Hanging his head, totally crestfallen at being unable to validate his theory of Aswa-da's involvement, Aby-od entered the hall.

The elders glared at him with disgusted, scathing expressions. How dare their leader corrupt the antediluvian laws? How dare their leader shirk away from the responsibility of dispatch? How dare he care for a planet that did not care about its people or its future?

Accusations of traitor fluttered through the elders in clandestine whispers. Whatever the outcome of Earth, it was clear he was dishonored. Maintaining his leadership in Kudamun would prove extremely difficult. Only a significant success would restore the high council's faith and trust in him.

It seemed that indeed now Ellie was his last hope.

Chapter 84

Jonathan D Treeborne stared out from his corner. The same corner he'd not moved from since Aswa-da had deposited him there on returning from the Pentagon. Treeborne didn't know what the thing was his god handled so gleefully, but as he watched the massive blood-red crystal pulsate, Treeborne became incredibly afraid. What did this all mean for his own destiny?

Aswa-da, unaware of Treeborne's descent into fear, had locked his attention on speeding up the Therab to its final stage of activation. Opening the panel underneath the dark-red crystal to expose its inner workings, Aswa-da was straightaway transfixed by the twinkling lights that arced from crystal to crystal making their connections. A slow, nefarious smile slithered across his face; his ancestors had been truly magnificent in designing the Therab using light-based engineering. In certain reverence, he placed his hand cautiously inside the sparking arrays, and with unaccustomed gentility, he changed the position of two crystals. Almost immediately, the massive crystal pulsed brighter. From deep inside the Therab, a low hum also began. Aswa-da nodded, pleased with the reaction, and started to turn one of the crystals he'd changed clockwise by 180 degrees. The low, audible hum rose in loudness, and different harmonies interplayed between the hum. Rapidly, the sound multiplied, shattering the chamber's age-old quietness.

Hunching in the corner, Treeborne shielded his eyes from the blinding, ferocious red light with his arms. Every second that passed, he felt that the light was increasing in intensity. Treeborne could feel the light burn through his skin and his bones. It seared through his eyes like a flame through paper. In parallel, he heard sounds burst forth, weird and strange. And loud, so incredibly loud. Harmonics emanated and formed vibrations that assaulted Treeborne's cells, threatening to crush them under the weight of each obscure, thunderous note.

Treeborne was aware of a piercing pain in his ears and a heavy popping, like his sinuses had exploded. Lifting a finger, Treeborne felt a trickle of blood dripping down each earlobe. The sound, not meant for humans, had perforated his eardrums and the blinding red light was in danger of robbing him of his sight completely.

On the floor, bleeding, shaking, Treeborne curled into a ball, his head deep between his knees and his arms over his head. A pitiful attempt to screen against the pulsating light and cacophonous sound.

It was obvious to Treeborne he should have vacated the chamber as soon as Aswa-da brought him there. Evil was everywhere. He could feel it palpably, rising amongst the sandstone, but like before, all those many decades ago, when he'd been a young boy, he'd been mystified. But even more than that, the darkness he'd been born with had connected instantly at that moment. Holding him captivated.

And now it was too late.

He couldn't move. Huddled tightly in a fetal position, the most powerful man in the world was now reduced to a shattered shell, a mere remnant of the indestructible force of persuasion, manipulation and trust he'd been a few hours before.

Aswa-da continued his work, completely unaffected by the light and sound, his senses able to withstand such an attack.

The halo of black, shining crystals spun so fast, they were but a blur of sparkling light. Underneath, like a heart from some fairytale giant, the red crystal beat in rhythmic time with the strange sounds.

Full of dark joy, Aswa-da raised his arms up in reverence. Ecstatic conviction flooded through him. After an eternity of dual-house policy, Kudamun would face a step change, and the high council would acknowledge that the House of Etima was the *only* house left to rule.

Chapter 85

Confounded faces inhabited the empty space where the president had been.

"Where did he go?"

"How did he disappear?"

"Who was that tall guy?"

Questions streamed from their trembling mouths and heads turned to Ellie for answers. Far from being the font of all knowledge they expected, Ellie unfortunately, was just as dumbfounded as the mortals that surrounded her. Helping the officer who'd been caught in the explosion recover with unnatural haste, Ellie responded to all the questions in a single delivery.

"I don't know what's going on." She pointed to the sandstone tablet she'd placed on the glass table and added, "But maybe that will reveal the truth."

Eyes gazed. The small rectangular tablet looked innocuous, but Ellie detected a strong, dark energy pouring from it. Staring at it, Sam was intrigued. "What is it?"

Ellie shook her head. All her inherent Kudamaz knowledge didn't tell her anything. She could only feel the resonance coming from the tablet, but she couldn't identify how the resonance had originated.

Reiner moved in to look at the tablet. "Is that what the president had?"

Weitz stared at the sandstone rectangle, contemplative, and an idea formed amongst memories of the unbelievable he'd been a spectator to. "Maybe that thing was how he fooled us." Weitz had no idea just how perceptively astute he really was.

At that moment, as if to signify what was at stake, the control panel behind Hutchinson crackled and spat sparks. Ellie looked around at the mess of burning wires and open circuitry. The president's blast had completely ruined the command and control unit.

Hutchinson followed suit, shaking his head. "Thank God the abort sequence got through."

Ellie's eyes lifted upwards to the missile display screen. Just a few minutes before she'd seen nothing, no missile blips or trajectories. But in a perverse reversal of fortune, the screen flickered, suddenly displaying all fourteen missiles, and the blocks were continuing to advance.

"Fuck!" Ellie's curse forced heads in her direction. "It must have been a malfunction."

Distraught and numb with terror, all looked at the screen. Other blocks had now appeared originating from China, Pakistan, Iran, and North Korea. The retaliatory strikes. They had been launched in response to the president's unprovoked attack. The path of self-destruction. Earth was following the rocky road to complete oblivion.

Ellie straightened and addressed her husband calmly.

"Sam, you've got to tell them the launch was an accident. You and Hutchinson are going to have to play the diplomatic card and buy me time to repair this panel."

Sam couldn't understand why Ellie didn't use her powers to blast the missiles from the skies. Making that suggestion, Ellie spun round. Sorrow flickered in her beautiful eyes.

"Maybe one or even two, but they're not like bullets or guns. They're extremely complex constructions, and it would take time. Too much time. We've got half an hour before simultaneous impact on all fourteen targets. The only chance we have is the control panel."

Ellie noticed that all four men were looking at her with frightened, baffled expressions. Hutchinson panicked. If this wonderful woman couldn't stop the missiles, what hope was there for the world?

"Are we going to die?" Hutchinson asked Ellie quietly, brave enough to speak the words all around him were thinking.

Ellie smiled and placed a comforting hand on top of Hutchinson. She stared into his scared eyes. "We are not going to die!"

Ellie's soft voice enraptured Hutchinson. He felt a quiet calm wash over him, and his panic vanished.

"But I do need the two of you to get on that line and start talking to the owners of those things." Ellie pointed to the new blips on the screen heading towards the US.

"We've got some bilateral communications to do. Come on, Hutchinson," said Sam. Then he caught himself and blushed, recognizing the man he'd so flippantly addressed was now the US President. "Excuse me, Mr. President, sir, but we have some rabbits to pull out of some very diplomatic hats. Please, let's hurry."

Hutchinson smiled broadly as he heard Sam address him as 'Mr. President'. He stood, intoxicated, basking in the moment, until Ellie's powerful voice scythed through his personal adulation.

"Hutchinson, start talking to them now. Otherwise, your position in office will be shortest ever!"

Chapter 86

Ellie's directness spurred Hutchinson into action. Taking the telephone abruptly, he requested connection with the president of China. Sam grabbed another phone and followed suit, requesting to be put through to the prime minister of Pakistan. As the leaders were called, and state protocols rapidly acknowledged, Sam and President Hutchinson dived into their simultaneous explanations as to why the US had launched nuclear missiles against their countries. Sam agreed quickly with Hutchinson that the story would be "a powerful artificial intelligence virus infiltrated the DoD computer, causing the computer to believe the US was being attacked, and thus it took the appropriate action with the missile launch." They couldn't tell them the president had gone postal!

While her husband worked his diplomatic magic, Ellie worked her own brand of supernatural trickery. Concentrating all her energies on repairing the weapons unit, onlookers watched as wires miraculously melded their severed connections. Circuitry, membranes, and boards straightened and smoothed from their once twisted structures. Chips, resistors, and transistors pulled back into position. Piece by piece, the incremental rebuilding of the unit took place.

Members of the Pentagon staff stopped working. With imminent annihilation from all sides, work seemed fruitless and immaterial. They crowded around Ellie and gazed with awe and baffled disorientation as she used her reconstructive powers at lightning speed. From darkened nooks inside the unit, lights started to flicker and glow. The buckled and blackened keyboard pushed outward, flattening, and pulled back into its original functional design.

Gradually, the control screen bubbled back to life in recognition of the weapons control unit coming back on line.

"We're back in business!" yelled Ellie across the room to Sam and Hutchinson. They raised a thumbs-up and turned back to their deep, placating discussions with world leaders.

A man in a navy suit pushed forward in front of the crowd.

"I've got the abort sequence."

He took his place at the restored control unit. With confidence, he typed in at speed the abort sequence for each missile. Unlike before when the launch codes were transmitted, set, and locked for concurrent deployment, the officer aborted each missile on successful transmission of the code. On receiving the abort sequence, the flickering oblongs on screen blinked out. In turn, the other oblongs with their lethal trajectories also started to wink out.

Smiling Sam revolved in his chair, speaking rapidly in Russian. Stunned, Ellie smiled back. Another revelation. She never knew Sam spoke Russian!

Hutchinson finished delivering his abject apologies and Sam finalized his conversation. In unison, both men breathed out, their fragile human energies totally spent.

The clock showed Ellie had exhausted twenty-nine minutes and forty-five seconds. A minute longer would have been a minute too late. The scared but relieved faces told her that this was over.

Only she knew it wasn't.

Chapter 87

Who was that Kudamun elder? Why did he take the president?

Ellie looked at the tablet she'd left on the table. Picking it up, an unmistakable power surged from it. What was it? Ellie was frustrated. She couldn't even read the inscription on it. Turning it over in her hand, a chill ran through her. A residue of pure darkness remained in the sandstone, jolting Ellie back to her primary mission. Looking at the numbers on the floating display, Ellie could see that although the speed of acceleration had been quelled, the numbers still were increasing. She had to activate the Therab quickly and reverse the balance shift.

Ellie looked at the people bustling around the room. Innocent people. Submersed in their daily lives. Their loves, their hates. Everything they were would cease to exist if she failed. She had a duty to her people and the place she had called home for six thousand years.

Thrusting the tablet into Sam's hand, she announced to the fearful but incredibly grateful throng she had to leave to prevent Earth from being destroyed. Sam visibly gulped down his anxiety. So cold, so clear were Ellie's words of mankind's extinction, that although he knew much more than others in the room, the blatant facts came no less devastating to him. Encasing his hand around the small sandstone tablet, he stuffed it into his jacket.

Following their surreal routine, Sam placed his arms around Ellie's waist and waited for the shimmer.

"We're going to Ur in Iraq. It was the birthplace of civilization and it is the secret resting place for the one thing that can bring this planet back to equilibrium."

"In Iraq?" questioned Hutchinson, amazed. "So it's not just about the oil. No wonder everyone wanted to get their hands on that country."

"Yes, the Therab affects humans."

"What in God's name is a Therab?" asked Hutchinson, deeply worried that there was a weapon of great power stuck in center of the renowned axis of evil.

Ellie stared at the floating numbers, increasing slowly but still increasing. The time for words, for discussion, was over.

"Mr. President, we've got to go."

But Hutchinson was insistent, refusing to let the matter rest. As President, he had a right to know everything. Ellie understood his doggedness, but she couldn't satisfy him with full discourse.

"The Therab will decide this planet's fate. It is a power beyond your comprehension. I can't say anymore, sir."

"Is it why so many wars have been fought there?" Weitz's perceptive streak once more taking hold.

Ellie nodded. "For humans, the lure to be with the Therab is great. Unfortunately, it has been the source of continual conflict in the region over the ages."

Ellie gripped Sam tightly and thought of the ziggurat in Ur, just as Abyod had told her. The pull of the Therab was unbelievable. Ellie could almost see the chamber materializing around her, even though she was still in the bowels of the Pentagon. She watched as the dusty sandstone walls interlaced with the stark glass and metal in a visual fusion of two places, pure quantum entanglement. Two locations in space at the same time. Ellie knew what she was witnessing was for her eyes only. No one in the room had the visual range to decipher the slight rip in the field of reality. They would never see the world so fluid and fluctuating as she could.

It was definitely time to go. Ellie told President Hutchinson this. He read the eagerness in her eyes. He touched her shoulder.

"Good luck, sweet stuff."

Ellie raised her eyebrows, hearing the new president's unexpected term of endearment.

"Don't worry, Mr. President. We won't let you or the rest of the people on Earth down."

Hutchinson flushed again, hearing the 'Mr. President' title.

"You know you're going to have to get used to it," added Ellie.

Hutchinson smiled, nodding, realizing that his own destiny was being fulfilled.

Whispering to Sam to get ready and close his eyes, Ellie submitted to the pull of the Therab, and the Pentagon's clinical, cold interior overwrote with sandstone and blasting heat.

Chapter 88

Aswa-da slipped his hands into his robes and removed a small device. Just above his palm, numbers formed in the air. The countdown to Earth's obliteration had started. He thought about Aby-od, backed into a corner, on pain of death, forced to commit his precious little planet to total oblivion. Aswa-da sneaked a smile as he wondered whether Aby-od had discovered the truth behind his involvement. He remembered how pathetically bureaucratic Aby-od had been. Blinkered by protocol. Blinded by politics. No, Aby-od would have reasoned that no accusation could be drawn against him, as so little, if any, evidence existed. Only when Aby-od had gone to the Great Hall would he have known that his absence at the proceedings held a deeper meaning. Then, at that moment, Aby-od would have comprehended the full impact of Aswa-da's actions and what they intimated for Earth, the universe, even Kudamun.

Aby-od's impotence at the situation facing him would have been a joy to behold. Aswa-da was disappointed that his timeframe did not permit a shimmer to Kudamun to watch Aby-od's squirming inadequacy and discomfort at facing such untenable odds, but his involvement in speeding up the Therab's activation had to be aligned precisely with Earth's dispatch.

The chamber, ablaze with dazzling, cardinal light, reverberated with shocking sound. The walls seemed to vibrate with the paralyzing harmonics bursting from the Therab.

Aswa-da flicked from watching the counter to the sparkling halo of ebony. Trepidation hit him unexpectedly. Like an impatient human waiting in a queue, he tapped his foot and muttered, "Come on," under his breath.

Considering the consequences of the activation malfunctioning, fleeting panic flashed through him and he shuddered. Unaware of his ominous thoughts, the ebony halo encircling the pulsating, angry, red heart of crystal continued upward to the zenith point.

Chapter 89

A massive holographic Earth floated in the Great Hall. The swirling clouds, the continents of green, and the deep oceans of blue. For an observer from afar, it looked to be one of the most peaceful planets in the universe. Such a great shame that its appearance did not match its performance, mused Aby-od desolately. And he looked down at the crystal he was expected to turn, to release the supercharged harmonic energy wave that would instantly obliterate the once beautiful planet.

The speaker pronounced Earth's sentence. Listening to the words, Aby-od shook his head in utter dismay.

"Great Ensi, Lord Aby-od, leader of Kudamun and head of the House of Giznu, under the order of Kudamun, you have the right and the power to dispatch Ki for the persistent breach of all antediluvian laws, and explicitly for Ki's latest action. It has placed itself on a path of self-destruction, making Ki, the Earth, a direct threat to all the other planets in its immediate vicinity."

Heads turned to stare at Aby-od. Elders from the House of Etima, pleased to see the opposition failing at last, sneered at Aby-od's obvious distress. Elders from the House of Giznu, ashamed and annoyed at the inadequate results delivered by their leader, glared at Aby-od.

"Please, Great Ensi, initiate the dispatch of Ki now," instructed the speaker with determined coldness.

Aby-od's hand rested on the crystal. With a slight sob in his voice, Aby-od delivered his dispatch address.

"Great members of the high council, we have assembled to witness the summary dispatch of Ki. As you are aware, I have already made my feelings towards this dispatch clear to you. I believe that unseen forces have played a significant role in placing Ki, the Earth, on its current fatal path, and I believe that dispatching the Earth is part of a greater plan. However, under antediluvian law, I have no evidence and thus, will not be placing accusations on any party. But hear this, honorable members. Faith in the Protector has not been upheld, and this action of dispatch is another example of our failure to really believe in the antediluvian laws that we so frequently use as justification to employ remedies against ourselves and the planets in our care. I will undertake dispatch, but I want it noted that I do so under duress. I still believe in the Protector. And I also believe that this high council has been manipulated to arrive at the conclusion I will soon be making." Aby-od stopped to take a breath. "Under the order of Kudamun, with honor, I hereby dispatch Ki, the Earth."

His words had pounded with raw, naked emotion. He didn't care anymore. They had to be told. A travesty of justice was being committed. As leader of Kudamun, it was Aby-od's duty to communicate this to the high council, whether they believed him or not.

Depressing the crystal, tears formed in his large black eyes, and slowly he turned the crystal to activate the lethal Harmon wave.

Chapter 90

In the cavern, Aswa-da looked on anxiously, willing the process forward. The Therab must have picked up on Aswa-da's anxiety, for in response the spinning particles connected with the crimson crystal's summit. Instantly, the blazing light and shattering sound stopped. For what seemed a second or two, all the light in the chamber sucked back into the crystal's core, sinking the dusty, ancient cavern into dark silence.

Aswa-da held his breath in the darkness. The only illumination was the countdown display floating before him, flaunting Earth's obliteration, a mere five seconds from that moment.

A tightness gripped Aswa-da's throat, as the display dropped to four and then to three. Feeling that maybe he'd undertaken the activation incorrectly, Aswa-da considered shimmering.

Then from deep inside the crystal surged a burst of such energy that could, if the Therab so wished, create a new world. The energy pulsed through the crystal's pinnacle point and shot forth a blinding red light. The halo of dark particles, now engulfed within the energy pulse, flowed into the red light and sparkled within its rays. The red light flooded upwards and disappeared straight through the skylight at the top of the ziggurat.

With considerable relief, Aswa-da shimmered outside to observe the effect of the red light. Tilting his head, he watched the light pour from the ziggurat like airborne lava from a volcano, turning the majestic, star-encrusted sky incandescent red. Aswa-da smiled. He was safe. Earth was safe, now cushioned by the Therab's force field that encircled the planet. A twinkling, ruby ring of protective particles, the trillions upon trillions of minute shields would serve as a buffer to whatever Kudamun was going to throw at Earth.

Shimmering back into the chamber, he glanced at Treeborne huddled in the corner, eyes shut, bleeding, shivering, and deeply terrified. He'd turned his body into a tight ball.

"Pathetic human!" muttered Aswa-da. Antipathy soaked his tongue and he continued to activate the second stage.

Chapter 91

Aby-od turned the crystal and watched the globe. Turning the crystal opened up the momentary rip in space-time. The Reality Gap that was always in existence and had been created by Kudamun was there to keep a minimum gap of one degree between the physical universe and Kudamun. Through the rip, Earth and Kudamun were aligned on the same plane for a mere nanosecond. To an onlooker in space, the harmonic energy wave would literally have leapt out of space, seemingly from nowhere.

Aby-od stared as the wave hit the Earth. He lowered his head. All the high council elders rose to their feet, dropped their heads down, and closed their eyes, feigning respect for the deceased planet.

The wave enveloped Earth completely. Aby-od waited for the shatter.

He imagined the people. They would feel nothing. Death would be painless and instantaneous. He thought of Ellie. She would be aware of the blast wave resonance but would be unable to escape. She would die with the humans she'd failed to protect. The blast would be immediate. Unlike the self-destruction of a nuclear world war, which would affect Earth's neighbors, the Harmon wave gave planetary annihilation that was both immediate and contained.

Aby-od raised his eyes upwards. Expecting to see nothingness, just space, he braced himself, and then almost fell to the floor in shock.

Earth was still there, floating peacefully in space. But instead of the greens, blues, and swirling clouds, a red, sparkling aura encased the Earth.

The Therab had been activated. It had sucked up the Harmon wave blast giving it the energy it needed to initiate its full chain-reaction capability. Without energy from Earth's dispatch, the Therab would not have possessed the requisite power to do what its creators had so unwittingly intended. Aby-od shivered as he stared, looking at the Earth. Planetary protection was the Therab's initial stage, and what followed would bring Kudamun and the universe to its knees. Ellie had neither the knowledge nor the understanding to activate planetary protection. But...He stared at the empty throne to the left of him. Aswa-da did. He would use the Therab to bring a reign of evil and darkness.

The elders stirred, gasping, and shook their heads, angry at Earth's miraculous survival. With a united tone of acrimonious incrimination, the elders shouted at Aby-od.

"What is the meaning of this treachery? How can Ki still be there? Lord Aby-od, provide your explanation now!"

The anger in their voices suggested that they wanted to continue with some form of execution, and that form could well be Aby-od. Lifting his hands up, palms vertical, he began to pat the air. The gesture quietened the hostile intonations of the elders. Assuming Aby-od would lie, they waited to hear him falsify events. The act of perjury was death by Harmon wave. The high council would *still* have their execution.

The speaker turned to Aby-od.

"Great Ensi, Lord Aby-od, the high council craves your indulgence to explain the events we are now witnessing."

Looking around the Great Hall, Aby-od wondered how many were complicit in Aswa-da's actions. Or was Aswa-da a rogue faction working alone? The truth had been buried for too long. He would not procrastinate further.

The time for truth was now.

Chapter 92

"Honorable members of the high council, Lord Aswa-da, head of the House of Etima, is not here. Surely, on such an important occasion as dispatch, the leader of the opposition should be here. Why is he not?"

Pointing his slender finger towards Aswa-da's throne, his voice boomed, powerful and confident. Elders turned to stare at the empty throne and Aby-od continued with renewed vengeance.

"Lord Aswa-da has fooled the high council. He has deceived us all. He has manipulated our antediluvian laws in his favor."

Ripples of dissension undulated through the high council members, but no one came forth to repudiate his forthright accusations.

"Lord Aswa-da discovered something, a device of immeasurable power, and he plans to use the device against Kudamun and possibly the entire universe."

"What is this device?" shouted Temenos, the deputy leader of the House of Etima, mortified that Lord Aswa-da had engaged in actions unbeknown to their house.

"Where is this device?" called Kurkur, another of Etima's elders.

Suddenly, the high council was awash with voices screaming questions, their vitriol made visible by the unexpected discovery of another's deceit and treachery.

Aby-od anticipated their reactions. With strength afforded by a tenacious determination for right to succeed, he continued his announcement of truth.

"The device is called the Therab. It was made by my ancestors. When the true power of the Therab was realized, the creators knew it couldn't remain on Kudamun, for fear that the power would be abused. They banished the Therab to Ki, the Earth. At the time, Ki as a planet was in its early formation.

Nothing existed. A dimensional lapse field protected the Therab and ensured its existence would remain a secret. Later it was time locked at six thousand Earth years, so it could never be accessed."

Aby-od stopped talking. The hall was silent. Not a whisper. Not a comment. Nothing. The high council was in shock. They were staggered by Aby-od's address. Paralyzed by the thought of a powerful weapon on such a primitive planet. Outraged that they had been for so long shielded from the truth.

"From the red aura we see encircling Earth, it's apparent that the Therab has been activated. When the Harmon wave hit Earth, the aura of Therab, absorbed the energy and channeled it back into its central power unit, boosting its capability."

The high council issued whispers of disbelief. Aby-od continued, unabated in his delivery of the truth.

"The absence of Aswa-da to these proceedings indicates his implicit involvement in this action. Before I was forced to undertake dispatch, I located his Kudamaz presence on Earth, but I was prevented from identifying his exact location. Had I been permitted to pinpoint Lord Aswa-da's location, I would have instructed the high council to extract him. The Therab's protective shield now prevents such an action. The aura is an impenetrable force field that protects Earth from any external hostility. Earth is now isolated from Kudamun. We can no longer shimmer to anywhere on Earth, nor can we locate and view anyone on the planet." Aby-od motioned to the hologram. "This is our only observation ability. We can see nothing else."

Aby-od noticed movement as heads flicked from side to side, talking to one another. Their fidgeting and interrupting nature had returned. Only Temenos was pensive. Listening to Aby-od's words, he called out asking the question Aby-od had feared.

"How powerful is this Therab? And why should our great Lord Aswa-da have interest in it?"

The Great Hall dropped to a mere hush again. The cavernous room reverberated with each rustle of a robe, each shuffle of a foot. They waited breathlessly, staring back and forth from Temenos to Aby-od like a surreal tennis match. Temenos tensed his muscular frame as he stood patiently. Aby-od squared his shoulders and breathed in. The high council had to know everything.

"Honorable members, Lord Temenos, I thank you for asking the question. With the accumulated power of both its own energy source and the Harmon wave energy delivered at the point of dispatch, the power of the Therab is immense. Reaching far beyond the confines of Earth. Once fully activated, the Therab's effect will be felt by every planet in the entire universe. To put it simply, the Therab is a multiplier and copier. The level of balance shift on Earth is taken as a base line and this is then multiplied. This will happen only after planetary protection has been instigated. Once Earth is totally absorbed in a massive level of balance shift to either the dark or light, the Therab will take Earth as the original and will copy its level of balance shift throughout the universe. Each planet's balance shift will change immediately to match the exact level of balance shift on Earth. The universe will be plunged into total chaos and confusion. With due respect to the honorable members of the House of Etima, I think it safe to assume that Lord Aswa-da does not intend to activate a balance shift to the light."

Viewing the reaction of his house and the opposition, he paused, giving them time to understand the revelation. They were horror-struck. Every elder knew the result of such an action. The universe would descend into utter darkness. Kudamun would no longer have the balance of light and dark. The House of Giznu would be removed. The House of Etima would reign for a short while, until the Ancient Ones learned of the corruption. The Ancient Ones would cleanse the universe of evil completely and Kudamun would cease to exist. All that the Ancient Ones had given them would be wiped out. Because of Aswa-da's insanely egotistical power plan for total and ultimate domination.

The high council members rose to their feet, screaming for Aswa-da's execution.

Aby-od quelled their blood lust. In a solemn, spiritual voice, he stated that not all was lost.

"Great members, through this abyss of darkness, there is still light. Our only remedy is the Protector. Let us come together with a collected conviction that the Protector will win. We failed the Protector before by not believing in her. Let us not make that mistake again. Believe in her and hold hope in your hearts. And trust in the hope that the balance on Earth will be restored."

Aby-od sat down, exhausted and shaking, but as he looked into the eyes of his fellow members, he saw conviction, he saw belief, and most of all, he saw hope. His words had stirred them. Impassioned them. Forced them to feel, perhaps, for the first time. Aby-od prayed that it was not too late for them. Or for Earth.

Chapter 93

Dry heat hit them coming out of shimmer. Sam repressed a cough as the dust in the ageless corridor lingered uncomfortably in his lungs. Ellie moved quickly. At the end of the corridor, a flickering red light radiated. She'd felt the Therab's resonance even in the Pentagon glass room. A strange sensation, different from other energy patterns. She could sense the Therab's resonance arching across the world.

Ellie looked down the corridor. Deep inside her Kudamaz brain, Ellie knew the Therab had been activated. This was the work of high council elders. Probably, the elder that had taken the president. She had to speak with Aby-od about this. Her responsibility was protection; his was politics. He had to be informed.

"I've got to go."

Sam stared at Ellie on hearing her unexpected announcement. "Go! Where? We've just arrived?"

"I've got to see Aby-od. I won't be long." Ellie was making it sound like she was popping off to the shops for a pint of milk.

Sam tried to say that leaving him in an unknown and potentially hostile place was not a loving act, but Ellie's kiss swallowed up his words.

"I'll be back in a blink. Anyway, you can take care of yourself, can't you?"

Sam started to say, "Yes, in normal circumstances." But Ellie had shimmered, her mind focused on the Hall of Umray in Kudamun.

Watching her shimmer, Sam shrugged, accepting that he couldn't tell Ellie anything, and sat down on the hot sandstone floor to wait on her return.

The air slipped and slid, glistened and sparkled, and Ellie materialized, but not slowly, gently as usual. This time, a painful jolt shoved her hard into the wall opposite. Jumping up, feeling the need to protect her, Sam held her in his arms.

"That was quicker than I thought."

"Sam, I didn't. I couldn't." Ellie pulled away from her husband and walked farther down the dusty corridor.

Sam was mystified. "I thought you could shimmer anywhere."

Ellie looked back irritably at Sam. Just for that second, she wished he had all the knowledge she possessed.

"I can. But I couldn't get to Kudamun. I couldn't slip through the Reality Gap. I couldn't leave the planet."

Sam had been just about ok about shimmering from country to country, but this 'Reality Gap' and 'couldn't leave the planet' talk confused him. It made him feel quite alone, a mere flicker of an outline of a shadow in the presence of Ellie's towering omnipotence.

"You travel to other planets?" He knew he would never fully comprehend his new, improved Ellie.

"Yes. How the hell do you think I returned?" Her once intelligent husband now sounded rather dumb.

"I don't know. Flying saucer or something." Sam's voice trailed off with embarrassment as he looked at Ellie's amazed face.

"A flying saucer! Please, Sam. What do you think?"

Ellie was aware that she was many millennia ahead of Sam in her knowledge and her perspective of the universe. She hadn't wanted to sound so demeaning to Sam, but her annoyance at not being able to shimmer and get to Aby-od had made her worried and somewhat irascible. And at that moment, she felt a little hacked off by the fact her husband was totally ignorant to her plight.

Flushing red with humiliation, Sam turned his face away. He'd always been the clever one. Now he couldn't even hope to match the power in her little finger. She was eons ahead. God, he felt so inadequate, so stupid. But most of all, he felt so hurt.

Ellie knew what she'd done. Moving forward, she tried to touch him, but Sam shrugged her away. She stared at him, her gorgeous eyes flashing inhumanly bright, like a photographer's light was shining directly at her.

"I didn't mean to hurt you. I'm sorry. It's just if I can't get to Kudamun, I'm lost. I need to get Aby-od's advice. You see, Sam, I don't know it all. Right now, I'm struggling. I don't understand this Therab. I don't know why an elder's involved. I'm not the supreme one. I'm out of my depth. I need Aby-od's help. But I can't even contact him. Earth is depending upon me. How am I going to do it? How am I going to get through this? I'm on my own."

Ellie's powerful eyes filled with tears. Fear crept across her beautiful face. Sam could see shadows of his old Ellie, all her insecurities, her frailties. He grabbed her passionately.

"You're not on your own. You've got me. I may not have your powers, but I know a thing or two about taking out bad guys. What are we waiting for?"

Sam's face was taut with determination. Ellie nodded, her strength regained.

They made their way softly down the remainder of the corridor.

Chapter 94

The panel underneath a jet-black crystal on the Therab had been exposed. Inky shimmering lights arced from dark crystals inside the Therab's base unit to make their light connections. A menacing power throbbed. It was as though the unit could only just contain the evil that taunted it, spurred it on to make that eventual release.

Aswa-da moved the inner dark crystals from one place to another. Two crystals the size of tennis balls, one black and one white, embedded into the middle of the control panel on the outside of the base unit started to react to Aswa-da's maneuvers. Gradually, the black crystal began to glow with powerful, pernicious energies, whilst the white crystal dimmed, its iridescent light becoming nothing more than a pale rock.

Turning around, Aswa-da shouted irritably for the tablet. President Treeborne, still curled in a tight ball, opened his eyes cautiously and squinted. With a slight pressure pop, he pulled his hands from his bloody ears.

"Didn't you hear me, you contemptible creature? Give me the tablet!"

Aswa-da's pleasant peacefulness had vanished. A disturbed scowl replaced his usually smiling features. His previously kind eyes now burned with ingrained hatred. Treeborne believed he was looking at Satan himself. He cowered into the corner, deeply confused and totally terrified.

Approaching Treeborne, Aswa-da loomed up like a Colossus over him, intimidating and threatening. Treeborne shied farther away, his back pressing painfully against the solid sandstone wall. He felt the rough, broken sandstone spike into him. He dearly wanted to dissolve into the wall. He wanted to get away from the villainous vision that had taken over his wonderful god.

"Did you hear me?" repeated Aswa-da, his anger at being ignored pouring from him like visual vitriol. "Give me the tablet now!"

Aswa-da's voice boomed around the chamber. Treeborne shook, his whole body petrified. Where was his god? What had happened to him? Who was this person?

Aswa-da bent down and picked Treeborne up by his jacket collar. The president shut his eyes, not wanting to look upon the evil image that had possessed his god. Aswa-da shook him like a rag doll.

"Give me the tablet!" screamed Aswa-da.

Treeborne fumbled in his pocket, pressing his fingers against the cloth, searching for the tablet amongst the folds of his expensive suit. But his search was in vain. The tablet was not there. Realization grew on his face. Aswa-da read his mind.

"You haven't got it, have you?" He threw Treeborne viciously to the sand-filled floor.

In his disoriented state, Treeborne hadn't noticed the absence of the tablet. He had been too scared to register anything. Somehow, it must have fallen out. But he didn't really know.

Treeborne looked up at the dark, ominous figure above him and shook his head pathetically.

Aswa-da screamed with inhuman rage. "Where is it?"

Treeborne pushed his mind back. He was holding it in the Pentagon. Just before his god arrived. He struggled to remember. There was a feeling…a hand. He forced his mind to recall that moment. There was something. Treeborne closed his eyes and tried again. The girl, she shimmered. He remembered that. Seconds before they left. What else? What else? That feeling…a hand, her hand, in his pocket. A sense of emptiness, that something had been removed. All the pieces slotted into place, and the memory flooded back, playing with clarity in Treeborne's mind.

"The girl. The girl has it!" shouted Treeborne, praying that his god would return. Aswa-da's face darkened further, if that were possible, and he gripped the president's arm savagely.

"What girl?" he snarled.

"The girl at the Pentagon. She moved like you."

Aswa-da regarded the president with malicious contempt.

"The Protector!" Slipping his hand inside his robe, he nodded. "The Protector has the tablet." He withdrew a small oval device. He pointed it at Treeborne.

"If the Protector has it, I've no use further use for you." Aswa-da pressed the device with a force. Treeborne's eyes widened. The device the creature held was a weapon. His god was getting ready to kill him. Remnants of courage returned.

"What about my destiny?" Treeborne screamed. "What about my leadership? You told me I would reign over the world. You gave me the quantum bomb to eradicate evil."

"Yes, I gave you the quantum bomb, but you couldn't keep your big mouth shut. That whore took it from under your very nose. I could have intervened. But why stop a good party? I let events take their own course. As it happened that Al Douri human had more sense than you."

Treeborne couldn't believe what he was hearing. Tears filled in Treeborne's eyes. His fury flowed at Aswa-da's vicious deceit.

"You told me I would be Earth's savior!" Treeborne shouted hysterically, and he stared with blame-filled eyes at Aswa-da. He was aggrieved. He'd been lied to, manipulated and played like a pawn. And now he was to die. For what? What was it really all about?

"I am the new Messiah. I will lead my people to a brave, new world. I am ruler over them, now and forever more."

The president's imp features quivered. He tried so hard to believe in the words he was reciting. But his conviction was waning.

Aswa-da laughed with malevolent relish. The pathetic human actually believed he was the chosen one.

"You? Rule the world! You can't even rule your life. I've been ruling you since you were a child. Everything you've said, done, and felt was because I wanted you to. And now I want you to die."

Shivering with ire, Treeborne looked at Aswa-da's evil, laughing face. He felt violated. He felt abused. His life had been a lie. His destiny, a misapprehension. And for what? What had it all been for? Why had this creature betrayed him?

"Tell me why!" yelled Treeborne, his pent-up fury pelting out with his pain at Aswa-da's monstrous deception.

"You do not need to know."

Aswa-da's voice was not shouting nor threatening. But the inference couched within the words was that Treeborne's life had been for absolutely nothing except Aswa-da's own pleasure. And now he would die without further knowledge as to why. It was the cruelest delivery Aswa-da could possibly have given.

A hot, uncomfortable tingling, rather like pins and needles, ran through his body. Treeborne looked down and saw with horror that his body was fading out. He pleaded for Aswa-da to stop. Smiling Aswa-da circled the president, who was paling by the second.

"You were prepared to kill millions of innocent lives to remove Al Nadir. Why should you care about one person?"

Panic-stricken, knowing he was dying, Treeborne fell to his knees, begging, his dignity lost back at the Pentagon.

"Please, Lord Aswa-da, allow me to stand at your side. I will be your faithful servant. Whatever you want, I shall give."

Jonathan D Treeborne, the former president of the USA and one of the most powerful men on Earth, groveled pitifully. His attempts to negotiate the halt of his demise were greeted with disgust and revulsion.

"You had the powers that I invested in you as a child. Powers that enabled you to change the minds of others, to manipulate and persuade people, and for them to have absolute trust in you. You could have used this gift I gave you to make the world a better place, to bring peace in places of constant war and conflict. But you didn't, as I knew you wouldn't. Right from a child, I could see what darkness lurked in you. Once you became of an age to acknowledge the full meaning of what your powers could bring you, those powers were used by you to abuse others. Innocents who trusted you became tools to be used in your selfish, depraved, and cruel world. You brutalized and dominated those beneath you with absolute impunity. Someone who could deliver such suffering to others is not a savior of them. You are not the Messiah. You are nothing. In fact, you are less than nothing. You are a pathetic excuse for a human. And you deserve to die."

Treeborne glared at his god through fading, sad, and pained eyes, as the Harmon wave coursed through him, blasting every atom in his body.

"I thought I would reign by the side of my god." The president sobbed.

"And so you shall!"

Pressing the device with vehemence, Aswa-da watched impassively as Treeborne screamed in abject pain. The Harmon wave tore at his cells, its unrelenting frequency literally ripping his molecular structure apart. Treeborne's form was but a shadow, vibrating with a vicious velocity.

Opening his mouth, Treeborne shrieked, "I hate you!"

In response, the Harmon wave reached its lethal pitch, shattering Treeborne into floating particles that evaporated in the searing heat.

Without a shred of emotion at what he'd done, Aswa-da turned back to the Therab.

Aswa-da's body vibrated slightly, sensing another Kudamaz resonance nearby. He shut his eyes, looked in his mind, and rapidly pinpointed the resonance's location. Opening them again, Aswa-da stared down the dark corridor. The Kudamaz resonance was approaching slowly. He smirked and moved to the antechamber at the side. Hidden from the entrance, he waited patiently for the other Kudamaz to arrive.

Chapter 95

Reaching the end of the corridor, the red light Sam and Ellie could see from the top of the corridor now burned fiercely in front of them. Ellie scanned the chamber for the president. She was sure she'd heard a scream, but no one was there. She detected a faint resonance of something, but she couldn't locate it exactly. It could have been Kudamaz or human. Or even a side effect of the Therab. In truth, she couldn't be sure.

Ellie approached with certain stealth into the heart of the chamber, for she still sensed a presence nearby. She signaled to Sam to be aware and alert. He acknowledged her advice, withdrew the Glock he'd taken from one of the Secret Service agents back at the Pentagon, and ran along the sandstone wall. Ellie raised her eyebrow as Sam turned around to her.

"What?" he mouthed.

She shook her head. Despite her 'new ability', Sam still took the lead. He couldn't help it. Some things Ellie knew would never change.

Ellie followed Sam inside the chamber. She found the Therab at the very end. She looked at it quizzically. Somehow in her mind, she'd imagined the Therab to be an immense structure, towering and magnificent. The squatty, modest-looking unit did not carry the presence to be titled 'a weapon of immeasurable power'.

She wondered whether Aby-od's intelligence had been accurate. Tentatively, she moved towards the Therab, her fingers brushing lightly its smooth translucent sides. Walking around the Therab, she noticed the empty recess. Reading the Kudamaz inscription above the recess, she knew it held a cobalt-blue crystal that, when in place, would set off the chain reaction of balance shift throughout the universe. Reading this, Ellie knew that this unassuming device was most definitely the Therab.

Looking over her shoulder, she beckoned Sam who was surveilling the rest of the chamber. He walked briskly towards her.

"Show me the tablet," Ellie whispered hurriedly.

Sam withdrew the small sandstone artefact from inside his pocket. Ellie held it, and the unmistakable power at its center reached out to her. Closing her eyes, she connected with the sandstone atoms that gave the tablet its form.

Sam watched on, stunned, whilst Ellie used her powers of atomic deconstruction to nibble away at the sandstone like a termite eating wood. Only Ellie wasn't demolishing, she was revealing. With each second that passed, the tablet got smaller and smaller. Suddenly, resistance started to kick in from all sides of the sandstone. Ellie worked, like a child painstakingly cutting out a cartoon from a book, and through her mind, she etched carefully around the resistance. The sandstone structure completely disintegrated. The last grains fell to the floor and mingled with the rest of the six-thousand-year-old dust. The big reveal now over, Ellie was left holding a small, brilliant cobalt-blue crystal.

"How did you know?" asked Sam, once again enthralled by his wife's ability.

Ellie smiled smugly at her husband. "Process of elimination."

Sam nodded, appreciating the line. Ellie Mark I always had a special way with words. It seemed Ellie Mark II was no different.

"This is a vital piece of the Therab's mechanics." Ellie gave Sam the crystal. "Hide it away. Don't let anyone have it. I need to work on how to get this thing started."

Sam thought how much more Ellie the Protector sounded like his old Ellie. The way she used to speak when she was trying to get her head around a software problem or a new device. If he ignored her superwoman powers, he could easily forget she'd changed at all.

Then he looked at her, head forward, furrowed in concentration, reading inscriptions he couldn't begin to understand, and sadly he realized she wasn't the same. She had a universe of knowledge in her mind. Oh yes, she'd told him she needed him, that she couldn't do it alone, but he knew that was just an act. Ellie had been so very good at acting, almost as good as she had been at convincing and persuading. The two went hand in hand. Ellie was supremely brilliant in the act of persuasion. That's why she'd excelled in business. She could sell anything to anyone, coals to Newcastle, condoms to the Pope. You name it, and she could sell it. But Sam knew what she was selling: the 'I'm still a fallible human' idea, he just wasn't buying.

He wished he could. It would have lessened his feeling of isolation. That feeling of remoteness, like he'd walked just too far out on a ridge and now he couldn't get back. He'd seen so much in his life, and should have been prepared for anything, but somehow, his wife's transformation was just mentally too much for him. Since his rescue, he'd felt at times incredibly hurt and alone. The connection he'd once had with Ellie was now so intermittent and undefined.

Standing there, illuminated by the eerie blood-red aura, Ellie looked even more alien than before. Suddenly, dark thoughts absorbed him, and he couldn't stop them. His 'other wife' would never be the same. His life would never return to what it was. He didn't have his Ellie back, just some supercharged copy. Why hadn't they both just died? They could then, at least, have found real peace together. Somehow, that would have been more natural and easier to accept, than what he'd had to come to terms with - his wife literally reborn.

Sam shuddered, deeply aware of a growing darkness within him. Coming to his senses, he cursed himself for such gloomy thoughts. Why should he have thought like that? Shouldn't he be eternally grateful? Hadn't he received the miracle he prayed for? Hadn't they both secured salvation?

Sam stared at the crystal in his hands. The smooth edges almost slid in his palm. It was unlike any crystal he'd ever seen. It didn't reflect light and its shine seemed muted, and as he looked deeper, he could see flecks of light inside the crystal, like quick, sudden starbursts. Gazing, entranced, Sam was drawn into the cobalt-blue universe like a magnetic force had fixed to his eyes. He had the sensation of being sucked in, like all his energies were streaming out of him, and finding their home in the small, inoffensive piece of glass in his hand. He forced his fingers over the crystal, momentarily breaking the unearthly attraction, and pocketed it deep inside his jacket. The crystal vibrated gently against his chest. Sam trembled and unease surfaced inside him. The crystal, like his wife, was alien. It originated in a place he'd never seen, been to, or even heard of before that day. Totally alien, and now it was next to him. Sam shook his head.

"I think I understand how this thing works," called Ellie, breaking into his thoughts.

"Huh?"

"I said I know how to get this show rolling."

At the mention of 'show', Sam's mind flipped back for a second to the satcomm room at Baba Heydar. The floorshow. Salim's face full of perverted pleasure. He remembered the way he'd begged Salim for Ellie to be spared such a death, but his pleading had only been met with salivating lips and salacious smiles. That last moment, when he'd turned, when Sabena had transmitted a few minutes earlier than planned, he believed that was it. The woman he'd protected, cherished, and loved all his life was about to be…His mind couldn't even register what was about to happen. If he didn't think it, how could it happen? How could it be real if he didn't say the words in his head? Glancing at Salim as the satcomm sprang into life, his eyebrow raised in anticipation, his smirk fast on his face, his eyes longing to watch the display that would soon take up the entire screen, Sam had known at that moment all was lost. Heavy nausea had risen in him. He'd gagged, swallowing down the sickness, for he knew that if he'd start, he'd not stop. He knew he'd give way to the dark forces and choke there and then on his own bile.

He'd brought Ellie to here. His life had brought her this death. His actions had brought her to this. To this end.

Shaking with gut-wrenching desperation, Sam had turned away from the screen. No torture he'd gone through matched the pain he now had. Someone had driven a screwdriver through his crotch and worked the tool up through his body, slicing him just that bit more apart with every move, pushing him away from his own being. Until eventually the screwdriver split his brain, delivering a state of sheer, desolated madness, an insanity created by the knowledge that he was waiting…waiting to watch his own wife be fucked to death.

Sam jolted back as the memory crashed through him, making him shiver. Oh God, he had nothing to lament over. Ok, she'd changed. But she'd been saved from *that* death. And if that meant transformation into a bloody Dalek, he'd have welcomed it rather than witness the alternative. God, he should be on his knees thanking Aby-od, not regarding him as the cause of their predicament.

Chapter 96

Ellie closed the panel on the black crystal and opened the panel underneath the white crystal. Aswa-da could see developments spiraling out of his control. Abruptly, he shimmered out of the antechamber and arrived, equidistant between Ellie and Sam.

Ellie whirled around as Sam shouted to her to watch her back.

Aswa-da's deep black eyes shone with malicious delight.

"So you are the Protector!" His tone was openly derogatory. Slowly, he looked Ellie up and down. Shaking his head disparagingly, he added, "The high council must be desperate."

Ellie smoldered at Aswa-da's blatant provocation but did not move from working inside the white crystal's panel.

"If I were Aby-od, I'd want my money back," sniped Aswa-da, goading Ellie to refrain from changing the crystals and retaliate. Ellie didn't jump and take the bait. She ignored him. Her sole focus was fixed on powering the white crystal to reverse the balance shift.

"Do you really think you can change things now? The world is rotten, vile, and corrupt to the core. And people want it like that. Nothing you will do will change what is meant to be."

"You're wrong," replied Ellie.

Inside the panel, her hands moved at lightning speed, making new connections between the crystals. Aswa-da watched the white light arc and spark, creating the Therab's light-based circuitry. Concerned, he tried a different line.

"Why should you care about these pathetic humans?"

His voice rattled her, penetrated her body, filling her with a crushingly portentous feeling that she had no wish to feel. Ellie would dearly have loved to have quietened him, but her powers had no effect on Kudamaz life forms.

"Join me." Aswa-da's tempting was too much for Ellie. The last crystal sparked and lit up as the circuit was made. The white crystal on the Therab's top panel fired up, ready for activation. On seeing this, Ellie turned to Aswa-da, her face full of defiance and cold indignation.

"You must be insane to think I'd join you."

"Well, you must be short of a full load. You are after all, trailing around with that primitive," Aswa-da remarked, indicating to Sam.

Hearing the inflammatory remark, Sam shouted angrily, "Hey, fucker, I'm off the scale at MENSA!"

Aswa-da looked with disdain at Sam, as if he was something unpleasant he'd stepped in. Sam recognized the look. Exploding with fury, he took his gun out of his pocket.

"Not so fucking pious now, are you?" Sam screamed.

Ellie looked horrified. Sam had no idea what he was dealing with. She called out to Sam to calm down, but her husband ignored his wife. Aswa-da smiled fascinated by Sam's primal instincts of protection.

"See, Protector, your primitive thinks he can kill me."

"I can kill you!" yelled Sam furiously.

He fired the gun.

Through his Kudamaz vision, Aswa-da watched the bullet for a split second and then stepped nonchalantly to one side, avoiding its lethal trajectory. Missing the target, the bullet slammed into the sandstone wall behind Aswa-da. To Sam's human eyes, all he saw was Aswa-da move faster than a blink. His movement was so fast it was barely perceptible. There was no ducking or dodging involved. Aswa-da was just swifter in motion than the bullet's velocity. Sam stared, shocked and unable to know what to do next. He'd been trained to deal with terrorists, people who got hit when he shot a bullet, not people who could move faster than light. No training could prepare him for that.

"What do you see in this primitive?" asked Aswa-da, seeing Sam's confused expression.

"Hold your tongue." Ellie's voice was powerful and booming. She was deeply offended. He was talking about her husband, blaspheming their love.

"I suppose it could make a good pet," continued Aswa-da, focused on riling Ellie to move away from the white crystal. "But you couldn't have sexual relations with such a creature."

Turning the white crystal forty-five degrees, Ellie faltered. Hearing Aswa-da's disgusting remark, her face reddened with rage. She'd tried to assuage the situation, knowing that the elder was pointedly provoking her, but his last delivery was unforgivable.

The elder was degrading her beloved, turning him into an animal, making their love seem unnatural and dirty. She was suddenly beyond anger. Moving her hand away for an instant, her finger extended in front of Aswa-da like an angry parent disciplining an errant child.

"Don't you dare say a word…"

Ellie stopped speaking as Aswa-da shimmered, his hands outstretched, ready to hold onto the black crystal the moment he materialized. His plan had worked. The Protector had played into the elder's hand.

Ellie berated herself for being so gullible, so weak. She was irritated at being so easy to fool, Ellie went to place her hands back onto the white crystal, but as she neared it, her hands were violently pushed back, slamming painfully onto the side panel.

The ebony-robed Aswa-da regarded Ellie's actions with pleasure.

"Having trouble, Protector?"

Chapter 97

Ellie stared wildly at the elder. His sly attitude infuriated her. How could she have been so stupid? That was why he was so intent on goading her. He knew the lockout process. And she'd walked straight into his trap. Screaming with frustration, Ellie threw her entire body onto the white crystal. Sam watched as she was flung back onto the sandstone floor. The force of the propulsion was enough to kill a human. Instinctively, Sam dove to the floor to help his wife, but she was back on her feet and smarting with fury before he could move two paces.

"Aby-od was clearly economic in his briefing to you. Listen and learn. When the white crystal is being activated, the black one is covered and contained by the Therab's force field and is effectively locked out from anyone touching it. And if the black crystal is being activated…Oh, I think you get the idea!"

With a patronizing sneer, Aswa-da turned back to activating the black crystal.

Ellie was desperate. Aby-od had told her so very little. She wasn't prepared.

"Protector, do you *know* who I am?"

Aswa-da thought it interesting to test her on whether Aby-od had even the slightest glimmer of understanding of his involvement in proceedings, and whether Aby-od had revealed his suspicions to the Protector.

"You're an elder of the House of Etima," answered Ellie fluently.

Aby-od had told her nothing. Aswa-da's smile grew wide and menacing.

"Not any elder. *The* elder. I am Lord Aswa-da, head of the House of Etima, and soon to be leader of Kudamun. But of course, that's something else Aby-od failed to tell you."

Ellie was mortified. The corruption went to the highest level. Why hadn't

Aby-od warned her? Why hadn't she been properly informed?

"And you know why he didn't tell you about me?" continued Aswa-da, splintering Ellie's thoughts. He flicked a mischievous grin at Ellie, licking his lips. *This was going to be good.* "Because he didn't know. He had his head so far up his ass he couldn't see the truth for politics and protocol."

Something about the way the elder described Aby-od made Sam smirk. Although Aby-od had saved them, he still felt he had contacted Ellie much too soon and that ill-timed contact precipitated events that eventually led to their incarceration and torture. Aby-od had still much to answer for.

Aswa-da stared at Sam, fascinated to witness how easily influenced humans were.

"Even the primitive recognizes that Aby-od is a useless, incompetent fool."

"Hey, hey, enough of this 'primitive' talk. Have a bit of respect!"

Sam was getting thoroughly pissed off by Aswa-da's hubris and arrogance. Ok, he couldn't kill him, but he'd be damned if he was going to sit by and listen to his condescending crap.

"Respect! It is you, primitive, who should show respect," Aswa-da sneered haughtily at Sam.

Bristling with fury, Sam pointed his gun again to shoot.

"Stop this!" screamed Ellie. "Aby-od is not a useless, incompetent fool. He values and upholds the antediluvian laws. The House of Giznu is a house of honor and pride. Aby-od would never stoop to manipulate a planet's future. He would never breach the order of Kudamun." Ellie's voice flowed loudly and confidently.

Sam couldn't help but be surprised by her outburst. Once again, she was saying words that held no meaning or understanding. Such moments only sought to underline how very far away Ellie was to him. He felt so terribly alone. They'd been so in touch, so connected. Now he felt adrift, still trying to love someone he couldn't even begin to really understand.

Aswa-da's vicious rebuke wedged into his own thoughts of emotional abandonment.

"Honor and pride. Ah! Protector, how little you know. The House of Giznu is a lie. They survived in power by breaking *all* the antediluvian laws. This Therab kept them in power for too long. Earth survived, although it should have been dispatched centuries ago. But that time is over. Dark will return and gain its rightful place. Despite Aby-od's best intentions."

Aswa-da paused.

Should he tell her? Hell, why not?

"Intentions that I played a small part in. His calling to you so early. You wondered why. At the time, I was watching you just like Aby-od was. I thought it would be helpful to speed up his observations, so I enhanced what he saw. Aby-od interpreted it as a positive connection and called to you. Such a pity he had such a terrible communication problem. I did what I could to assist. I think my intervention may have scared you a little. Sorry! I was only trying to be a team player!" Aswa-da smiled, enjoying the moment. He was well aware of the devastating news he'd imparted.

Sam and Ellie were staggered. The ill-timed communication from Aby-od triggered the scream and so much that followed. Sam had been sure it was Aby-od's fault. His incompetence. He'd blamed him openly, and silently hated him. But now, this new revelation chilled him. His vengeance had all the time been misplaced. The creature before them had carved out the chain of confusion, pain and death. Aswa-da was responsible for everything that had happened to them over the last five days. And now all the bastard could do was gloat over the tremendous ignorance he'd bestowed on all parties.

Tear Aswa-da apart. That had been Sam's first thought on how to avenge against the utter torment they'd been subjected to, but his trick with the bullet meant Sam would never get close. Being Kudamaz, he'd shimmer at the moment of impact.

Sam stared at Ellie. She was silent, her face pained and drained. Sad eyes spoke volumes. The knowledge that she wasn't special, that she was just a pawn in Aswa-da's grand game, crushed Ellie. And Aswa-da's final words appeared to finish her completely.

"You have failed, Protector."

Chapter 98

Ellie looked on, appalled. The black crystal had started to glow, radiating a silver hue. After all they'd been through, it couldn't end like this. Ellie was sure there had to be a way. Destiny didn't stop here. There had to be hope. Her anguish made her shiver. A human emotion. She could still feel so much. So much goodness and so much evil. And soon there would be no more goodness. The energies of light she could now sense when she reached out, all the kindness, charity, and love would soon be overwritten with cruelty, greed, and hate. The pain of this change would kill her, of this, she was certain.

I have to find a way.

If only she hadn't been so blind to Aswa-da's scheming. If only Aby-od had told her more. Now all she could do was feel the light energies across the world rapidly descend into darkness. Desolation took her. Aswa-da sensed her misery. Witnessing her despondency at her inability to change the situation, Aswa-da shot her a smooth, satisfied smile.

Deep within her, something stirred. Ellie could feel the light energies, but there was more. The light energies were building inside her. Ellie's eyes widened as she remembered Aby-od's words. "All I know is you are the conduit. You will find a way. The power is in you." It all became clear. She knew what she had to do.

Ellie closed her eyes and concentrated. Sam looked at her. At first, it appeared that Ellie had yielded to Earth's inevitable fate. That she had acceded that Aswa-da had won. But he knew his Ellie of old wasn't a defeatist, and whatever else she was now, that determination would not have left her. In her great mind, she was devising a scheme to thwart Aswa-da and fulfil her mission. Suddenly, Sam felt connected again. The detachment he'd sensed earlier had gone. He gazed at Ellie, renewed love in his eyes, and hope filled his heart.

The huge crystal had started to flicker from red to black. Aswa-da watched as the rectangular crystals that had returned to the base after the red light had been released gradually started to revolve, their speed increasing as he looked on. The second stage had begun.

Nothing could stop him.

He cast a glance towards Ellie, who'd dropped to silence since his last revelation. Her eyes were closed as if in meditation. *Sleep, Protector. Never wake. Your assistance is no longer required.* Aswa-da turned his attention back to the Therab.

Ellie could feel the light energies growing inside her. She knew that before very long, the energies would reveal themselves. She had to act fast. In parallel with collecting and building all the goodness across the world inside her, Ellie began to focus the encapsulated goodness onto the white crystal. With immense might, the energies burst through the Therab's force field and headed for the white crystal.

Consumed totally by evil, Aswa-da felt nothing, sensed nothing, saw nothing. As powerful as he was, he was no match to the Protector. Light energies poured unhindered into the white crystal, unseen, under Aswa-da's very nose.

Turning to face Sam, he requested coldly, "Give me the crystal."

Ellie, deep in concentration, heard the words. She flicked open her eyes. Immediately, all channeling of the light energies halted. Sam was in agony, caught in a mental battle. His left hand was partially raised towards his inner pocket, but Sam was grappling with it, trying to push it back down. His face was strained. He was fighting with his own body.

Ellie was stupefied. How could Aswa-da control Sam? He could only use the black crystal to control people if they had darkness in them. The inscriptions clearly stated this.

But Sam was good. Sam was true. Sam was love.

Ellie tried to convince herself, as she did the one thing she'd not done before. She reviewed Sam's level of balance shift.

Ellie's eyes filled with tears. Sam was almost ten per cent to the dark. How could this be? Sam was a good man. He hadn't harmed anyone. Why should he...Then, it all came flooding back. His job. In the kitchen, standing there, with his gun ready to fire. His words. 'Ellie, darling. I'm sorry. I'm MI6. My work is to identify, undermine, and take down international terrorist organizations that are deemed a threat to national security.'

His work at MI6 had clearly caused his darkness. Ellie thought again, rationalizing her hypothesis. But surely in his work, he was removing terrorists and removing evil. He was one of the good guys. That wouldn't have caused a dramatic shift to the dark.

The deeper she thought, realization hit. Malta. His breaking had caused so many deaths. Oh, this wasn't fair. He'd broken to save her.

She looked at her husband. Each movement Sam made was packed with resistance like he was walking against a hurricane. But little by little, he was edging towards Aswa-da.

Fight, my sweetness. Fight. Ellie was powerless to help her husband. Now that he was falling under Aswa-da's influence, only activation of the white crystal could save him.

Breathing in, with tears streaming, Ellie closed her eyes and commenced her channeling. She summoned all her power, every inch of that superhuman strength she had to speed up the process, for now it wasn't just Earth, Kudamun and the universe that was at stake. It was Sam. And he was more important to her than all the other three put together.

Chapter 99

Ellie upped the velocity of capture, and the white-light energies flooded into her. Unable to contain them, the energies seeped through her body. They filtered out and found their own way onto the white crystal. Now a towering pillar of shining light, Ellie stood and forced the white crystal to come alive. Slowly, the crystal began to flicker, desperate to live.

Aswa-da glanced over at Ellie, his eyes leering, his face patronizing her pitiful attempt to control the Therab. *Shine your light, Protector, and watch me devour it.* Unconcerned by Ellie's gleaming display, he turned his attention back to the Therab.

The seconds passed and gradually the flicker in the white crystal grew stronger.

Every semblance of good across the Earth, no matter how small or how seemingly insignificant, poured into her. From a small boy in Ecuador nursing an injured kitten to a mother in Afghanistan, ready to do anything to protect her family from Taliban raiders. All the kindness, the bravery, the courage that was humanity was captured and focused onto the white crystal. It glowed, fierce and strong. Ellie could see it although her eyes were still tightly shut. But absorbing Earth's goodness wasn't enough. There just wasn't enough good in the world to reverse the balance shift. She had to activate the Therab and multiply the white-light energies. Somehow, the crystal had to be turned.

She visualized the white crystal in her mind. She could see its seven-sided structure. Perfect facets. Smooth sides. Engineered for good billions of years ago.

"Help me, Ellie. Don't let me do this!" Sam's frantic, scared voice screamed out.

Ellie shivered and tears flowed from her closed eyes. She could not help him. From his voice, she knew that he was falling farther under Aswa-da's control. His special ops training in combating mind control would have helped him initially, but Aswa-da's power aided by the dark crystal would have broken through his flimsy mental shield. Resisting Aswa-da's control had caused Sam intolerable pain. He could not hold out much longer. Listening to her husband's cries, Ellie was racked with consuming guilt. She wanted to help him so much.

"Oh God, Ellie. Please help me. Please, for God's sake, help me!"

"Give it to me, Sam. Save yourself. Embrace the dark side. You know you want to. Remember all the people you've killed. All the lives you've taken. All the pain you've caused. You're at home in the dark. It's what's in your soul. I can feel it. You can't change destiny. You can't change what is to be. You're evil, Sam. Always have been. Come to me, Sam. Come to me. Give me the crystal."

Penetrating and powerful, Aswa-da's words rocked Ellie. She could never believe Sam was evil.

"The people I killed were bad. I've never killed a good person!" shouted Sam, his terror sounding clear as he tried to counter Aswa-da's vicious statement.

"How do you know they were really bad?" Aswa-da's retort ripped through Sam's conscience. Ellie knew Aswa-da's game. Stay strong, sweetness. Stay strong. Guard your conviction. Hold your belief.

"They would have killed me and … other … innocent … people," Sam gasped, suffering the full impact of Aswa-da's influence. He strived to deliver his reasoning, but searing pain tore at him. His muscles ached. A tremendous force crushed his brain, and his skin was so blisteringly cold, it burned him.

"They were evil. I'm not!" screamed Sam, letting forth a howl with such a pain-drenched force that Ellie almost stopped concentrating on the white-light energies and ran to him to halt his agony.

Perplexed, Aswa-da watched Sam's progress. It was all too slow. He couldn't risk moving his hands from the black crystal for fear that the Protector would lock him out. But he needed Sam to bring him the crystal quickly to initiate the chain reaction of dark energies. The crystal had to be in situ before the final stage was activated. Once the revolving crystals had reached the zenith point, the cobalt-blue crystal had to be back in place. Without it, nothing would work. Time was ticking. He needed that crystal. Aswa-da regarded Sam. For a human, he had great strength. He had to find his breaking point.

"Remember Malta, Sam. Do you know how many lives were gone in an instant because you valued your wife more than them? 578,119. That's a lot of innocent lives you've destroyed. All because of your selfishness. You knew what Salim was going to do. You knew those people were going to die. But you saved your wife and yourself and let them die. All 578,119. Men, women, children. Every single one innocent. None of them were bad, and none deserved to die. But they did, Sam. All because of you. And that makes you evil."

Aswa-da's smug smile widened, witnessing the effect his well-chosen words had on Sam.

"Stop it! Stop it!" yelled Sam. Recalling the images of the ravaged island, his resistance crumbled. "They would have killed her. I'm her husband. I couldn't. I couldn't let them do that. I couldn't watch while they did that. I love her." Sam's drained voice rang through the chamber. "I loved her." His body shook violently.

Aswa-da's power was so strong, so vicious. By concentrating on his fractured conscience, he was breaking through Sam's armor, destroying his defenses.

Ellie heard Sam's broken replies. Her lips trembled. She wanted to run to him, to stop his pain. But his only salvation was in her activating the white crystal.

"You placed her life ahead of 578,119 innocent people."

"Yes."

"Then you are selfish. And your decision was cruel and evil."

"But I loved her. I couldn't see them kill her like that."

Sam was distraught. This was all wrong. He wasn't evil, just a victim of terrible circumstances. He had been pushed too far. But hearing Aswa-da's words, and the scathing truth that they were laced with, Sam knew he was losing. Aswa-da's dark control was slipping between the cracks in his conscience. His shaking left hand moved slowly up towards his jacket pocket. Observing the gesture with pleasure, Aswa-da issued further encouragement.

"Come on, Sam. Come with me. The dark side is fun. No worry. No commitment. No responsibility. You'd love that, wouldn't you? No responsibility. Nothing to worry about at all. You can have it. Just give me the crystal and you can be free."

Sam was trapped between the good side and the bad side. The battle was tearing him apart.

"Come on, Sam. You know you want to."

Sam was falling. He was lightheaded, dizzy, intoxicated by evil. His eyes swam. The black crystal's power had made him insatiable. He felt free. He felt like he could do anything, be anyone. Thrusting his hand into his pocket, he withdrew the crystal. Clutching it, he held it out towards Aswa-da.

'Stay strong, sweetness.'

Hearing Ellie's voice, he wrenched his head around to look at her. She was in a trance.

'Stay strong, my sweet Sam.' Like before, her voice was loud and clear in his mind.

"Come on, Sam. No responsibility. Only fun. Only freedom. Just give me the crystal."

Sam couldn't hold out much longer. Even Ellie, bathed in all the world's goodness, could still sense the absolute darkness that had invaded the chamber.

She focused. And she felt the good.

In a world obsessed with evil, it called to her like the sweetest dawn chorus, its clarity, its strength overpowering. The kindness, charity, and love sought her out. From polite gestures to outstanding courage. Every experience. The essence of goodness. Humanity poured into her. Filling her totally. Illuminated by the measures of mankind, she concentrated, and slowly the crystal turned.

But the movement was minute. Ellie forced her mind to work faster. On the other side of the Therab, out of Aswa-da's field of view, the white crystal rotated.

Above her, the huge crystal was almost totally black. The rectangular crystals now spun at speed, edging ever closer to the center of the crystal. Harmonies flew from the top of the scale to the bottom, like a crazy orchestral rehearsal was taking place without a musical sheet. But the sound, unlike the devastating noise the president had heard, was no longer harmful to humans.

Sweat dripped down her face. With every ounce of mental force, Ellie concentrated on finishing the white crystal's revolution.

'Good, Sam. Just a little more. Come on, Sam.'

Her husband was seconds from breaking. Aswa-da mustn't have that crystal. Ellie pushed harder. Her brain was on fire, ready to explode. One more push. Ellie screamed out in pain and relief as the white crystal clicked into place. Its revolution was complete.

Chapter 100

Aswa-da jumped at Ellie's scream, clearly not expecting the sound. For a moment, his concentration wavered, and he lost control of Sam. The vile connection severed. Sam reached for his gun, turning it full on to Aswa-da.

Flecks of white dotted through the black inside the huge crystal. The tiny white specks grew rapidly in size, eating more of the black.

Noticing a change, Aswa-da stared around him. The chamber was getting brighter. He stared in anger at the huge crystal. The white energies ate away voraciously at the dark.

Glaring at Ellie, he noticed her aura had vanished. She stood still, her arms by her side, eyes still closed. Aswa-da was amazed. She had not moved. She had not touched the white crystal. How could the white light be activated?

"Damn you, Protector!" Aswa-da shrieked

He tried to turn the black crystal. Barely an inch away and his hand, like the Protector's before, was slammed to the side. He was locked out. Enraged, Aswa-da tore off the panel underneath the black crystal. No sparks. No arcs. Nothing. The circuits were dead.

The dark luminescence that had pervaded through the chamber had been consumed by the brilliant white light. The love of the world suffused the chamber with a glorious feeling of hope and joy. Aswa-da choked back his disgust. The sheer goodness of humanity reverberated in the walls. He could feel it soaking into his skin. The sensation made him shiver. He couldn't stand being so close to pure goodness. Shaking with frenzied rage, he watched the ring of crystals, now nothing but a spinning blur, rise towards the top of the giant crystal. Activation of the second stage was almost over.

Detecting the last whisper of darkness gorged on by the white light, Ellie snapped open her eyes and took in the scene. Sam was a foot away from Aswa-da. His hand was outstretched, clasping the cobalt crystal in one hand. His gun, trained on the dark lord, was in the other. Terror and agony were etched on his face. Aswa-da's hands were deep inside the black crystal's panel.

Seething with anger, Aswa-da screamed, "What have you done?"

Ellie glared back at him. "I did what I was told to do. Aby-od briefed me well, did he not?"

Aswa-da listened, infuriated that Aby-od, by-the-book, bureaucratic, bloody Aby-od, knew something that he didn't about the T'herab.

Ellie reveled in Aswa-da's sudden impotency. "Goodness will always win. Light will always be more powerful than dark. That's destiny. Accept it."

"Hey, Aswa-da, you wanted your crystal, then have it." Sam's contemptuous voice erupted with strength as the white-light energies coursed through him. With a flick, he tossed the cobalt crystal into the air. Drawing his gun, Sam's sharpshooter training came to the fore in the split second the crystal was airborne. Eyes like lasers focused on the crystal's center. Pulling the trigger, full of revenge for the unbelievable pain Aswa-da put him through, he yelled, "Have your fucking crystal!"

Aswa-da screamed out, "No!"

The bullet hit at close range, shattering the crystal and sending shards of cobalt at the elder's feet.

At the same time, the spinning halo had reached the top of the giant crystal and the energies connected. The chamber exploded into blinding white light. Instinctively, Sam shielded his eyes from the supernova. The huge crystal pulsed out the white light, sucked it back in, held it for a second, and then burst forth the white energies. Released, they sped towards the skylight. Aswa-da stared on as the white light surged out. Watching, he knew his destiny had flown away in unison. It was over. He stood silent.

Turning to face Ellie, staring through orbs of total evil, Aswa-da spoke.

"You have taken what was mine. Now I shall take what is yours."

Ellie glared at him. His right hand had slipped inside the folds of his sleeve. Something shone out from the silken fabrics, virtually indiscernible to the human eye, and meant nothing to Sam. But to Ellie, meaning was as big as a billboard. She knew Aswa-da's next move.

"Sam, he's going to kill you!"

The words dropped from her trembling lips. But it was already too late.

Aswa-da had shot his Harmon gun, his face burning with vindictive hatred.

Chapter 101

Sam leapt behind a sandstone block, but his movement was far too slow. The Harmon wave had already hit him in the shoulder. Sam collapsed. Ellie screamed, watching her husband drop. Instantly, she felt the connection cut. No life-force.

Oh God, he's dead.

Mad with sudden grief and seeing Aswa-da gearing up to fire again, Ellie charged at him, flinging her body weight and pushing him to the sandy floor. Pinning Aswa-da to the ground, Ellie snatched the Harmon gun and threw it into the next chamber out of his reach. Although her strength was formidable, Aswa-da could see that emotionally, she was falling to pieces. A waterfall of hurt and misery streamed from her frenzied eyes. Such weakness. Seeing his opportunity, he brought his leg down hard on her back. Splintering pain shot up her spine, but she didn't let Aswa-da go. Her face close to his, she pulled his collar tight in her fist, the cloth cutting into the elder's throat.

He sneered at her. His malicious eyes fixed coldly on her own, eye to eye, black to blue, unblinking, unflinching. "It hurts to lose something you love."

Ellie's primal strength surged inside her, and she smashed Aswa-da's head against the sandstone floor. If Aswa-da had been human, his head would have split like a cantaloupe on a chef's chopping board. Instead, he gathered in his muscle, focused, and hit Ellie hard in the stomach. She took the blow without reaction, her hands fastening around Aswa-da's huge, muscular neck. He clawed at her slender fingers, but her vise grip only tightened in response. Bringing up his knee, Aswa-da thrust it viciously hard into her groin. Ellie gasped, her grip loosening for a second. Aswa-da saw his chance. He pressed up and rolled Ellie onto her back. With her hands still around his throat, Ellie kicked out, hitting Aswa-da's massive chest.

"You'll never win. Evil will always be more powerful."

"You think?" countered Ellie fiercely, rolling Aswa-da onto his back again. Her hands closed in tighter. Aswa-da tried to shimmer, but his strength was draining against the Protector's incredible might. Ellie sensed his pitiful attempt. "You're going nowhere but hell!" Her eyes narrowed, her teeth gritting hard.

"Ellie."

Sam's voice. Ellie heard it. Love enveloped her. Her grip momentarily loosened. Aswa-da felt it. He wrenched his knee up and, with a tremendous thrust, kicked Ellie full in the stomach. The energy in the kick threw her off Aswa-da, and she slammed into the wall.

"Ellie."

She turned to see Sam move. Aswa-da took the moment her sudden disorientation offered him. He centered his remaining energies and shimmered out of the chamber.

Ellie watched powerless and livid as Aswa-da shouted through the shimmer, "Hate killed love!"

She grabbed at his form, but he was too quick, and all Ellie ended up grabbing was a faint swirling black shadow that vanished once he'd dematerialized.

"Please, Ellie."

Hearing Sam's voice, Ellie ran frantically to her husband's side and cradled him in her shaking arms. She could feel his life-force slipping away. Kissing his hair, she smoothed his face with her tender, soft hand. "Oh my darling, my darling."

"I love you, Ellie," Sam whispered, his voice barely there. "Let me go, Ellie. Let me go!"

Every word was carved out in agony. Sam closed his eyes. His chest rose and then lowered. Each time, the movement slowed even more. From the time Ellie had cradled him, she could see his breathing had deteriorated to a shallow gasp. He was dying. After everything that had happened. After everything they'd gone through together, he was now the one who was leaving her.

"No, no," she murmured, caressing him. "I'm not letting you go. I'm not letting you go."

Laying Sam softly on the floor, Ellie ran to the Therab. From reading the inscriptions earlier, she'd worked out how to turn off the force field. She quickly touched a number of small crystals in a particular sequence inside the panel beneath the white crystal. Immediately, the resonance she'd sensed before arcing across the world vanished. Returning to Sam's side, she could see he was fading out. The vicious Harmon wave was blasting through his molecular structure, literally obliterating him alive. He'd fallen unconscious. Ellie was thankful. No longer was he aware of the blinding pain that tore ceaselessly at his fragile cells.

She gathered Sam in her strong arms and pictured the Hall of Umray in her mind. Ellie closed her eyes and pulled her husband close.

"Hold on, my sweetness," she whispered.

Then the two of them were swathed in a cloak of flickering, sparkling rainbow lights.

Chapter 102

Aby-od with the rest of the high council had watched anxiously events as they transpired. The holographic Earth bobbed in the center of the Great Hall, still encased in the red aura of Therab's force field. But for a second, it suddenly gleamed, resplendent with a bright, sparkling white light. The brilliance of the light completely overpowered the red aura, and for a brief instance in time, the Earth shone like a glorious new sun.

Closing his eyes to the blinding but beautiful sight, Aby-od could feel tears of jubilation erupt inside him. He allowed their passage down his weary face before they fizzled, sparkled and disintegrated.

The white light dissolved but its effect was immediate. Flashing red numbers went into free fall. The balance shift to the dark reversed at rapid speed. Earth was out of the Dark Zone. The elders stared, captivated by the fleeting numbers. The point of Great Risk passed and still the numbers continued to fall. The elders in the House of Giznu broke into smiles as the balance shift entered into the five per cent borderline. Even the elders in the House of Etima, knowing that their very existence had been put at stake because of Aswa-da's action, cracked their stone faces with relieved smiles. Aby-od nodded to both sets of elders, his face a radiant expression of joy. Gratitude showed through his exhausted face. Gratitude to them for holding onto the hope. For having the strength to believe. But most of all, gratitude to Ellie, the Protector, who had saved them all.

The counter blinked continuously to show that equilibrium had been restored on Earth. The balance shift had been completely reversed. A collective cheer rippled through the high council. Aby-od knew that they were cheering not because of Earth's survival but because they had secured their own. The threat posed by Aswa-da and the activation of the Therab to create such a shift to the dark would have culminated in the total cleansing of the universe and the destruction of Kudamun. The Ancient Ones would never have permitted such utter darkness to remain. All the elders knew this. When they watched the force field embrace the Earth, all they had in their defense was hope and faith, and a belief in the Protector. But those weapons were defense enough to win. *Thank you, Ellie. Thank you.*

Aby-od stared at Earth. The red aura flickered and then disappeared. The Protector was returning. He turned to deliver his euphoric address to the high council.

"Honorable members, something happened today. Something terrible. Something wonderful. Let us always remember this day. Let us make a fresh start. The power vested in us should not be regarded as a duty, a protocol, a procedure. It is commitment to a belief that we can make a difference for all the planets in our care. That we can help them when they need help. And most of all, that we can still remember to feel. Like the inhabitants feel on the planets we oversee. And we should never, never lose faith in hope. For it is hope that gives us purpose. And it is hope that helped us win today."

Aby-od sat down graciously to a standing ovation. As dreadful as the situation had been, maybe the high council had needed a jolt to their system. The terror they had felt had brought them alive. Aby-od knew that the high council would never act with piety and supercilious impassiveness again.

Of course, it would be all change in the House of Etima. After his actions, Aswa-da would no longer be the head of the house. Lord Temenos would take the mantle by default.

Aswa-da would be tracked by the high council supreme guards, and when arrested, would face summary execution for grand treason against the order of Kudamun. His resonance pattern had already been programed into the planetary security scanners, and when he shimmered anywhere, an alert would be sounded. He would be immediately collected by the supreme guards and returned to Kudamun to be tried. Aby-od knew he'd try to run, but with all their safeguards in place, he had nowhere to run to. The high council would find him eventually.

The speaker closed the session of the high council and all the elders shimmered out.

Aby-od headed for the Hall of Umray, knowing that the Protector would return there. Arriving in the opulent hall, he sensed the air in the center of room waiver. The swirling, materializing form appeared to be larger than the Protector. Thinking it could be Aswa-da, Aby-od charged his Harmon gun and primed it to fire on full power once the shimmer had solidified. Pensive, Aby-od watched the shimmer form into two bodies and not the one as he had first thought. Sam and Ellie. Aby-od breathed deeply. He didn't like confrontation, but he would have killed Aswa-da without hesitation.

"Aby-od, help me! Sam's been hit by Aswa-da's Harmon wave. He's dying!"

Ellie's intense voice thumped into Aby-od like a punch in the face.

What could he do? Sam was human. His framework was fragile. Easily extinguished. Aby-od knelt by Ellie. She held Sam's albeit lifeless body in her trembling arms. He felt totally at a loss. He shook his head as Ellie implored him with sad eyes.

"Please, Aby-od," she cried hysterically, "do something!"

"I can't Ellie. He's human."

"For fuck's sake, Aby-od, do something!" screamed Ellie, staring at Aby-od. Her words and her manner were more like the old Ellie than he ever could have believed.

Aby-od was helpless. "He's human. They're fragile. Too fragile."

Ellie looked down at Sam, her face heartbroken. If only he'd been Kudamaz. There could have been a way.

"Aby-od, please!"

She couldn't believe, wouldn't believe, that it was all going to end like this. Not after the hell they'd been through.

Chapter 103

Aby-od was deeply ashamed by his obvious inadequacy. Ellie had saved them and now, when she needed his help, he couldn't give it. All he could do was repeat the same damn words like an old, tired record stuck in too deep a groove.

"There's nothing I can do, Ellie. He's human. I can't help him."

Ellie grabbed Aby-od's arm tightly. "Yes, he's human, and so was I. Remember what I was like before you reconstituted me? I was half-dead. Maybe not as bad as Sam, but I certainly wasn't doing any cartwheels. But you repaired me. You brought me back. If you did it for me, you can do it for Sam."

Ellie was desperate. It had to work. Aby-od could do it. But once again, the elder was shaking his head.

"It worked for you because you had the Protector's life-force code inside your DNA. You had a Kudamaz framework buried inside you. I had something to work with. But with Sam, I have nothing. And even if there was a way, reconstituting a natural human has never been done. I don't know what would happen."

"He's dying, Aby-od. Just try something!"

Her heart was holding strong, holding on. She wasn't letting go.

"But reconstitution has to have a Kudamaz framework," persisted Aby-od, feeling terrible for stressing the obvious to Ellie.

Ellie stared at Sam. He was blinking in and out. The phases between were getting more prolonged. He was longer 'out' than 'in'. Ellie knew he had just minutes before his structure broke down completely. He would then be 'out' forever.

Ellie thought about what was needed. Reconstitution needed a Kudamaz life-force. And where could she get a Kudamaz life-force? The Library of Ummia blasted into her great mind. The place where the Kudamaz place their life-forces when they have done everything they need to and wish to retire their life-forces. The solution became clear.

"Use the Library of Ummia. Find a Kudamaz life-force framework, align Sam's life-force with the new Kudamaz one, and overwrite Sam's life-force."

Ellie knew what that would mean. Sam, her Sam, would be gone, but he would be alive in some form. And from there they'd find a way. Somehow...

"Ellie, what you're suggesting has never been done with any species outside of our own. I just don't know whether it could be done."

Aby-od's voice was grave and reasoned, but Ellie wasn't listening. She had found a way to save Sam. She wasn't letting go.

"Aby-od, choose any male life-force and overwrite Sam's now!" Ellie shouted.

Her eyes flashed with vivid determination. Aby-od knew he couldn't win the argument, and he had to agree this idea gave Sam a chance, and a slim chance was better than no chance at all. Nodding, Aby-od shimmered out of the hall.

He materialized in a cavernous room. All around him, row after row of crystal shelving stretched up and up, almost touching the Reality Gap that floated high above him, which was constantly moving, fluctuating and exploding in colors of deep blue, orange and silver. The place he was in was the Library of Ummia, also called the Library of Lives. It was the place of past Kudamaz life-forces. On each of the shelves, cocooned inside translucent boxes, crystals sat displaying a variety of colors. Aby-od headed for the male life-forces and was inexplicably drawn to one pale-violet crystal midway through one of the rows. Trusting his instincts, Aby-od grabbed the crystal and returned to the Hall of Umray.

Ellie waited impatiently on his arrival. Out of shimmer, Ellie looked at the crystal Aby-od held. She could see the sparkling network of nodes inside the crystal. The Kudamaz framework.

"Hurry!" shouted Ellie, as the beautiful mosaic floor could be seen with increasing clarity through Sam's body.

Aby-od inserted the crystal into a half moon panel in the side of the wall. Slowly, a huge crystal high above them began to lower. Aby-od maneuvered it to hang directly above Sam's lifeless body.

"Leave him," ordered Aby-od with harsh authority and he pulled Ellie away.

By Aby-od's side, Ellie watched as he worked with haste. His hands seemed almost charmed, like he was being guided by a helpful spirit. Ellie looked on as the pale-violet crystal released its content: the Kudamaz framework. The life-force code manifested itself as a beautiful rainbow. Aby-od skillfully controlled the rainbow arc to connect with the giant crystal suspended directly above Sam.

The great crystal began to pulsate, and in concert, the harmonies started to ring out.

"Come on. Come on," muttered Ellie impetuously.

Aby-od whipped around at Ellie. "Don't rush things. I know you want to save Sam, but now we have to let the reconstitution process take its course."

The harmonies rose in pitch, and the giant crystal glowed with bright violet light. The sound reached a deafening crescendo. With an explosion of light and sound, the giant crystal discharged its Kudamaz resonance energies directly onto Sam's lifeless body.

Sam's body, now saturated, glowed with violet light. His body shone brighter and brighter until his human features were erased completely, leaving only a body filled with pure Kudamaz energy. A harmonic way above human hearing sounded, and in unison, Sam's body burst into flickering rainbow particles.

Ellie watched absolutely dumbstruck and horrified by the unusual spectacle. Although her in-built knowledge told her the process, witnessing it first hand was something very different, and she was profoundly disturbed.

"Fuck! Aby-od! Was that supposed to happen?"

Her use of profanities was strangely endearing to him. She was certainly a unique Protector. He smiled gently, understanding her concern, and placed his hand over hers.

"Ellie, you know you went through much the same sort of process. Look." He pointed. "See how the particles are using the framework to find their designated return positions."

Ellie stared in amazement as the once shattered particles whizzed back, following an invisible path to restore Sam to a whole person again.

Frightened, Ellie closed her eyes. Oh dear God! What had she done? Realization hit her. She had overwritten Sam with…Who?

She may have Sam's form back, but it wouldn't be Sam. Her Sam.

She may have overwritten Sam with someone who was horrible, someone for whom she had no feelings. No love. She was terrified to look into Sam's eyes and see only a stranger.

"Ellie, it's over."

Chapter 104

Ellie composed herself and got ready for the inevitable, the shock of seeing Sam but feeling absolutely nothing.

Cautiously, she opened her eyes. Sam stood in the center of the hall. Evidence of the Harmon wave attack had vanished in the same complete way all her injuries had been erased.

He stood, surveying the room slowly. His shoulders were square, his body muscular, more muscular than before. His stance was strong and self-assured.

Nervous and afraid, Ellie stared. This wasn't Sam. This was an Adonis from years gone by. Her eyes rose to gaze upon the stranger's face. The sculptured jaw line and high cheekbones were still unmistakably Sam's. Her gaze lifted higher. Their eyes locked. Deep, so deep inside her, Ellie felt something that had once been lost was found again. Reconnection. Her heart raced. Her mouth drifted into a smile.

She'd been staring at this man all her life.

A strong passionate smile flooded his face. Whispers of Selema's life filtered into Ellie's mind.

"Dumuzi."

Ellie reached out to touch him, but it was Selema's action, not one of her own. Selema and Dumuzi had been lovers. After Selema had given her life-force to create the Protector, Dumuzi had requested for his life-force to end. Being an elder, his request had been accepted, and his life-force had been captured and contained in the Library of Ummia.

It was the very same life-force that Aby-od had so hurriedly snatched just minutes before. Instead of being overwritten, Sam's life-force had somehow melded with that of Dumuzi's.

Now, after thousands of Earth years apart, Dumuzi had found his love again.

Sam walked over to Ellie. She trembled, her eyes filling with tears. Sam bent his head and kissed her with enraptured passion, with a desire that had been suspended in time. His arms crept around her, pulling her nervous body closer.

Feeling awkward, Aby-od stepped to the side.

Backing out of the kiss, Ellie looked into Sam's eyes, and she could hardly dare to ask, "Is that you, Sam?"

Déjà vu. Not so very long ago, Sam had asked the same of Ellie. Now she understood his fear and pain.

Sam smiled, smoothing back her hair with his familiar tenderness. "It's me, Ellie. But I feel different."

Ellie wondered what he was feeling. She wondered if he could 'feel' Dumuzi in the same way she could 'feel' Selema.

"All my emotions are more intense." Sam's voice was deeper and more masterful, but strangely, his slight accent still remained intact. "It's like I've been sleeping all my life and suddenly woken. Everything is new. I'm bursting with feeling. Oh Ellie, I love you. I've loved you all my life."

Sam pressed his lips onto Ellie's before she had a chance to reply.

Aby-od analyzed Sam's emotional display. He was incredibly confused. What was happening should not be happening. Not according to how the laws worked. Sam's framework, everything that he was, should have been overwritten. Sam should not now exist as someone to whom Ellie could relate to, let alone love. At least, that's how he thought it would work. Certainly, if a Kudamaz overwrote one life-force with another, no shred of the original Kudamaz life-force would be seen. Obviously, humans were different. But there again, in a library of millions upon millions of life-forces, he'd sped in and chosen one, and that one just happened to be Dumuzi's life-force. The odds on such an occurrence, Aby-od couldn't even begin to consider. He just had to believe some other force had been at work, something beyond even his own formidable understanding. And something that should remain that way.

Turning to face the lovers, Aby-od coughed, embarrassed, as Sam's passions overflowed to dramatic effect in front of his bashful eyes. Ellie dipped out of Sam's increasingly sensual embrace.

"How do you feel, Sam?" asked Aby-od, eyeing him, waiting for any delayed reaction to the reconstitution process. But apart from his incessant need to not let Ellie out of his arms or away from his lips, he had not displayed any other anomaly to the process.

Sam kissed Ellie's neck. "I feel alive!"

Aby-od could see his eyes inflamed with pure love. Aby-od tried again. This was surely a momentous occasion. A Kudamaz life-force had been used to restore a human. Bringing him back from the point of death, no less. Aby-od had so many questions. But he could see that Sam had interest in but one thing.

"Can you feel anything else?" questioned Aby-od, not to be deterred from understanding the moment.

"I can sense Dumuzi, if that's what you mean. The same as I know Selema's life-force is in Ellie. We were always meant to be together. And now we always will be."

Ellie's eyes shone bright. Looking into Sam's, she felt Selema's undying passion for Dumuzi. Ellie reached out for Sam and kissed him longingly.

"My sweetness, it's good to have you back," she whispered, nuzzling his neck. "I thought I was losing you. But I never let go."

"I felt your love inside me. It gave me something to focus on to. It got me through the torment and pain. You have been my strength. You have been my savior. I shall love you forever."

"But no one lives…" started Ellie, remembering her words.

But Sam was too fast. He dropped his lips to hers and took her breath away. In that moment, Ellie knew that forever, for them, could last a lifetime.

A SORT OF AN END?

NO, NOT REALLY - ELLIE AND SAM
CONTINUE THEIR ADVENTURES IN

THE REFRACTED

END OF BOOK THINGS

The Refracted
Part Four * Book Four

From the dark…

Just under four months had passed since the world had almost fallen to Al Nadir. Of course, the world didn't know that they had almost been crushed under the weight of Lord Aswa-da's mighty hand. But what they didn't know couldn't hurt them.

Ignorance had a kind of bliss attached. A rosy, warm feeling when you know, deep down, everything will be alright.

Oh, how wrong the world is…

Preface

The boy dove further, his body minuscule against the massiveness around him. A glorious turquoise sea, rippling with light, enveloped his thin frame. Shoals of iridescent fishes flashed past him. He gazed in wonderment at the world within a world so rarely seen. Everything was glistening, reflecting the brilliant sunlight above the waves. He sensed everything around him. The great light that saturated. The soft movements in the sand. The little undulations made by things unseen. All had a harmony. A living connection.

The boy stared at the seabed. It sparkled as if diamonds had been laid instead of sand. Shifting amongst the jewels, a starfish emerged and crawled across the bed. The boy was mesmerized. His eyes followed the starfish's trail. Another movement suddenly attracted him. Maybe it was a crab or even a stingray. Hoping for a stingray, the boy watched…

A tip poked through the sand. Grains tumbled down as the object started to reveal itself. Curious by the unfolding, glittering peak, the boy moved forward. Thinking it must be buried treasure and valuable, the boy reached out to snatch it.

His hands touched its smooth sides. The boy felt heat for an instant. Then he felt as though a double-decker bus had smashed into him.

The force sent the boy hurtling backward and the coral behind broke his fall. On impact, his mouthpiece dislodged, and oxygen rushed out. The boy saw the bubbles streaming but did not move. The mouthpiece floated in front of him. It was now an unnecessary accessory. Smiling, he breathed again as if the sea had always been his natural habitat.

The peak rose to its full height. The boy nodded, acknowledging its arrival. Uncovered, the object was a seven-sided crystal standing no more than two feet high. Inside a burning white light pulsed rhythmically.

Intrigued and unafraid, the boy advanced again. This time, his hands were outstretched, as if welcoming an old friend. Wrapping his arms around the crystal, like a son's embrace of his father, the crystal was soon hidden by the boy's body.

The warmth was comforting and reassuring. Like a parent's love, it was bold, undemanding and always there, a love of such strength that had borne life. It filled him with hope. Tighter, he enfolded his arms. He never wanted to let go of that feeling. Inside, and all around him, was complete goodness. Nothing could harm him. Nothing could touch him. He was as old as time. But out of time. He was everywhere. And he was nowhere.

His hands glowed. He smiled. The light was coming. Expecting the surge, he gripped tighter still. White shining light poured into him. He smiled and smiled and smiled. Water molecules moved away from him. His skin was dry, as if he was standing on land. The light infused with purity. Unencumbered goodness raced through his shining body. Totally submerged in light, the boy stood like a gleaming torch on the seabed.

Slowly, the light in the crystal pulsed and the boy's torch-like appearance faded.

Releasing the crystal from his hold, he moved away. The crystal blinked and its light dimmed. Watching as the crystal lost its luminescent light, the boy felt pain. Tears streamed. The last vestige of light blinked, and the crystal shuddered. Its clarity clouded. Turning angry grey like the sky before the rain, the crystal burnt out.

The boy cried with a sorrow he could not comprehend. All he knew was that his heart hurt. He could feel it ripping apart inside him, flooding blood through his body until he drowned in those ruby rapids.

Sinking to his knees, he felt transparent. Barely there. Barely existing. In response, the crystal descended into the sand. Second by second, the grains swallowed up the small opaque tower. Scrambling desperately through the sand, the boy searched for the crystal, but it had vanished.

Resting back on his heels, he stared at the point where the crystal had been. He knew it wouldn't return.

He stood up. It was over. Now, the beginning. *The new chance.*

And he would not fail them…

Chapter 1

Earth Date – 28 March 2017

Crystal encases me. Day and night. If day and night existed. But here in Kudamun, we have no natural dawn or dusk. It's important to understand the difference between 'in' Kudamun and 'on'. For Kudamun is not a planet. It is a complete inner dimension that is everywhere and nowhere, and crystal defines this world. From the opulent rooms upon rooms to the staircases and towers, all is created from crystal. But this crystal lives. It is sentient and offers nourishment to us, enabling continuation without the need for food. I still haven't found out how this happens. It just does.

Kudamun is separated from the known Universe by the Reality Gap. Walking through the corridors, sitting in my quarters, wherever I am in Kudamun, the Reality Gap floats high above, removing the need for a ceiling. I stare up at it and imagine it's a sky. Deep blues, bursts of vibrant orange, and silver streaks left by the quantum particles in constant fluctuation. Lines crisscross, shine, and explode then coalesce and vanish. As I understand it, the degree of tilt of these shooting quantum particles keeps Kudamun from being seen by anyone in the physical world, which, I guess, is a good thing. It stops us from breaking through at inopportune times, such as, well, those times you need to be alone, or alone-ish....I'm sure I don't need to spell those moments out for you!

Sorry, I didn't introduce myself. I'm Ellie Noor, a Kudamaz-human hybrid attuned to the resonance pattern of everything on Earth. Yes, it is quite a mouthful.

I could, of course, say, "Hi, I'm the Protector of Earth." It's a little shorter, but it also sounds like I've just stepped out of a Marvel movie.

But you know what? I think I'll just stick with, "Hi, I'm Ellie Noor, and I'm a bit different."

It has been a very strange journey, and one, I can honestly say, I'd never want to repeat.

I've been here just over two Earth days. Strictly speaking, I haven't been here a second, as there is no time in Kudamun. Our lives here and any time passing is defined by the planets with which we are connected. Through symbiotic interactions with the planets in our care, we age. But it's not how humans age. In truth, the Kudamaz are almost ageless. A young Kudamaz may have an Earth age of millions of years.

It is a difficult concept to explain, let alone fully comprehend.

I mean, I am one of them. But even I have some difficulty in realizing that both Sam and I will live forever. Or until the time when we surrender our life forces to the Library of Ummia.

I look at Sam and I see it in his eyes. Although he would never admit it, Sam still holds himself responsible for what happened. Despite the fact that Aswa-da was the orchestrator, he feels answerable for the hell I went through.

Those last five days of my human life, I still remember with vivid clarity. Although my strength overpowers the memories during consciousness, they burrow up like maggots in my unconscious mind, rising from a dark place. When I sleep, the nightmares come.

That reality of knowing with absolute certainty your final breath will soon be drawn in the sadistic hands of Al Nadir, I came to know it. I whispered my peace. I shall never forget the vision. It captured and tore apart my soul. Sam, bound and broken in a chair, his size made even larger by the massive screen before me. Defiance radiated throughout his body, but his eyes were sullen, opaque orbs. Those beautiful, laughing eyes I remembered had lost their light. He had no fear. Just sorrow. Deep, trembling sorrow for a life followed that would lead to another's death.

The death of the woman he loved.

At that moment, I tried to give him strength. Through those satellite waves, I attempted to restore his faith. He was already adrift, but I had to try.

I couldn't break. He had to see the force of my resolve. Despite my then human frailty, the Kudamaz code in my DNA had started to break through, increasing my resilience to Al Nadir's barbaric interrogations.

Awash with selflessness, I accepted my fate. Beyond husband and wife, our lives were joined in the common goal to save thousands of lives.

As it was, those lives were a statistic, a flashing headline of breaking news to horrify and plague those governments who had allowed infiltration into their ranks. It was a time of turning. The reassertion of a battle for dominance at an eventually universal level.

And a struggle that would change me forever.

We all search for a purpose in life. Including me. How strange that my purpose in life was death. Okay, I'm alive now. But Ellie, old Ellie, Mark I Ellie, has gone. Well, more accurately, her corporeal body has gone. Ellie is still alive in me. I'm the Protector. Although, as I say, I still can't bring myself to be called that. It sounds too weird, too out-there.

Does that sound wrong? I am the Protector of Earth. I have been imbued with unbelievable, mind-blowing powers. I did save Kudamun, Earth, the Universe and, most of all, Sam. But, inside, where no one can see, I'm still that frightened woman who saw her husband with a gun and whose world shattered from that moment.

I was never the same after Aby-od's call. The scream, the confusion, the sheer terror of seeing a glimpse of a power no human should ever see, of experiencing the point of death before it happened. I felt emotions with no rational explanation. Even when I replay the memory, the pain is still too much. I can't control it. The memory delivers an agony greater than all of the torture Ellie suffered.

Without that moment, nothing else would have happened. The Protector would not be here. Ellie would still be alive, in her human form, and still blind to the truth by Sam's lies.

Aby-od often asks me if all is well, as if he knows. He is such a sage. A man of wisdom. And a man much maligned by Aswa-da's actions.

Sam hated him at first. But he's come around since his reconstitution.

Of course, destiny is written. Even mine. Or perhaps especially mine. A destiny of seven thousand years in the making.

Sam loves being Kudamaz. He always was a leader, always had super intelligence, and as I found out recently, was also a rather badass kind of guy. The transformation for him, I can see, has been a good thing.

I'm not so sure about me.

Everything happened so fast. I had no choice. It all ran away from me and out of my control. I gave my human life so that others would not die. I should be proud. So why do I feel a little cheated?

Why do I feel that I was betrayed by my own destiny?

I guess no one really asked me what I wanted. I was forced to accept such a dramatic change. There was no alternative. I had to evolve. As Darwin says, "to change is to survive."

After his reconstitution, Sam became obsessed with returning to Earth. A thirst for retribution carried him forward. He had a desire to annihilate all of Al Nadir so that they never had the chance to regroup again or do to another innocent what they did to me. That was the reason I supported Sam and entered into a whirlwind execution of evil.

No one in Kudamun can give an explanation as to why Sam wasn't overwritten by Dumuzi's life force. But I know, however, that the truth is very simple. It's very, very clear.

Sam was saved by love.

Chapter 2

Two Earth Days Earlier

Ashton sat at his desk, staring in silence at a point in the past. He'd dimmed the lights to just a flicker and shut down his laptop. He should've been hearing nothing, but Godley's scream played at full volume in his mind. Ashton closed his eyes. He'd seen Godley fall to his sudden death on those shiny, marble steps in Whitehall, and his scream still reverberated with ceaseless persistence. When he'd seen the contents of that foolscap file on Maide, he'd wanted closure on the whole Sam and Ellie thing. But he never expected the actions that Godley had taken.

Abduction, torture, death. He could never countenance what Godley had done.

The level of deceit.

How could he, the prime minister of the UK, not have known that members of his own Cabinet were Al Nadir? With all his past training. His private intelligence networks. Why couldn't something have been seen? How could he have been such a fool? How many secrets had ended up in Al Douri's hands?

Ashton chided himself for being so blind to what was really happening in his House. With the exception of Jensen Stalbridge, his confidante, Godley had been his closest ally. He was always Mr. Fix-It when Ashton needed a job solved, and not just in politics. It was true that Godley had enough skeletons to topple the entire government and decimate him completely. It was perhaps a blessing he'd died so quickly.

Of course, if he hadn't died and Sam had still identified him as the turncoat in his Cabinet, Ashton would have enjoyed creating the conditions to see true pain in his eyes. Never one for being squeamish, he would have pulled the trigger when the time eventually came.

In many ways, Godley had gotten off lightly.

Ashton wondered why Godley had become a spy. What drove a man like Godley, who seemed so principled, to embrace the dark side? Money, power, influence? Or was it just that he couldn't stop himself? An inherent, festering streak of evil that manifested and metastasized throughout his body?

In his life, Ashton had seen a lot of what mankind could do and he realized that 'kind' had no place in 'man'. He'd often gone to the very edge of the abyss. In killing for his country, he'd never questioned the reasons why. Like Sam Noor, he always believed it had been for the greater good.

Accept that and you could literally do anything to anyone.

Unexpectedly, the beautiful, naughty face of his lover Judy Katzenberger, or as he called her, Katzy, drifted into Ashton's mind, but then the vision was superseded with the horrific present delivered by Al Nadir's resident sadist, Sabena Sanantoni. The present was Katzy's heart and her eyes had been embedded into the fleshy muscle of literary love. The recall shook Ashton, forcing bile up inside him, and he shuddered so violently he had to wrap his fingers around the edge of the desk to steady himself.

Yes, man (and woman) are capable of doing anything to anyone.

Ashton breathed in. He had to calm his nerves. Despite his compartmentalization training, sometimes alcohol was the only thing that enabled that siloing of emotions. He dipped his head down toward the drawer at the side of his desk and pulled out the Talisker. He tipped the aged malt into a glass. As he lifted it to his lips, he noticed a stream of red light glint through the glass and reflect across his desk. At the very same second, screams and yells pelted from outside. He leaped to the window. All of Downing Street was daubed in a strange, eerie, red light. People had massed below, despite it being the most private and guarded street in England. Number 10 staff, police, and other officials had poured outside to stare at the strange phenomenon in the sky. Ashton followed suit and looked upwards.

The night sky, no longer black, twinkled and rippled with hues of crimson. Ashton watched the people below. They were terrified. He wondered why he wasn't.

Maybe what he'd seen already fortified his resolve.

Ellie turning up announcing she was a Kudamaz alien and doing that weird vanishing act. And now this strange aura. The two occurrences were too unbelievable not to be connected. Of this, Ashton was positive.

What had Ellie said about some high council wanting to obliterate Earth? Could this be a precursor to total destruction?

Ashton didn't have time to consider it further. His door flung open and security personnel stormed inside.

"Prime Minister, sir, we have to take you to the secure location. Your family is already heading there."

Ashton didn't respond. He looked down at the people milling below him. Their screams and shouts still resounded. He looked at his security team. Their eyes were frightened despite their rock-hard demeanors and years of training. He had to ask himself again: if this truly was Armageddon, why wasn't he frightened?

Something inside made him feel calm. He remembered the incredible force that was Ellie Noor. Whatever was happening, she was at the heart of it. And she would win.

"Of course," said Ashton, grabbing his briefcase and jacket.

Security personnel took up their positions in a diamond formation around the PM and ran down the back staircase to the waiting car at the back entrance.

The secure bunkers that his predecessors would have used in such an emergency were no longer viable. They'd been destroyed by Al Nadir after they'd infiltrated into Special Branch, London's elite police force. Al Nadir spies had used their embedded positions to deploy nano-bombs, and now the bunkers underneath Whitehall, Horse Guards Parade, and Pall Mall were mere rubble and dust.

Now Ashton's route to safety was via a secure armed escort with an armor-plated, bulletproof Range Rover.

"Does anyone know what's happening?" asked Ashton, once safely inside the car.

His chief security advisor shook his head and shrugged. "No, sir. All we know is this red sky is everywhere across the world. Intelligence sources say it's originated from Iraq. It has to be Al Nadir, sir. Some gas or airborne biological weapon."

Ashton nodded, but inside he knew it wasn't anything to do with those lunatics.

"Anyone died?"

"No, Prime Minister, but we're not waiting to find out."

Ashton looked out from the darkened windows and shuddered. He definitely didn't want to hang around to discover what came next.

READY TO CONTINUE THE RIDE?

Dear reader,

It all looks like a happy ending, doesn't it?

Sam and Ellie are together forever. Al Nadir's vicious Salim Al Douri and his demented, sexy sidekick Sabena are dead. Treeborne's plan of nuclear destruction has been thwarted. Earth, Kudamun, and the Universe have been saved by Ellie (aka The Protector of Earth) from descent into darkness and certain obliteration by the Ancient Ones. Lord Aby-od has seen the Balance on Earth return to Equilibrium and, in doing so, his leadership in the inter-dimensional realm has been restored.

So what more is there to say?

A teaser to twist your mind.

They start with the first
To focus on the last
Greed is still the thirst
But it's written in the past

The Refracted will do what it says on the cover. It will change the direction of something (in this case, your perception) when it enters at an angle.

It will take you down into channels of light and dark. It will challenge you and amaze you. It's controversial. And it doesn't hold back on anything.

Nothing you've experienced so far in *The Trusted Thriller Series* will prepare you for the next explosive installment.

Are you ready?

You better be. Because once you're between those pages, there's no going back. You've just got to dive further in, and down, and hope someone comes along with that oxygen canister.

For your breath will already have left your body.

Continue with the adventure
Download The Refracted here
https://geni.us/IBdEELG

GET OPERATION SNOWDROP FOR FREE

You may have heard about Operation Snowdrop in this thriller series. Now is your chance to get the inside track on what really happened. Get exclusive access to Operation Snowdrop and get the truth behind the mission that crossed the line.

If you want to get insider intelligence on Sam and Ellie next adventures, early bird discounts on all future releases in *The Trusted Thriller* series, access to competitions or instant access to me, Michelle Medhat, then subscribe by hitting the link below and we can continue this journey together.

Operation Snowdrop Feedback

"OMG! Talk about edge of your seat, grab you by the ba... The author kept the book moving at a good pace with plenty of twists and an ending that will make you question the world around you!"

"Snowdrop is a fiercely paced book. Characters are dynamic, & powerful. A great spy thriller good versus evil gets blurred. Looking forward to next book."

"Kept me guessing and enthralled right up to the end. Looking forward to reading the next book"

"A very well written, suspenseful book. The description of the agents emotions and conflicts was very well done."

"I loved the constant adrenaline rush in this book. Looking forward to the next book. "

"So similar to the situation in the world today that it's hard to read. Well developed"

"This book is exactly why I read new authors as often as possible. The intrigue and characters are heart-stopping. 5 stars +"

GET ACCESS TO OPERATION SNOWDROP

https://dl.bookfunnel.com/nz69zq8lp2

ENJOY THIS BOOK? YOU CAN MAKE A DIFFERENCE

You have probably heard this before, but for an author, reviews really do make a difference. It takes no time at all to type in a few words, a sentence at the most, but it means the world to an author.

Honest reviews help others to find out about books they wouldn't have heard of before.

If you have enjoyed this book, I would be very grateful if you could leave a review on the book's Amazon page.

You can jump straight to the review page by hitting the link below.

LEAVE A REVIEW HERE

https://geni.us/HUxW

Learn more about Michelle Medhat

www.forever-connected.com
michelle@forever-connected.com

THE TRUSTED THRILLER SERIES

This Thriller Series is an edge-of-your-seat, ruthless, non-stop ride packed with gripping spy action, provocative sci-fi suspense, sex, political intrigue and amazing sci-tech to push Bond into the background! If you're searching for something that's nail-biting to the very end - you've found it in this extraordinary Thriller Series.

If you've read this book first, and haven't discovered the rest of the series yet, you need to read these books. Don't miss out, get them now and get the full story!

The Trusted (Book One – Part One)

He's a husband, a killer, and the only man who can save the world…

Sam Noor keeps his double lives separate with expert precision. But when the MI6 agent's wife discovers the lie, he fears that both his worlds may shatter. Distraught and conflicted, Noor concentrates on his latest mission and discovers a weapon that could cause a global catastrophe…

Drawn into the fight against a sinister terrorist group with powerful connections, Noor must uncover the faction's secrets by any means necessary. Even if it puts the woman he loves in the line of fire.

But Noor has no way of knowing that a supernatural war rages within his nation. And the winner could take charge of humanity's very soul.

Against forces that defy his reality, can Noor protect millions of innocents from a bloody end?

The Dominant (Book Two – Part Two)

One spy's war on terror could decide the fate of humanity…

MI6 agent Sam Noor isn't afraid to get his hands dirty to protect his homeland. While overseas interrogating an enemy terrorist, he's horrified to learn his beloved wife suffered the same brutal tactics from his own men. Determined to expose the betrayal and extract bloody justice, Noor uncovers an unbelievable fact: his wife died and somehow came back to life…

Swept up in an international power struggle, Noor goes rogue to uncover the eye-opening truth. The fallout from Sam's revenge ripples from the Oval Office through the CIA and MI6. As he fights tooth and nail to turn back the doomsday clock, cosmic forces wage their own battle for Earth's future. And Noor fears that preventing nuclear destruction may sacrifice the love of his life.

Can the maverick agent protect his wife and save his world from annihilation?

The Resonance (Book Three – Part Three)

World War III rages. What can she do to protect the innocent?

Ellie Noor's hope hangs by a thread. Tortured to within an inch of her life by sadistic terrorists, she's horrified to learn her husband's efforts to free her cost a half-a-million lives. But grief must wait as Ellie is swept up in an interdimensional attempt to stop all-out nuclear destruction.

Shocked to discover the key to saving the universe lies inside her, she becomes a potent instrument to respawn Earth's lost protector. But with the world's atomic arsenals locked and loaded, and sinister beings on the attack, she fears only an unfathomable miracle can halt humanity's extinction.

Can Ellie unleash her hidden power and prevent her planet's annihilation?

The Refracted

She's now a fully-fledged Protector. But her formidable extraterrestrial powers may not be enough to save humanity from itself.

Ellie Noor longs for an end to the constant fighting on Earth. Now fully alien and nearly invincible, she and her superhuman husband are busy stamping out terrorist armies worldwide. But her heart breaks when a new global alliance for peace makes its first initiative a mass execution of its enemies.

Suspicious of the motives of the movement's creator, UK Prime Minister Ashton, Ellie's search for answers only leads to startling revelations. And her former-MI6-spy husband isn't helping matters by kowtowing to the British leader. With political havoc and cosmic dangers threatening, one wrong move could spell disaster for millions...

Can Ellie balance the forces at play before humankind is wiped off the interstellar map?

A WORD FROM THE AUTHOR

Being a writer is a strange and often dichotomous thing.

You spend your days and nights isolated, locked over a keyboard, feverishly creating, in a world of your own (and in my case quite a twisted one at that!), only to shove your work up on Amazon (or whatever other book platform you use) and await the response and ridicule of the masses.

Are we writers, therefore, all masochists at heart?

It's a question I ask myself whilst typing until the early hours after a day of back to back, stressful meetings, when my eyes can only just stay open enough to see the screen.

But really us writers do what we do because we love to write.

I could write about anything, but I chose to write these unpigeonholeable (I have dibs on this word!) thrillers that weave a world of the fantastic that feels, at times, almost like an adult comic. I've been told my books are guilty pleasures. Things people know perhaps they shouldn't be reading, but hell, let's do it anyway.

In SciTech innovation, which is my background and my day job, we talk about the art of the possible. This reference is often made when you take an idea and stretch it to its very limits. So you're just about skirting the impossible.

That's what I do when I write.

I imagine the scene running in my mind. I then stretch it, mix it up, and make it an unbelievable, jaw-dropping moment. But I do so ensuring that, somehow, it still has a touch of the possible about it.

I've already said before that *The Trusted Thriller Series* has become a part of me. The characters are my friends (yes *even* Salim and Sabena), and I imagine their lives, their feelings, and their emotions. This connection brings them to life. And hopefully, it makes them more real to you, the reader.

Sometimes I'll hear a song and think, yep, that's definitely reflecting Ellie's life. Or a song will somehow click with a whole chapter. That's why I've created playlists, which accompany the books. I'm still working on *The Resonance* playlist and this will be in a future edit of my newsletter *Fearless Spies, Amazing Realms and Ice-Cold Villains.* Make sure you sign up and get a free copy of Operation Snowdrop.

I've created playlists for *The Trusted* and *The Dominant* on the next pages.

Music is a great vehicle to inspire and many songs have driven entire scenes in my books, and *The Resonance* is no exception. Mark Kingswood's *Strong* played furiously in my head whilst writing some of the toughest scenes in this book. Look at the lyrics and you'll know why.

I'll let you into some intel. I had intended to finish the series on this book. However, I listened to Paloma Faith's *Do You Want The Truth or Something Beautiful* and it triggered a new, dramatic, and, needless to say, twisty storyline in me.

And suddenly, *The Refracted* (book four) was born.

I'm always on the receiving end of inspiration. Believe it or not, I was faced with a chicken (real, not frozen) and I immediately pictured how I'd visualize one of the new characters in book four. (And there's a signed copy for anyone who can figure out which character it is 😉 – email me).

What I'm really saying is inspiration is packaged in all kinds of guises.

Just be ready to recognize it, grab it, and make something wonderful from it.

The power to create is in us all.

Michelle Medhat

Find out more
www.forever-connected.com/thedominant
michelle@forever-connected.com

Twitter @theconnected1 Facebook @michellemedhat

The Playlists of *The Trusted Thriller Series*

The Trusted

Everlasting – Take That
Secrets – One Republic
Have I Told You Lately that I Love You – Rod Stewart
Rock You Like a Hurricane – Scorpions
Khalina Lewahdina (Let's stay alone together) – Amr Diab
E.T. – Katy Perry
Solsbury Hill – Peter Gabriel
Angel with a Shotgun – The Cab
Only Love can Hurt Like This – Paloma Faith
Who Wants to Live Forever – Queen
Rule the World – Take That
Fighting Suspicions – Rebecca Ferguson
The Architect – Paloma Faith
Rewrite the Stars – Zac Efron & Zendaya
The Last of the Secret Agents – Nancy Sinatra
New Divide – Linkin Park
Army of Two – Olly Murs
Demons – Imagine Dragons
Shine a Light – Bryan Adams
Don't Stop Believin' – Journey
What Part of my Body Hurts the Most – Rob Fowler & Sharon Sexton
Please Don't Leave Me – P!nk
Set Fire to the Rain – Adele
Guilty – Paloma Faith
Almeno Stavolta (At Least this Time…) – Nek
Candlelight – Jack Savoretti
I Belong to you – Caro Emerald
Try – P!nk
Redemption – The Strange Familiar
Nothing Breaks Like a Heart – Mark Ronson (Feat. Miley Cyrus)
Many Shades of Black – Adele & The Raconteurs
See Who I am – Within Temptation

The Dominant

Secrets – P!nk
La Tortura (The Torture)– Shakira
L'Altra Dimensione (The Other Dimension) – Måneskin
Amor Eterno (Eternal Love) – Fonseca
My Immortal – Evanescence
Revenge – P!nk with Eminem
Killer Queen - Queen
So Am I – Ava Max
Any Way You Want It – Journey
Me – Taylor Swift & Brendon Urie
Lucy in the Sky with Diamonds – The Beatles
Some Guys Have All the Luck – Rod Stewart
Perfetto (Perfect)– Gianna Nannini
Half the World Away – Aurora
Raise Hell – Brandi Carlisle
The Pretender – Foo Fighters
Too Good to Lose - Rebecca Ferguson
Maybe – Lewis Capaldi
Something's Gotta Give – One Republic
Torna a Casa (Come Back Home) – Måneskin
I Want to Break Free – Queen
Amo Soltanto Te (I Only Love You)– Andrea Bocelli & Ed Sheeran
Love at First Sight – Kylie
Whisky Tango – Jack Savoretti
Wonder – Naughty Boy with Emeli Sandé
Retribution – Jeff Scott Soto
Ayami Beek (My Days With You) - Elissa
Wasted – Jack Savoretti
Light My Fire – The Doors
We Share the Same Sun – Stereophonics
Surrender – Paloma Faith
What Have You Done – Within Temptation
Out of the Frying Pan and Into the Fire – Meatloaf
Rockstar (Salim's Theme) – Nickelback
Radioactive – Imagine Dragons
Back for Good – Take That
Danger Zone – Kenny Loggins

What Doesn't Kill You (Stronger) – Kelly Clarkson
Sweet But Psycho – Ava Max
Welcome to The Jungle – Guns and Roses

The Resonance
Strong - Mark Kingswood
Hiding – Florence + The Machine
The Sound of Sunshine – Michael Franti & Spearhead
All of My Heart - ABC
Toxic – Britney Spears
Burn it to the Ground - Nickelback
On Top of the World – Imagine Dragons
The Scientist - Coldplay
Blood on My Hands – Jack Savoretti
Music's Too Sad Without You – Kylie Minogue & Jack Savoretti
Suspicious Minds – Elvis Presley
Girls Just Wanna Have Fun – Cyndi Lauper
Traitor - Daughtry
Torn – Natalie Imbruglia
Dear Mr. President – P!nk
The Prayer – Celine Dion & Andrea Bocelli
The Winner Takes It All - ABBA
Guilty – Paloma Faith
Strip Me – Natasha Bedingfield
Won't Get Fooled Again – The Who
Changing – Paloma Faith
Drops of Jupiter – Train
Liar – Camila Cabello
Bring Me To Life – Evanescence
Venus – Bananarama
WW3 – Paloma Faith
Find U Again – Mark Ronson (feat. Camila Cabello)
Get Lucky – Daft Punk (feat. Pharrell Williams & Nile Rodgers)
Dancing in the Dark – Bruce Springsteen
Rescue Me – One Republic
Superheroes – The Script
Get Outta My Way – Kylie Minogue
Set Fire to the Rain – Adele

Who's Crying Now – Journey
Pain is So Close to Pleasure – Queen
Dark Night of the Soul – Van Morrison
Maybe Tomorrow – The Stereophonics
One Last Kiss – Kylie Minogue
Any Other Way – Jack Savoretti
Truth Hurts – Bullet for My Valentine
Stuck in the Middle with You – Stealers Wheel
Firework – Katy Perry
Red Light Spells Danger – Billy Ocean
Breaking Your Own Heart – Kelly Clarkson
Everything is Broken – Bob Dylan
Simples Corazones (Simple Hearts) – Fonseca
Greatest Mistake – Jack Savoretti
When Love Takes Over – David Guetta (feat. Kelly Rowland)
Shine – Emeli Sandè
I Saved the World Today – Eurythmics
Cold – James Blunt
Hold Me Close – David Essex
We Are Bound – Jack Savoretti
The Power of Love – Huey Lewis & The News

ACKNOWLEDGEMENTS

The name that has made this book a reality is Sam Medhat, my husband. He is my inspiration, and without him this series, would never have been created. He is the one who listens to every word written. He is the one who endures my frustrations when I have writer's block. He is the one who is constantly woken up by my unsuccessful attempts at creeping into bed in the wee small hours, after I've become lost in my writing world.

Without Sam, no writing would have happened.

Whilst writing this series, I lost my brother, father, and mother. None of them lived to see this in print, however their love is embodied within the words, and I hope, somewhere, they can see the result of the faith they had in me to achieve.

I would like to thank my fabulous editor, Ceri Savage, who has been with me on this journey, and who has been incredible in her support and advice.

Michelle Medhat

Printed in Great Britain
by Amazon

11000645R00198